P9-BYN-194

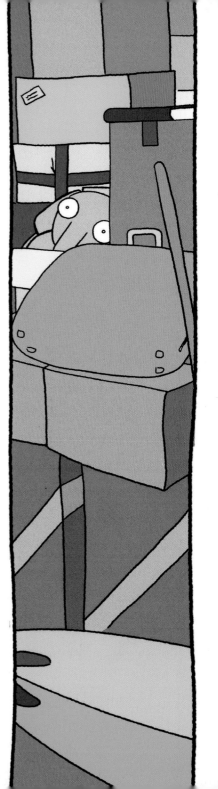

THE ODDS

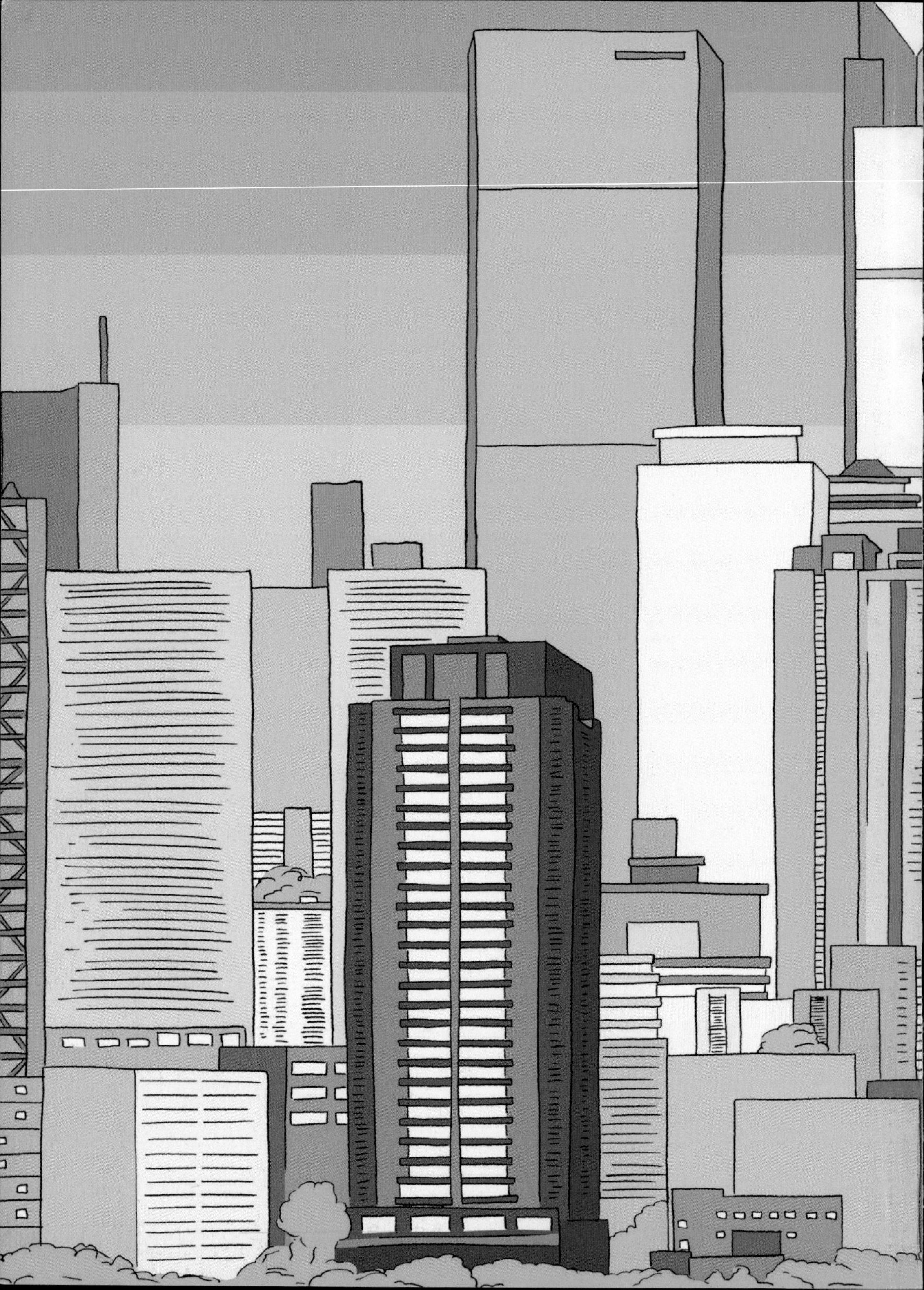

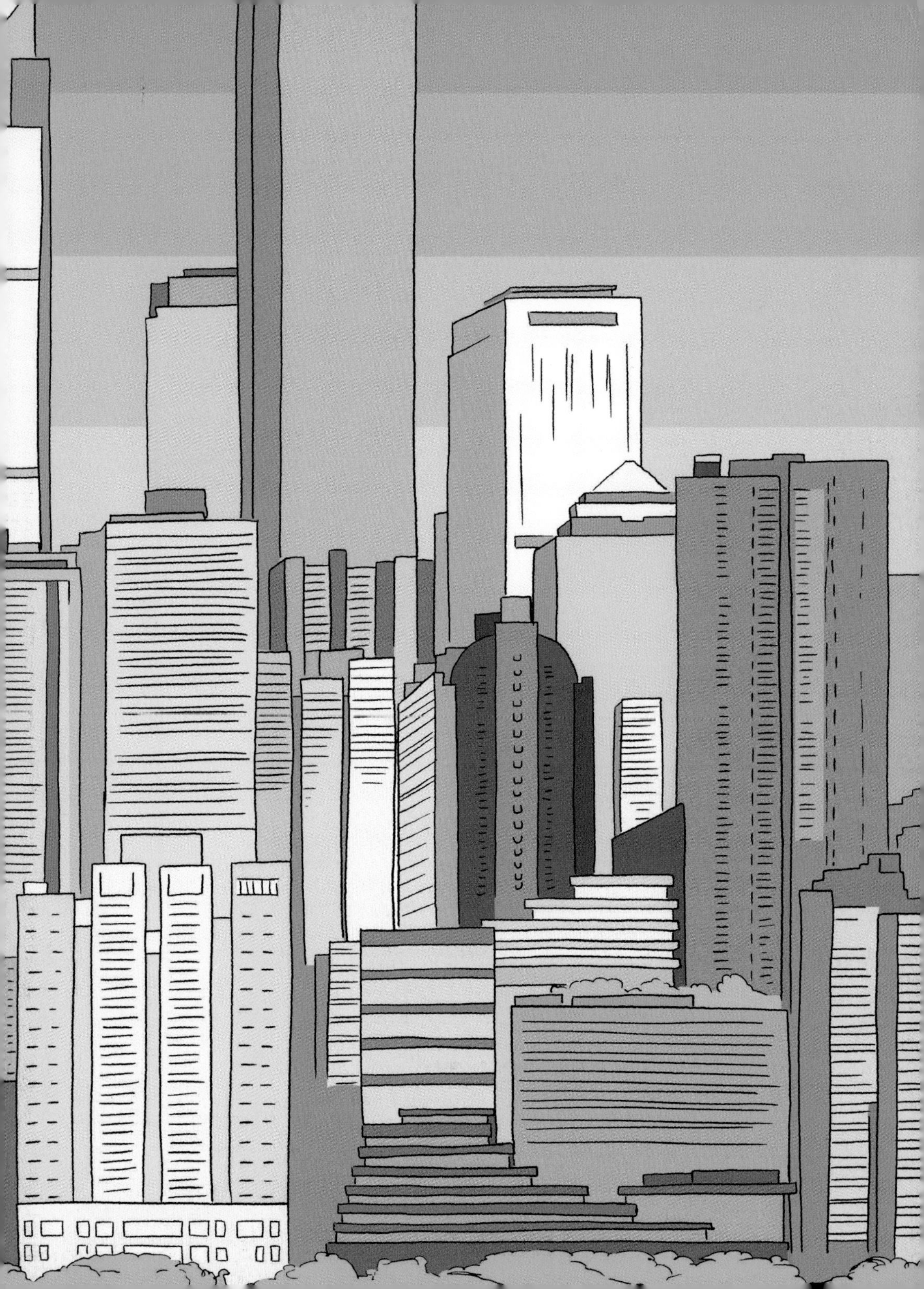

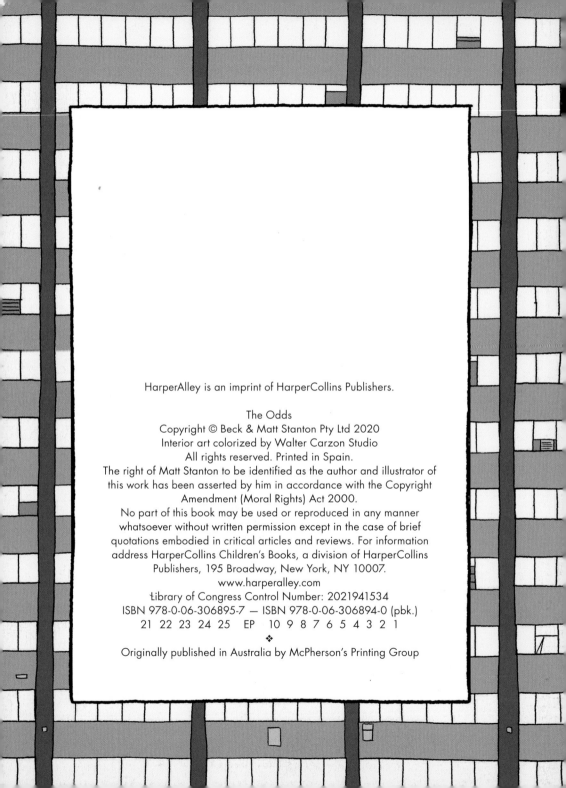

HarperAlley is an imprint of HarperCollins Publishers.

The Odds
Copyright © Beck & Matt Stanton Pty Ltd 2020
Interior art colorized by Walter Carzon Studio
Library of Congress Control Number: 2021941534
ISBN 978-0-06-306895-7 — ISBN 978-0-06-306894-0 (pbk.)
21 22 23 24 25   EP   10 9 8 7 6 5 4 3 2 1
❖
Originally published in Australia by McPherson's Printing Group

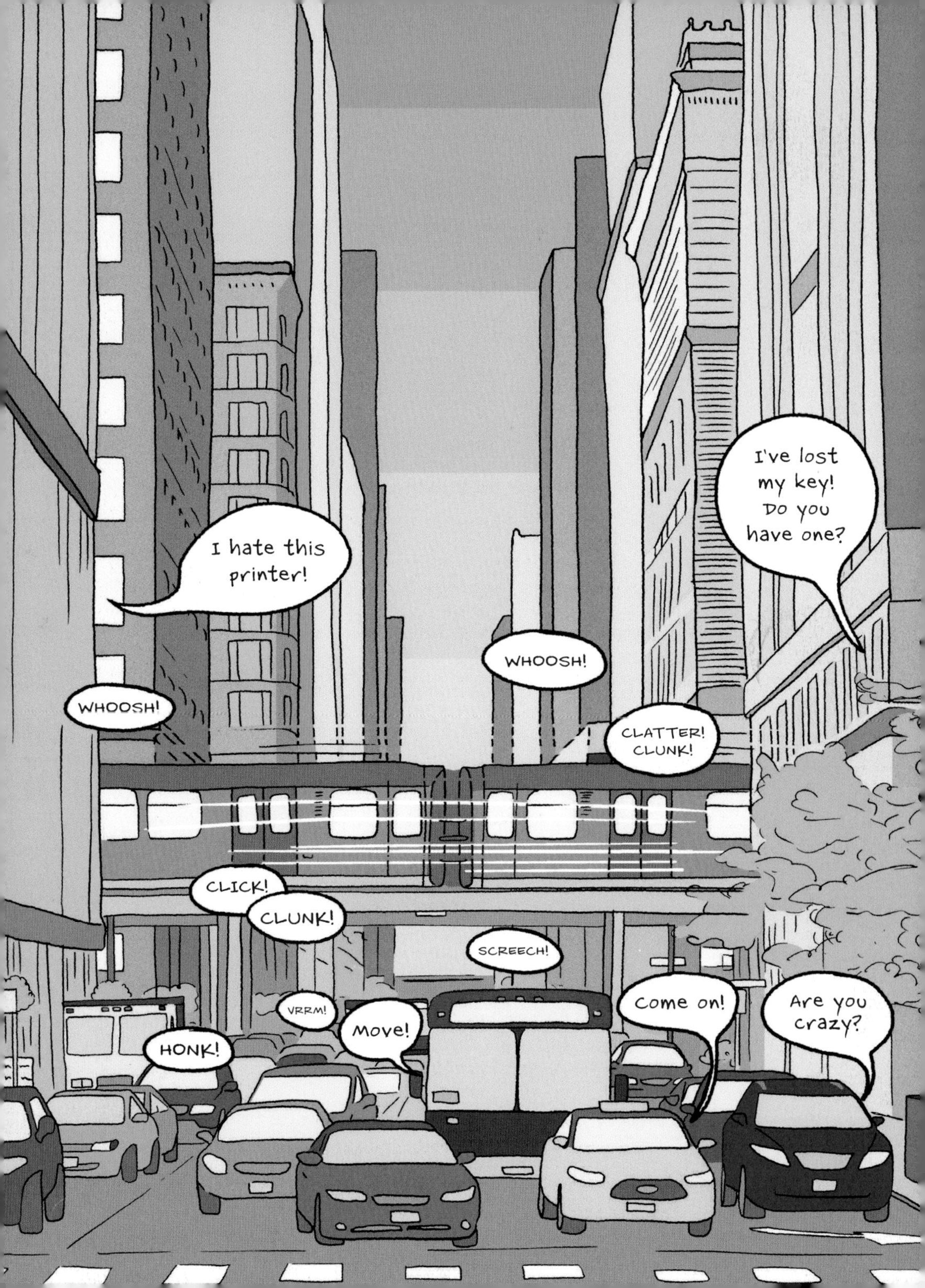
I hate this printer!
I've lost my key! Do you have one?
WHOOSH!
WHOOSH!
CLATTER! CLUNK!
CLICK!
CLUNK!
SCREECH!
VRRM!
HONK!
Move!
Come on!
Are you crazy?

For Beck

Thank you for seeing me,
knowing me, and
loving me.

Dreaming with you
is my favorite
place.

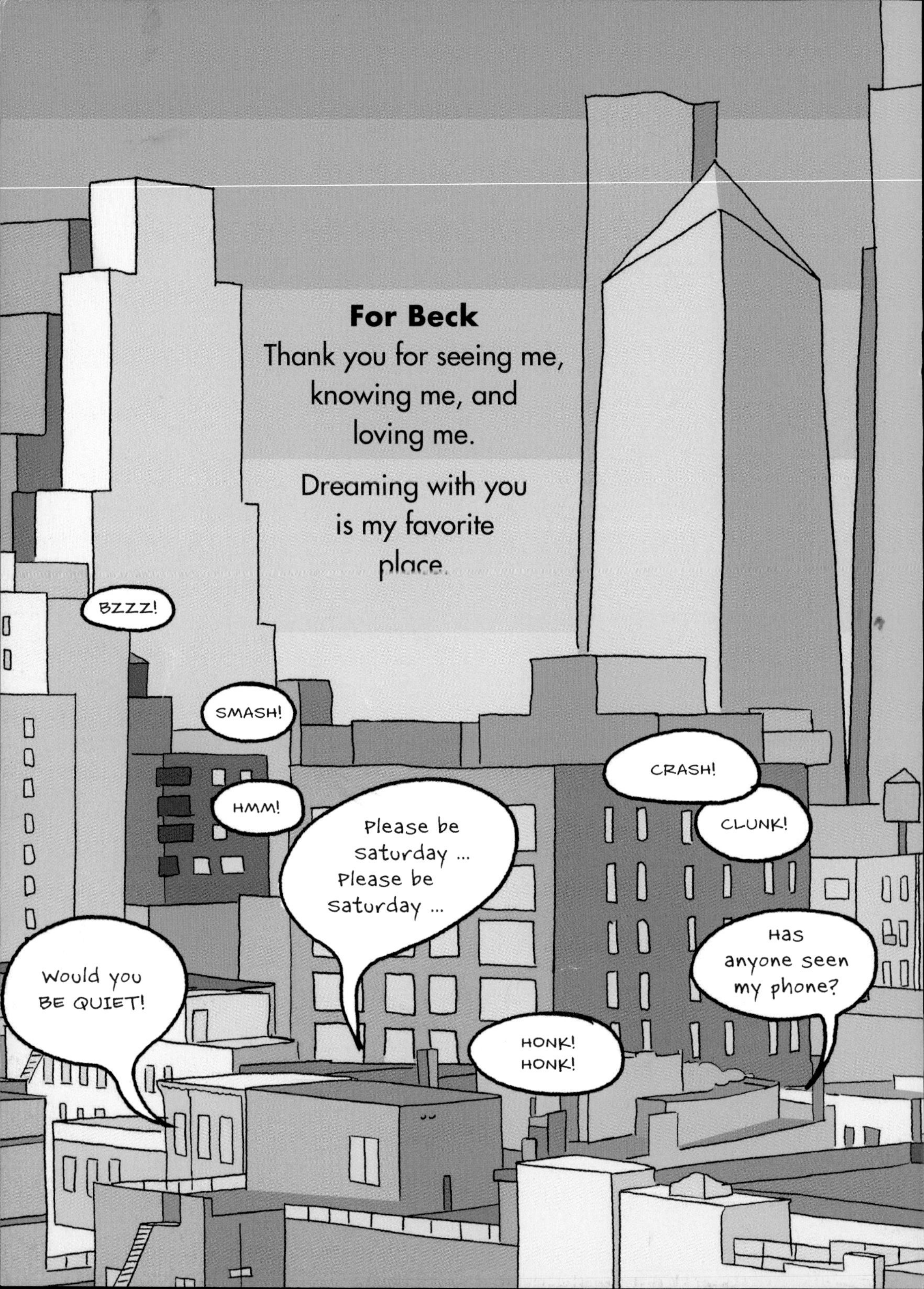
BZZZ!
SMASH!
CRASH!
HMM!
CLUNK!
Please be saturday ... Please be saturday ...
Has anyone seen my phone?
Would you BE QUIET!
HONK! HONK!

THE ODDS

words and pictures by

Matt Stanton

HARPER alley
An Imprint of HarperCollinsPublishers

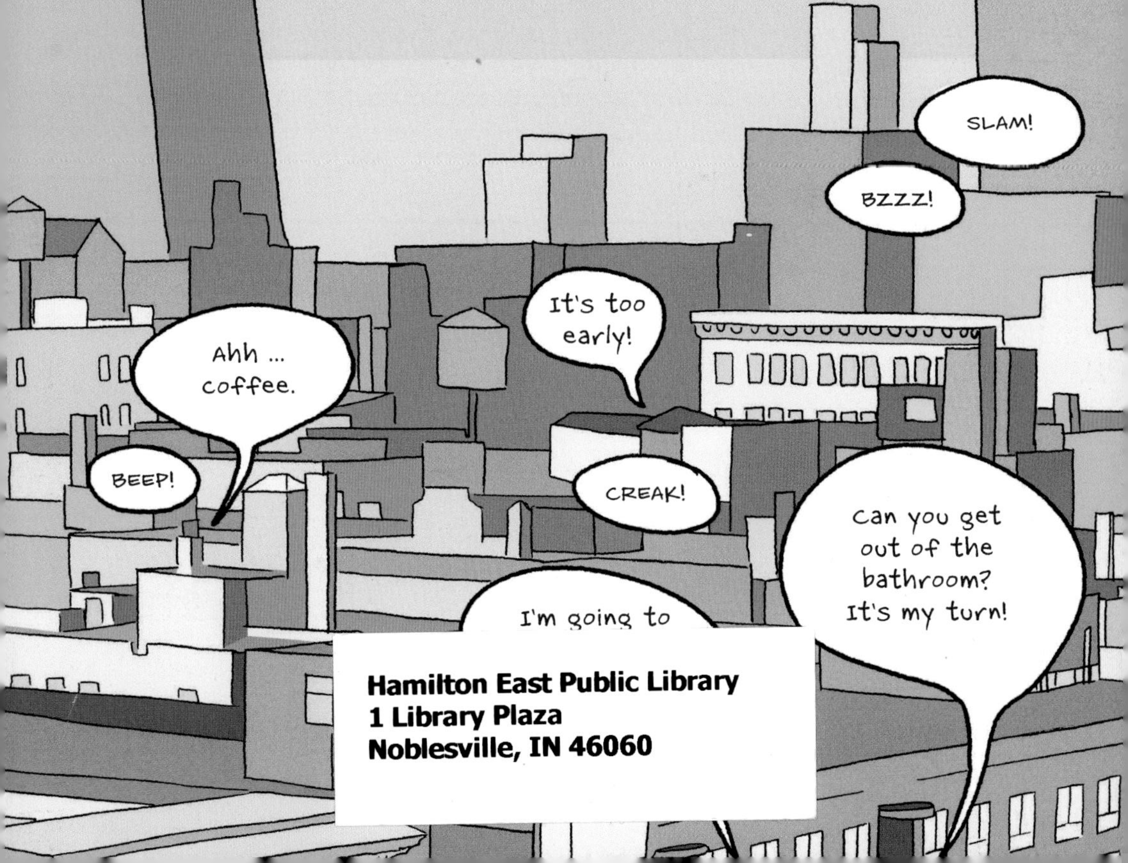
SLAM!
BZZZ!
It's too early!
Ahh ... coffee.
BEEP!
CREAK!
Can you get out of the bathroom? It's my turn!
I'm going to

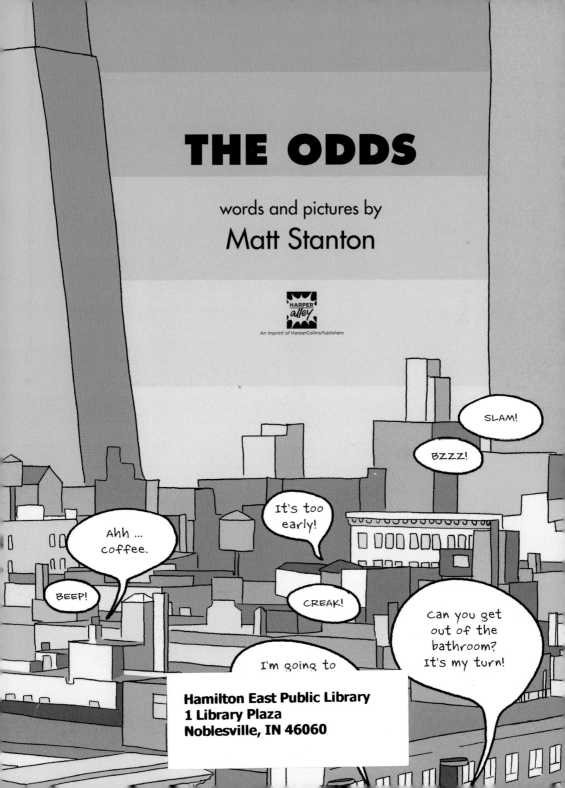

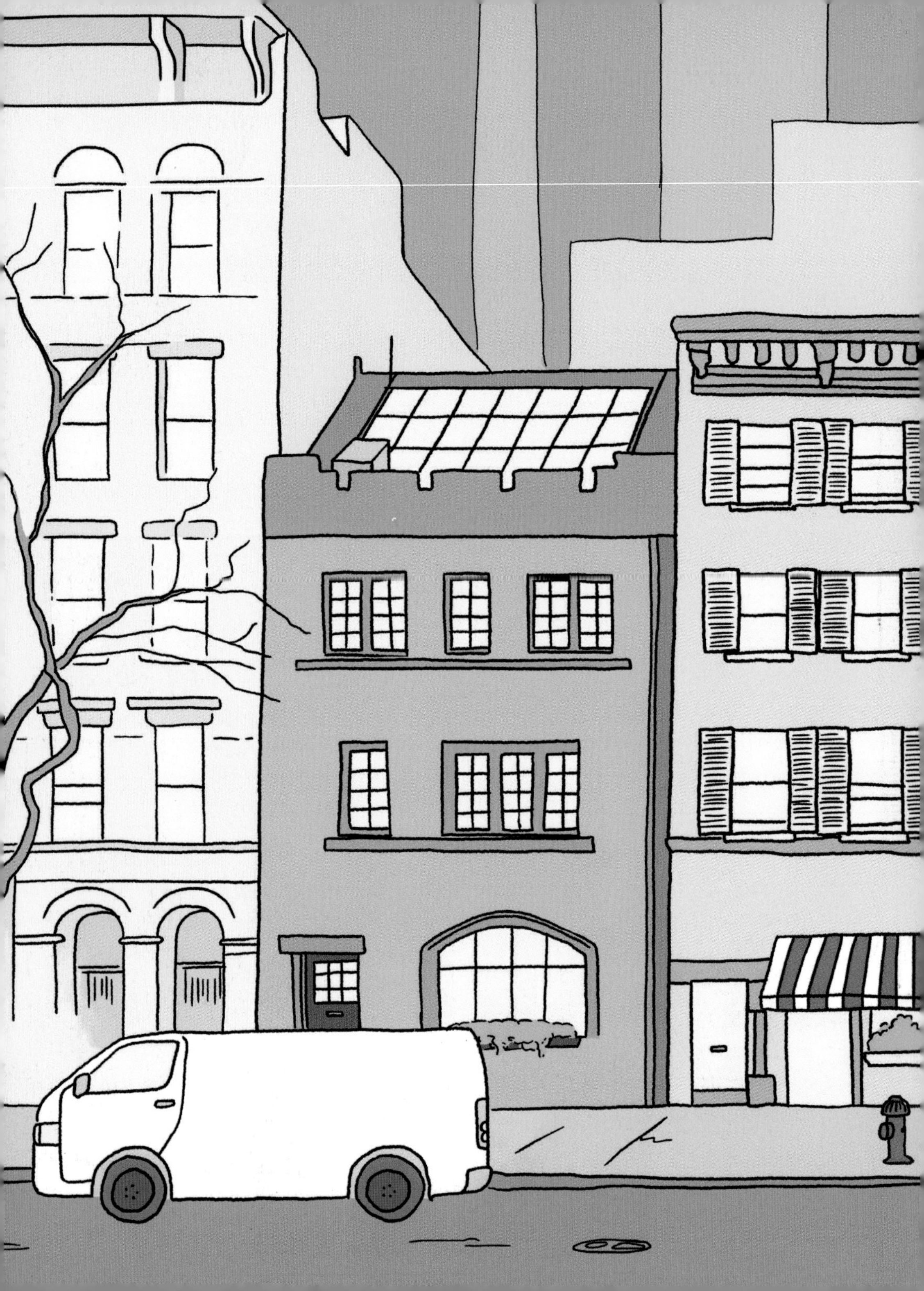

CHAPTER ONE
The Odds arrive uninvited

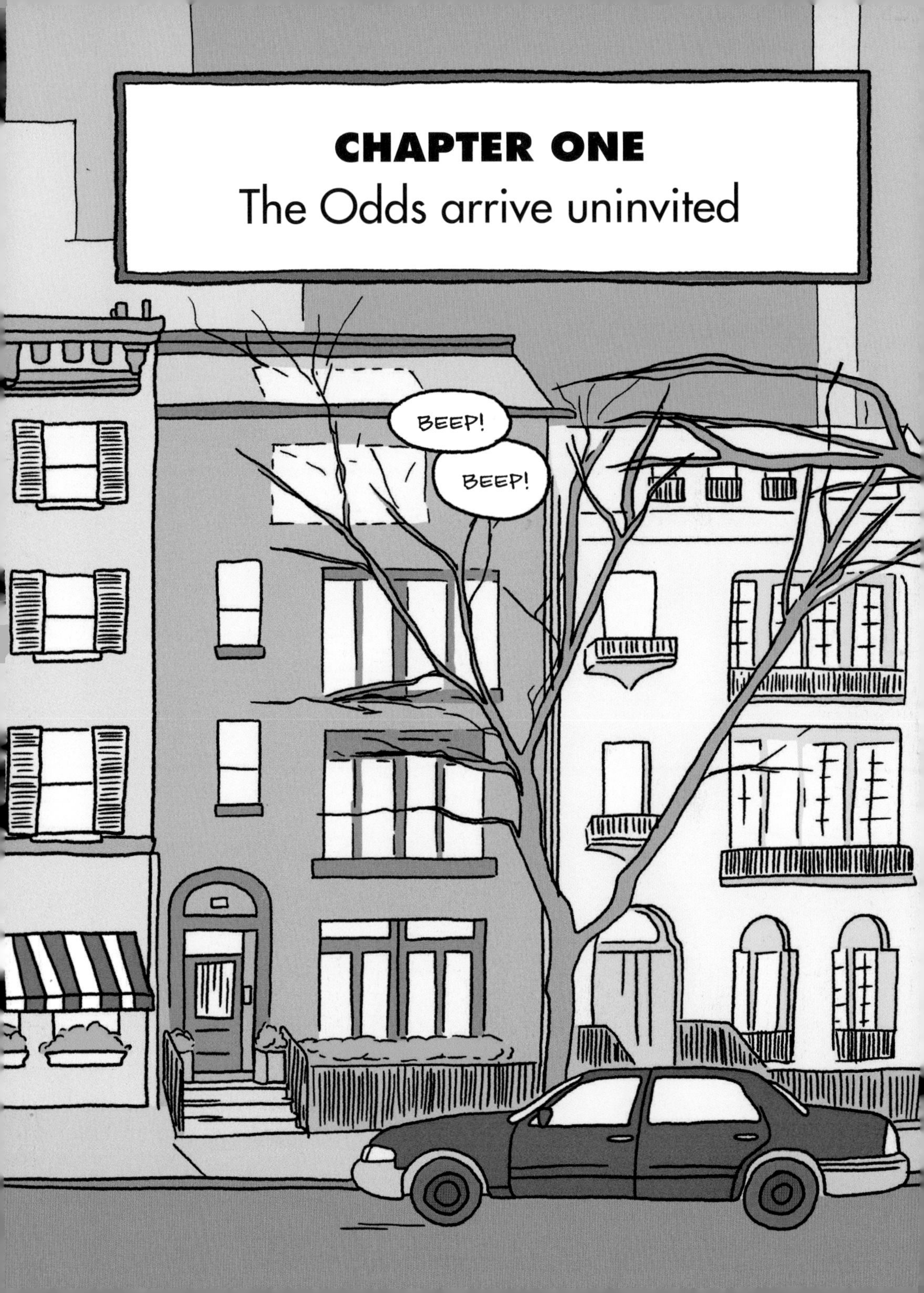
BEEP!
BEEP!

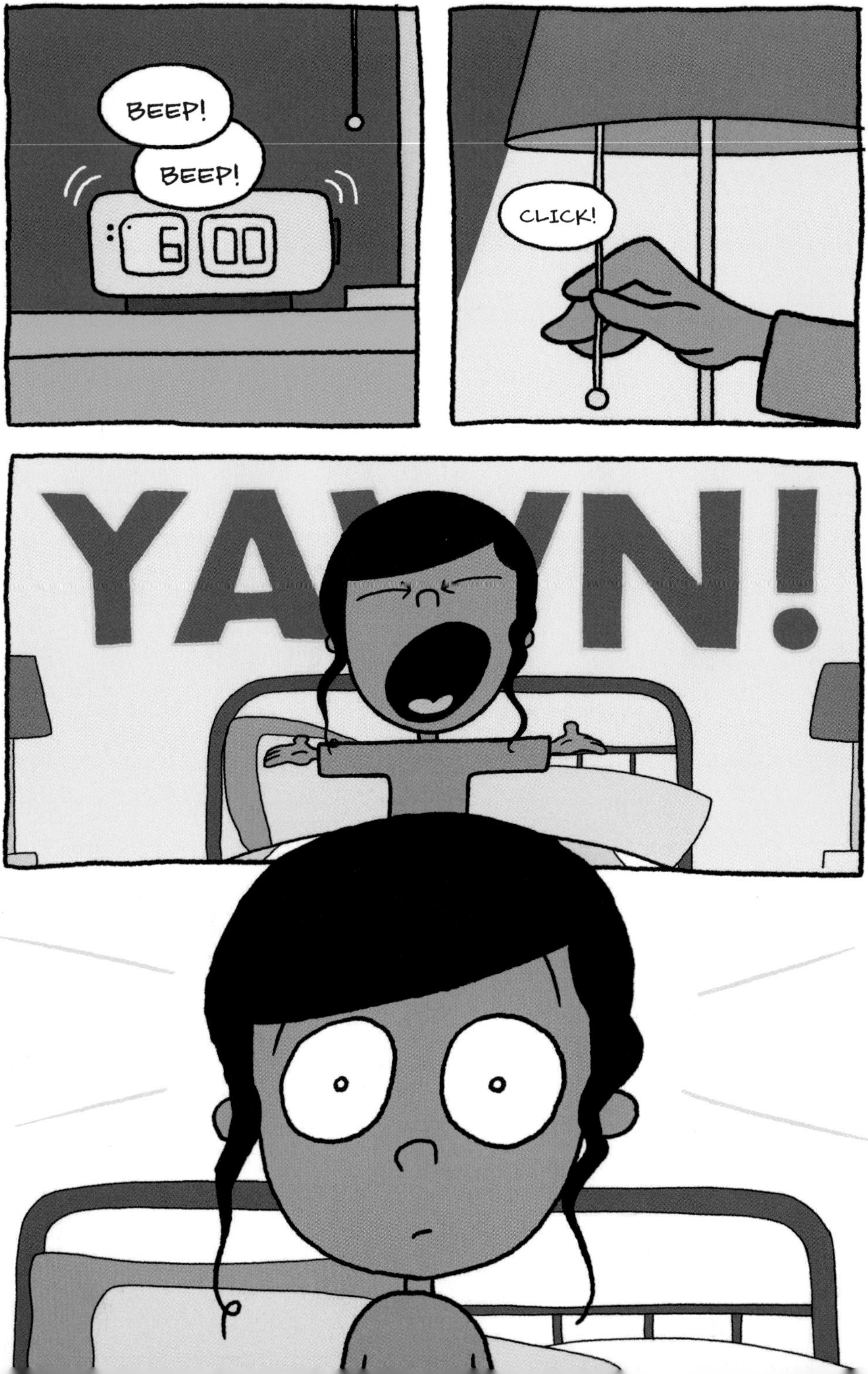
BEEP!
BEEP!
6:00
CLICK!
YAWN!

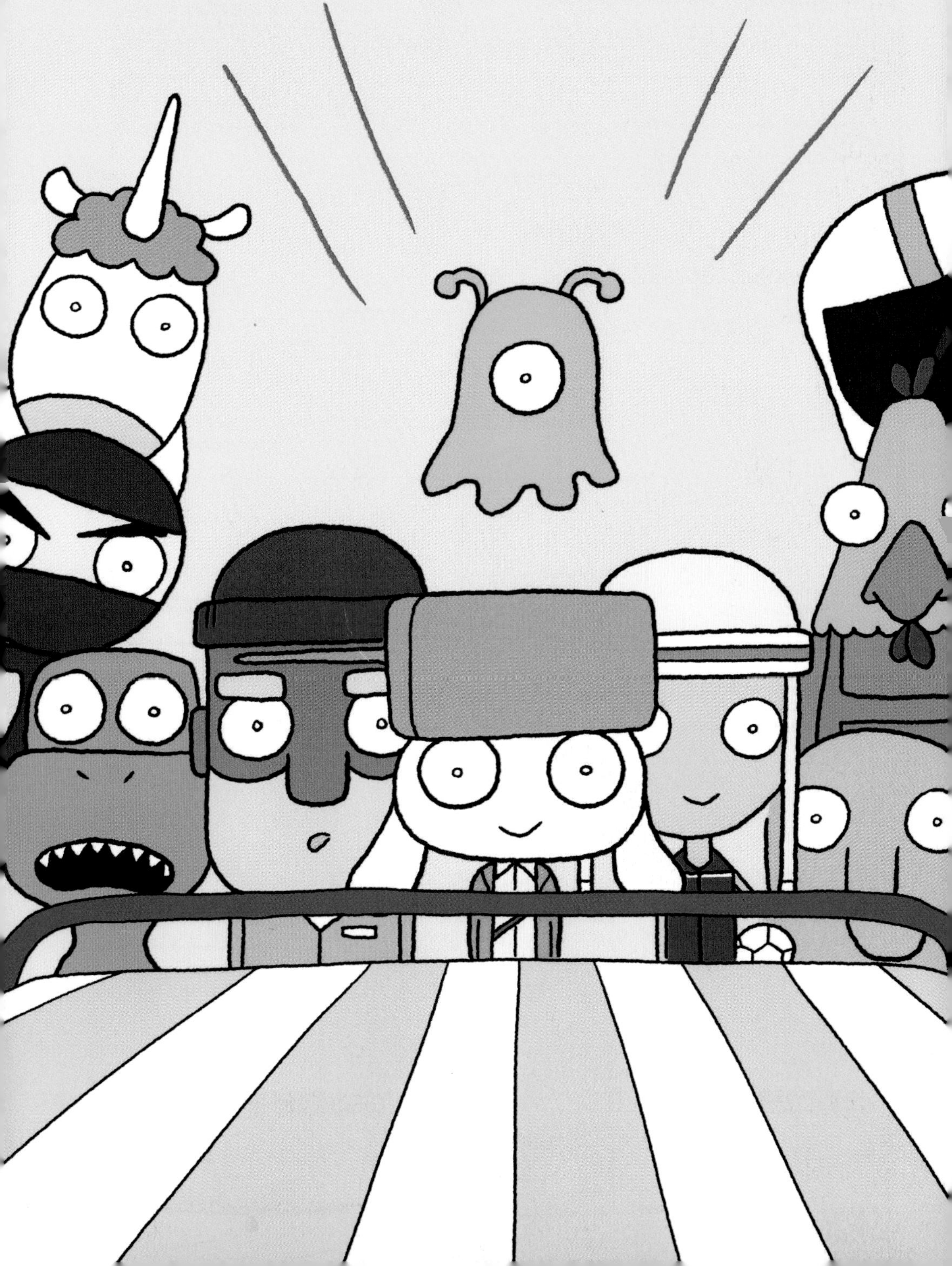

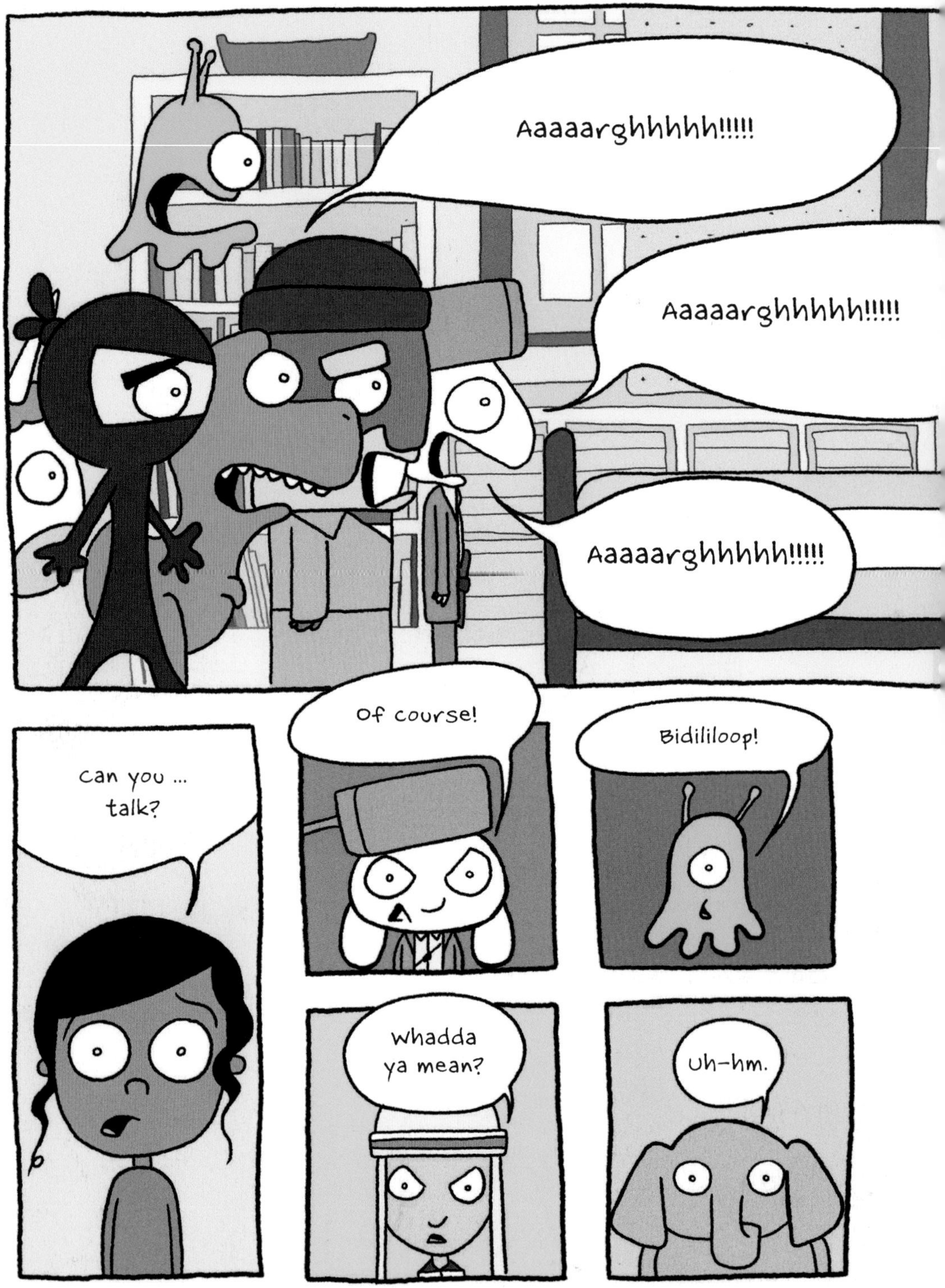
Aaaaarghhhhh!!!!!
Aaaaarghhhhh!!!!!
Aaaaarghhhhh!!!!!
Can you ... talk?
Of course!
Bidililoop!
Whadda ya mean?
Uh-hm.

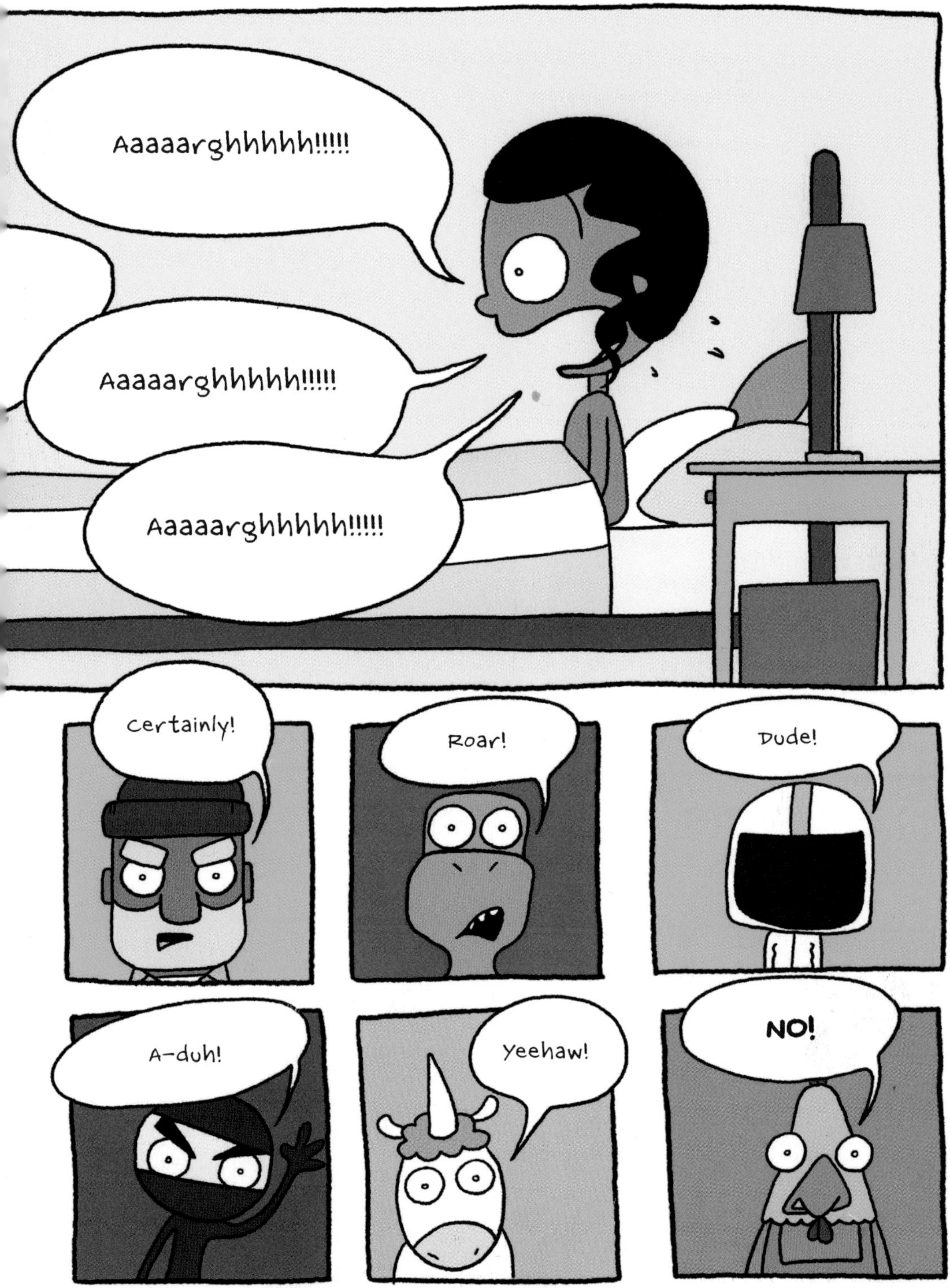
Aaaaarghhhhh!!!!!
Aaaaarghhhhh!!!!!
Aaaaarghhhhh!!!!!
Certainly!
Roar!
Dude!
A-duh!
Yeehaw!
NO!

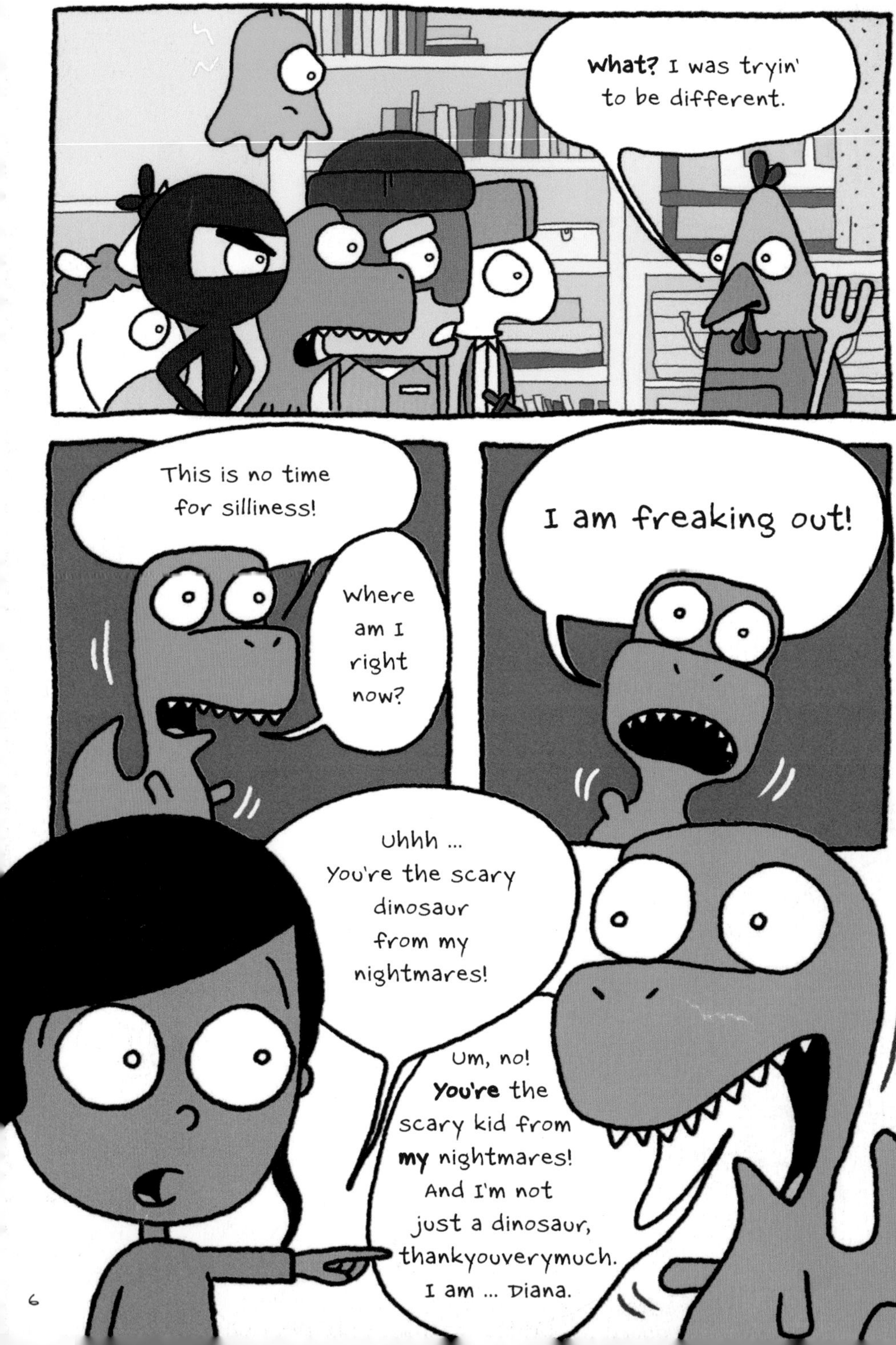

What? I was tryin' to be different.
This is no time for silliness!
Where am I right now?
I am freaking out!
Uhhh ... You're the scary dinosaur from my nightmares!
Um, no! **You're** the scary kid from **my** nightmares! And I'm not just a dinosaur, thankyouverymuch. I am ... Diana.

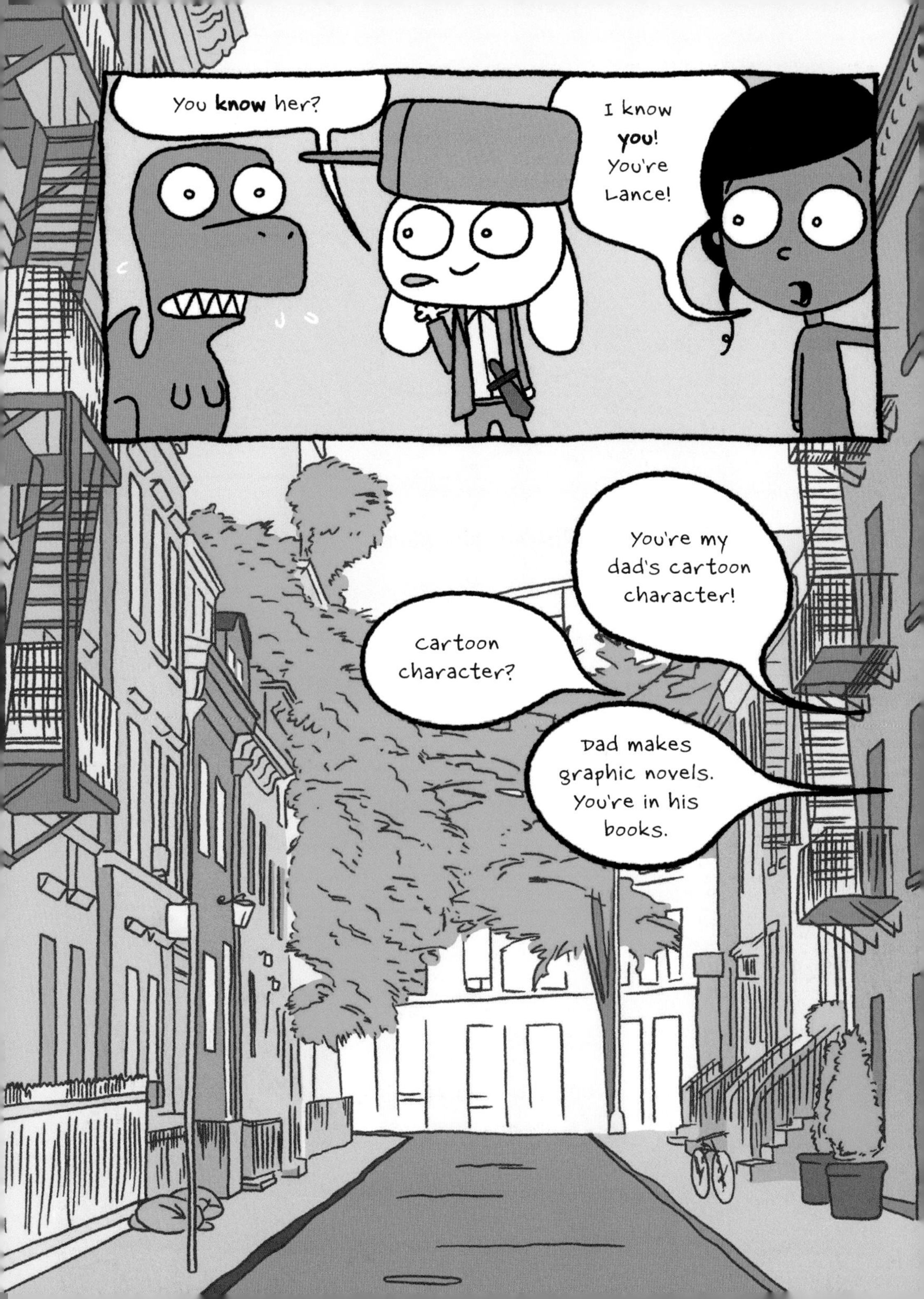
You **know** her?
I know **you**! You're Lance!
You're my dad's cartoon character!
cartoon character?
Dad makes graphic novels. You're in his books.

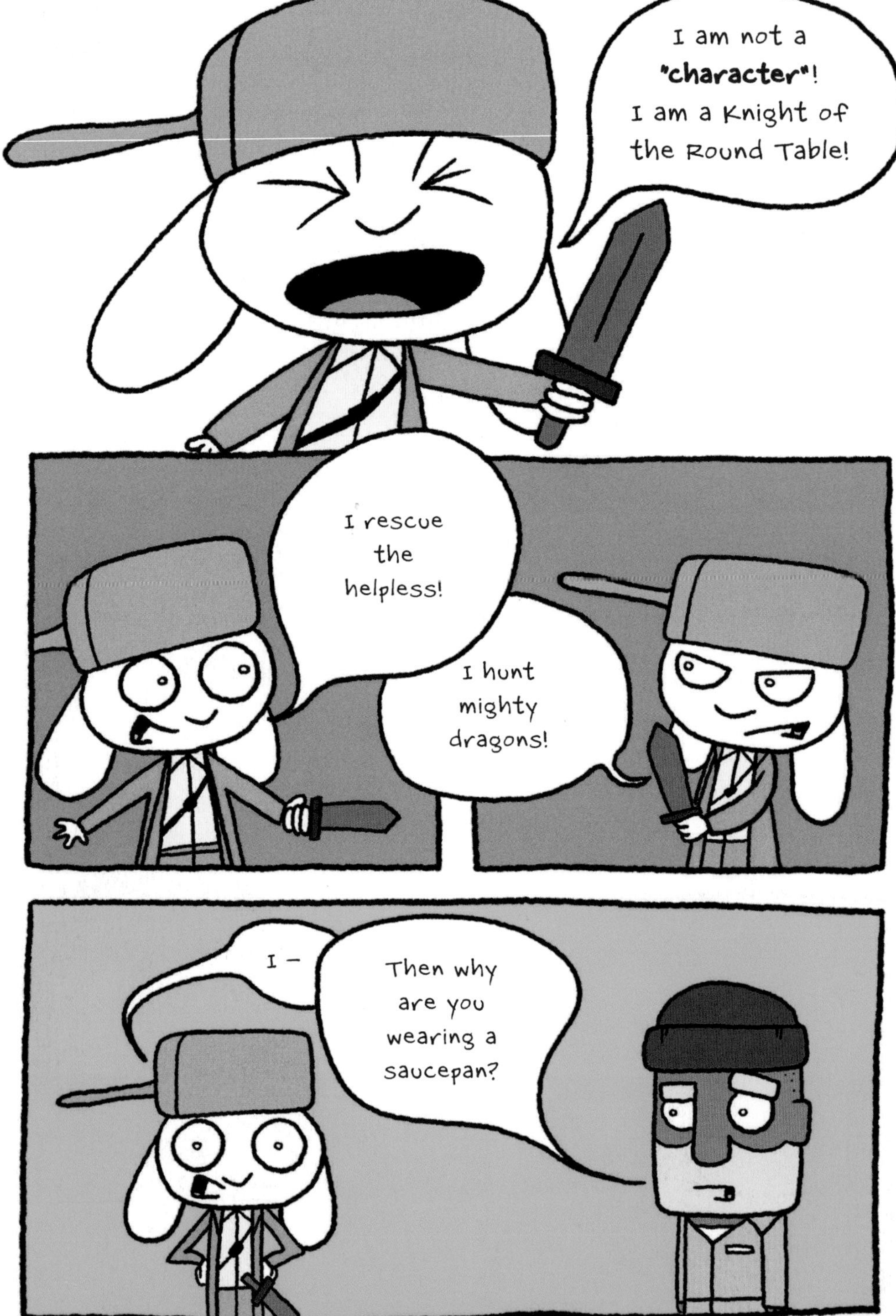

I am not a **"character"**! I am a Knight of the Round Table!
I rescue the helpless!
I hunt mighty dragons!
I –
Then why are you wearing a saucepan?

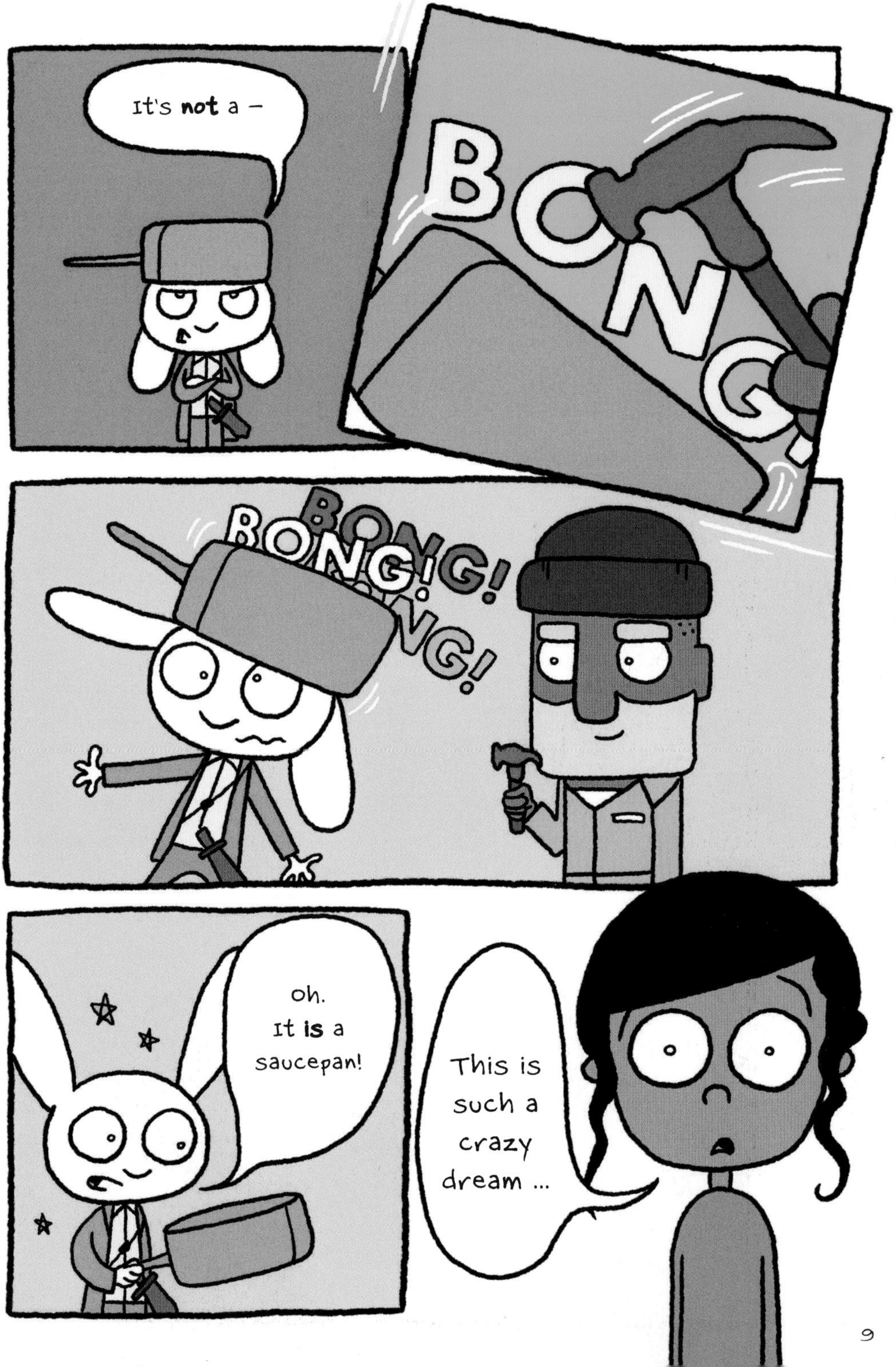
It's **not** a –
BONG!
BONG!
BONG!
BONG!
Oh.
It **is** a
saucepan!
This is
such a
crazy
dream ...

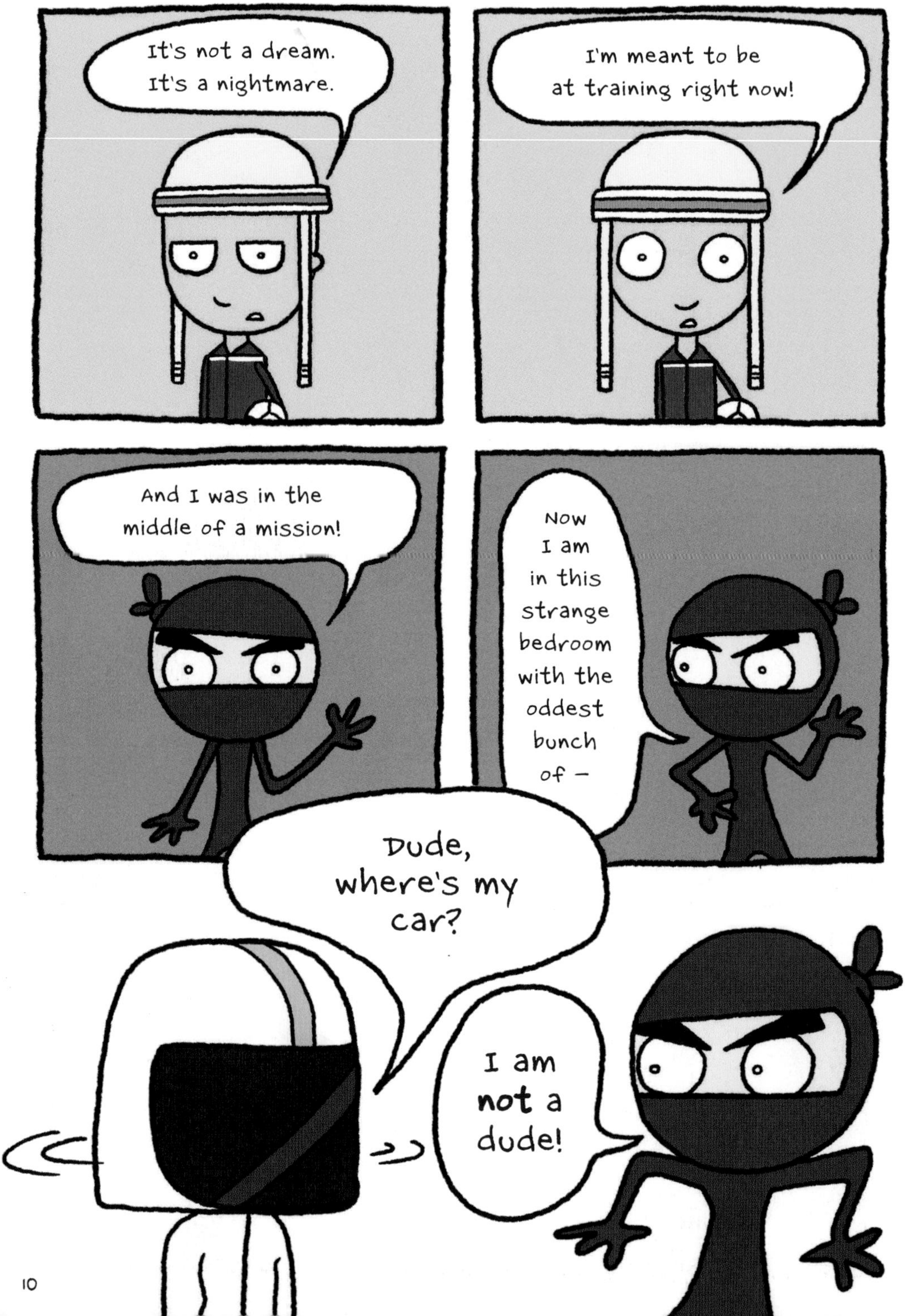
It's not a dream. It's a nightmare.
I'm meant to be at training right now!
And I was in the middle of a mission!
Now I am in this strange bedroom with the oddest bunch of –
Dude, where's my car?
I am **not** a dude!

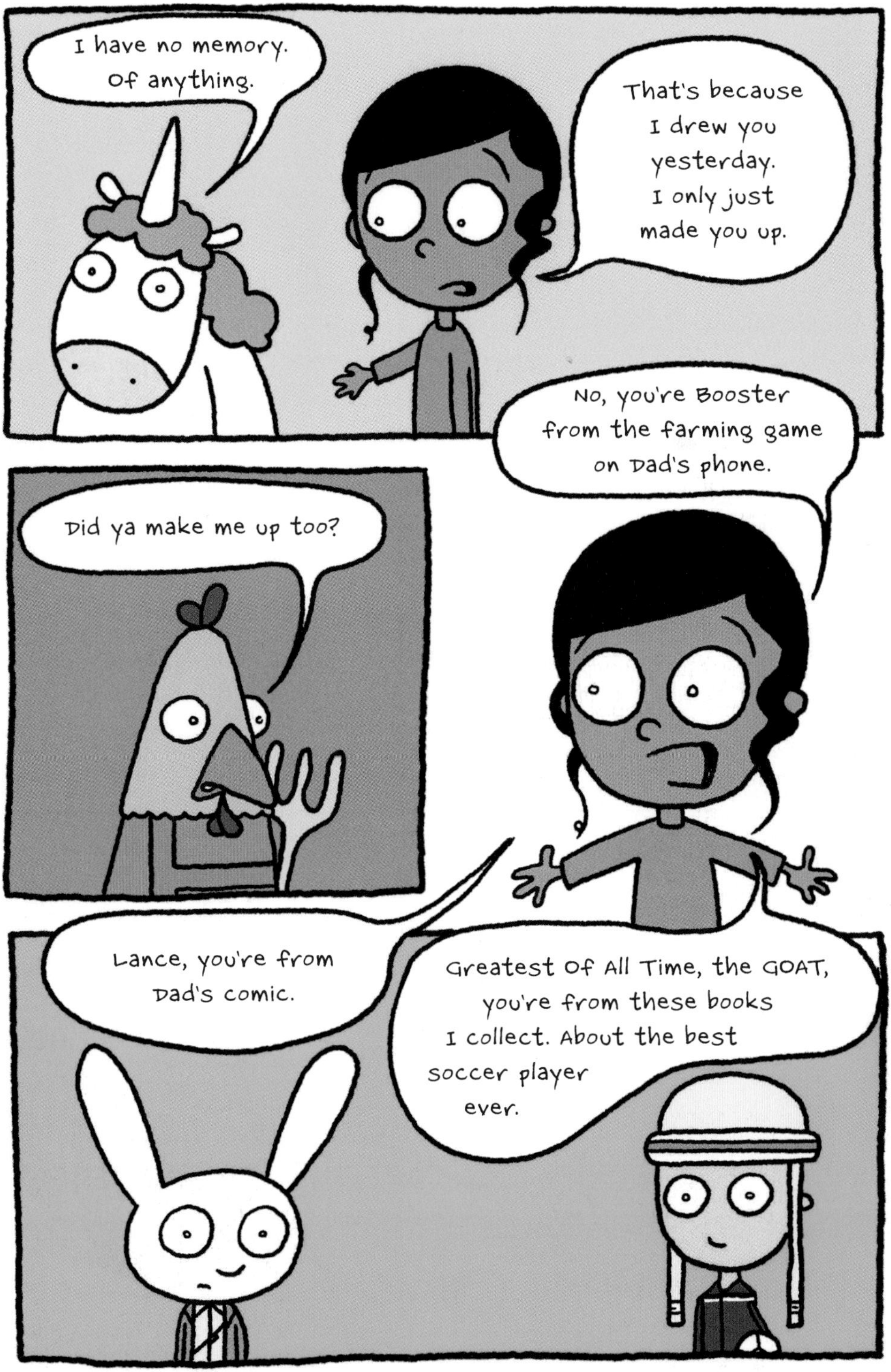
I have no memory. Of anything.
That's because I drew you yesterday. I only just made you up.
No, you're Booster from the farming game on Dad's phone.
Did ya make me up too?
Lance, you're from Dad's comic.
Greatest Of All Time, the GOAT, you're from these books I collect. About the best soccer player ever.

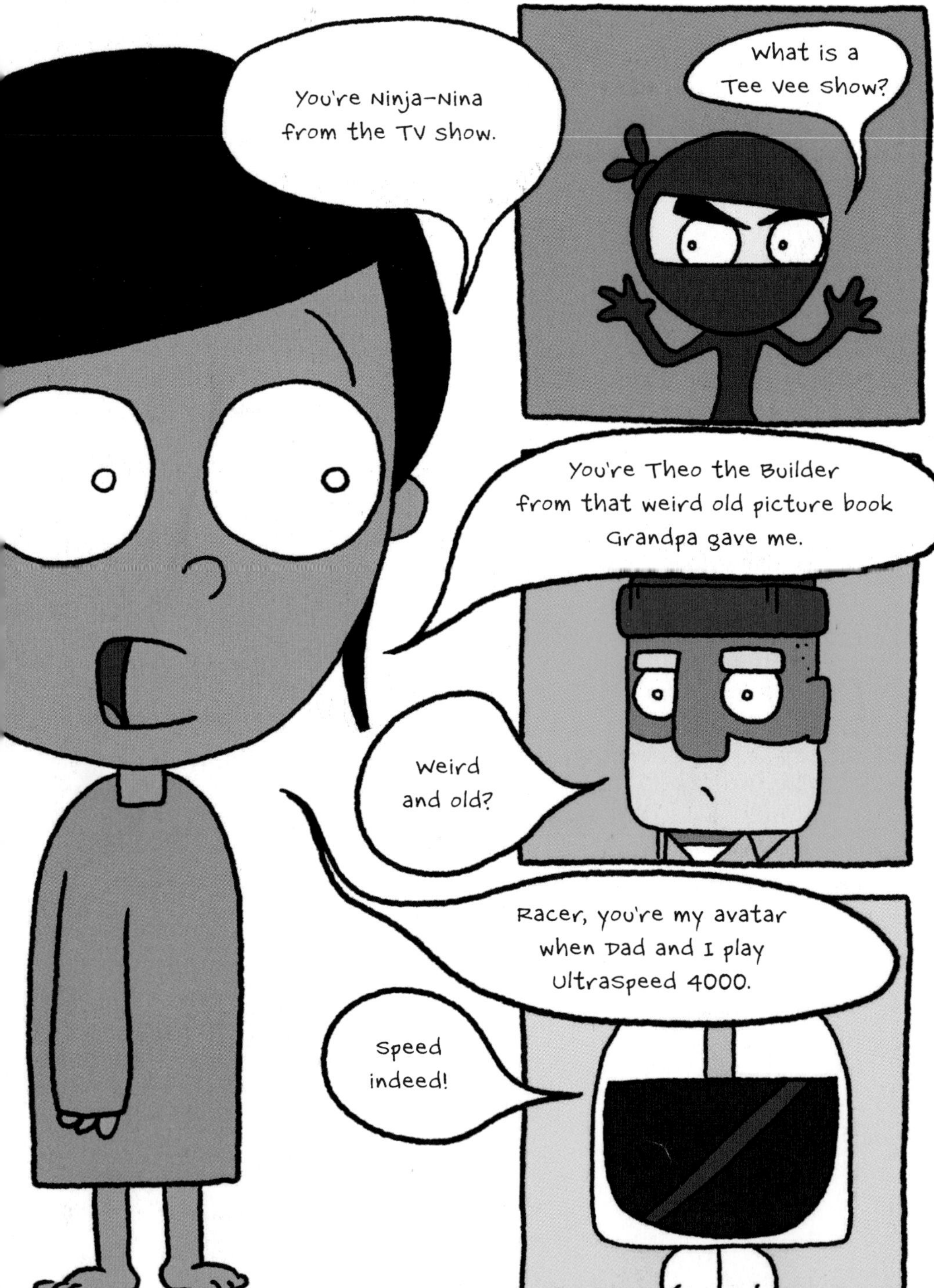
You're Ninja-Nina from the TV show.
What is a Tee vee show?
You're Theo the Builder from that weird old picture book Grandpa gave me.
Weird and old?
Racer, you're my avatar when Dad and I play UltraSpeed 4000.
Speed indeed!

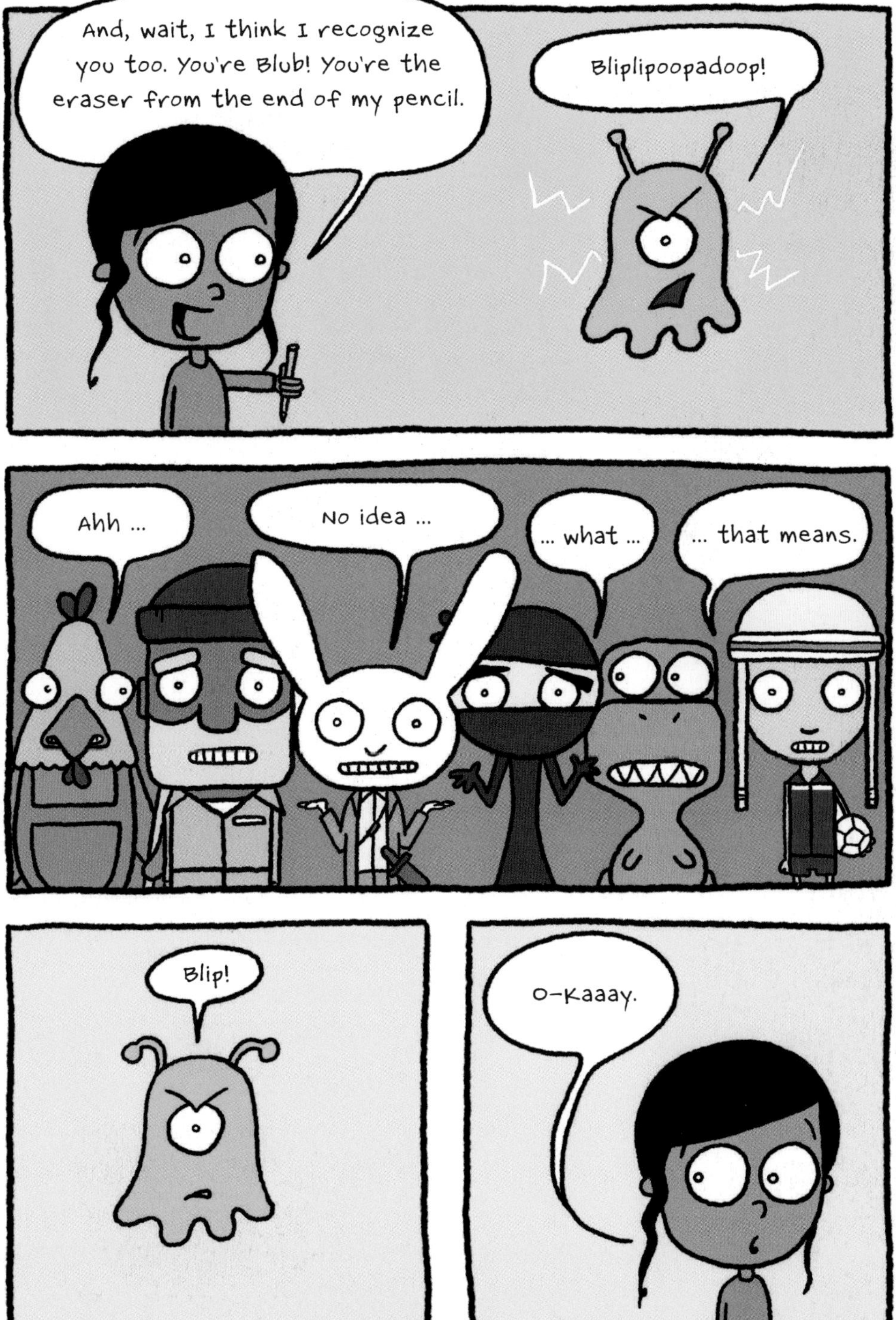

And, wait, I think I recognize you too. You're Blub! You're the eraser from the end of my pencil.
Bliplipoopadoop!
Ahh ...
No idea ...
... what ...
... that means.
Blip!
O-Kaaay.

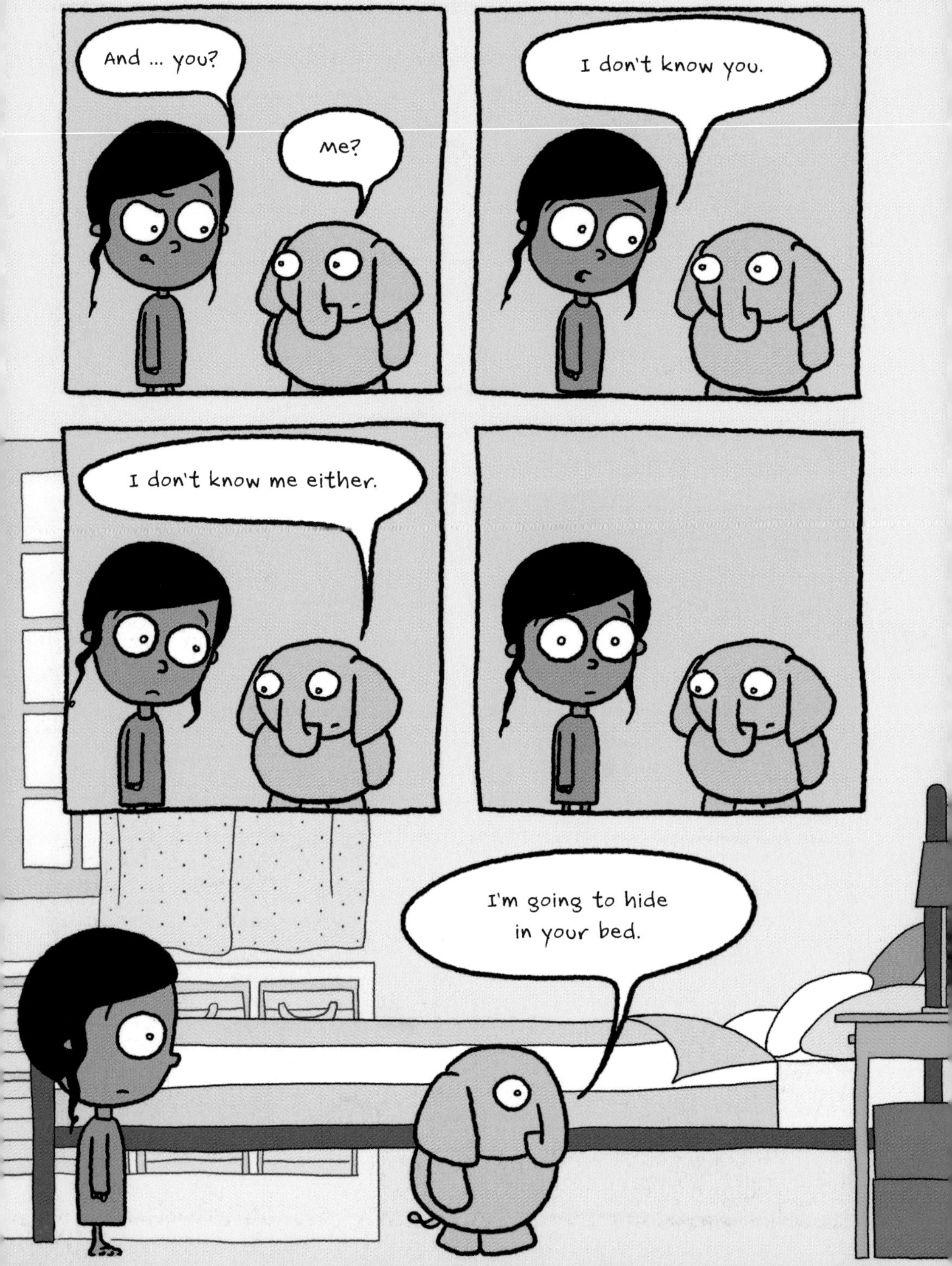
And ... you?
Me?
I don't know you.
I don't know me either.
I'm going to hide in your bed.

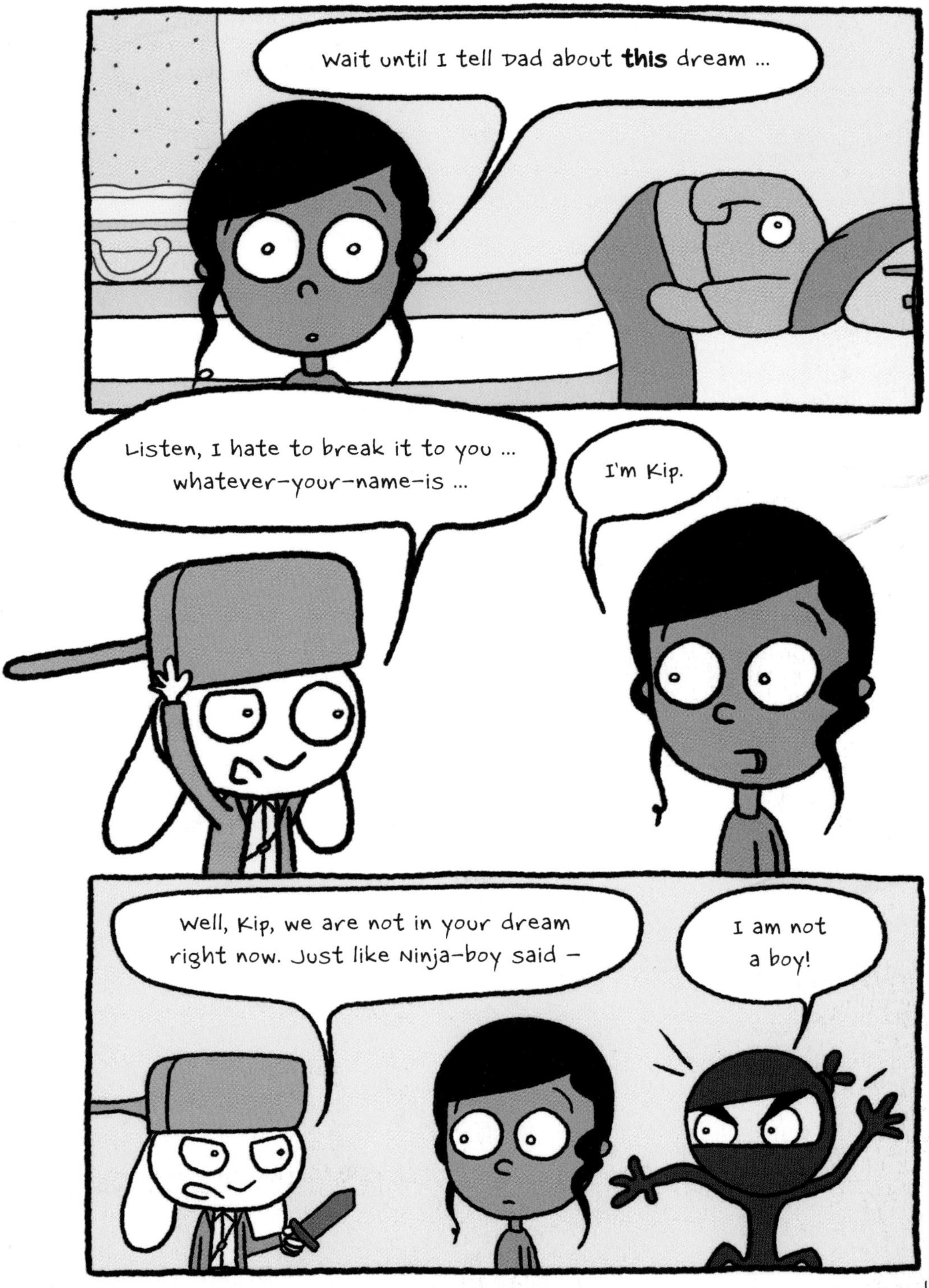

Wait until I tell Dad about **this** dream ...
Listen, I hate to break it to you ... whatever-your-name-is ...
I'm Kip.
Well, Kip, we are not in your dream right now. Just like Ninja-boy said –
I am not a boy!

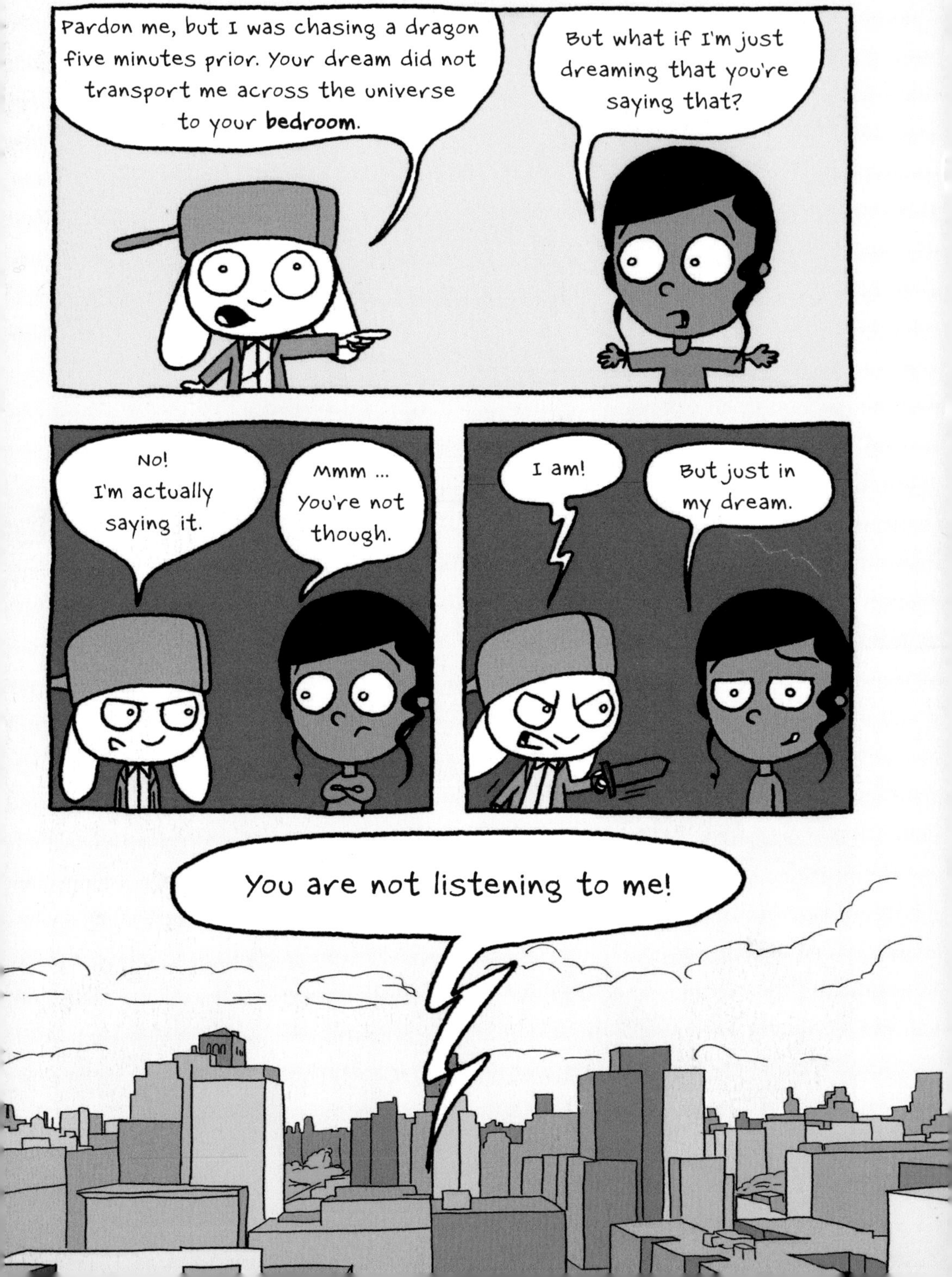
Pardon me, but I was chasing a dragon five minutes prior. Your dream did not transport me across the universe to your **bedroom**.
But what if I'm just dreaming that you're saying that?
No! I'm actually saying it.
Mmm ... You're not though.
I am!
But just in my dream.
You are not listening to me!

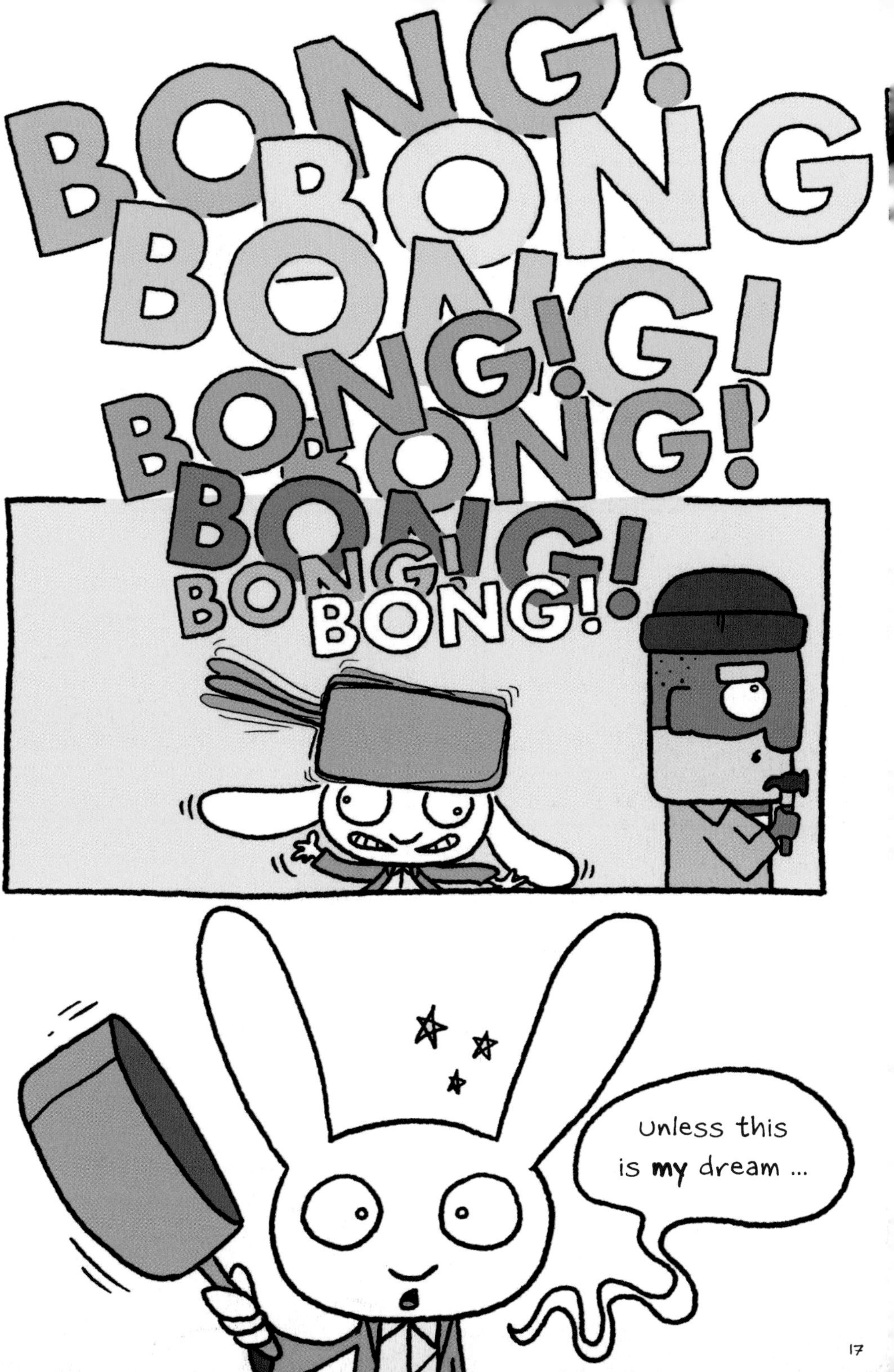
BONG!
BONG!
BONG!
BONG!
BONG!
BONG!
BONG!
BONG!
Unless this is my dream ...

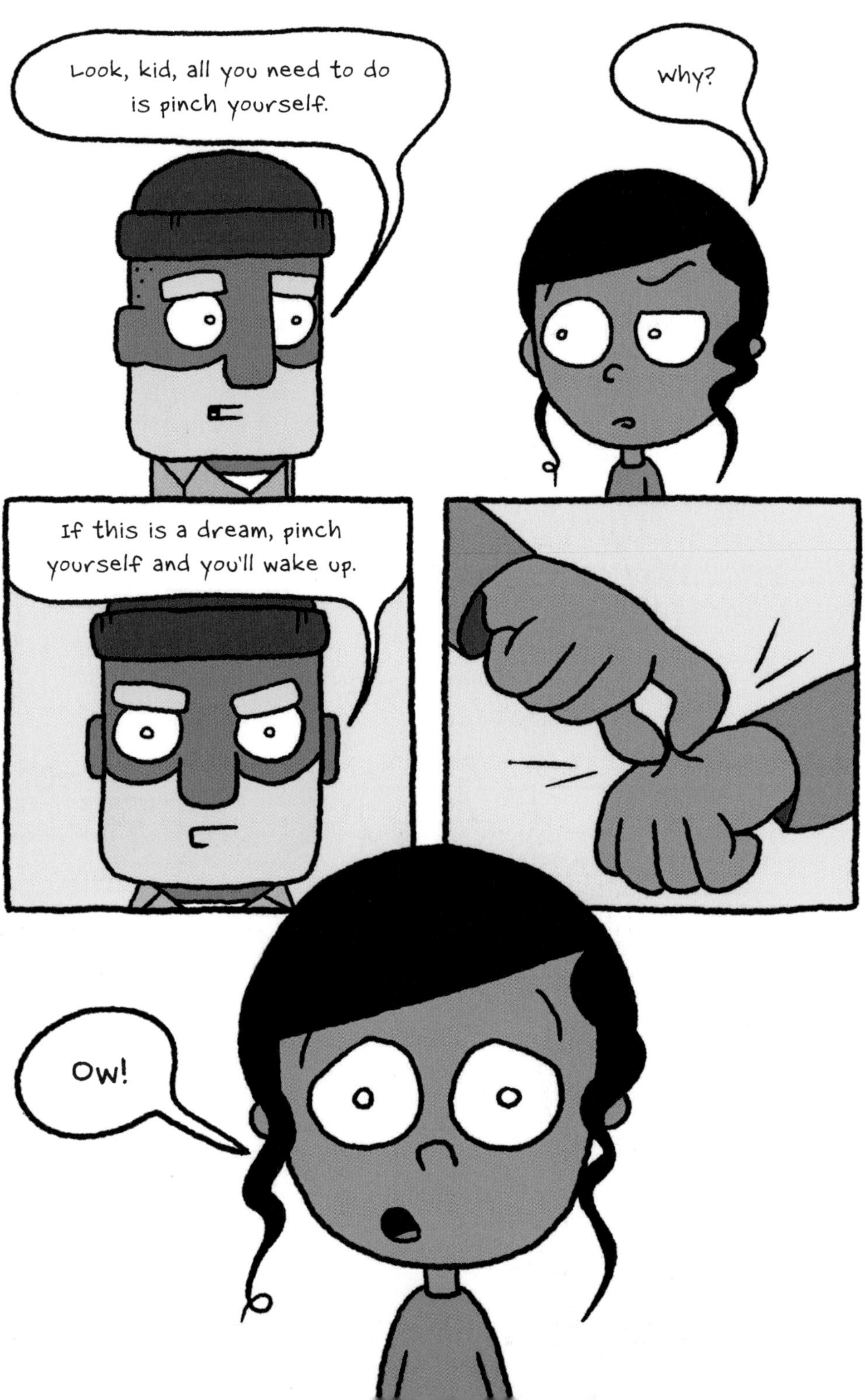
Look, kid, all you need to do is pinch yourself.
Why?
If this is a dream, pinch yourself and you'll wake up.
Ow!

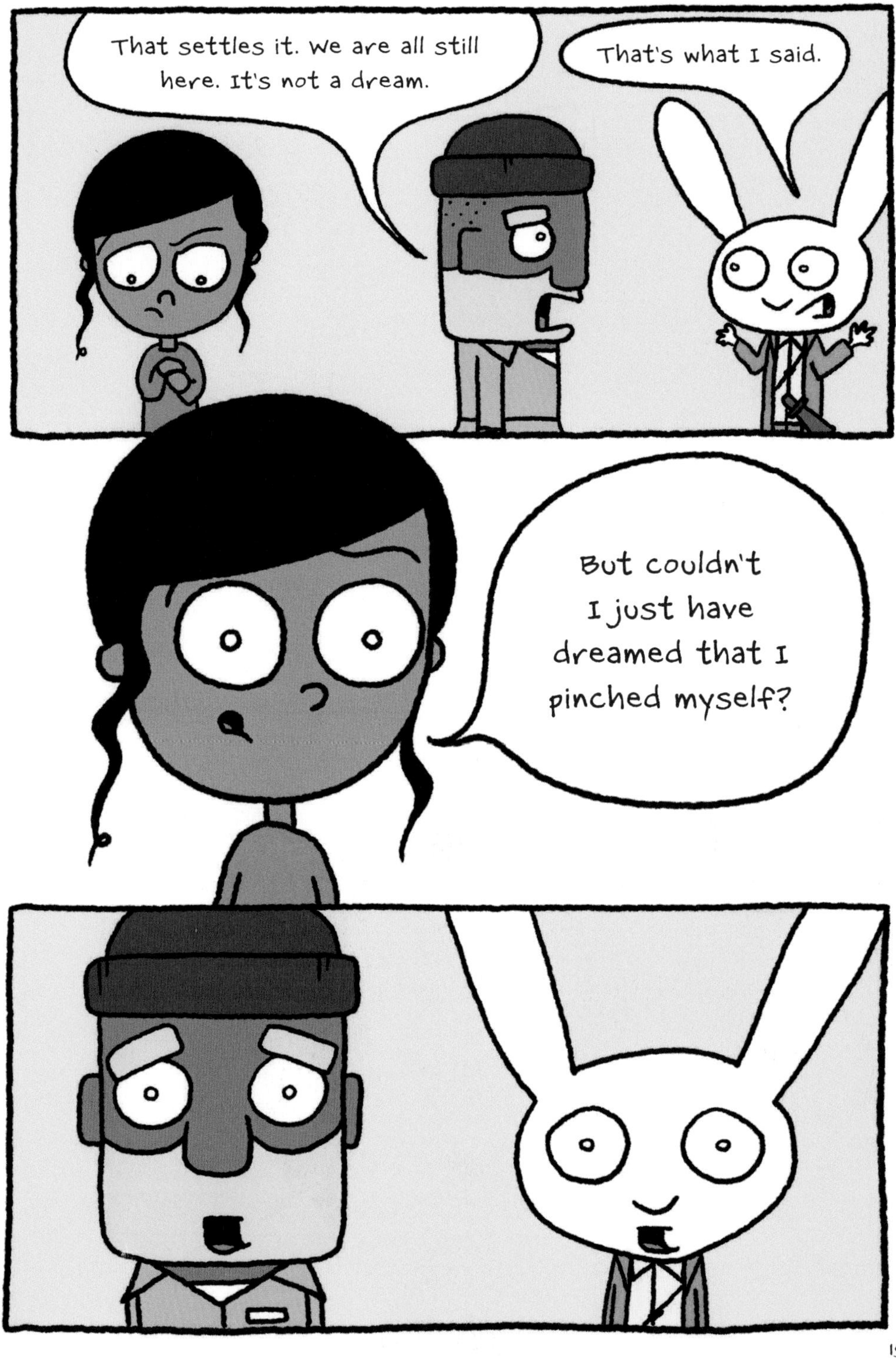
That settles it. We are all still here. It's not a dream.
That's what I said.
But couldn't I just have dreamed that I pinched myself?

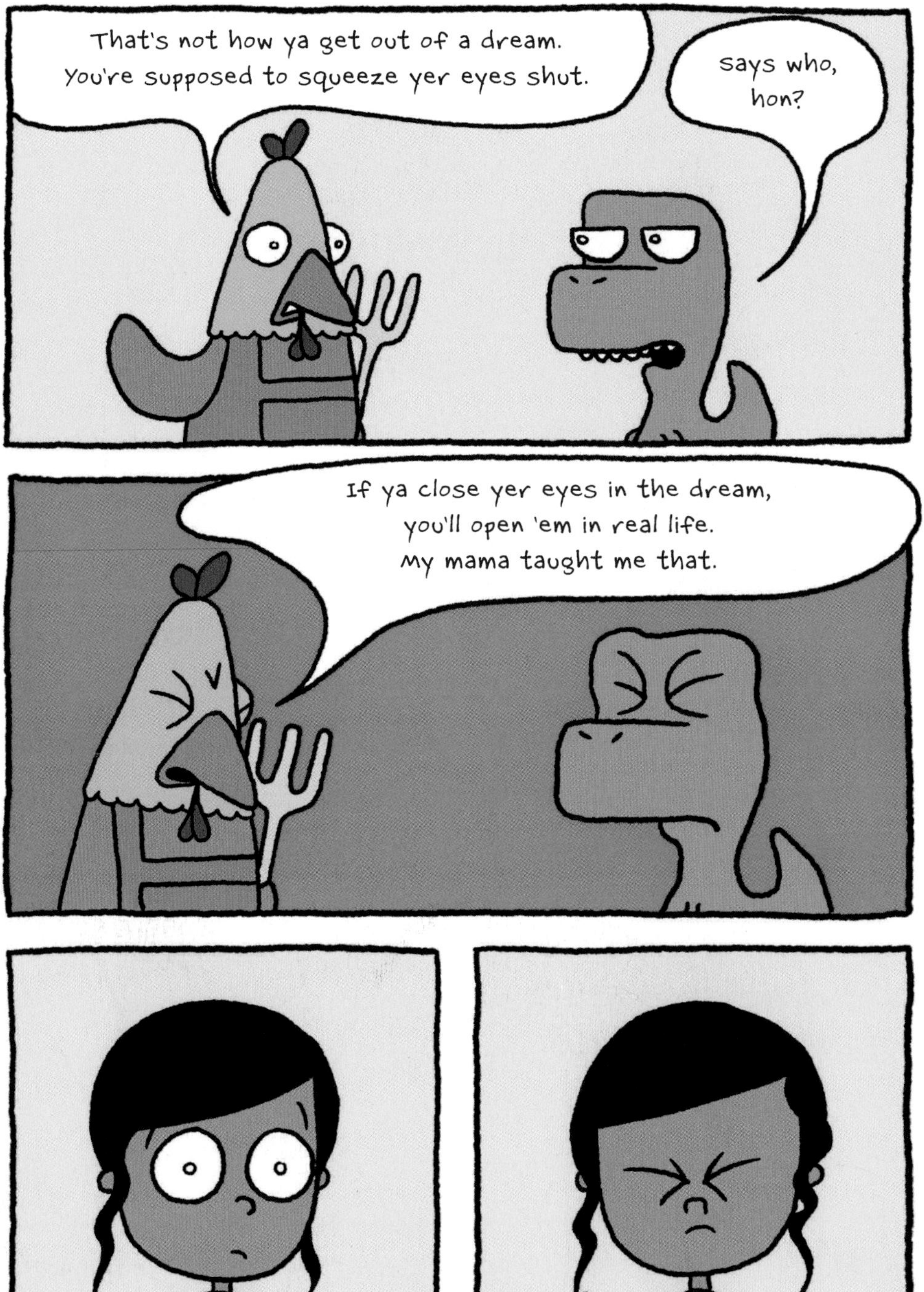
That's not how ya get out of a dream. You're supposed to squeeze yer eyes shut.
says who, hon?
If ya close yer eyes in the dream, you'll open 'em in real life. My mama taught me that.

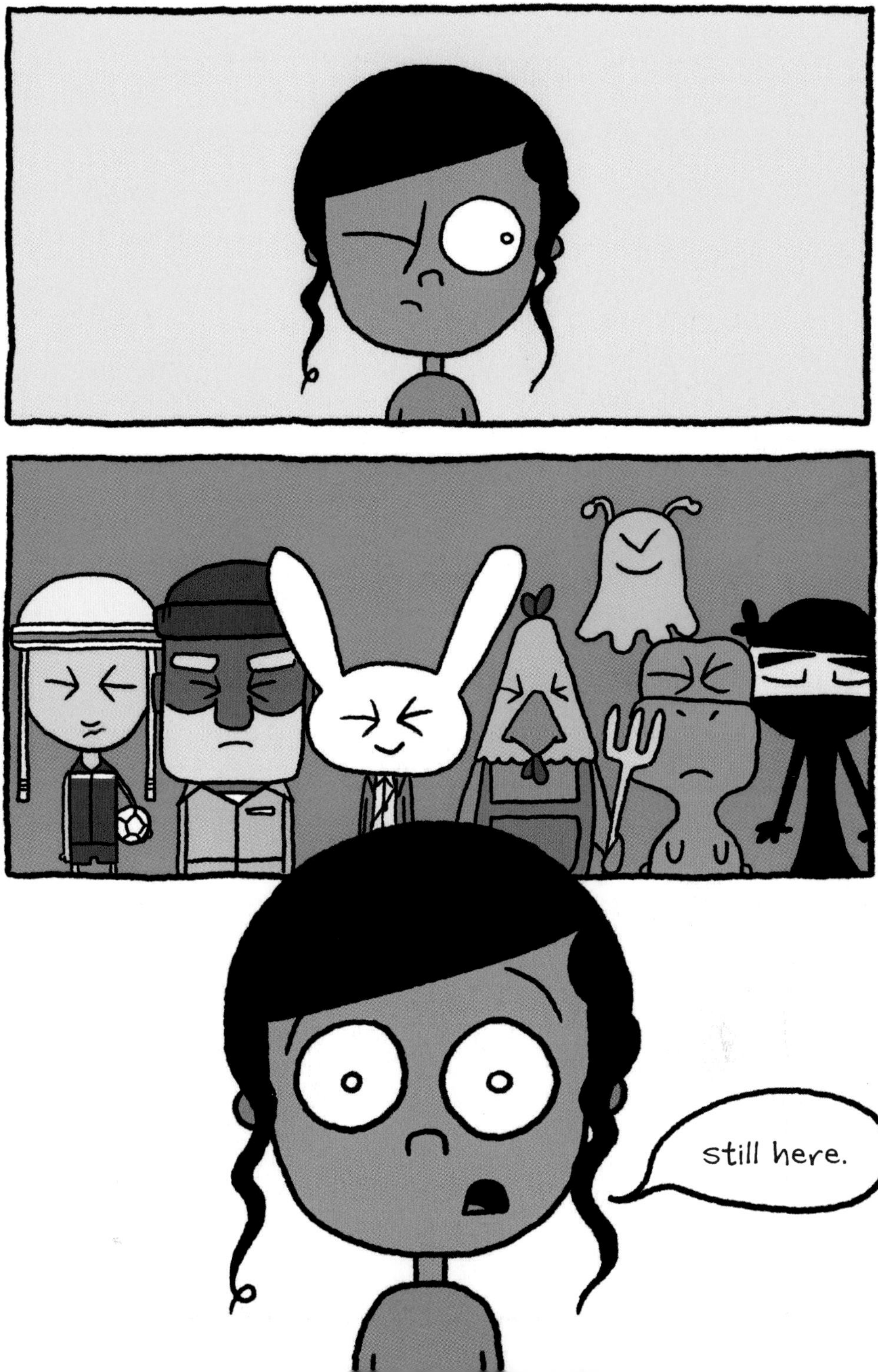
still here.

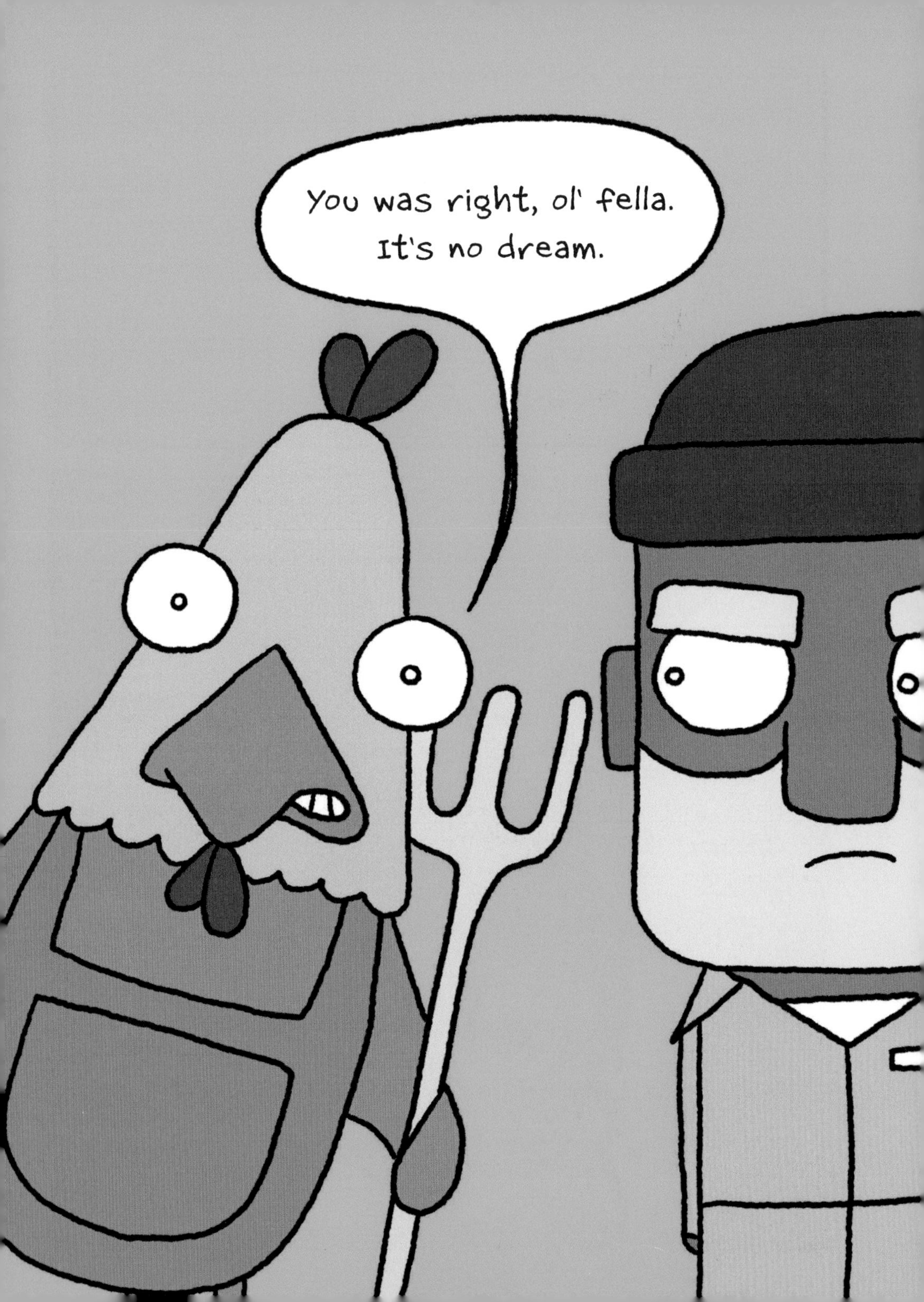
You was right, ol' fella. It's no dream.

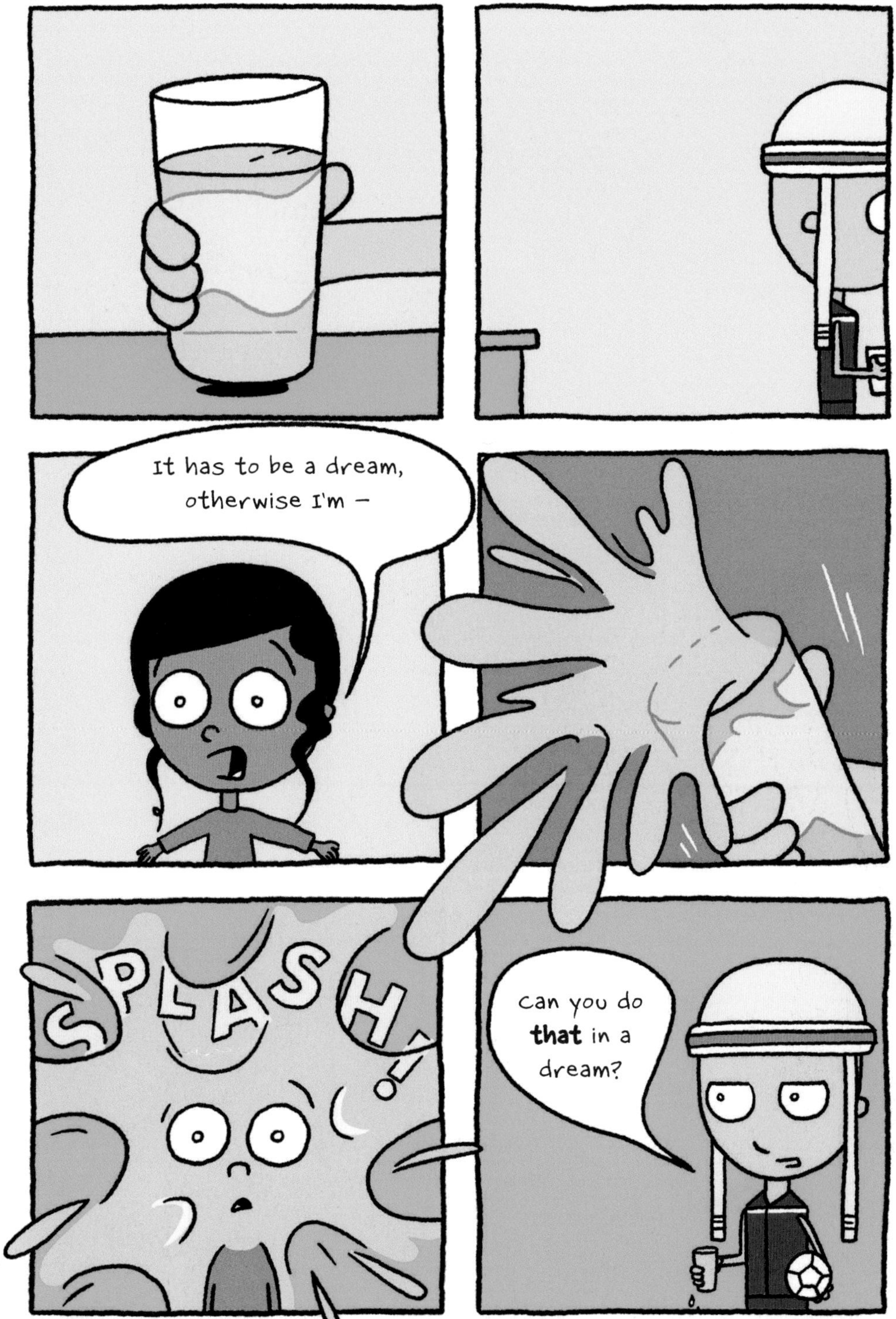
It has to be a dream, otherwise I'm –
SPLASH!
Can you do **that** in a dream?

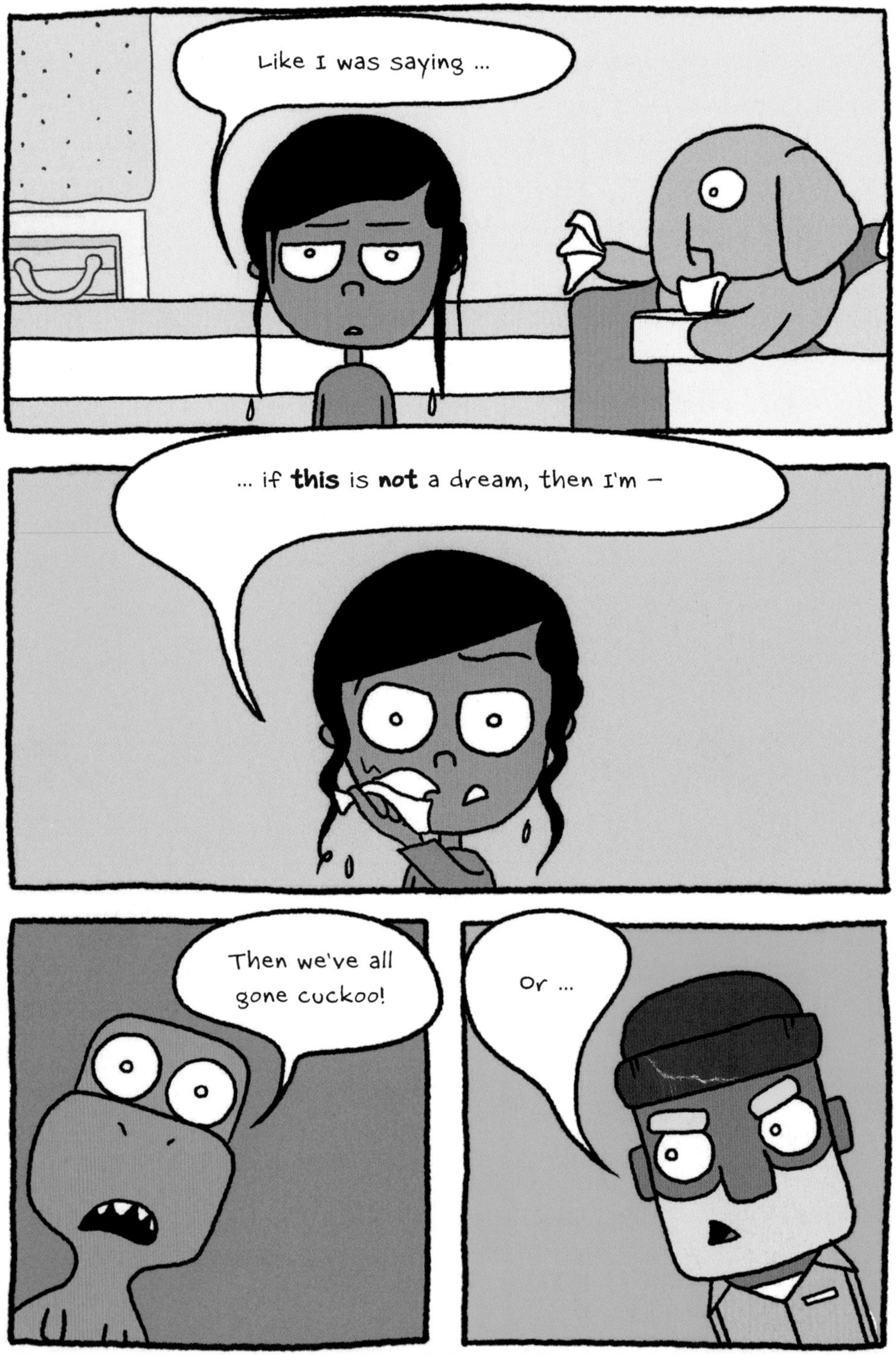

Like I was saying ...
... if **this** is **not** a dream, then I'm –
Then we've all gone cuckoo!
Or ...

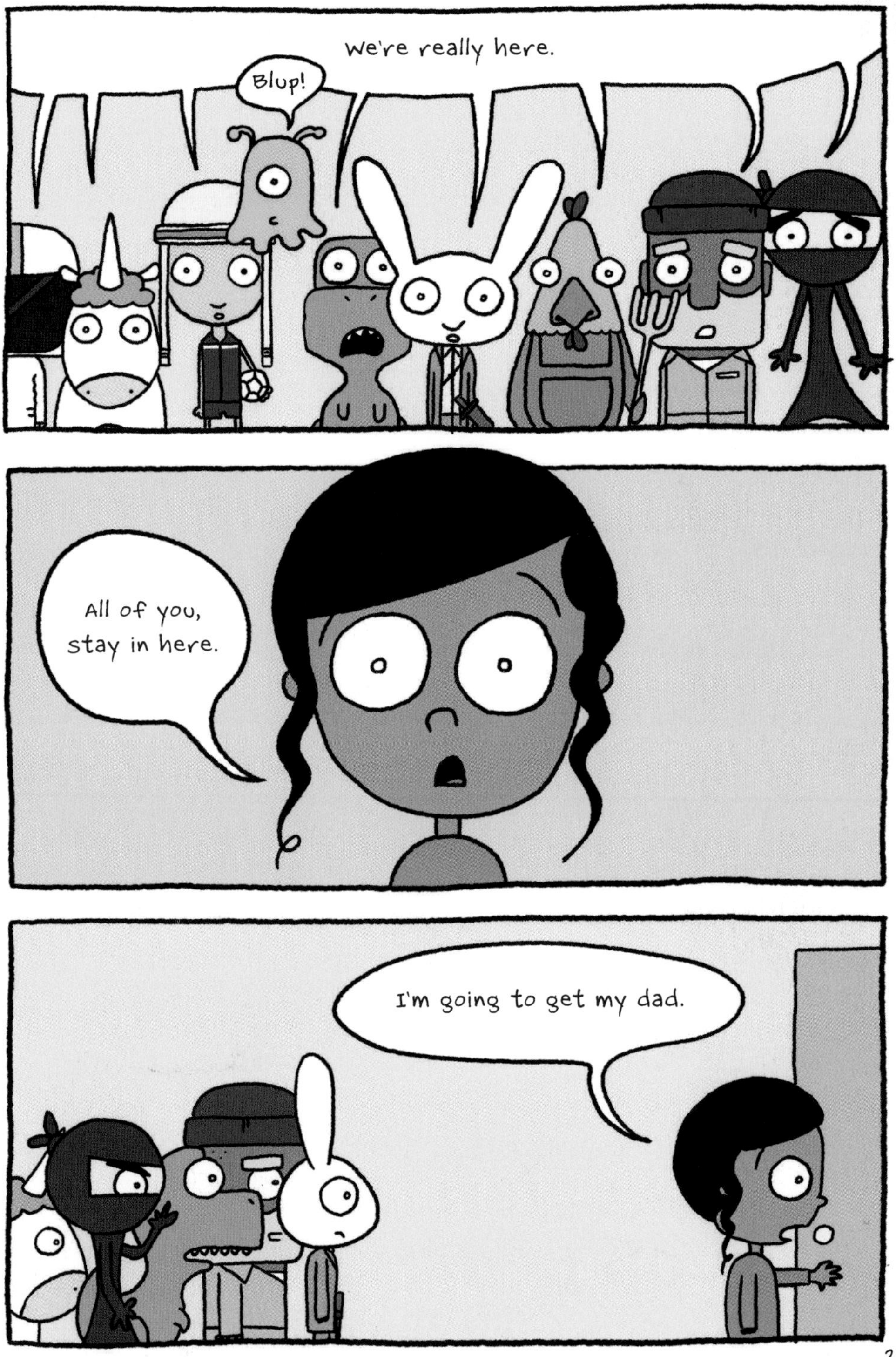
We're really here.
Blup!
All of you, stay in here.
I'm going to get my dad.

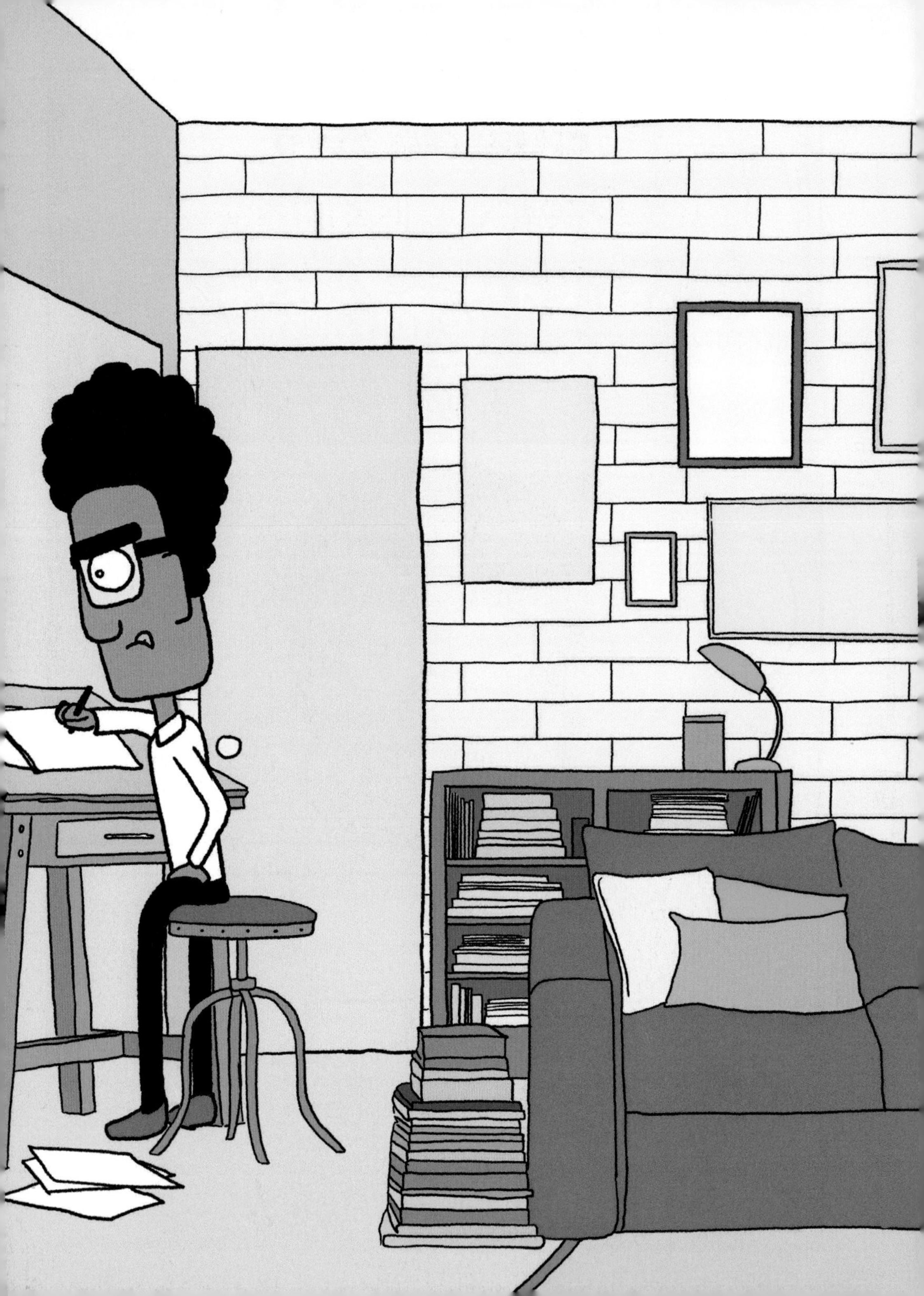

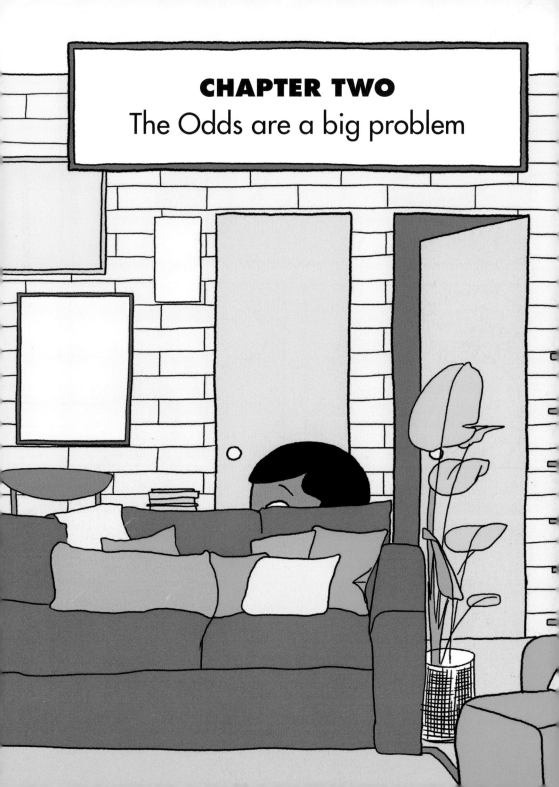

CHAPTER TWO
The Odds are a big problem

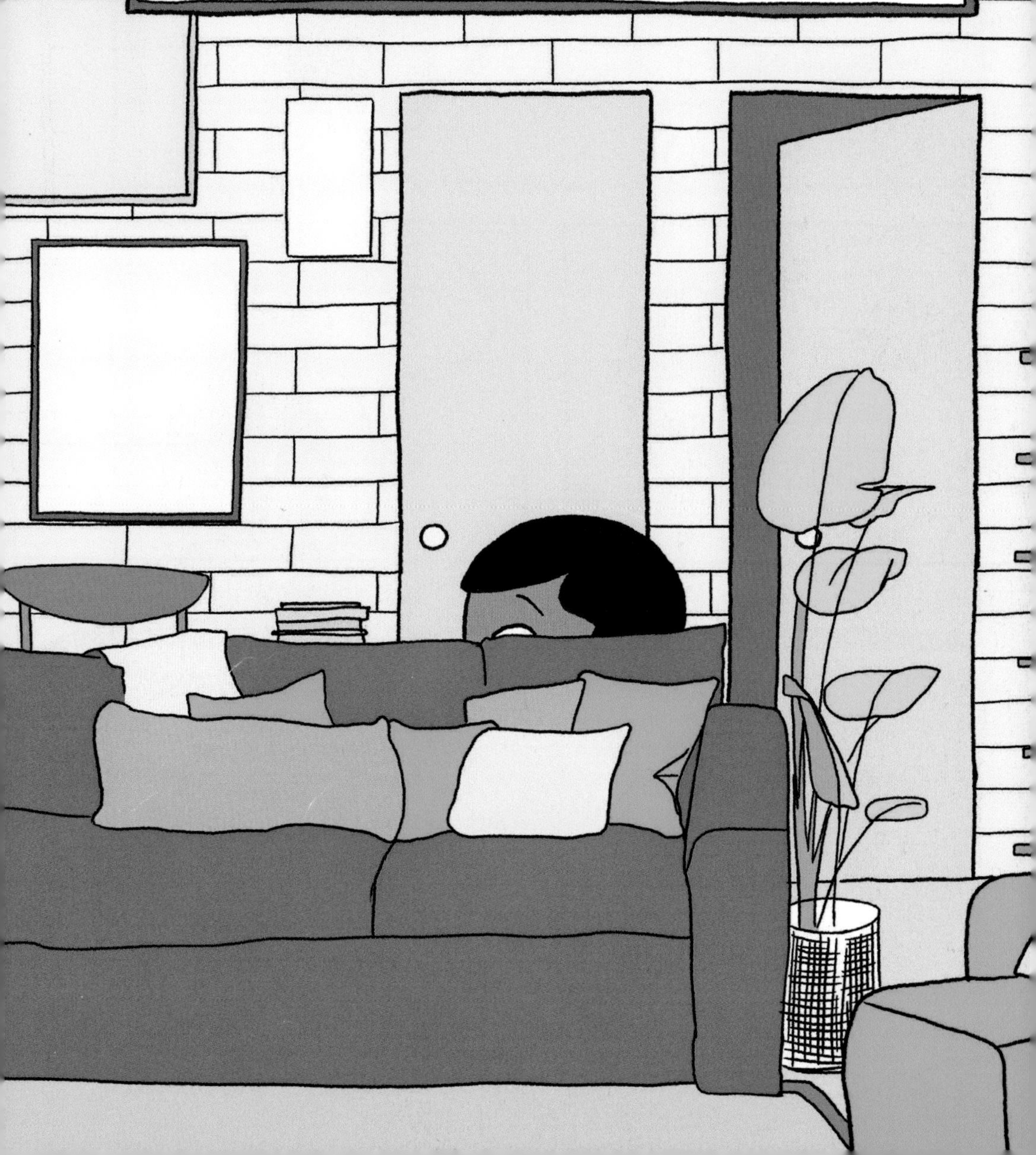

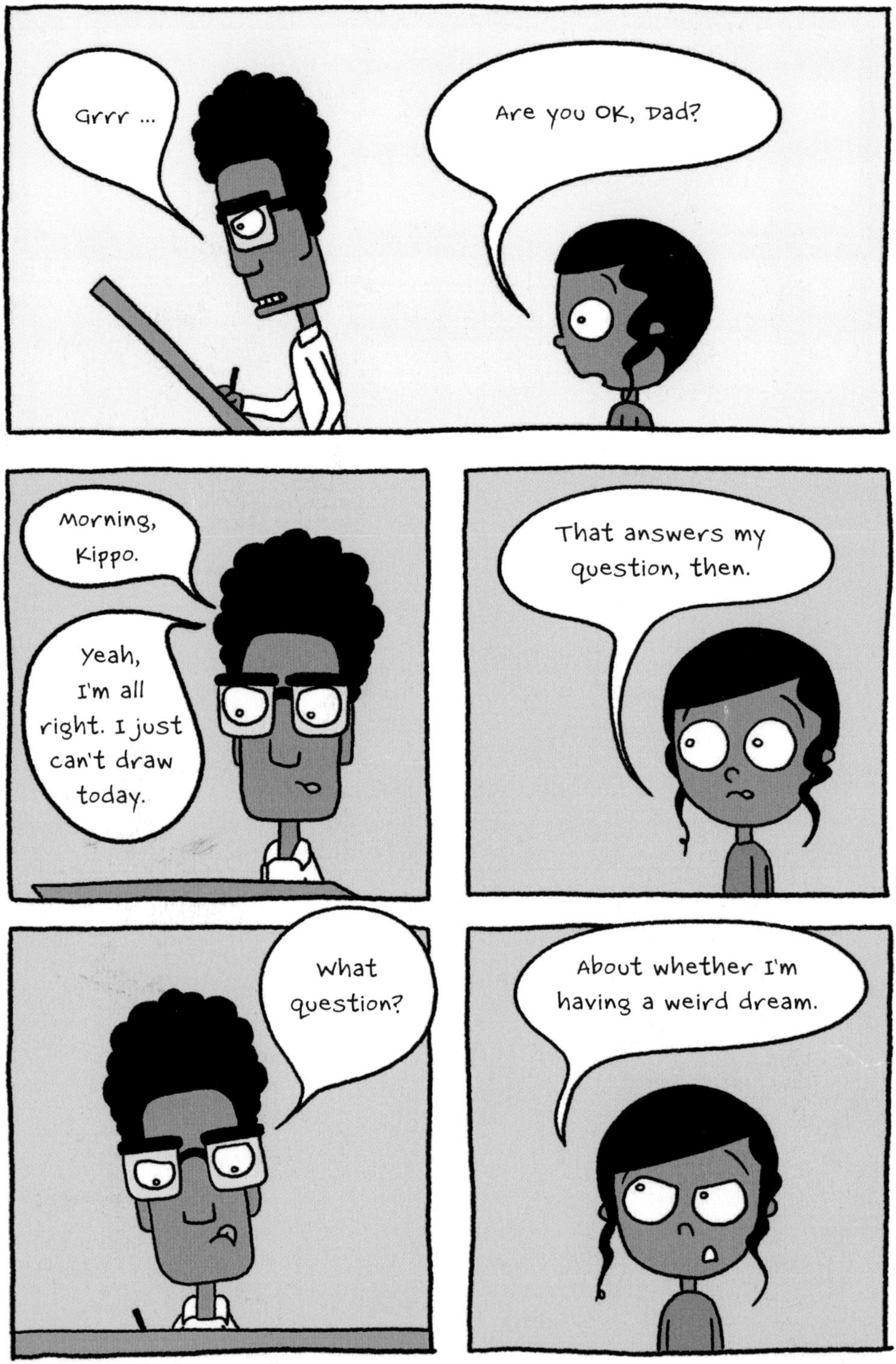
Grrr ...
Are you OK, Dad?
Morning, Kippo.
Yeah, I'm all right. I just can't draw today.
That answers my question, then.
What question?
About whether I'm having a weird dream.

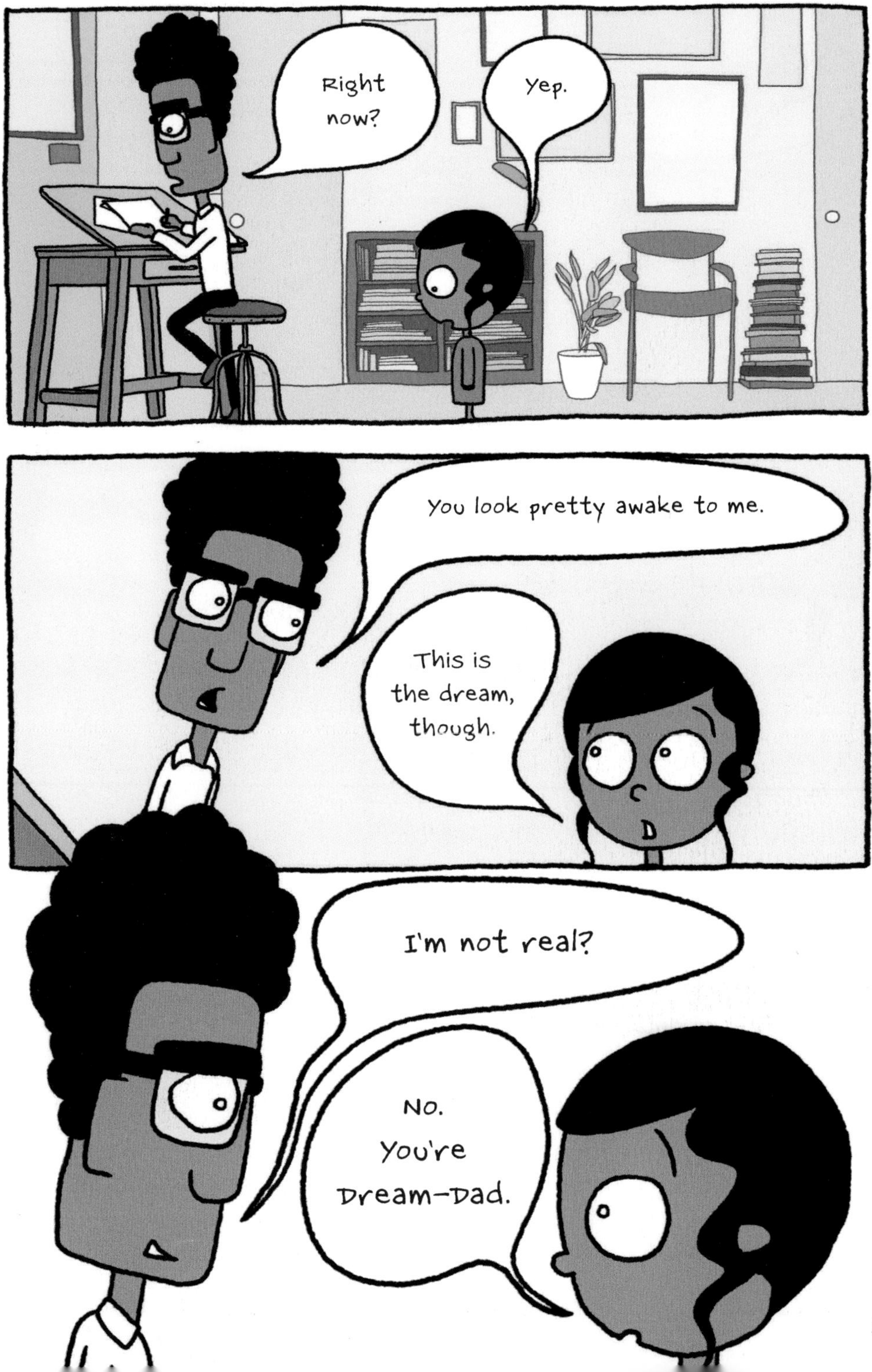
Right now?
Yep.
You look pretty awake to me.
This is the dream, though.
I'm not real?
No. You're Dream-Dad.

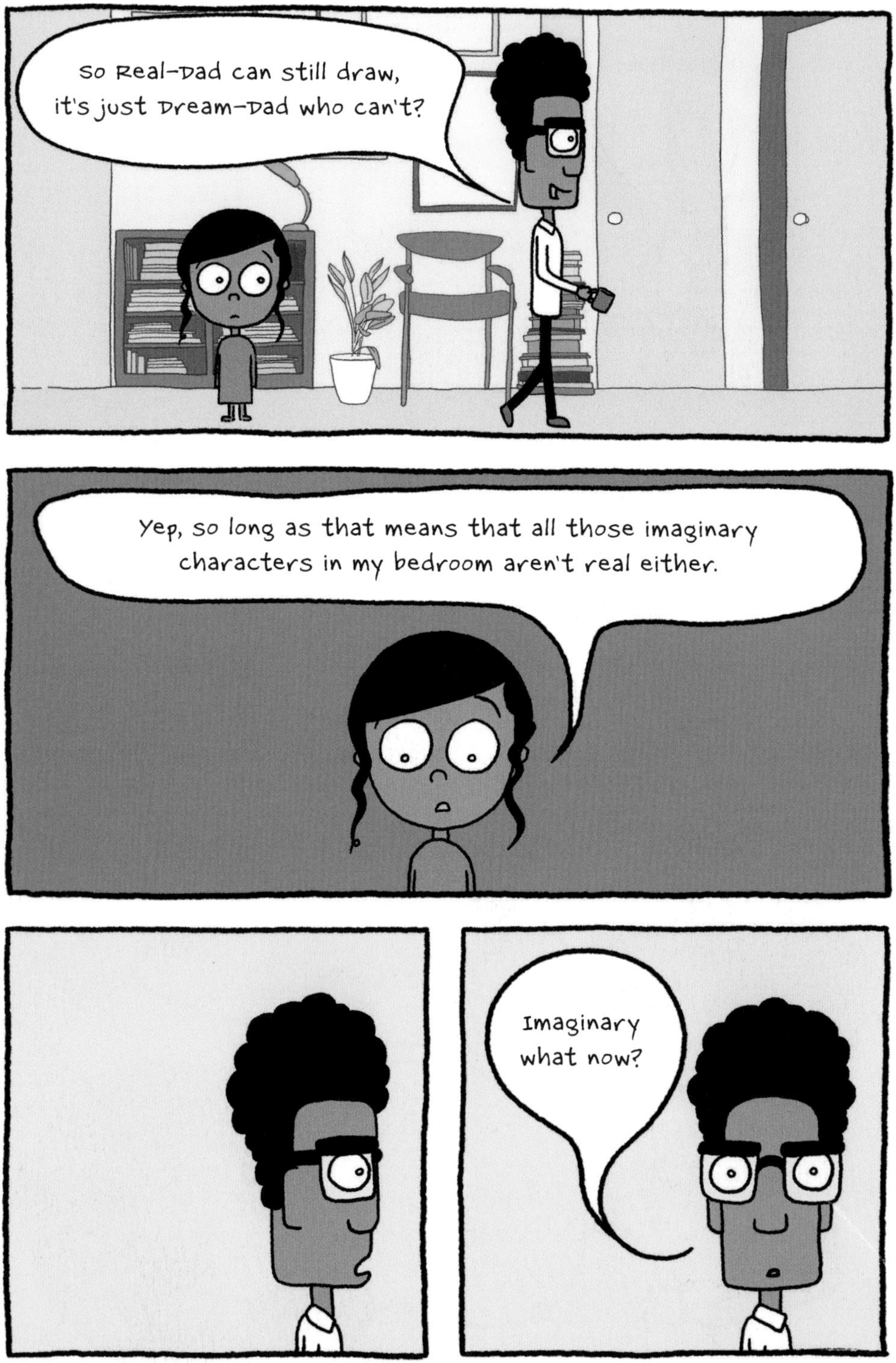
So Real-Dad can still draw, it's just Dream-Dad who can't?
Yep, so long as that means that all those imaginary characters in my bedroom aren't real either.
Imaginary what now?

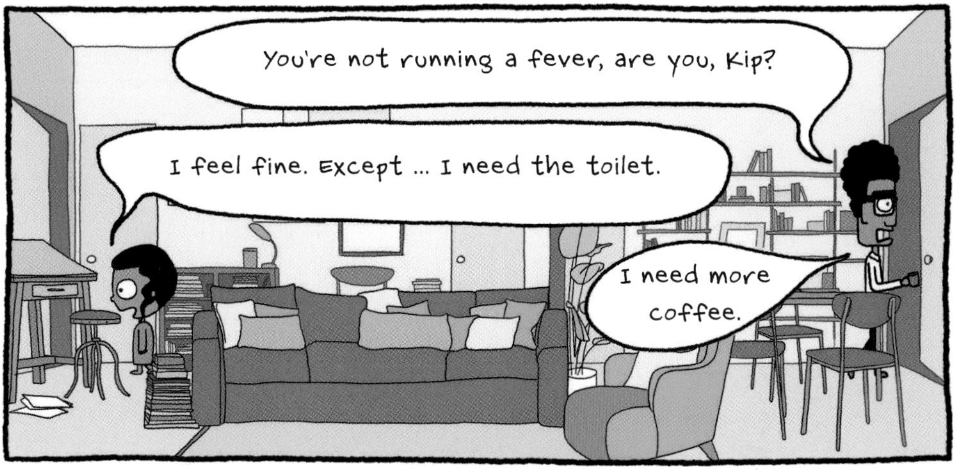
You're not running a fever, are you, Kip?
I feel fine. Except ... I need the toilet.
I need more coffee.

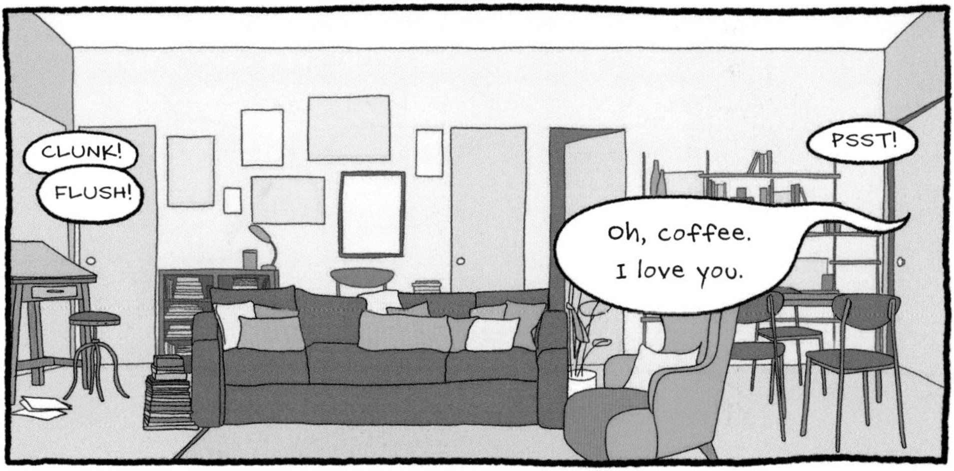
CLUNK!
FLUSH!
PSST!
Oh, coffee. I love you.

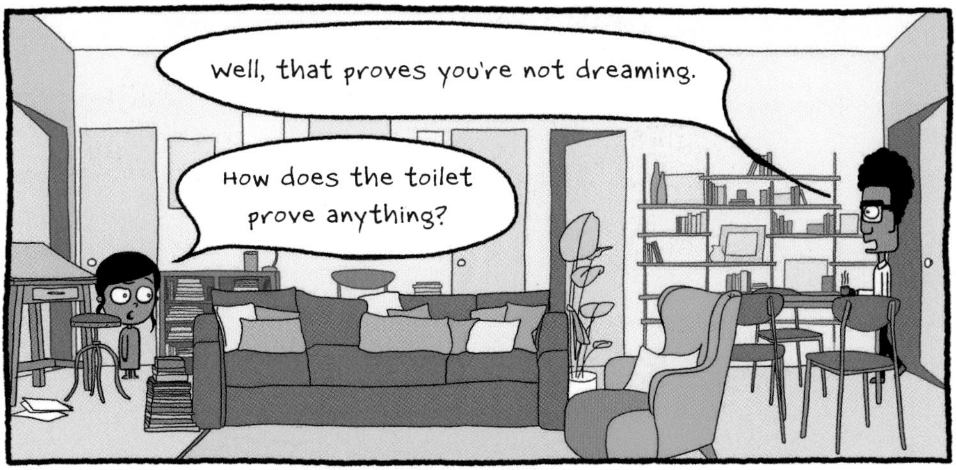
Well, that proves you're not dreaming.
How does the toilet prove anything?

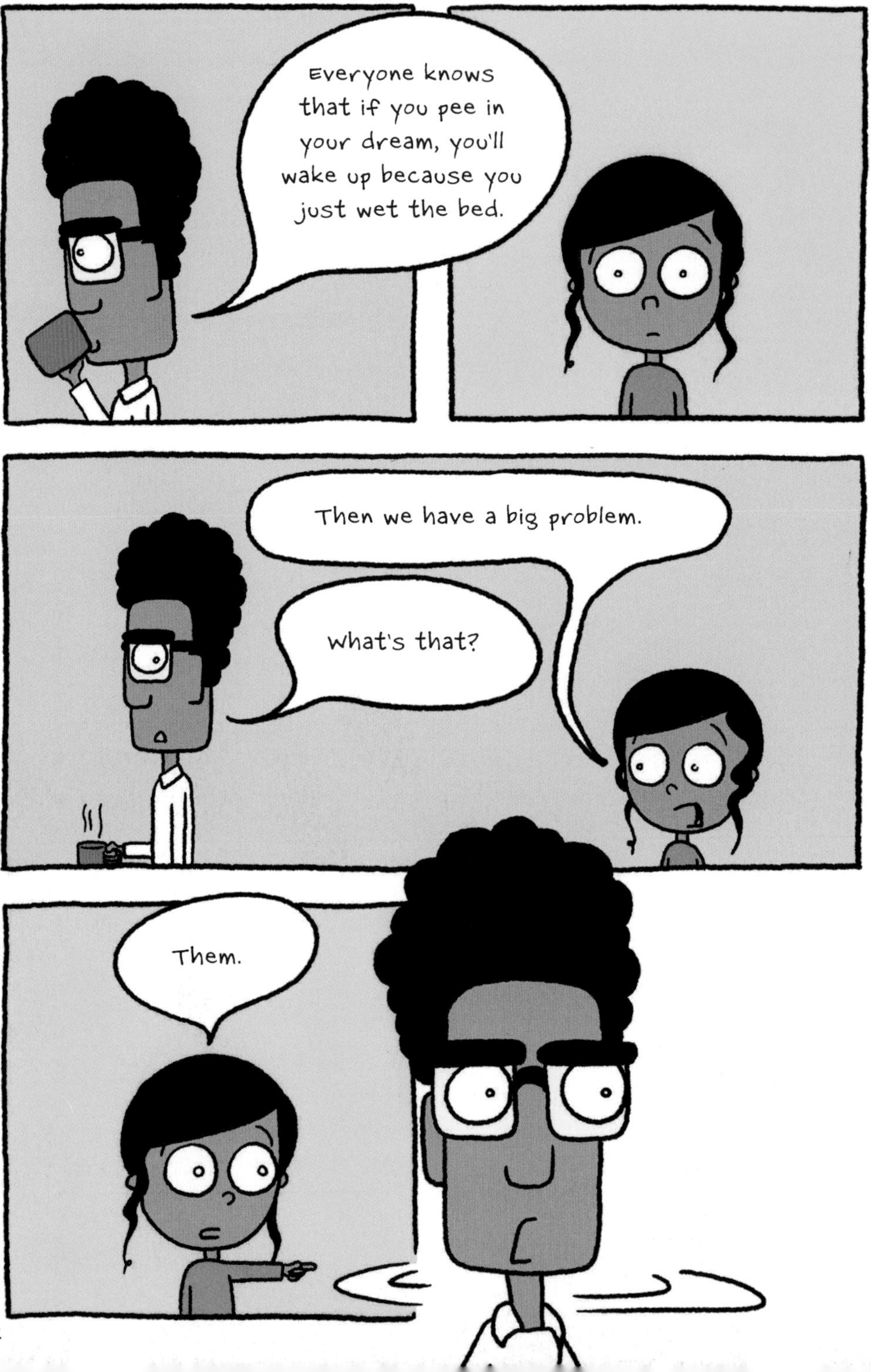
Everyone knows that if you pee in your dream, you'll wake up because you just wet the bed.
Then we have a big problem.
What's that?
Them.

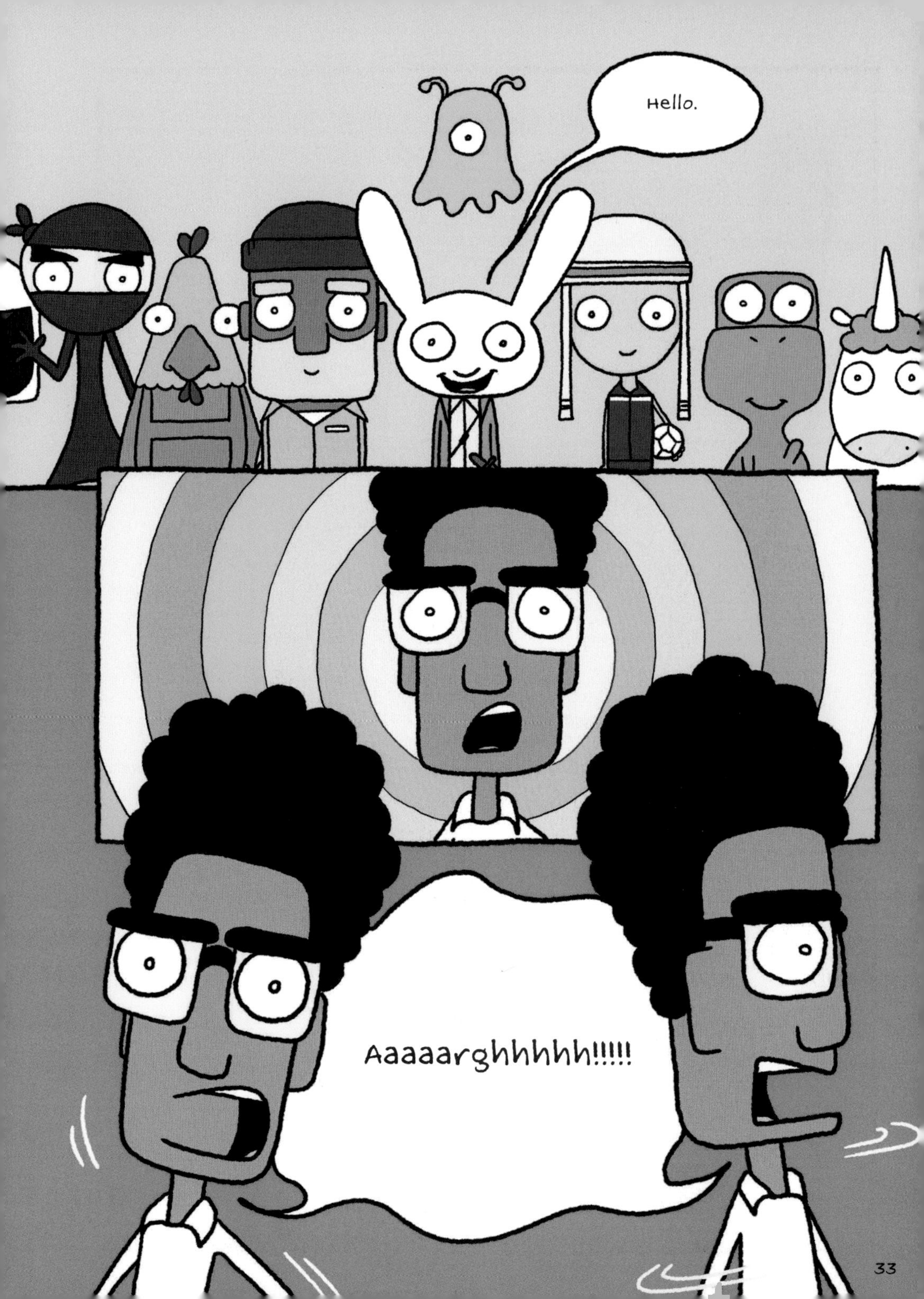
Hello.
Aaaaarghhhhh!!!!!

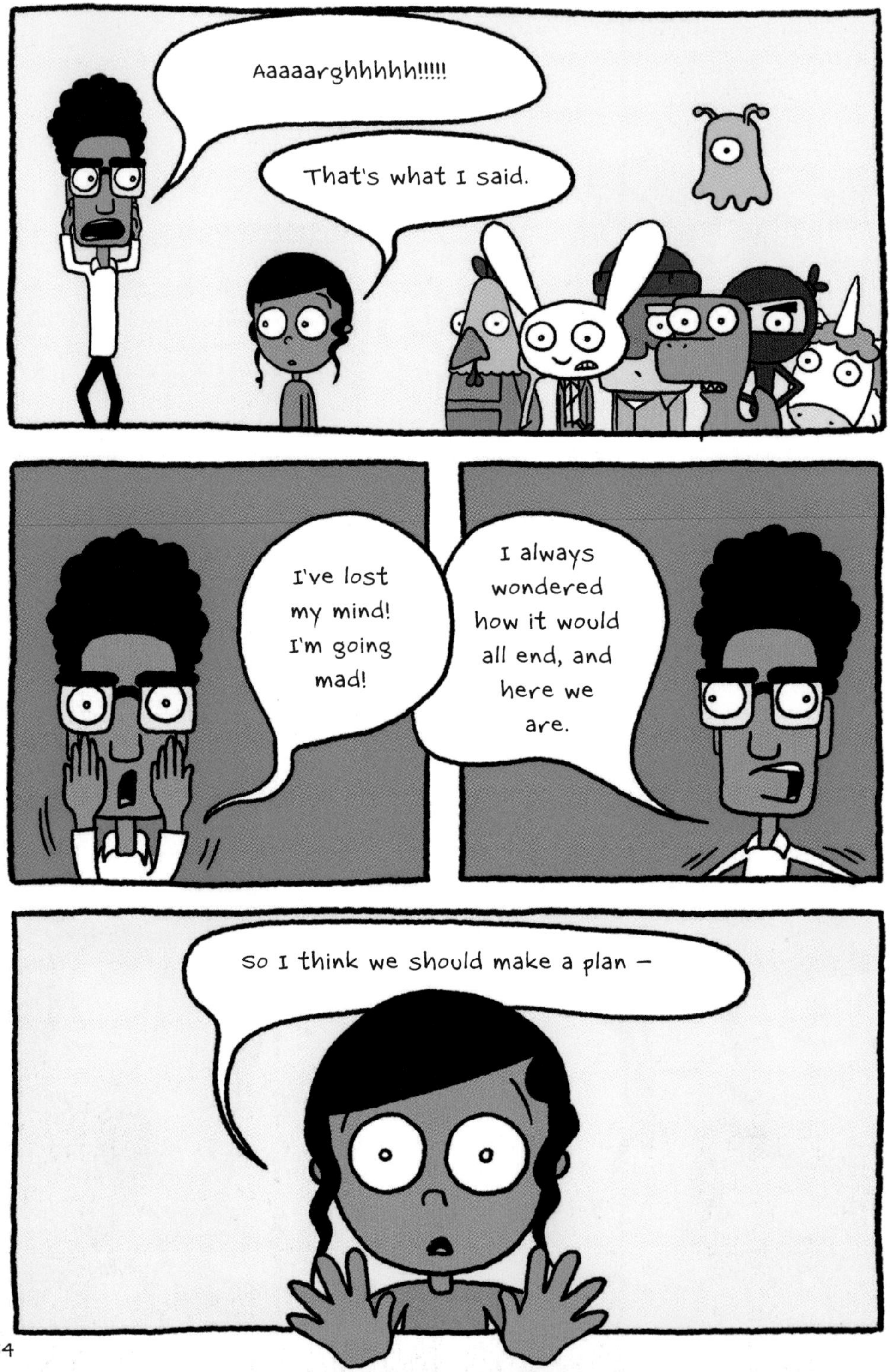
Aaaaarghhhhh!!!!!
That's what I said.
I've lost my mind! I'm going mad!
I always wondered how it would all end, and here we are.
So I think we should make a plan –

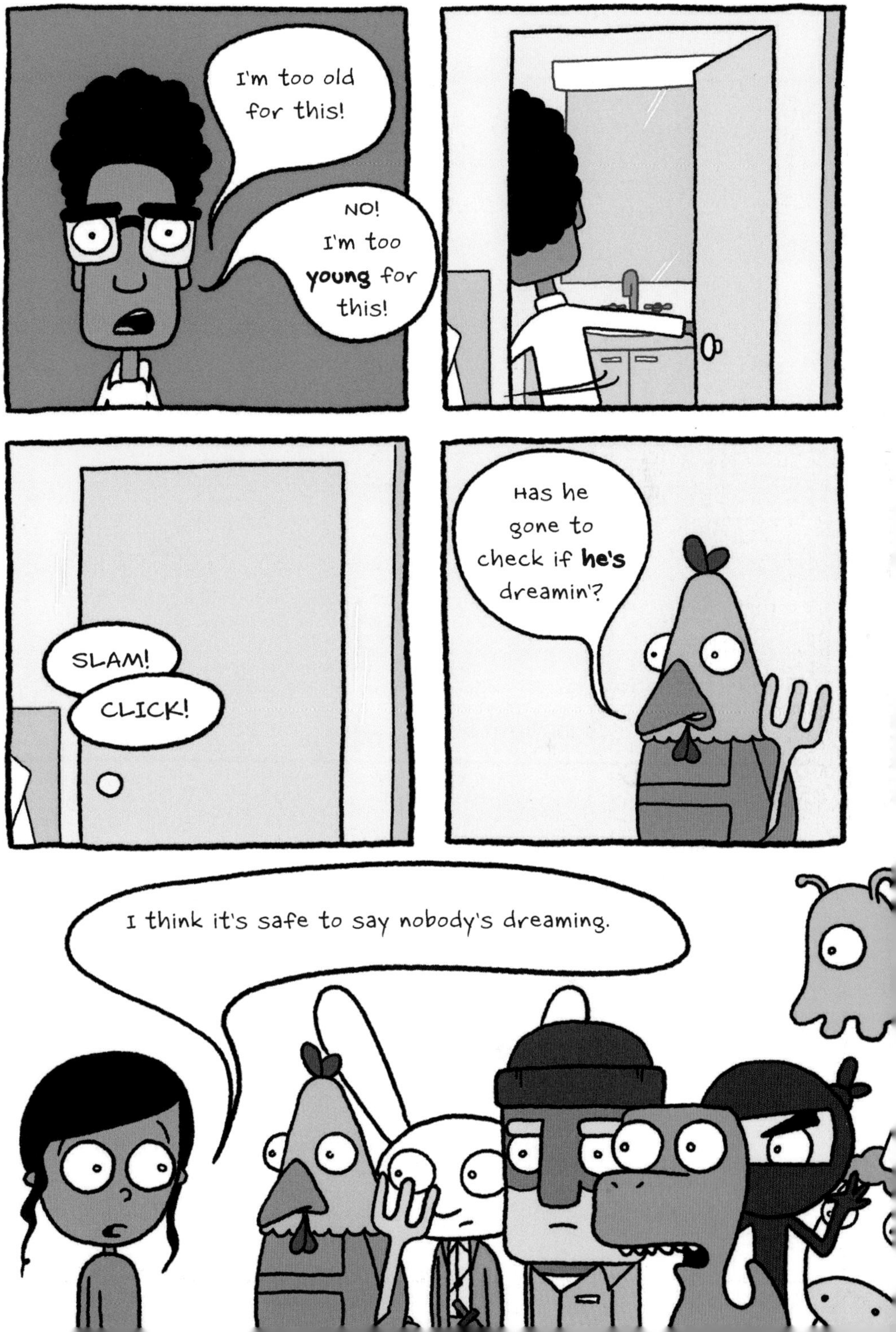
I'm too old for this!
NO! I'm too **young** for this!
SLAM!
CLICK!
Has he gone to check if **he's** dreamin'?
I think it's safe to say nobody's dreaming.

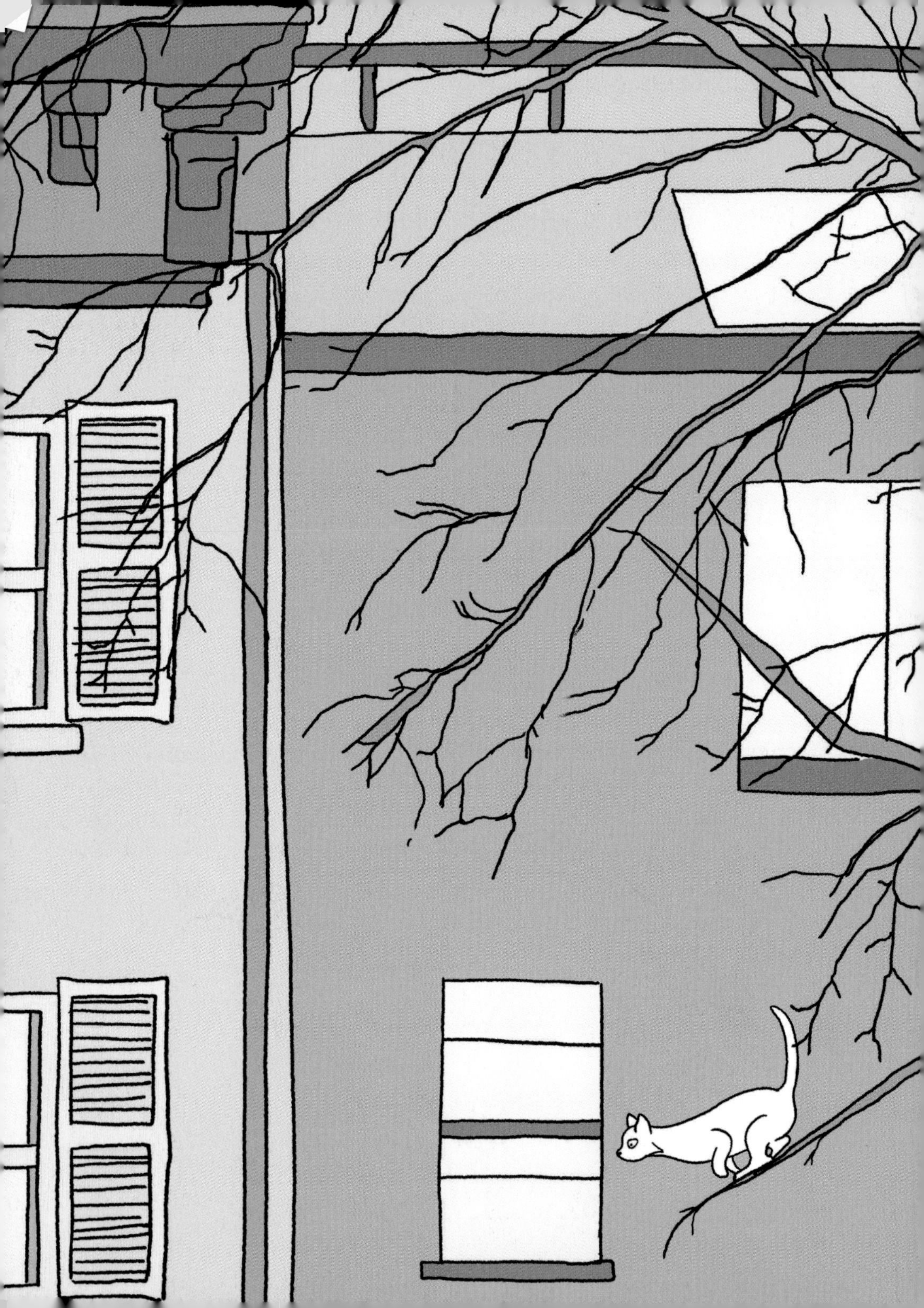

CHAPTER THREE
The Odds make themselves at home

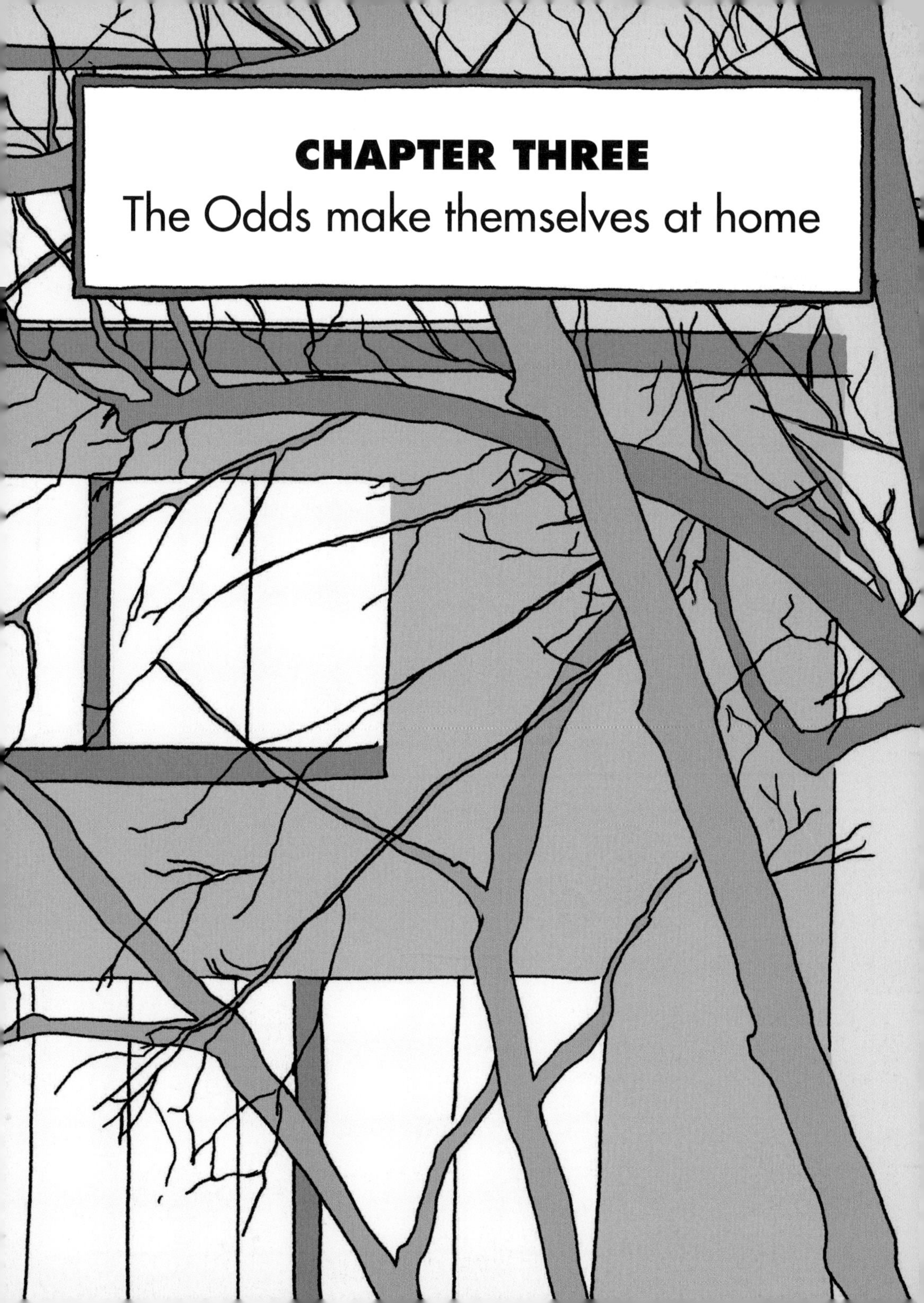

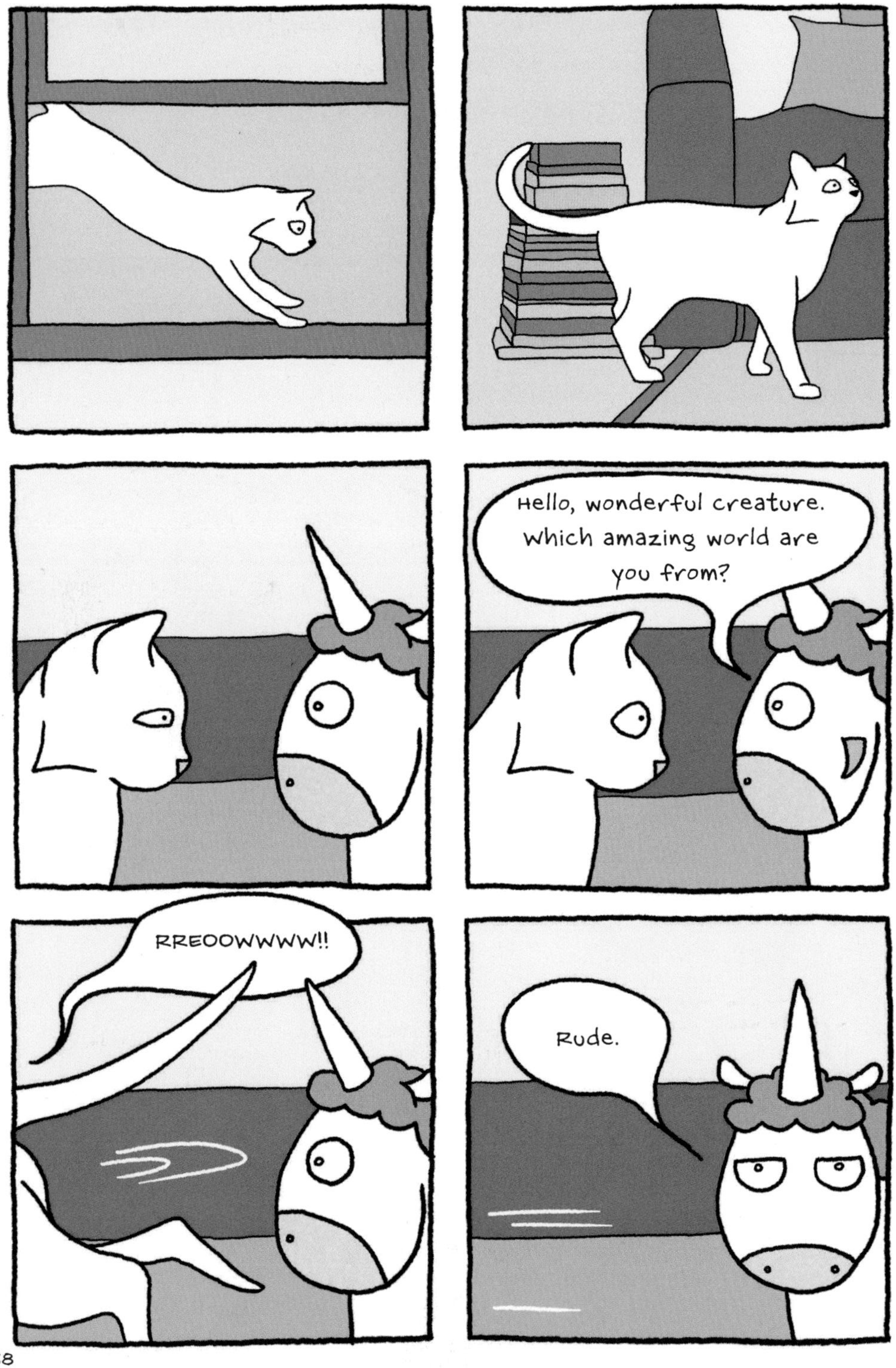
Hello, wonderful creature. Which amazing world are you from?
RREOOWWWW!!
Rude.

40

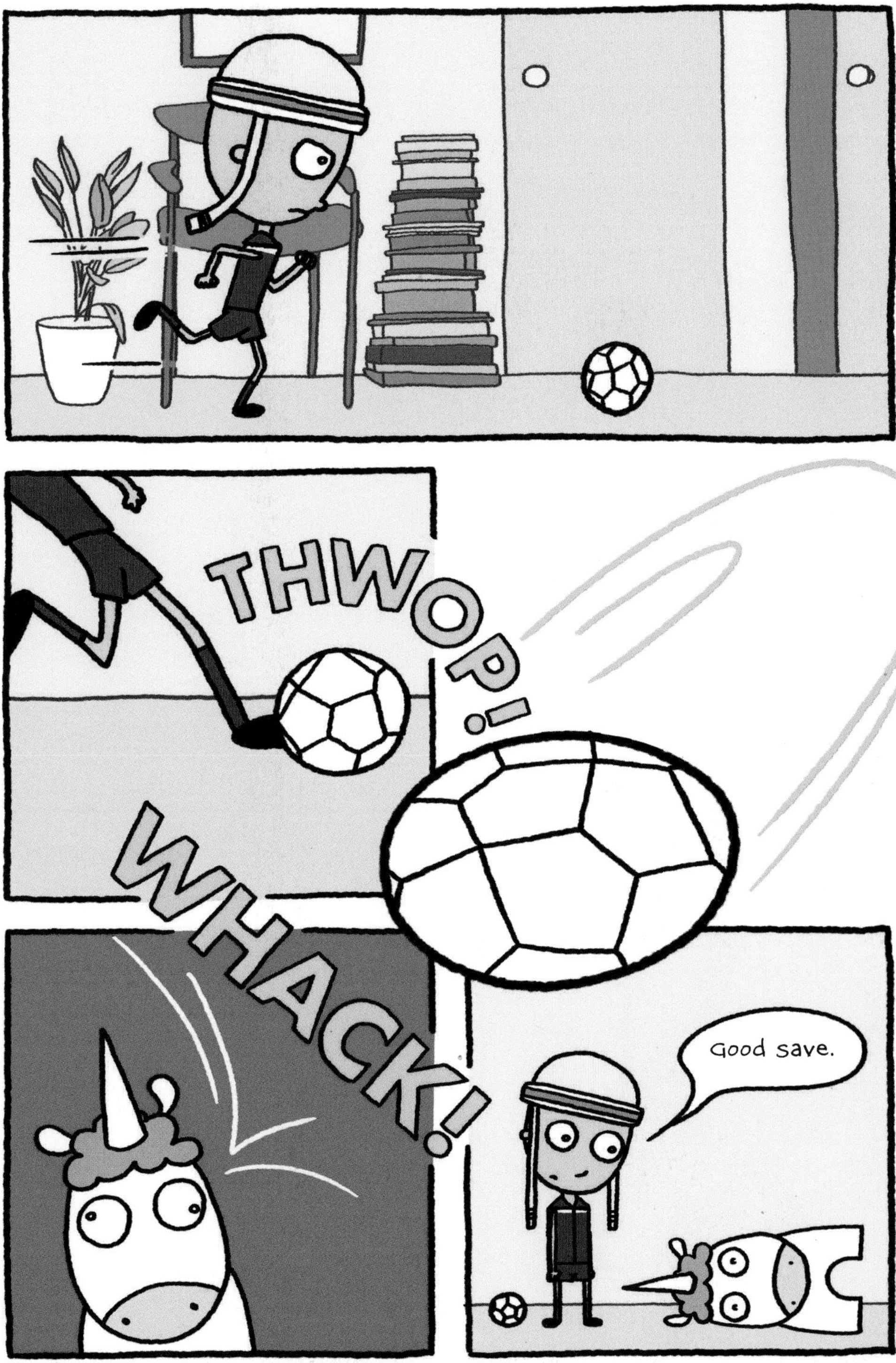
THWOP!
WHACK!
Good save.

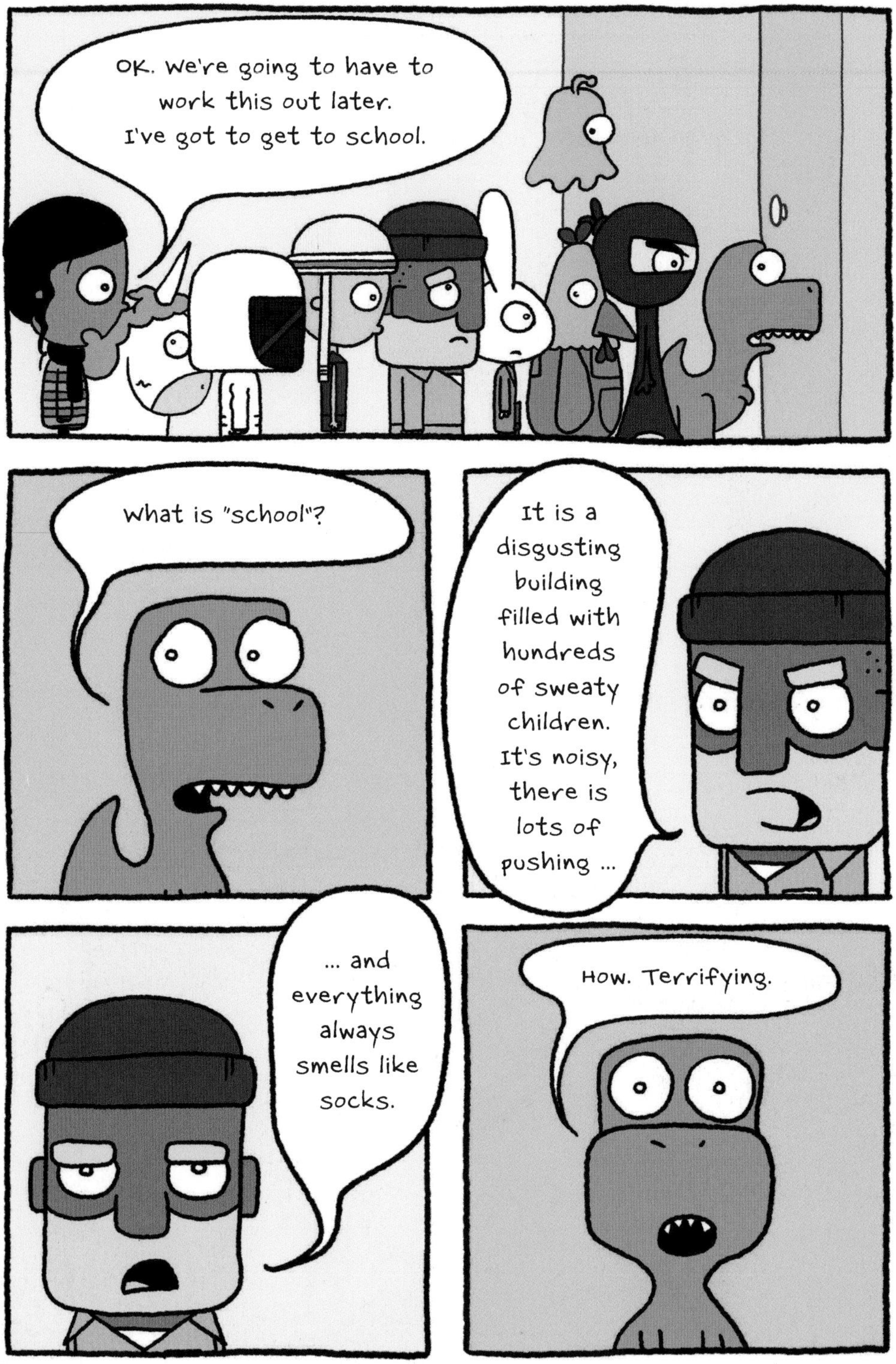
OK. We're going to have to work this out later. I've got to get to school.
What is "school"?
It is a disgusting building filled with hundreds of sweaty children. It's noisy, there is lots of pushing ...
... and everything always smells like socks.
How. Terrifying.

43

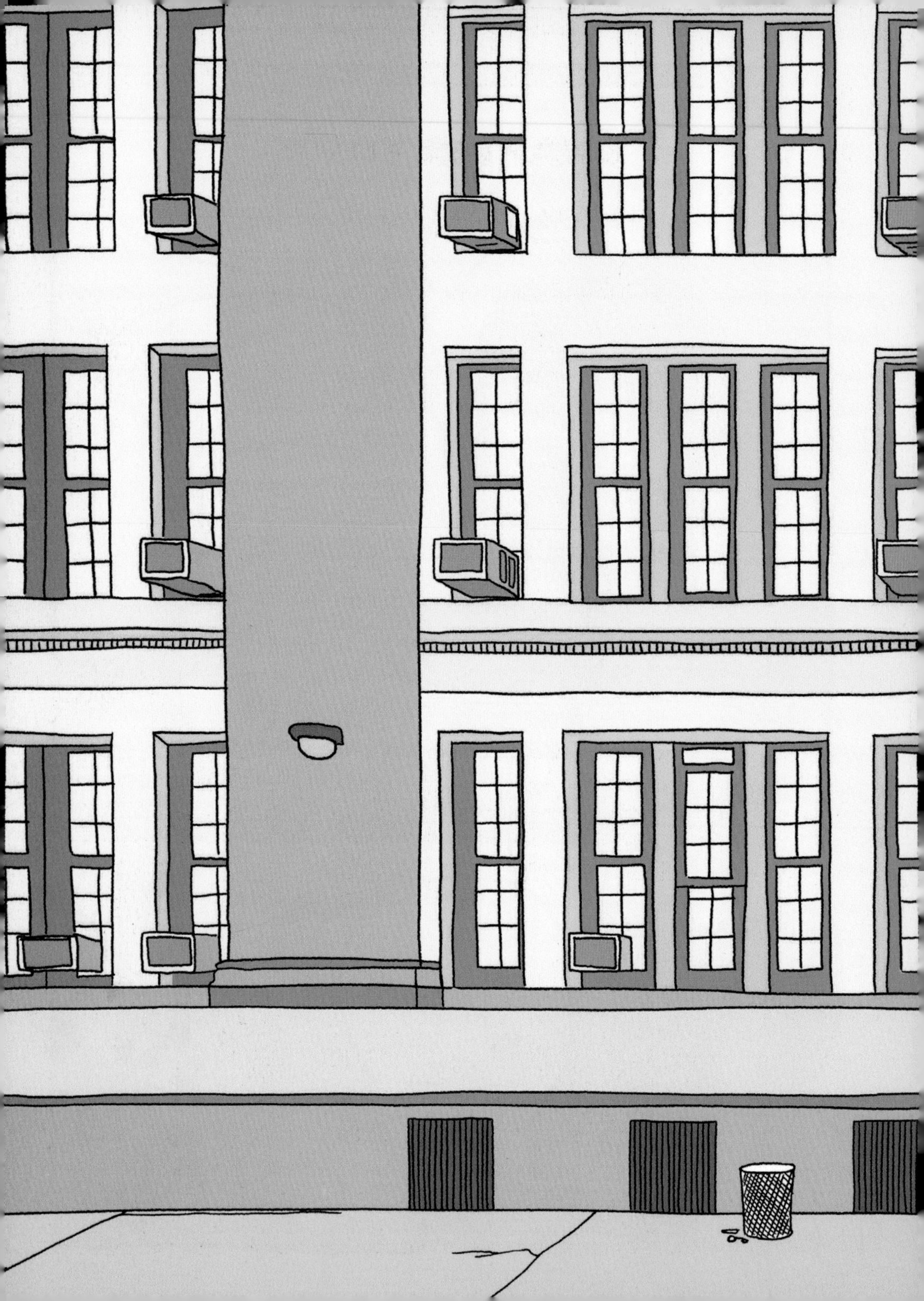

CHAPTER FOUR
The odd one out

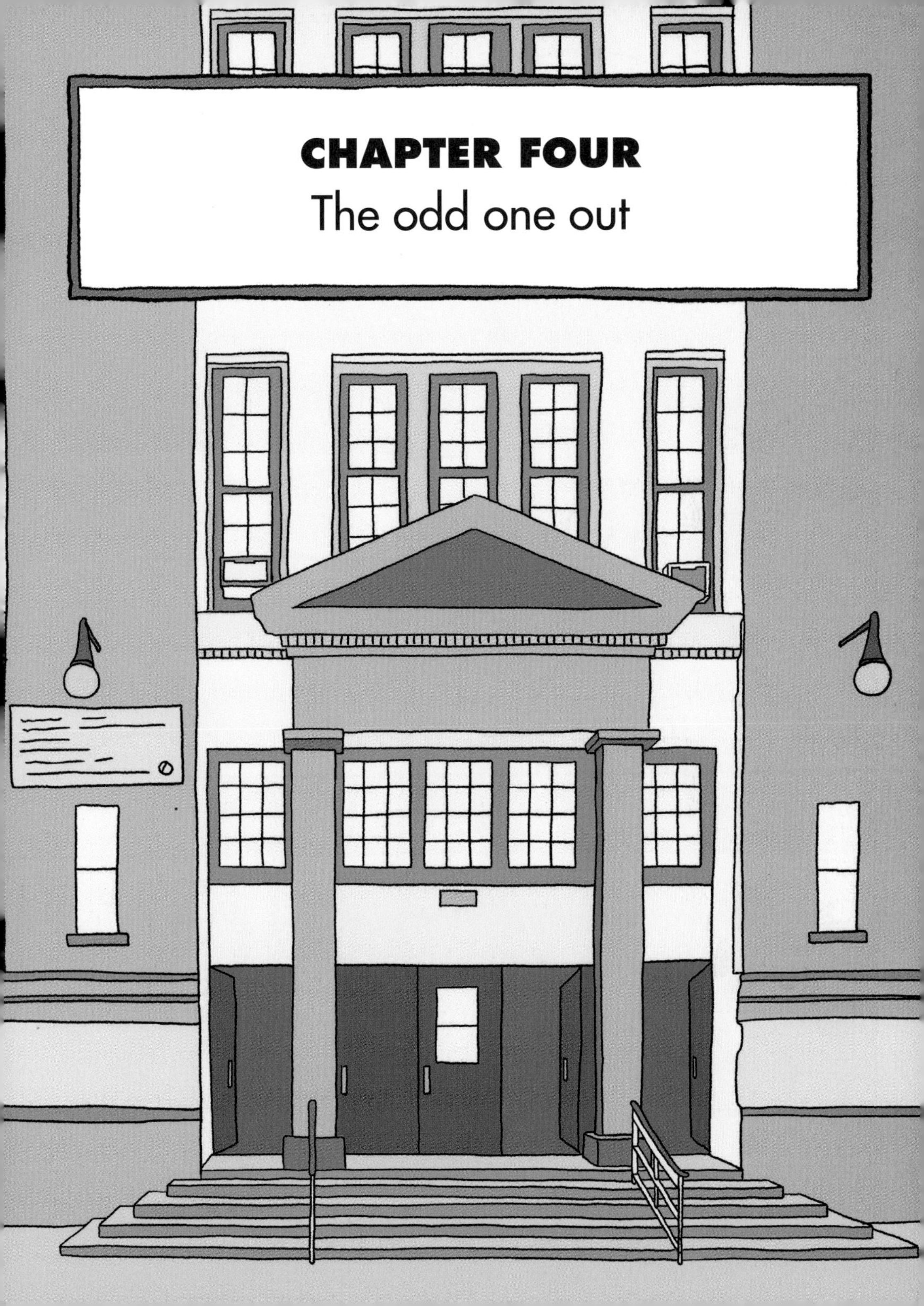

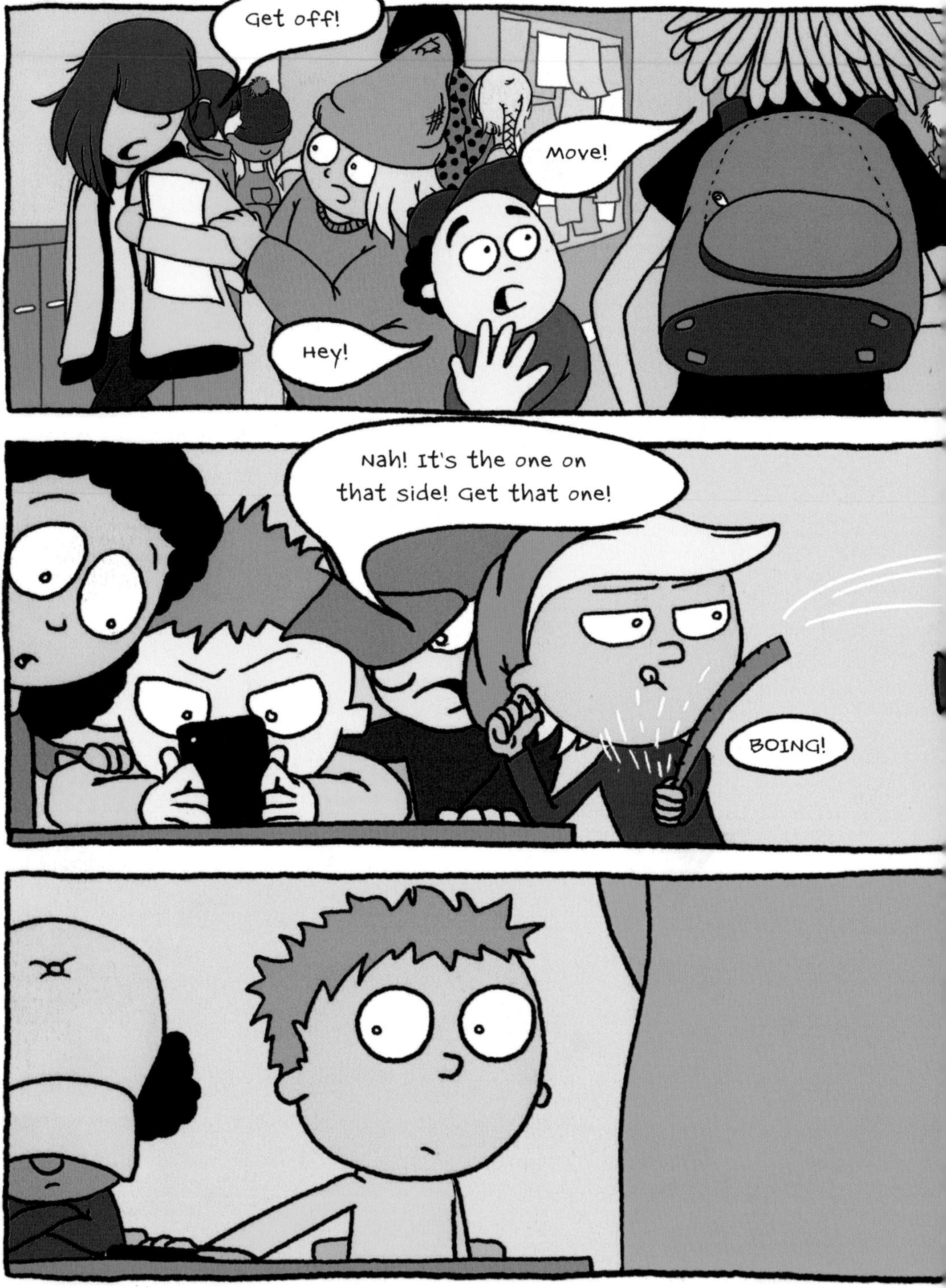
Get off!
Move!
Hey!
Nah! It's the one on that side! Get that one!
BOING!

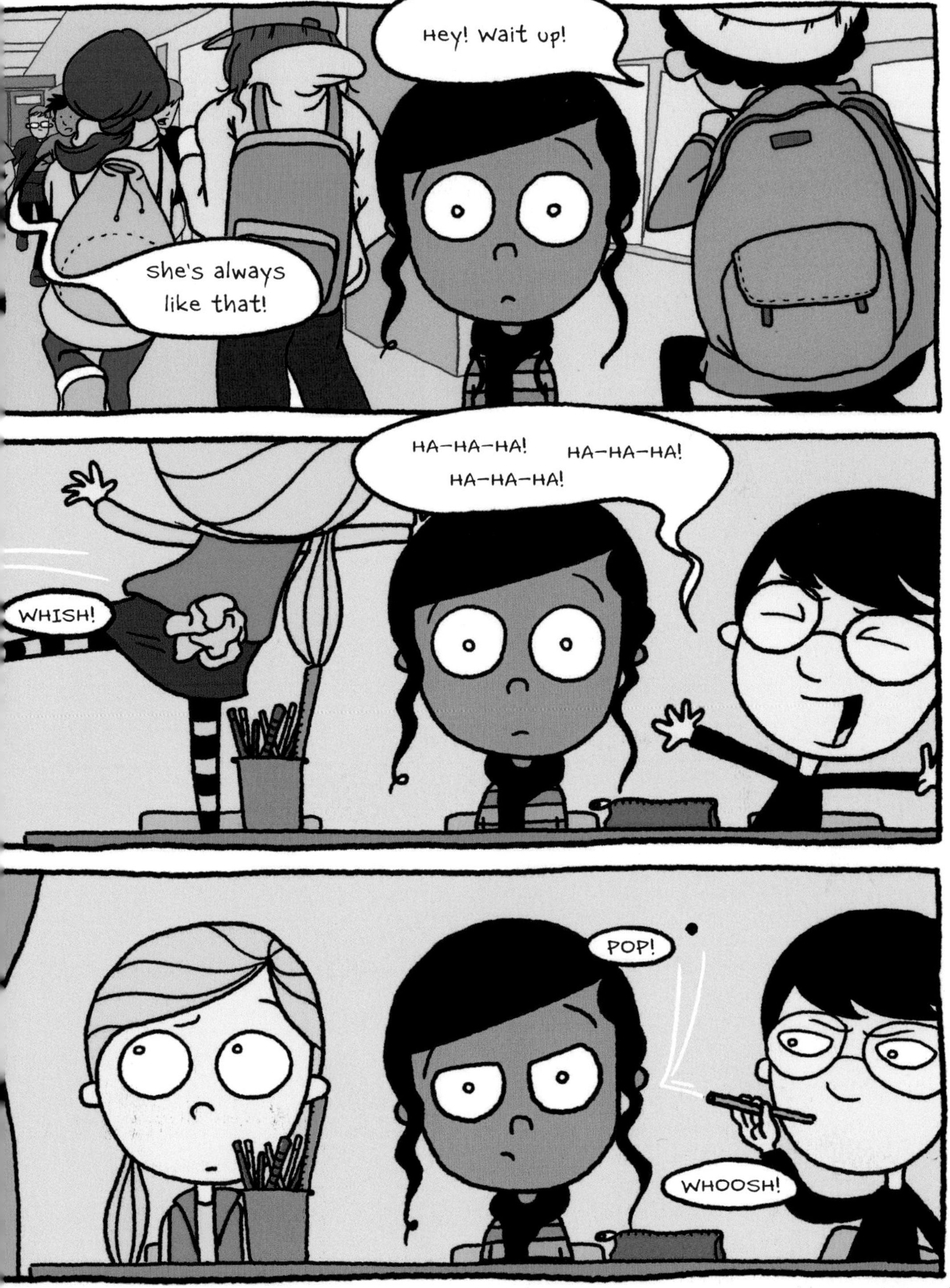
Hey! Wait up!
She's always like that!
HA-HA-HA! HA-HA-HA! HA-HA-HA!
WHISH!
POP!
WHOOSH!

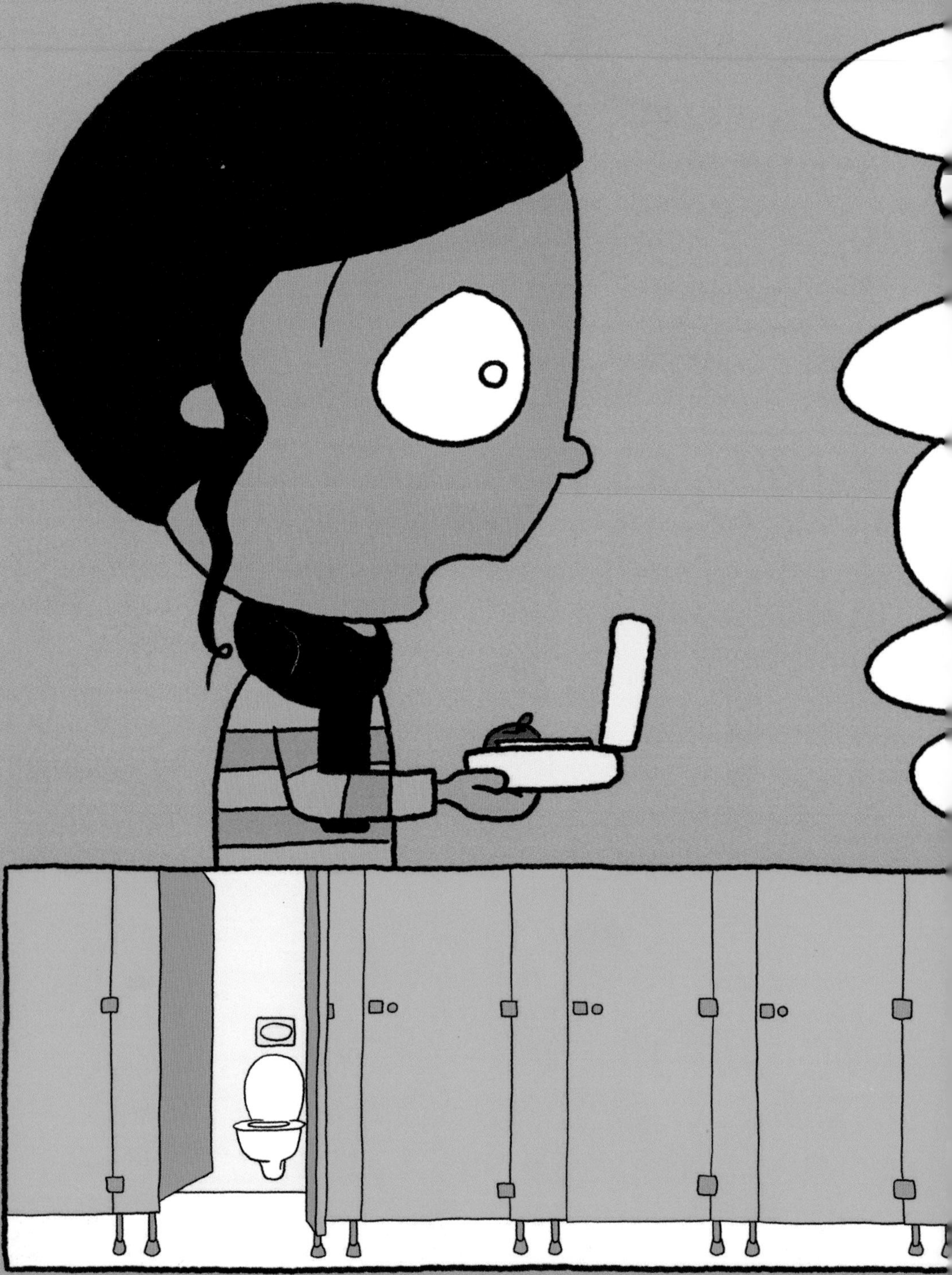

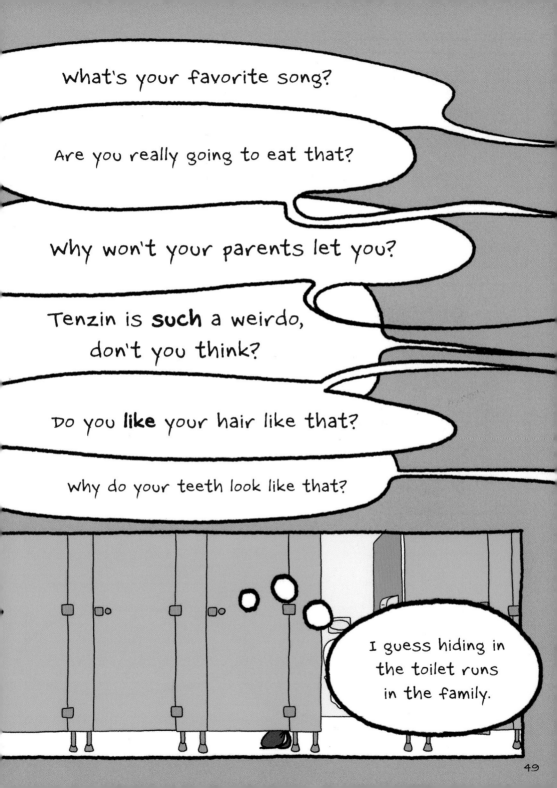

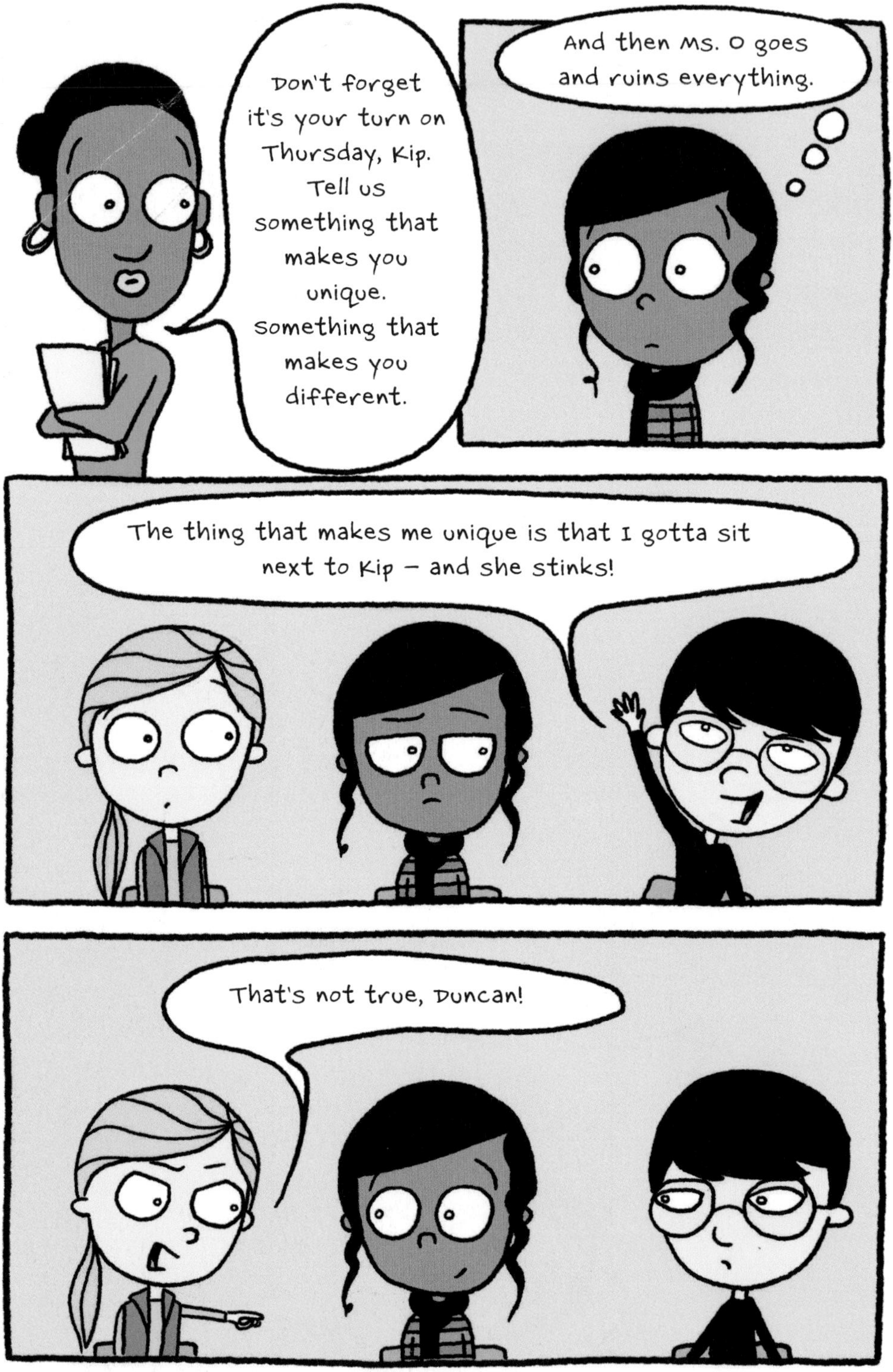

Don't forget it's your turn on Thursday, Kip. Tell us something that makes you unique. Something that makes you different.
And then Ms. O goes and ruins everything.
The thing that makes me unique is that I gotta sit next to Kip – and she stinks!
That's not true, Duncan!

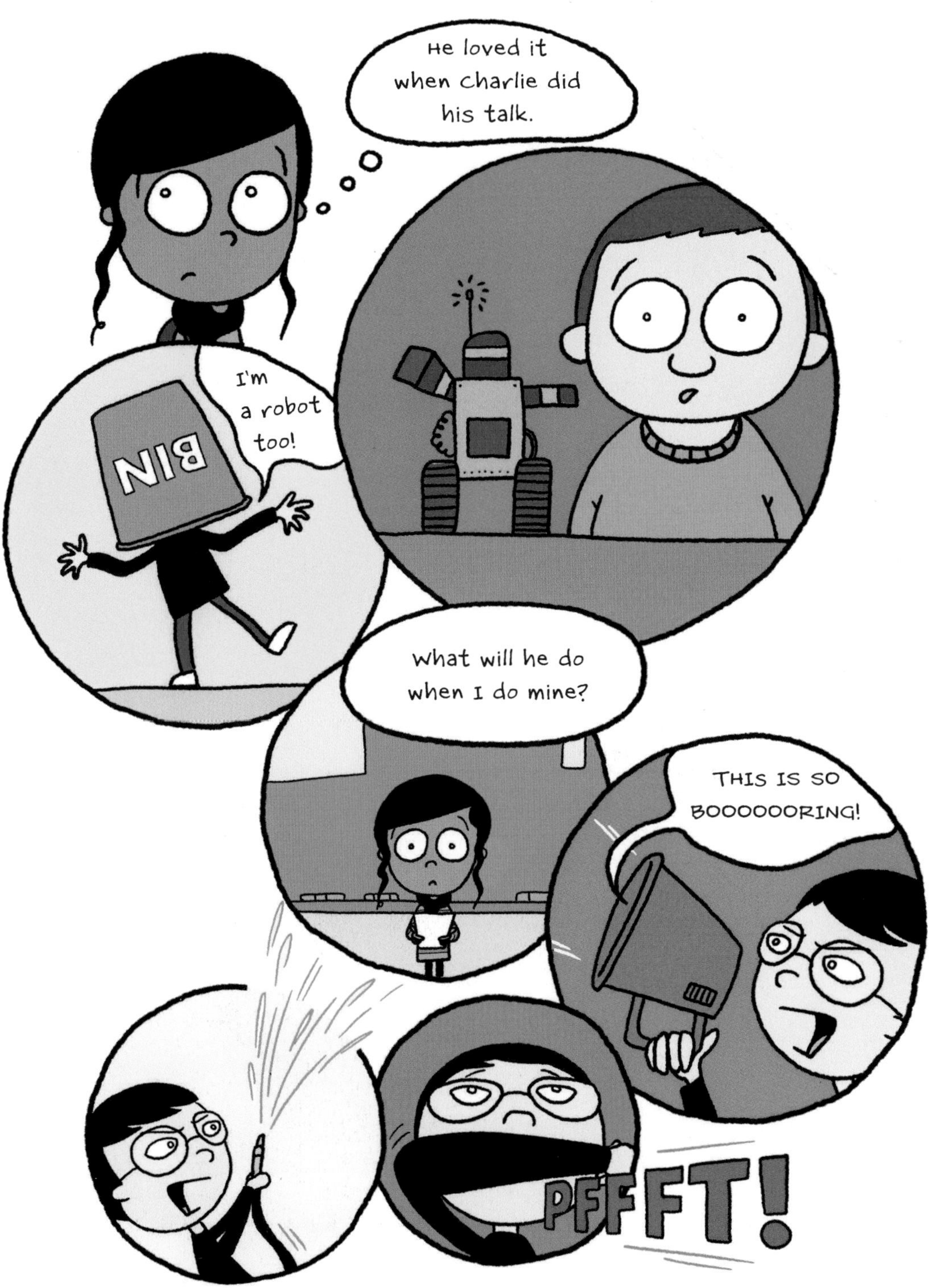
He loved it when Charlie did his talk.
I'm a robot too!
BIN
What will he do when I do mine?
THIS IS SO BOOOOOORING!
PFFFT!

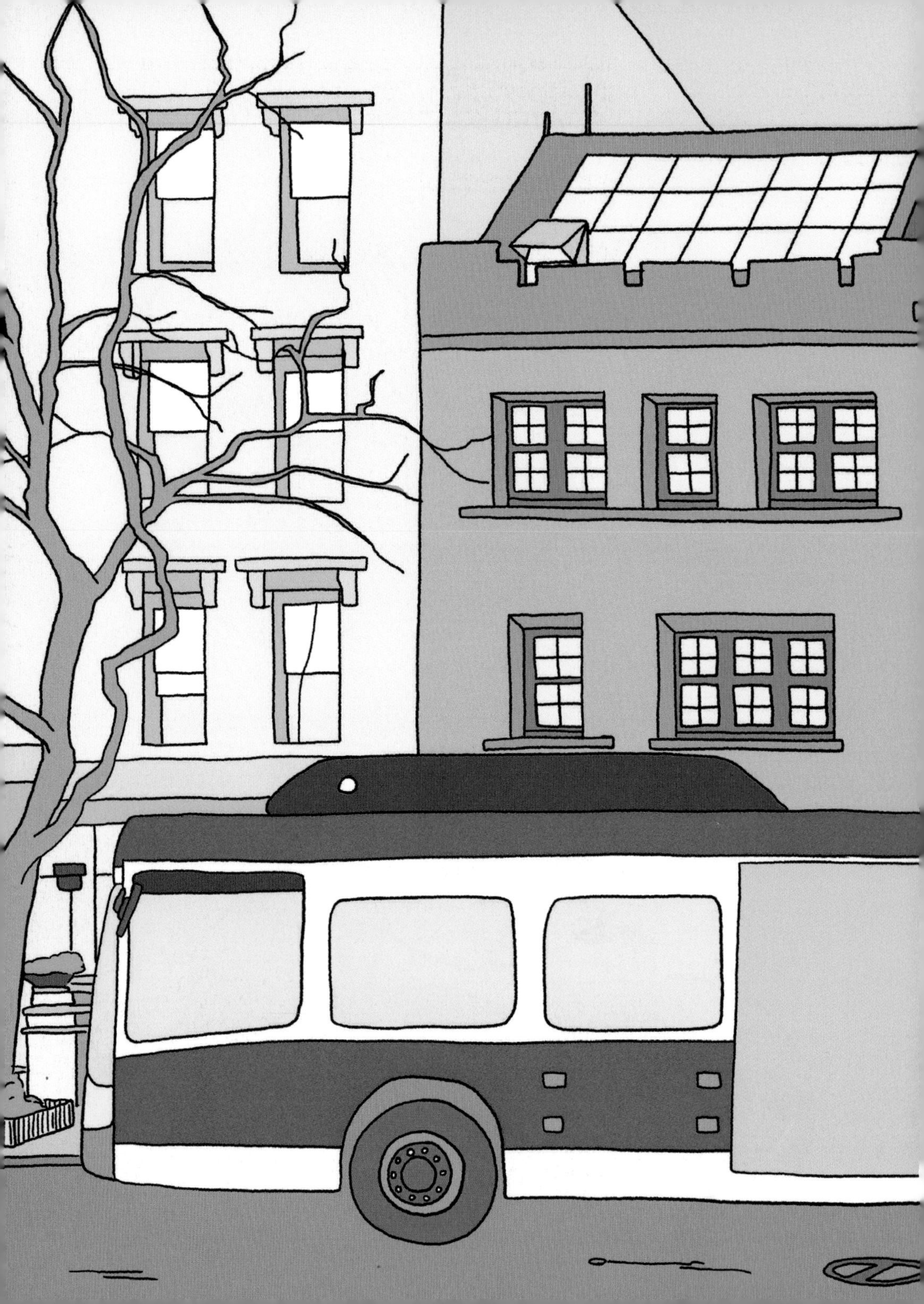

CHAPTER FIVE
The Odds take charge

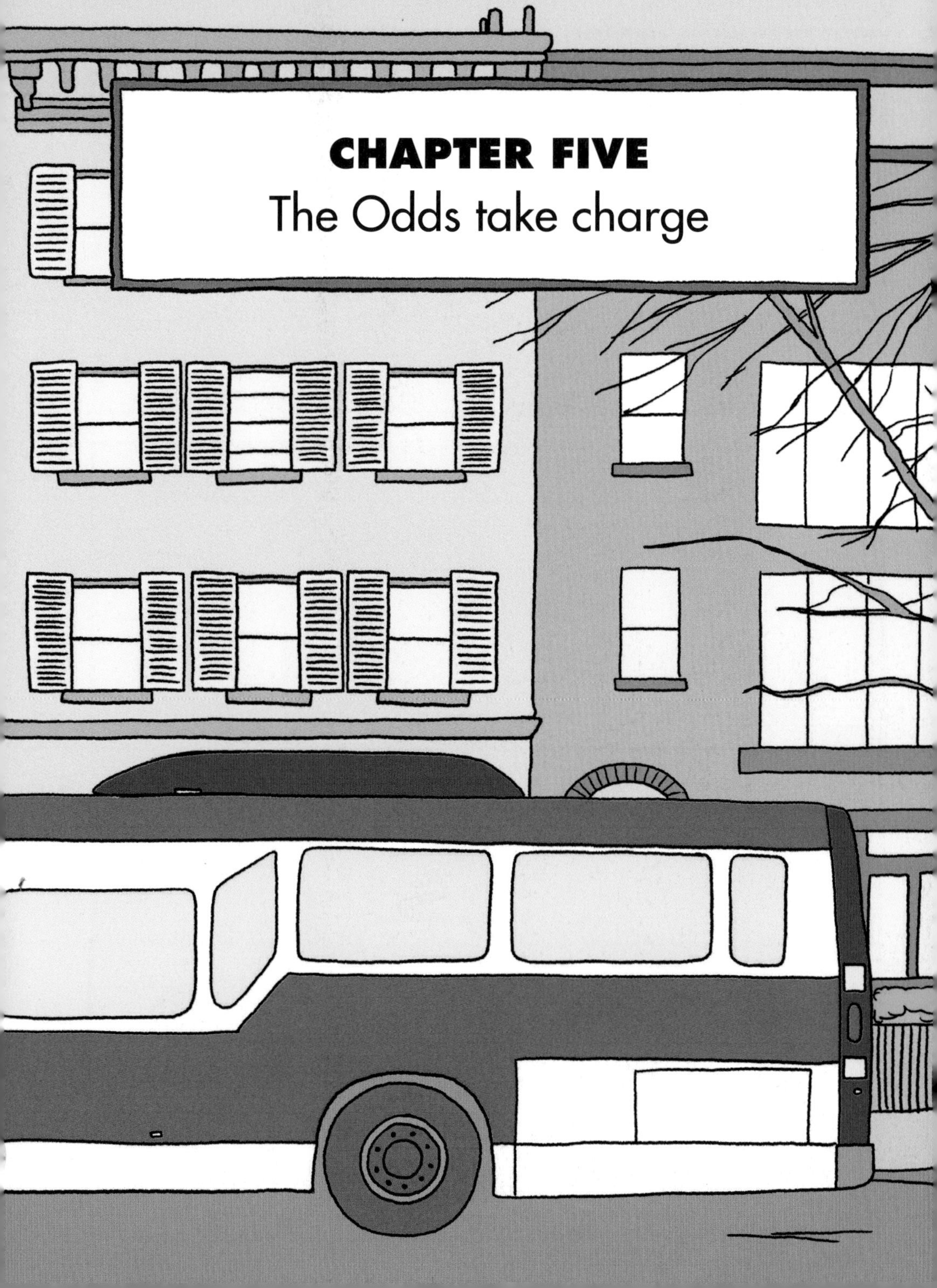

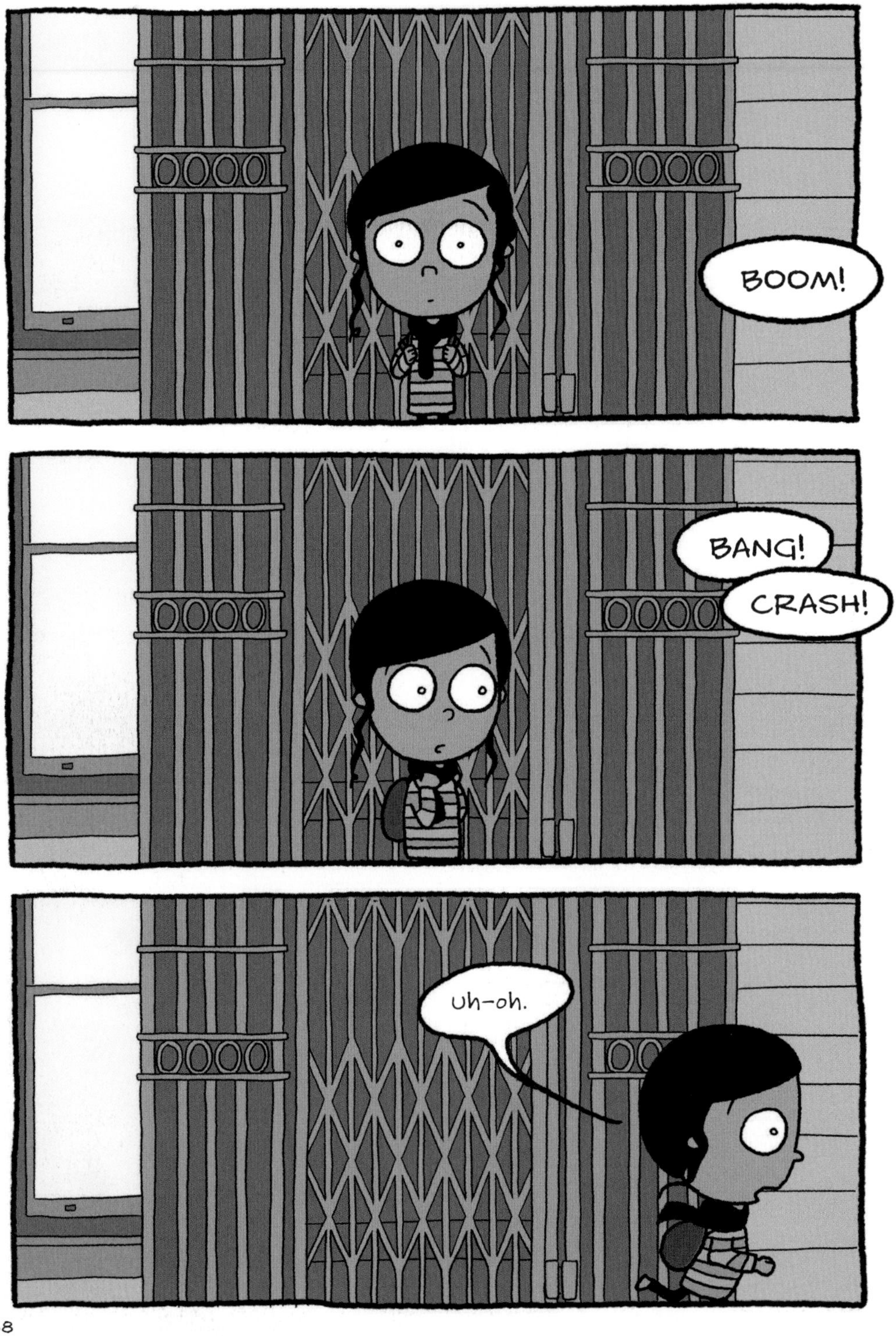
BOOM!
BANG!
CRASH!
Uh-oh.

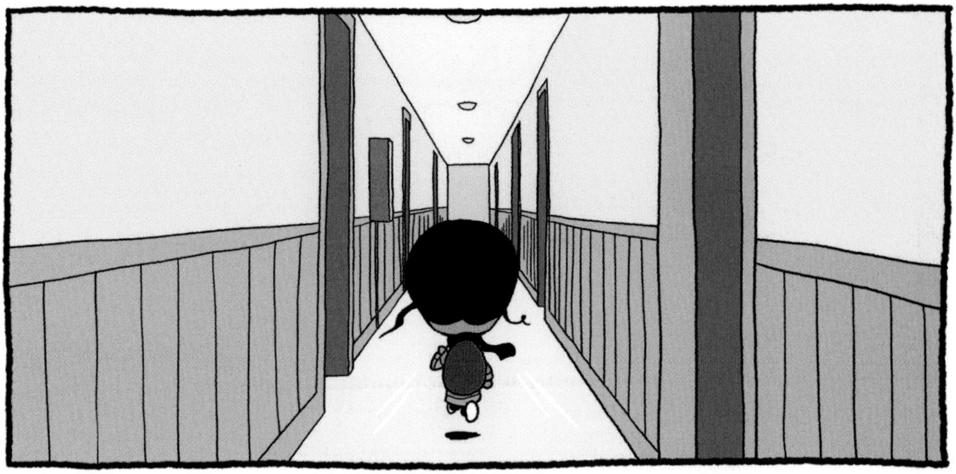

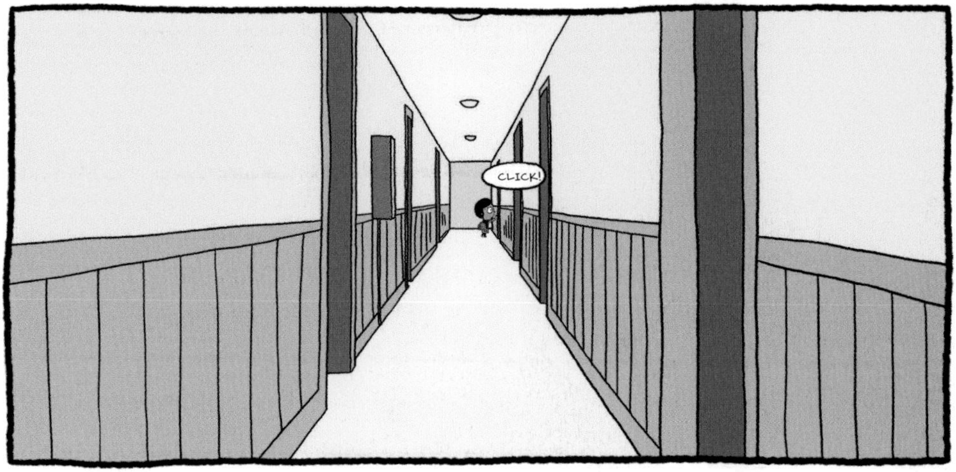
CLICK!

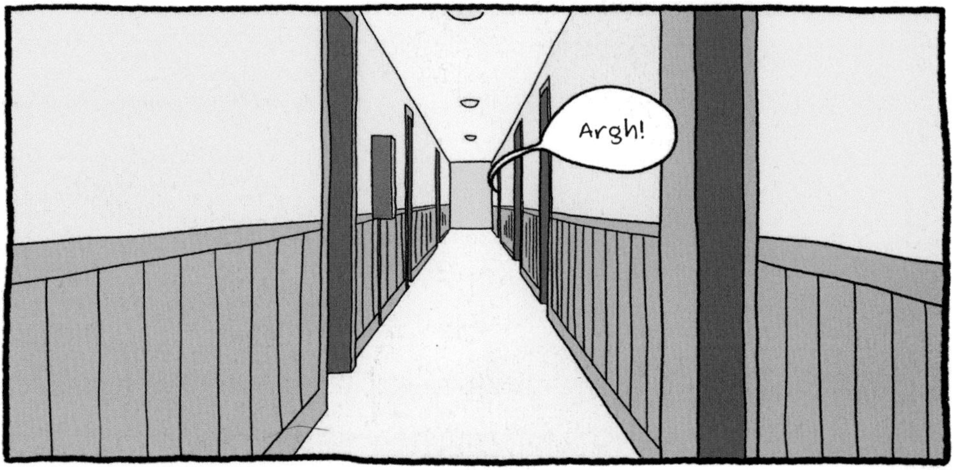
Argh!

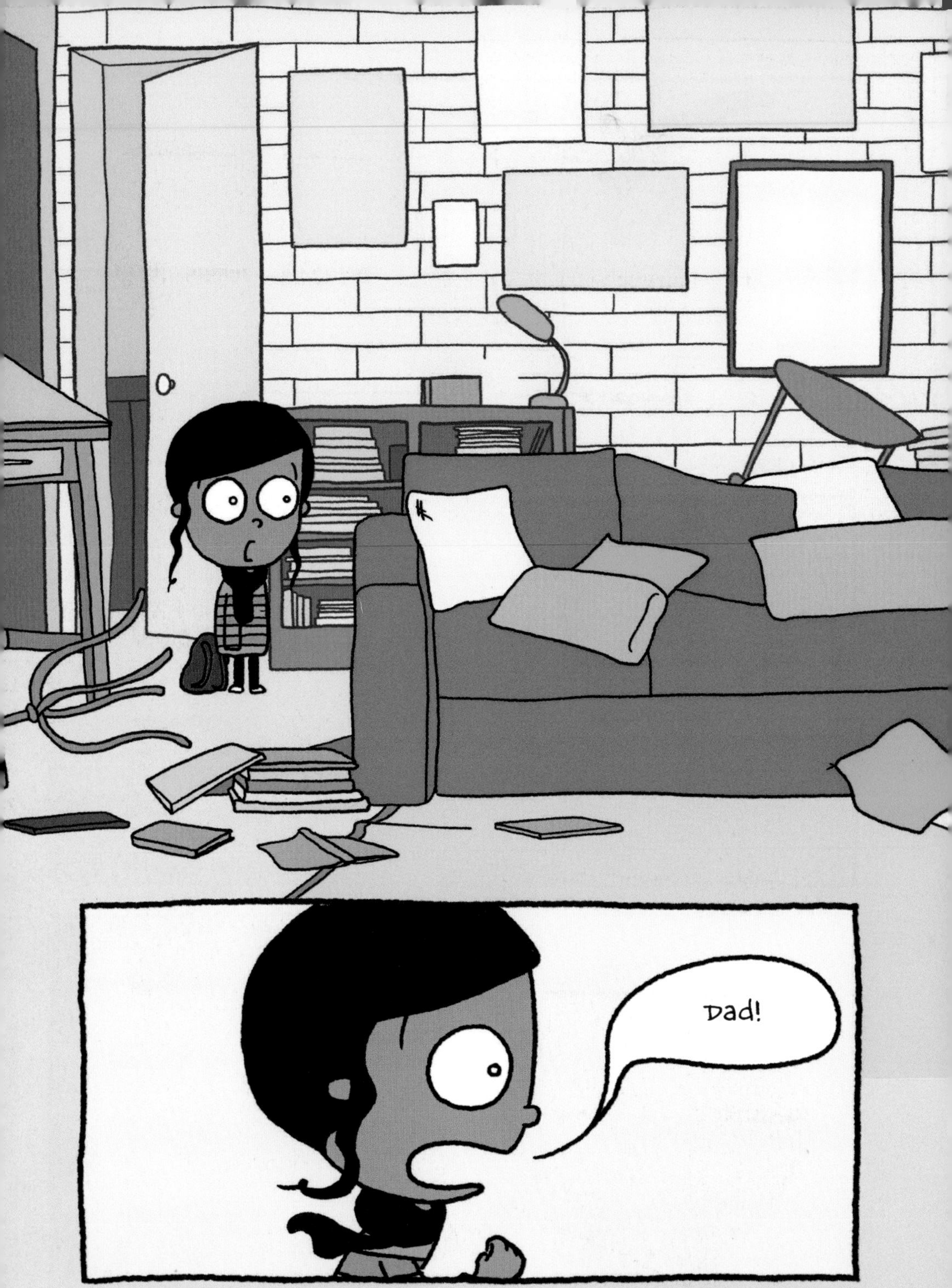
Dad!

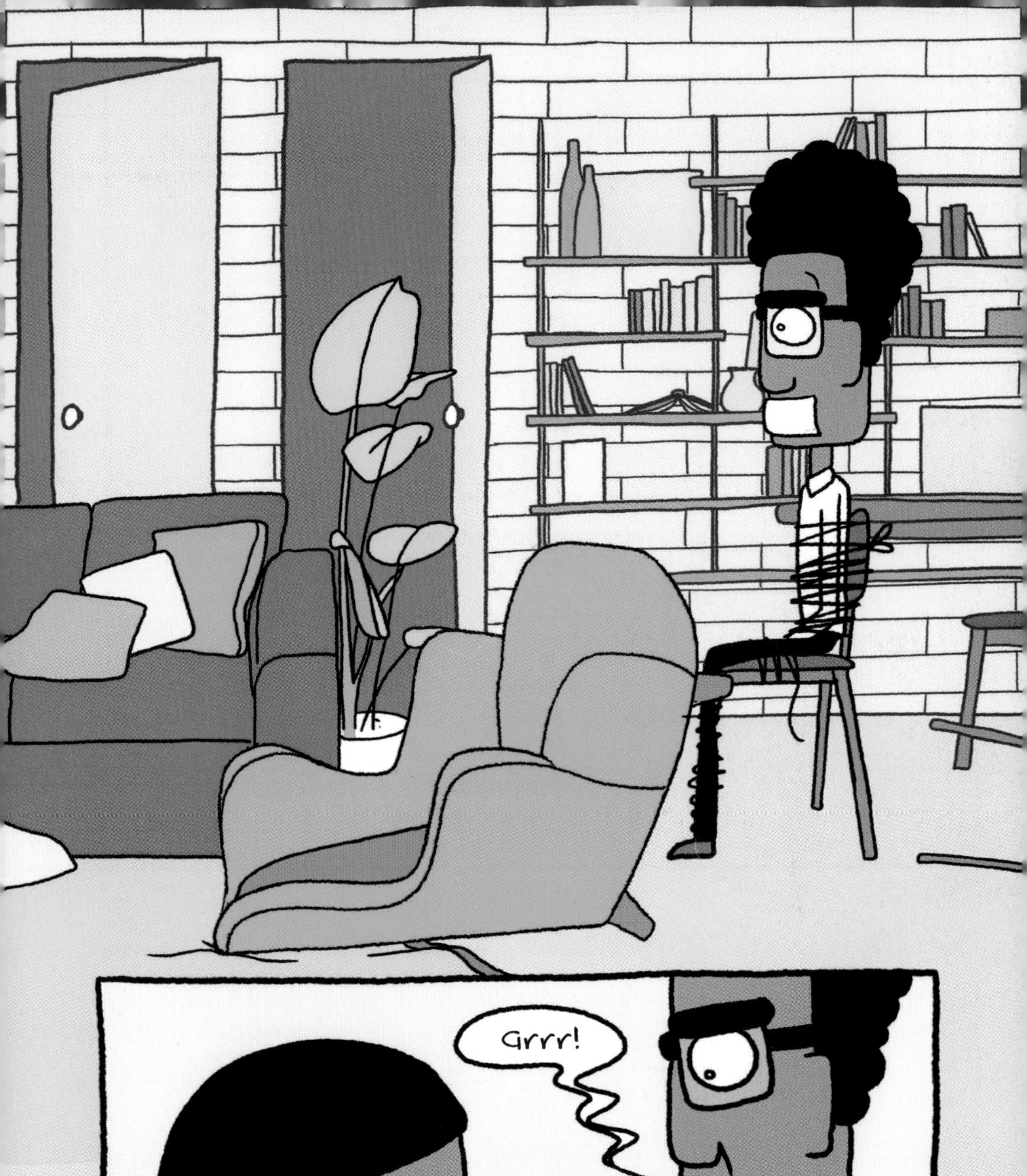

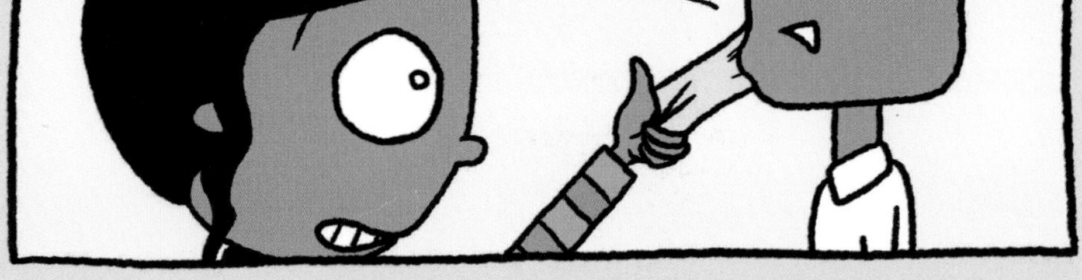
Grrr!

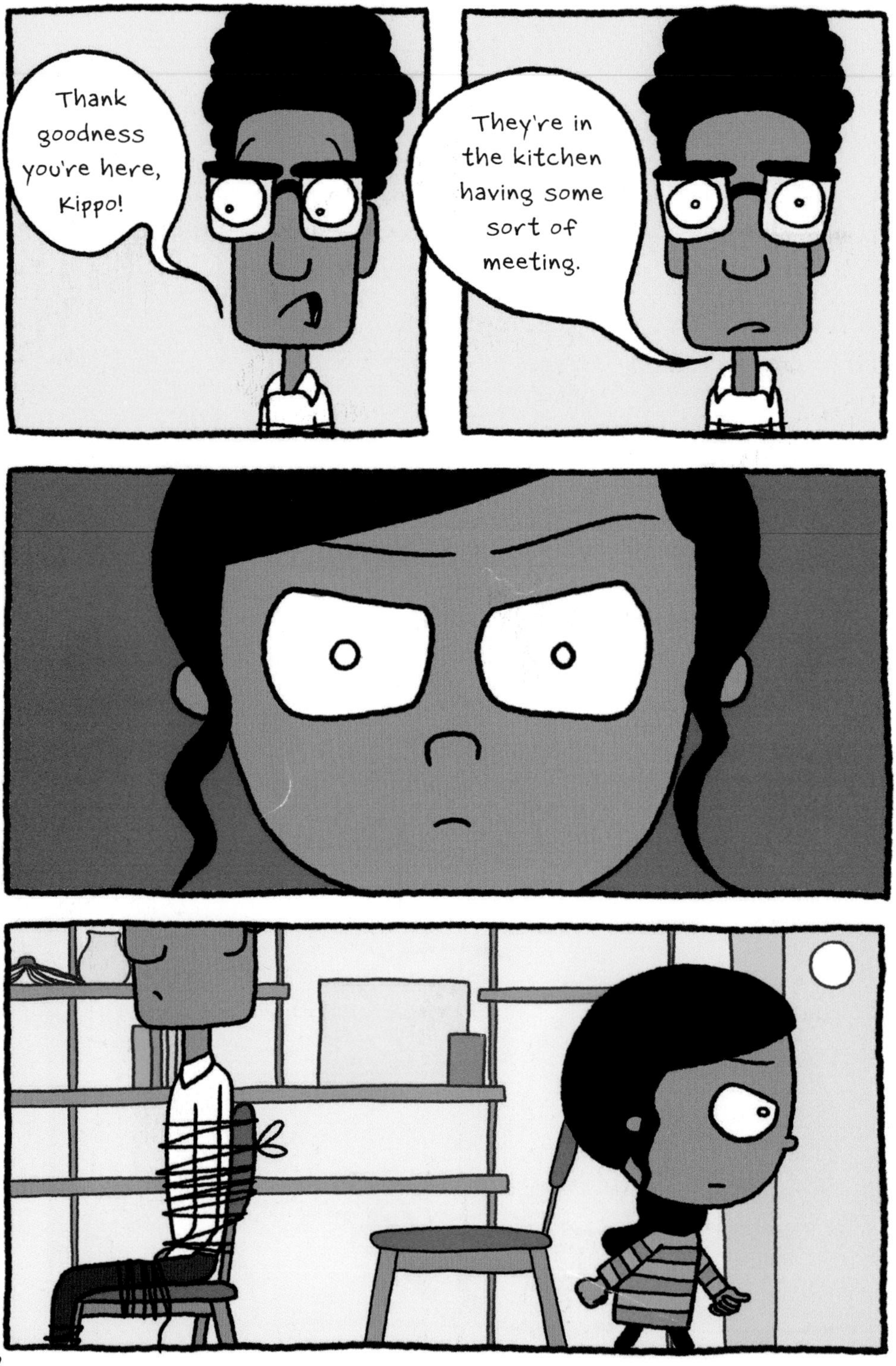

Thank goodness you're here, Kippo!
They're in the kitchen having some sort of meeting.

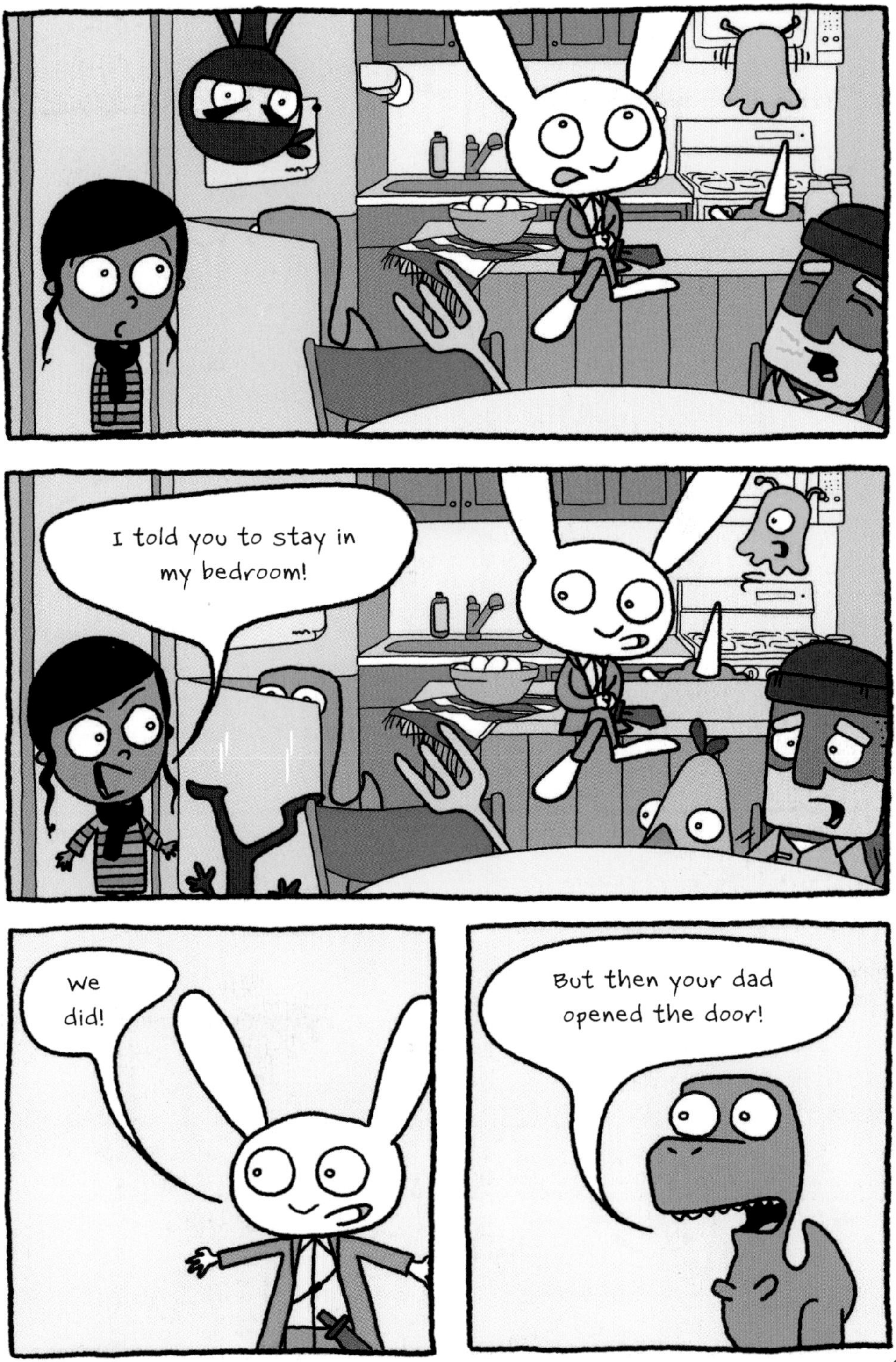
I told you to stay in my bedroom!
We did!
But then your dad opened the door!

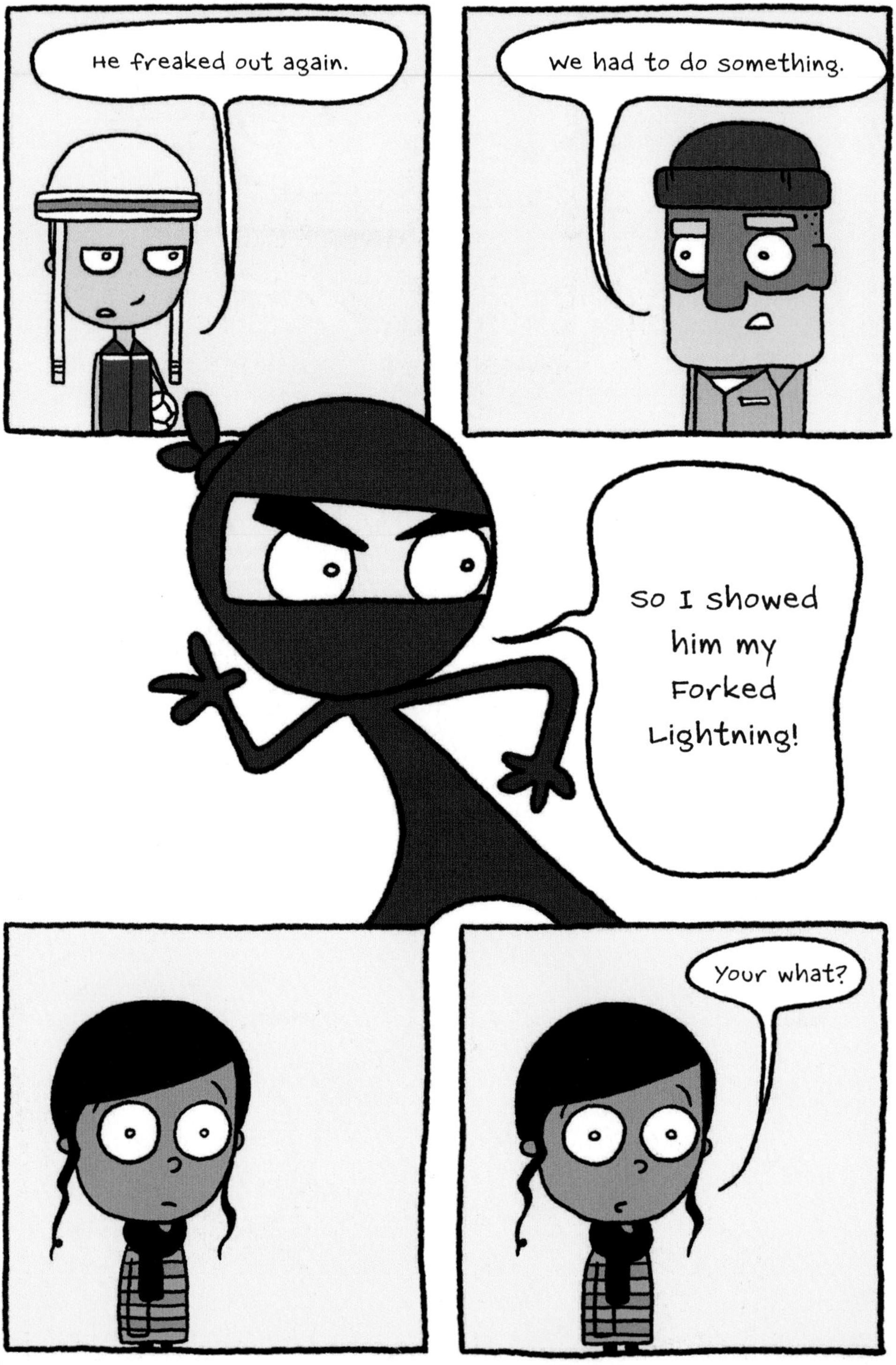
He freaked out again.
We had to do something.
So I showed him my Forked Lightning!
Your what?

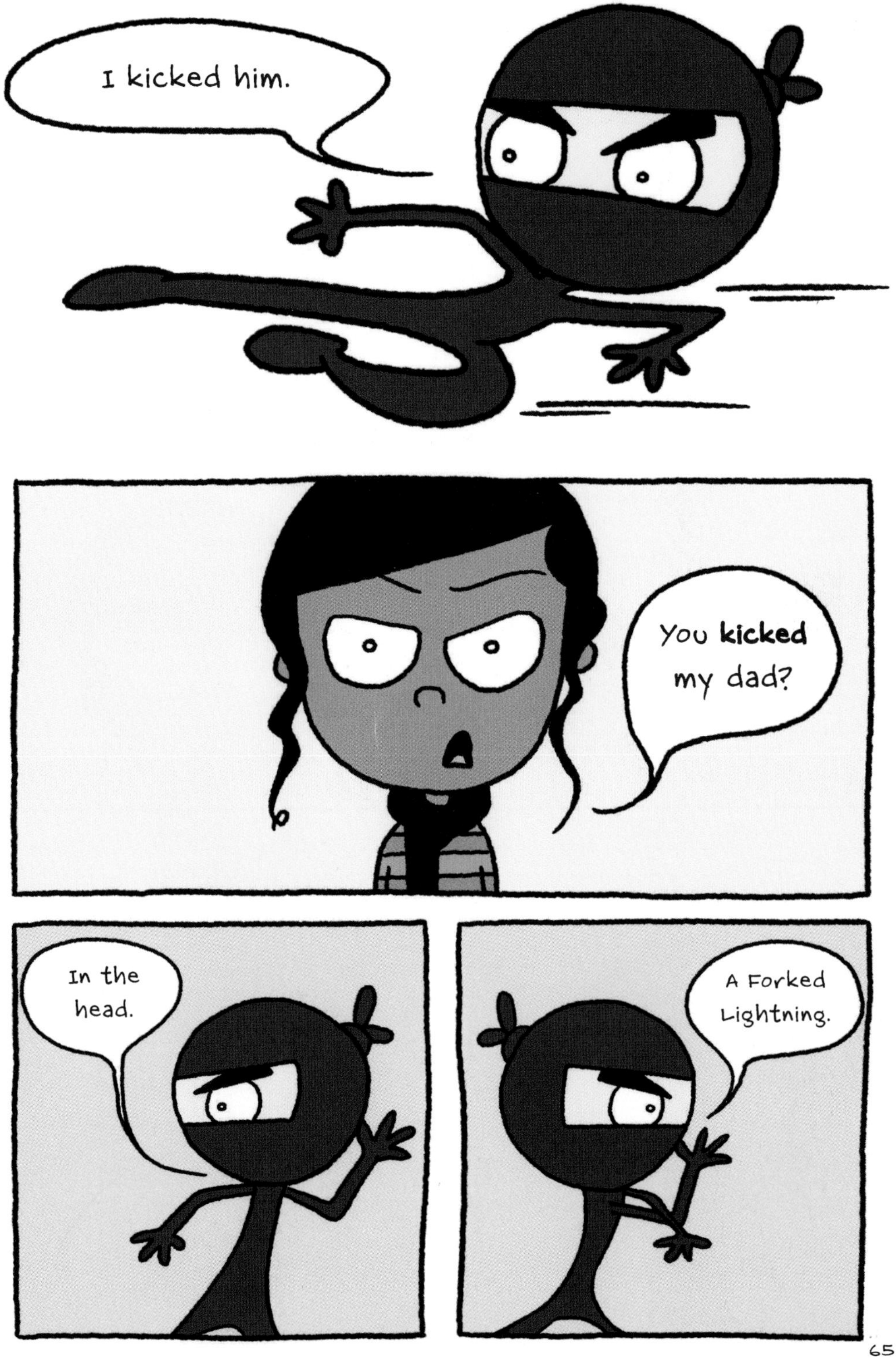
I kicked him.
You **kicked** my dad?
In the head.
A Forked Lightning.

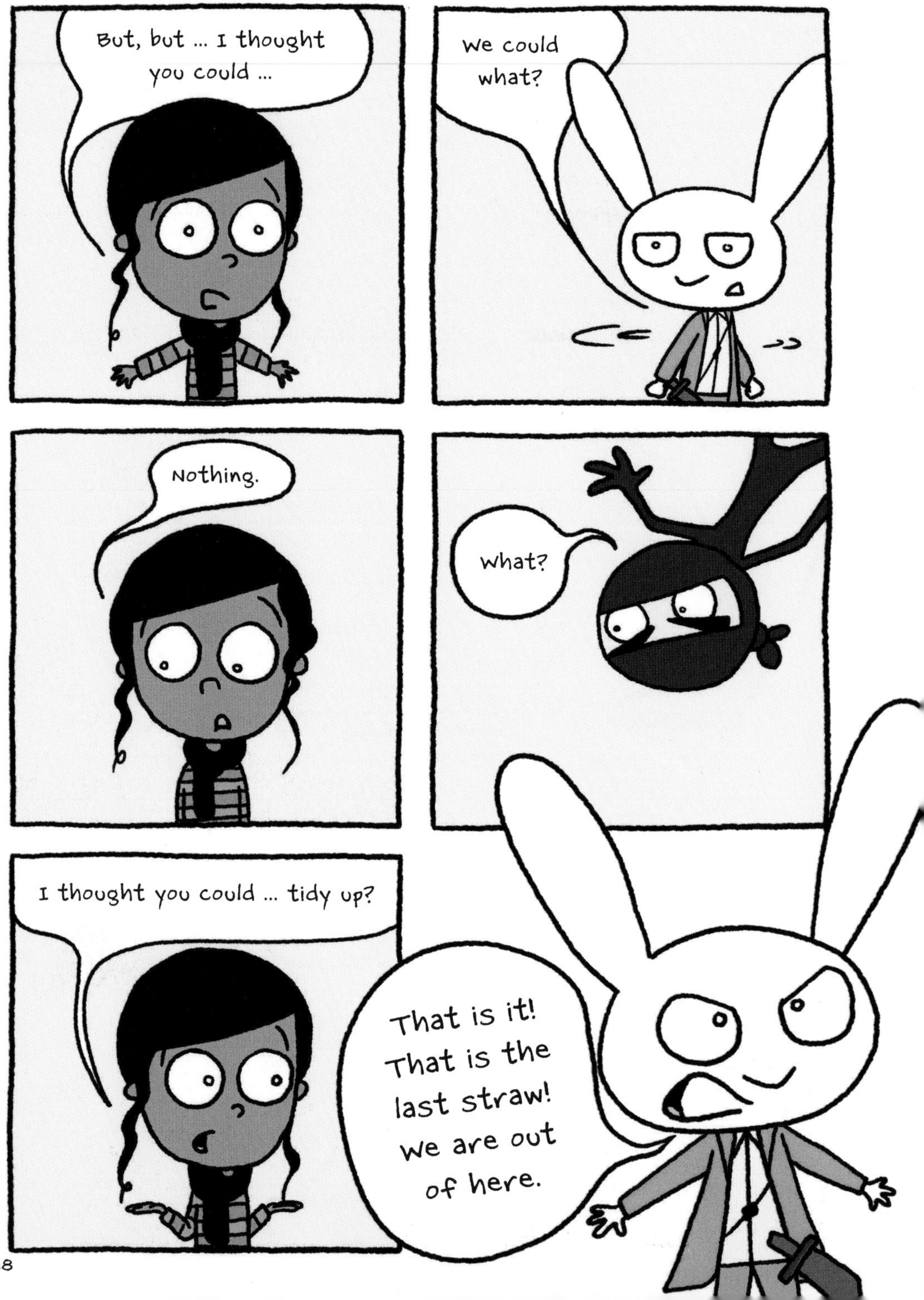
But, but ... I thought you could ...
We could what?
Nothing.
What?
I thought you could ... tidy up?
That is it! That is the last straw! We are out of here.

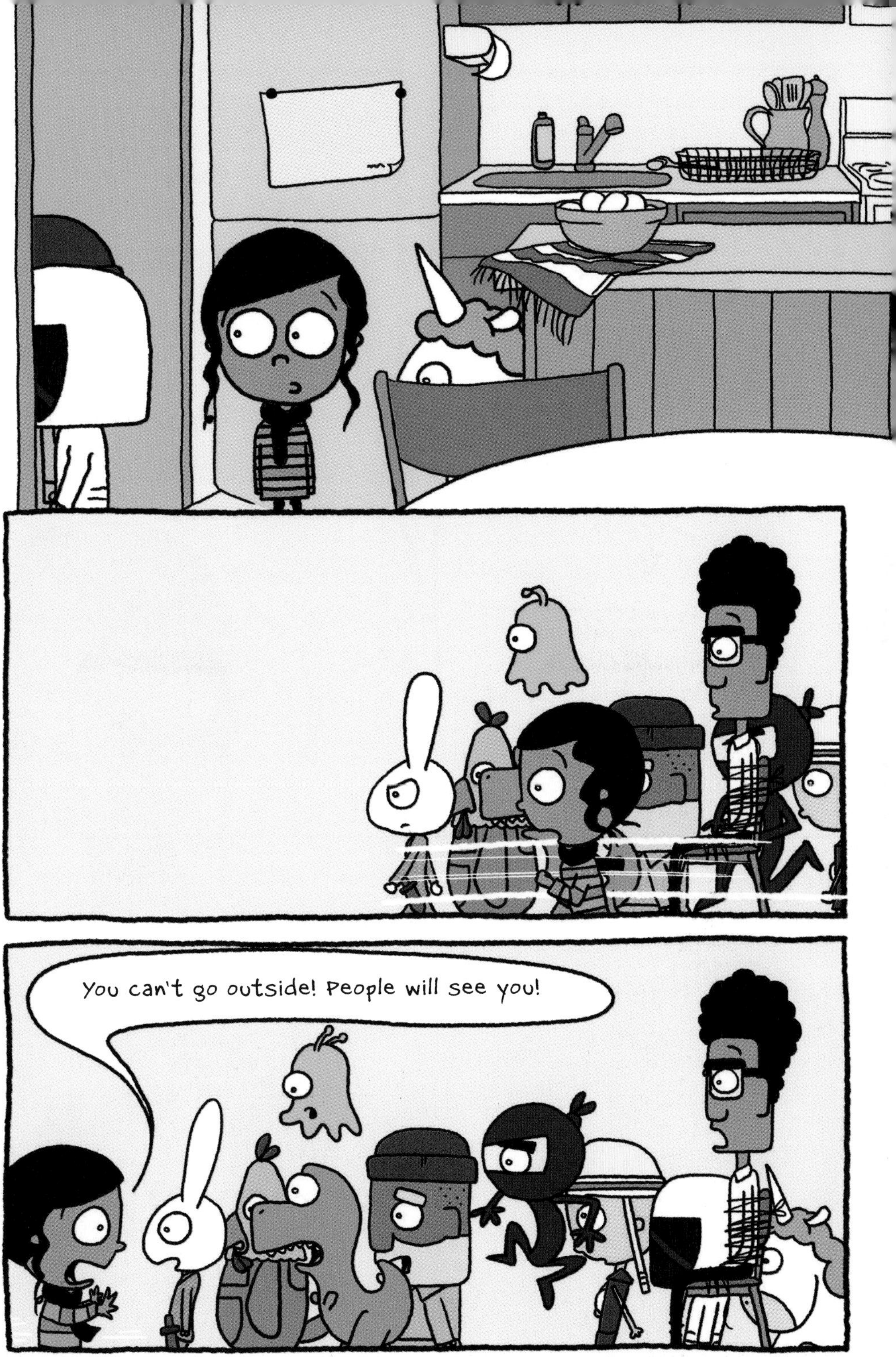
You can't go outside! People will see you!

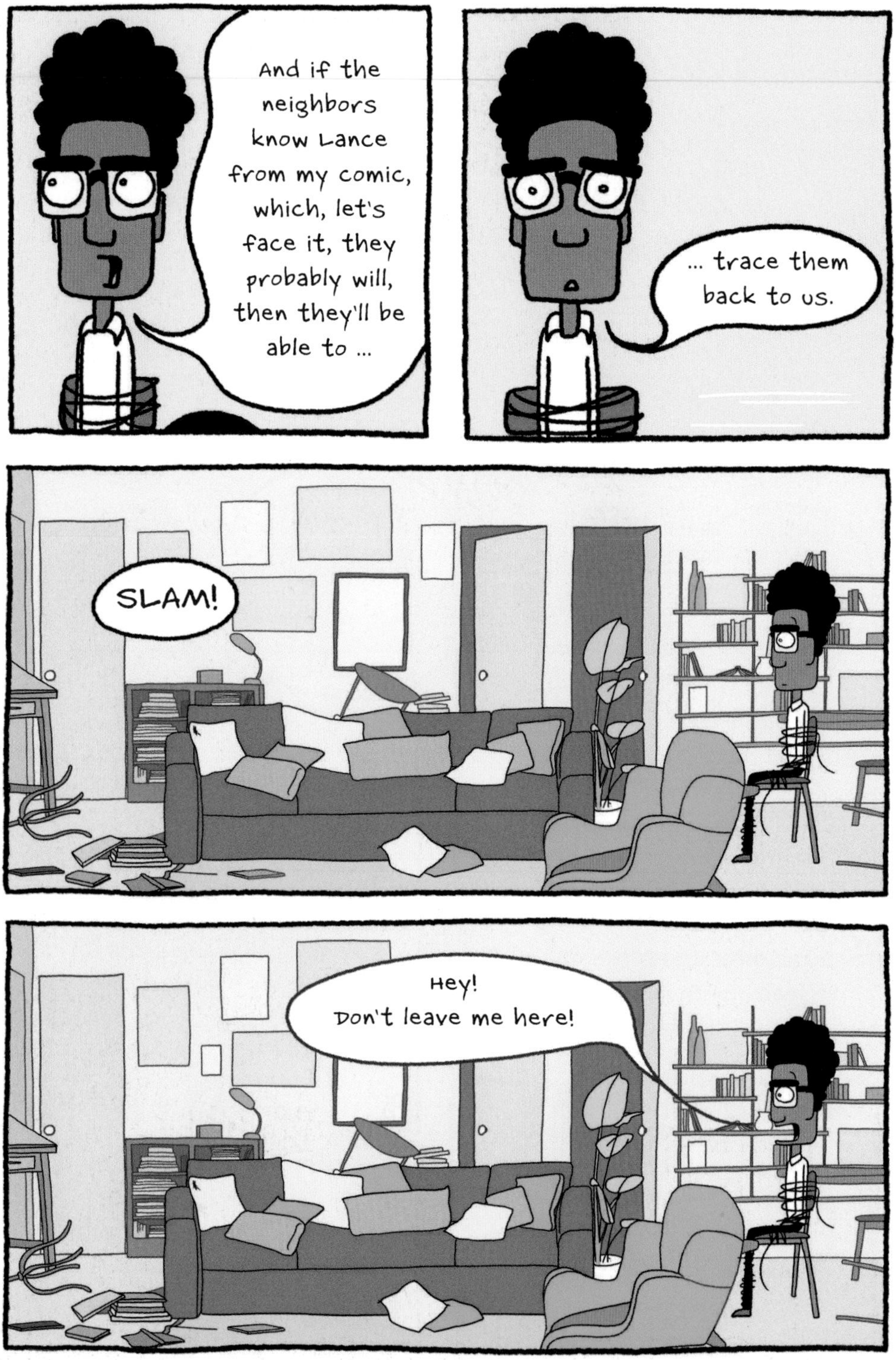

And if the neighbors know Lance from my comic, which, let's face it, they probably will, then they'll be able to ...
... trace them back to us.
SLAM!
Hey! Don't leave me here!

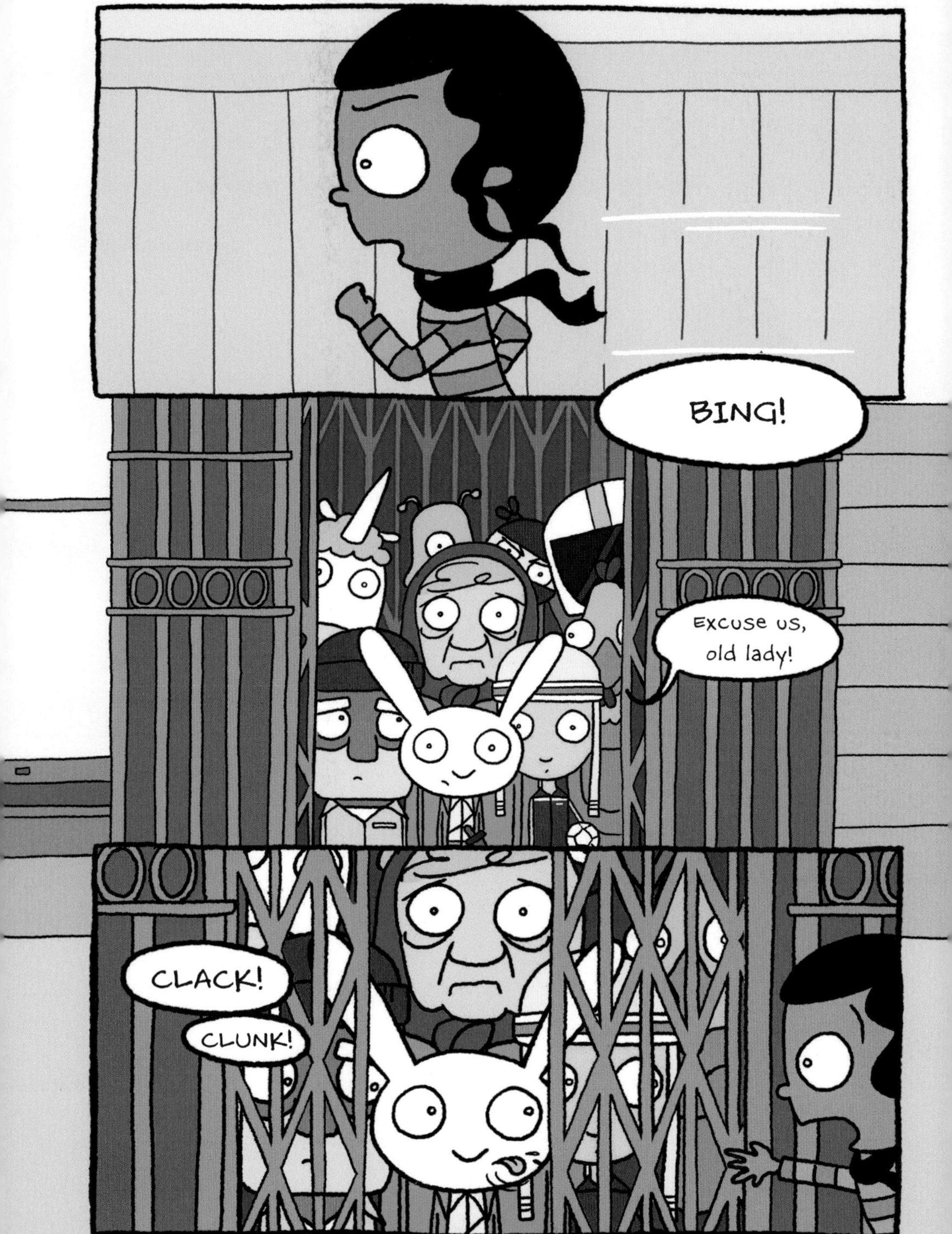
BING!
Excuse us, old lady!
CLACK!
CLUNK!

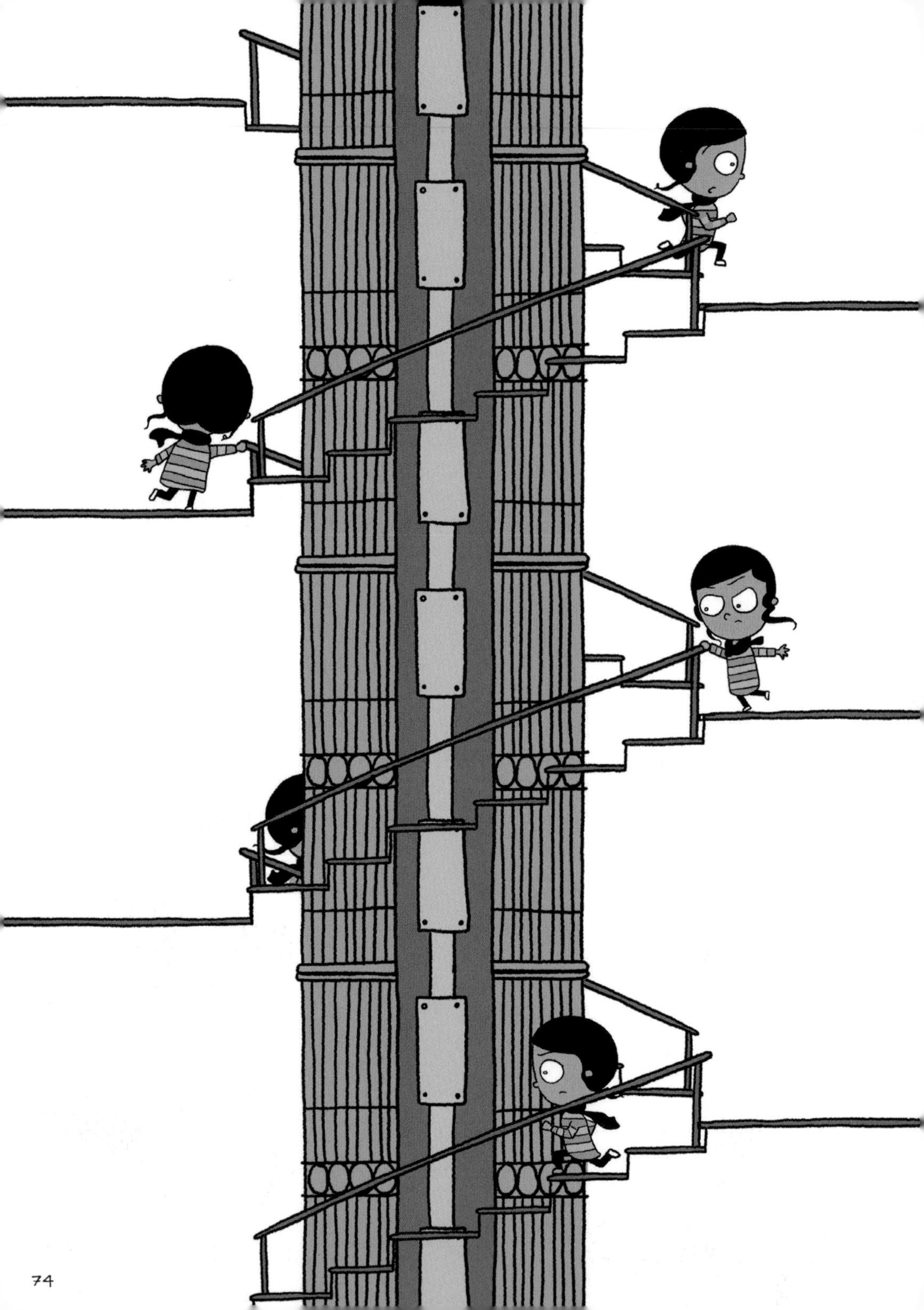

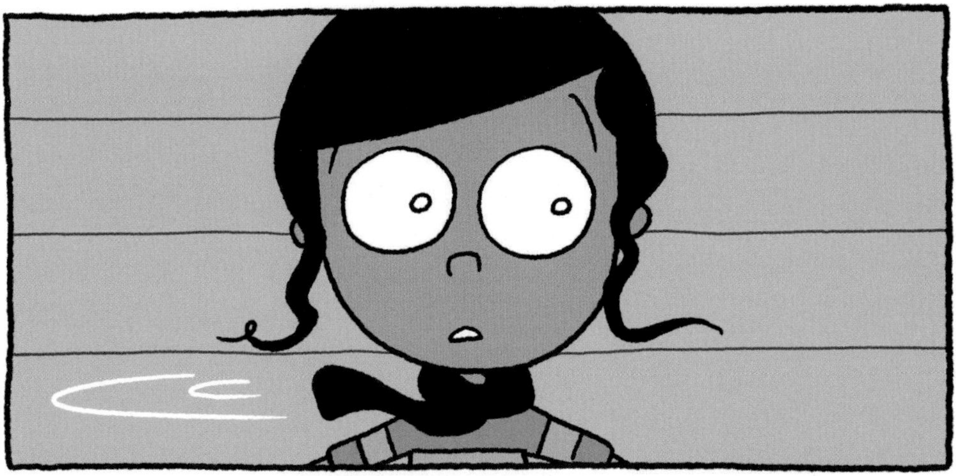

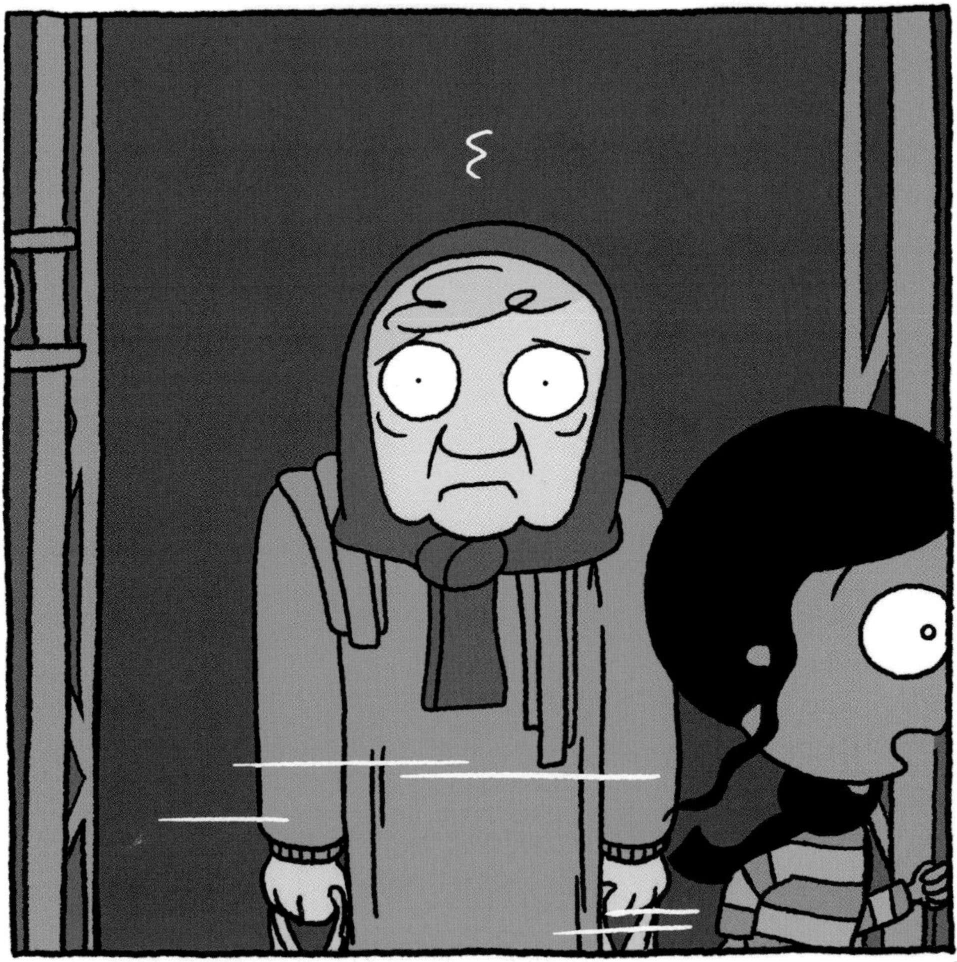

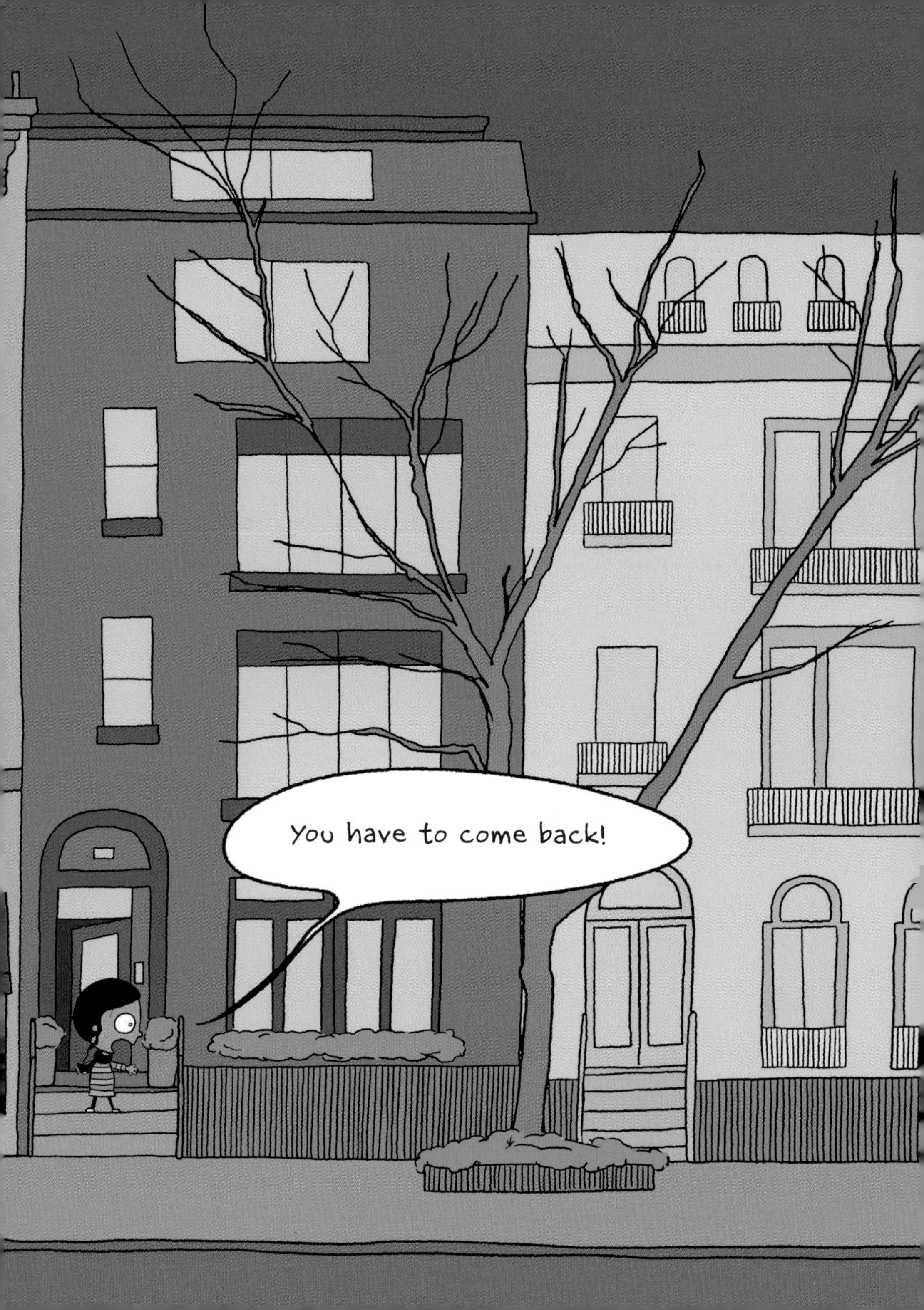
You have to come back!

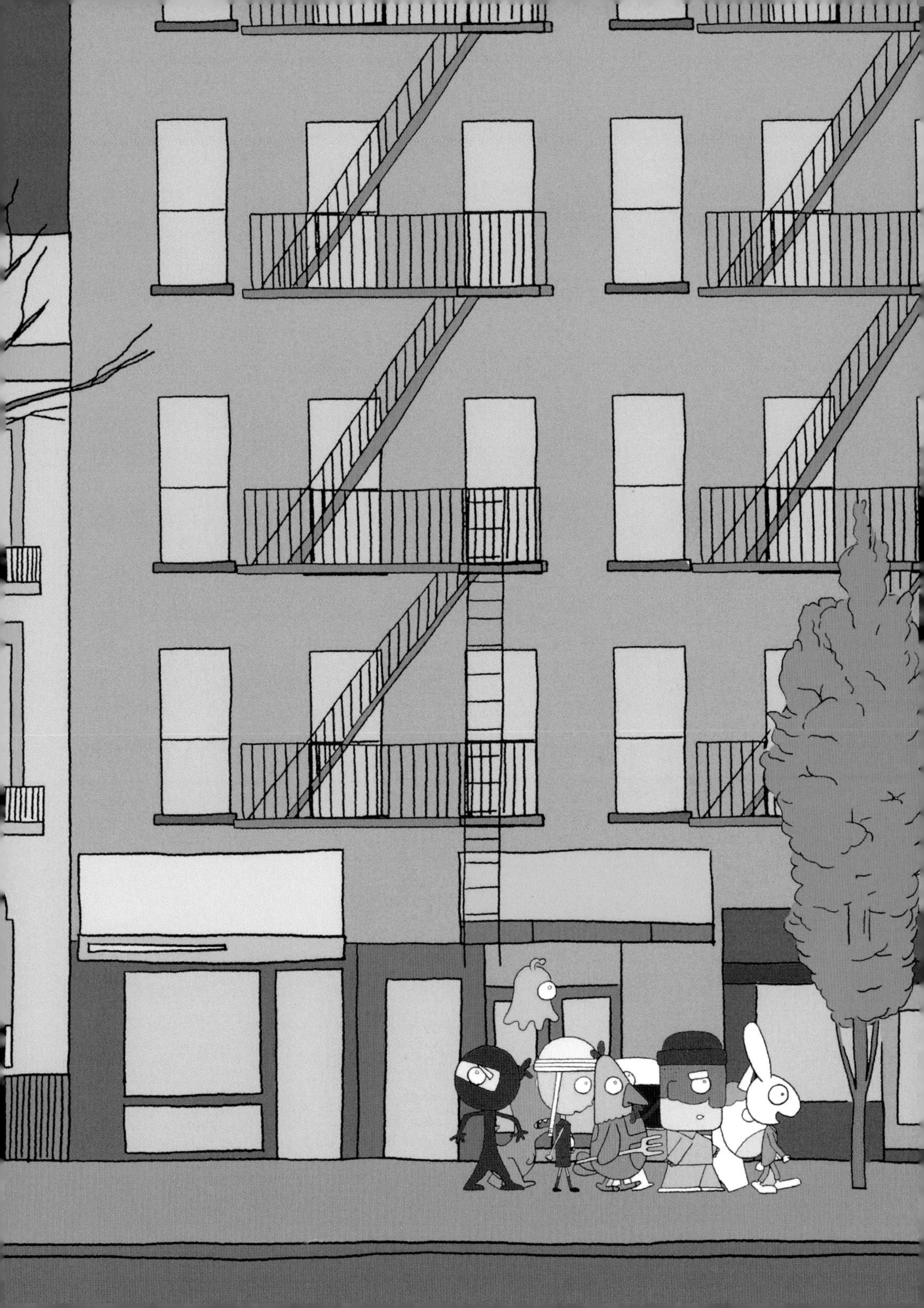

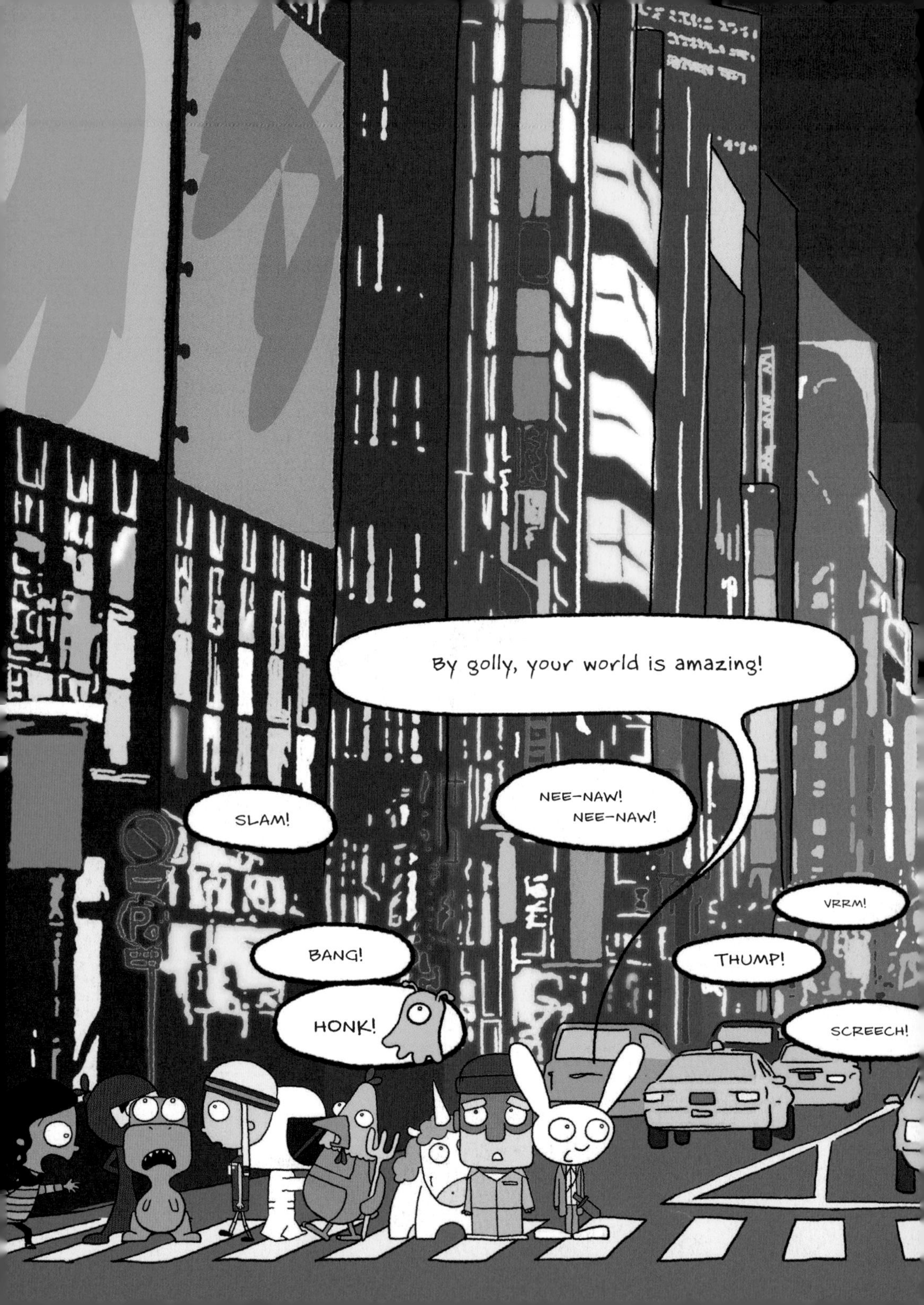
By golly, your world is amazing!
SLAM!
NEE-NAW! NEE-NAW!
VRRM!
BANG!
THUMP!
HONK!
SCREECH!

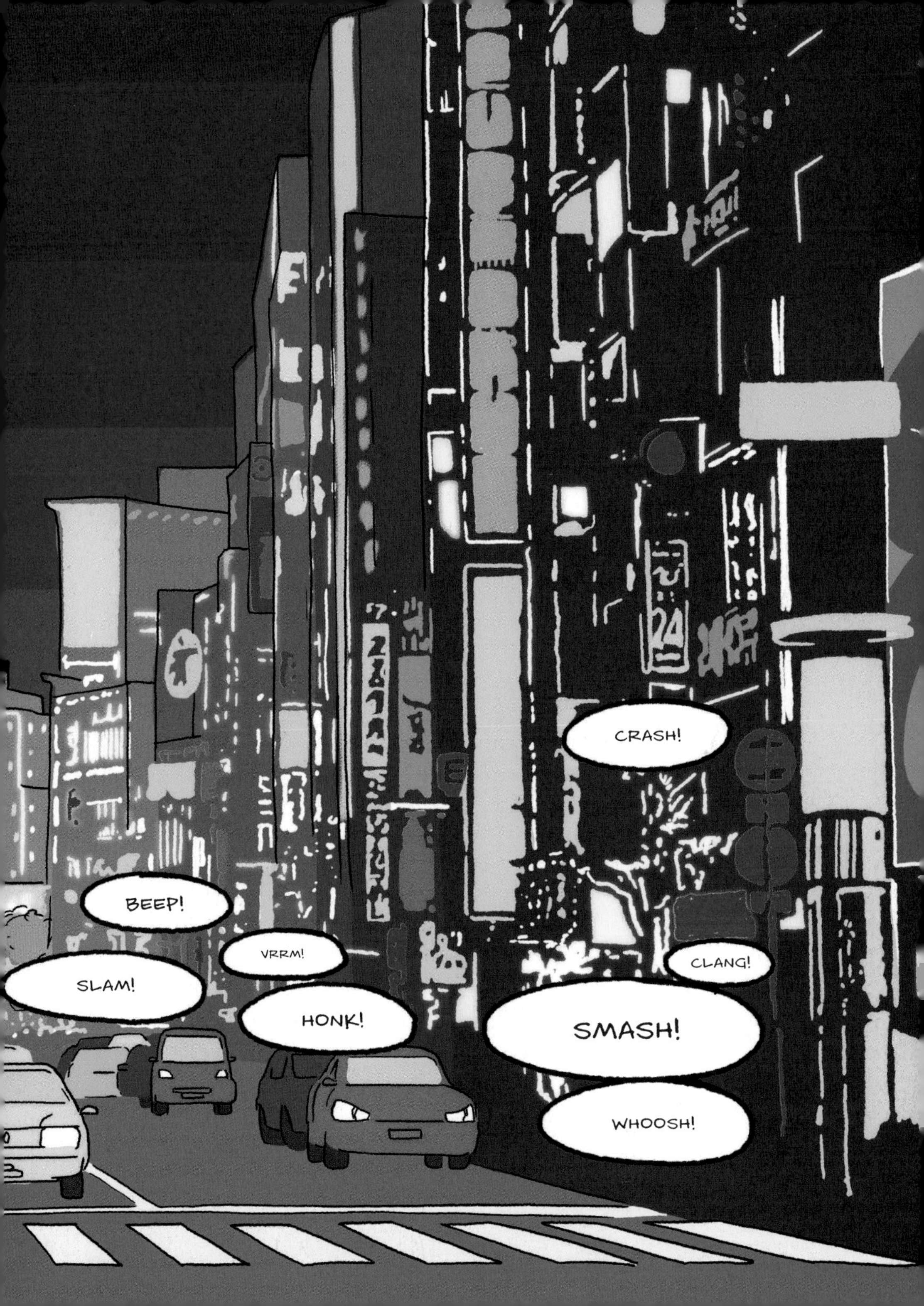
CRASH!
BEEP!
VRRM!
SLAM!
CLANG!
HONK!
SMASH!
WHOOSH!

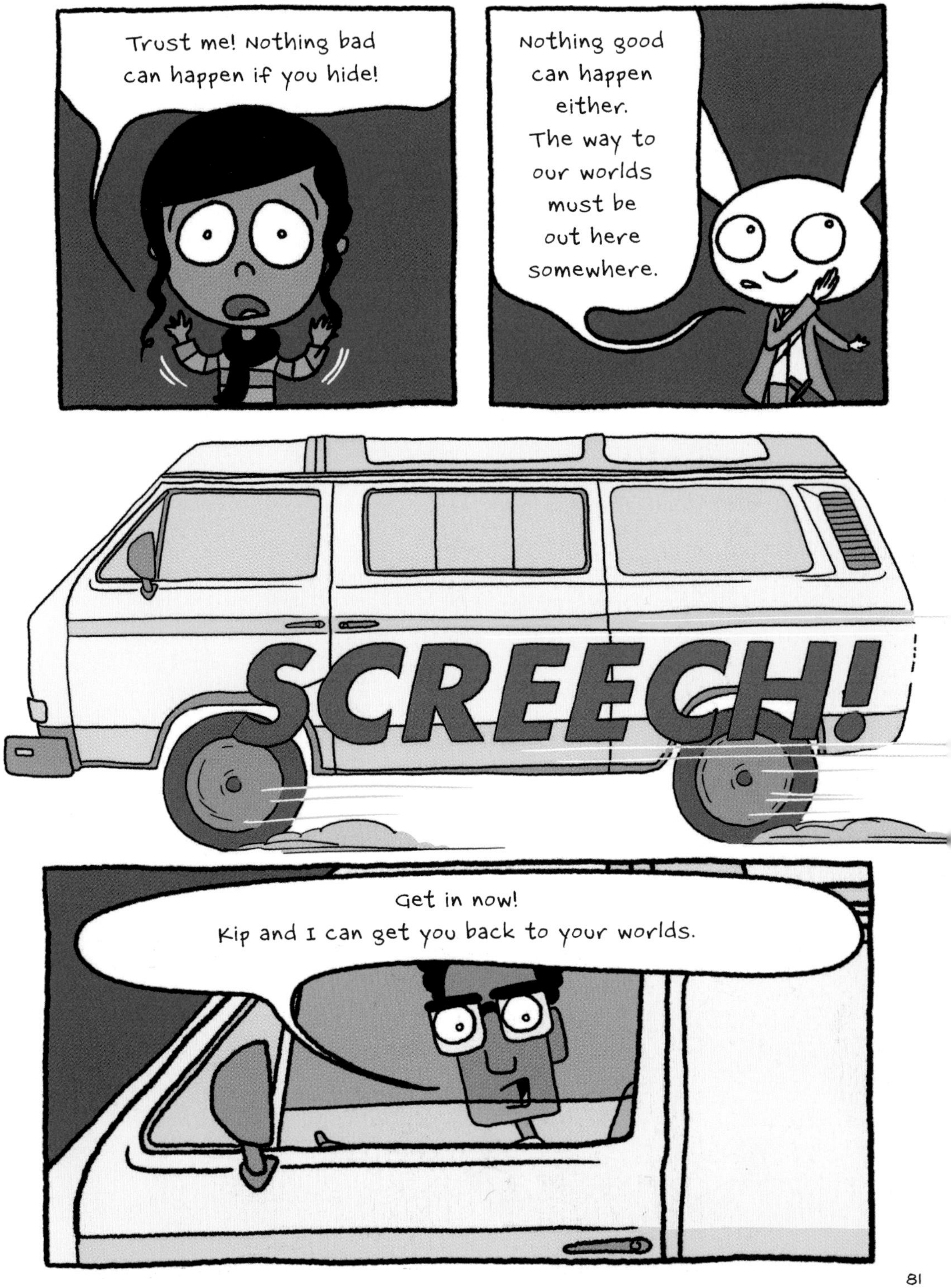

Trust me! Nothing bad can happen if you hide!
Nothing good can happen either. The way to our worlds must be out here somewhere.
SCREECH!
Get in now! Kip and I can get you back to your worlds.

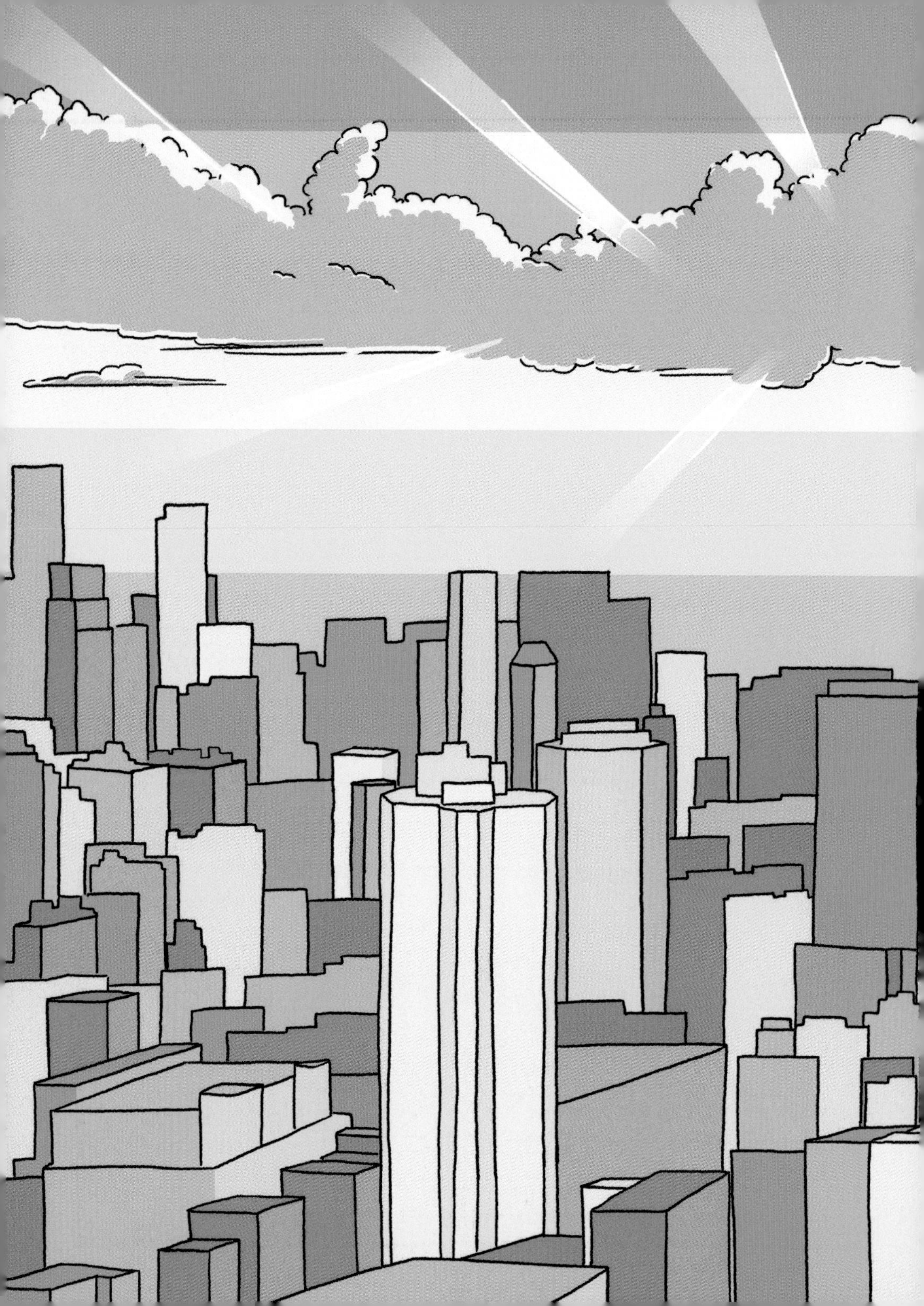

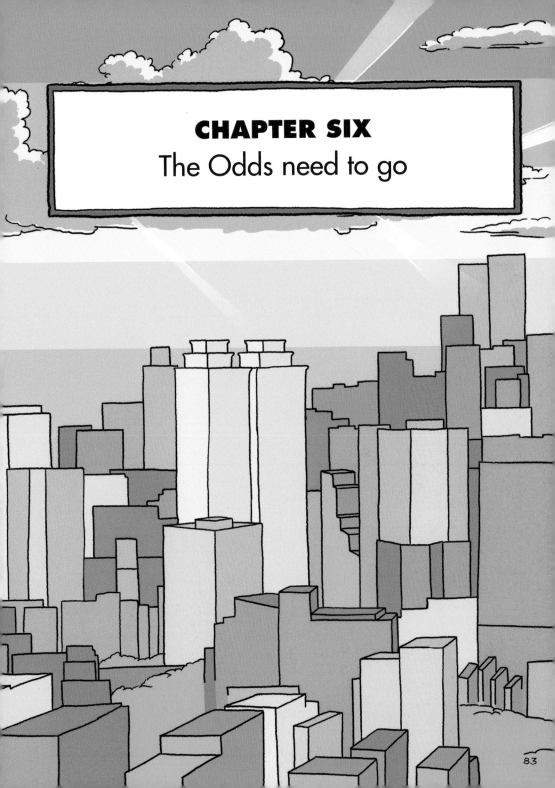

CHAPTER SIX
The Odds need to go

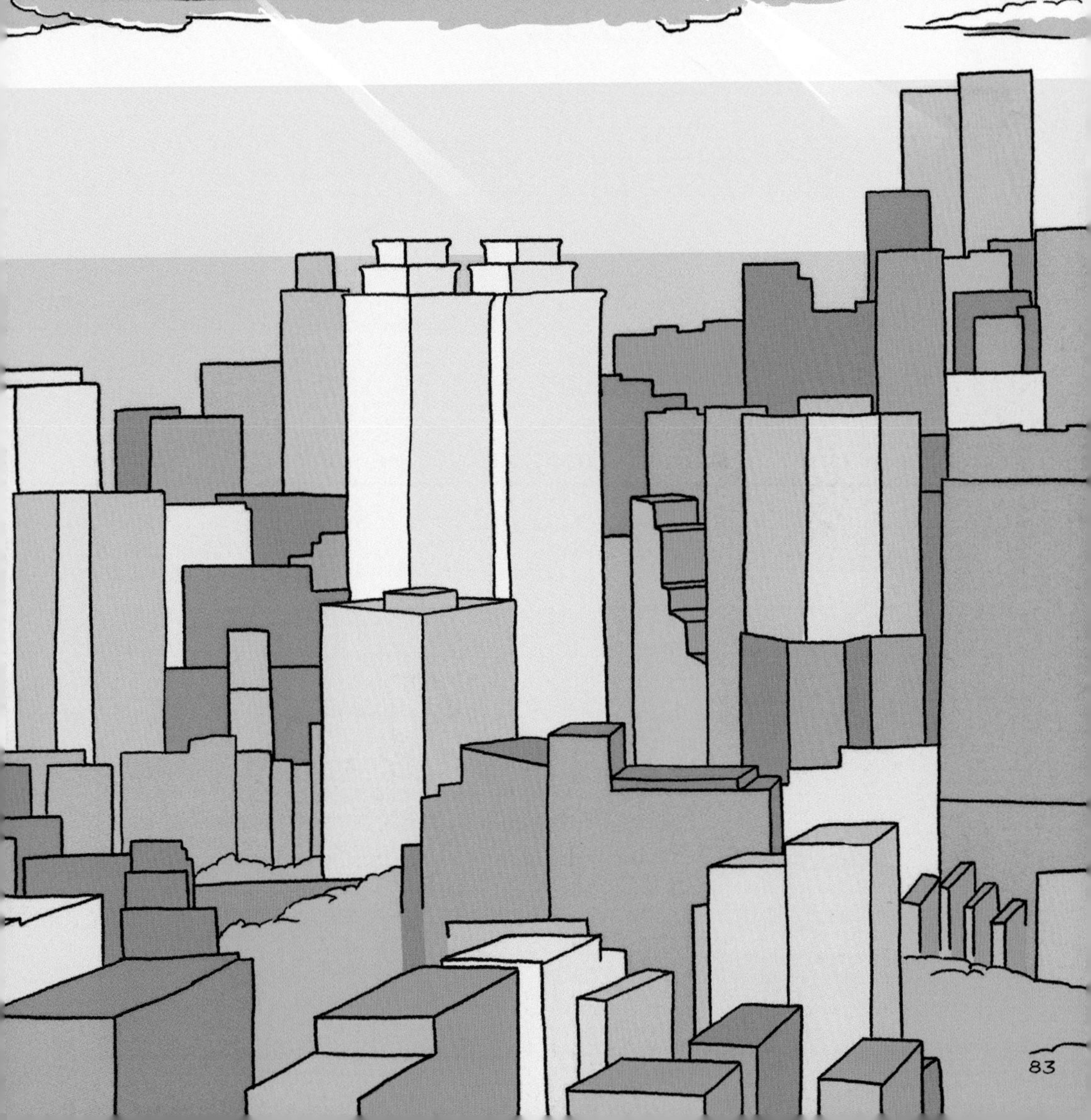

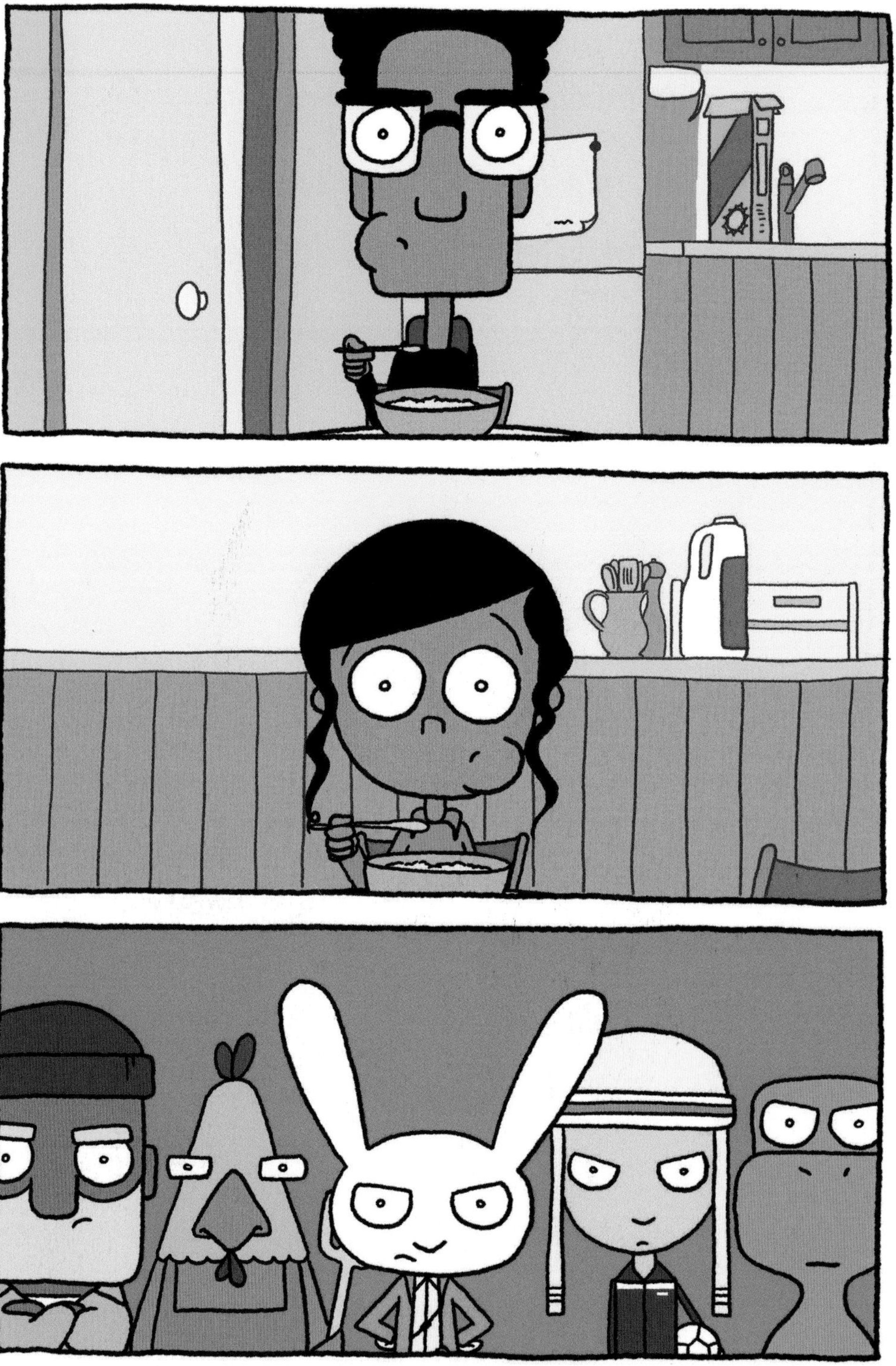

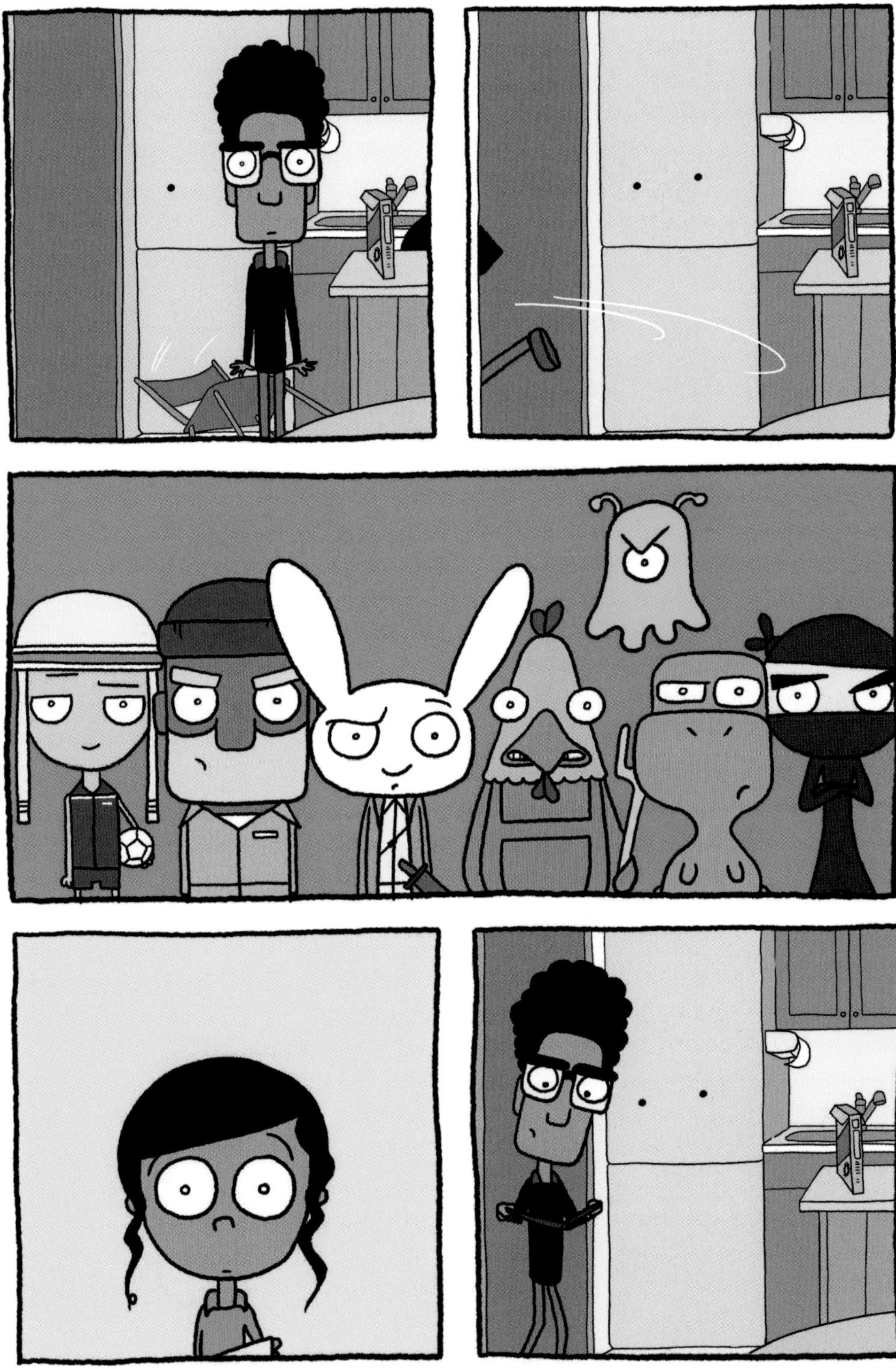

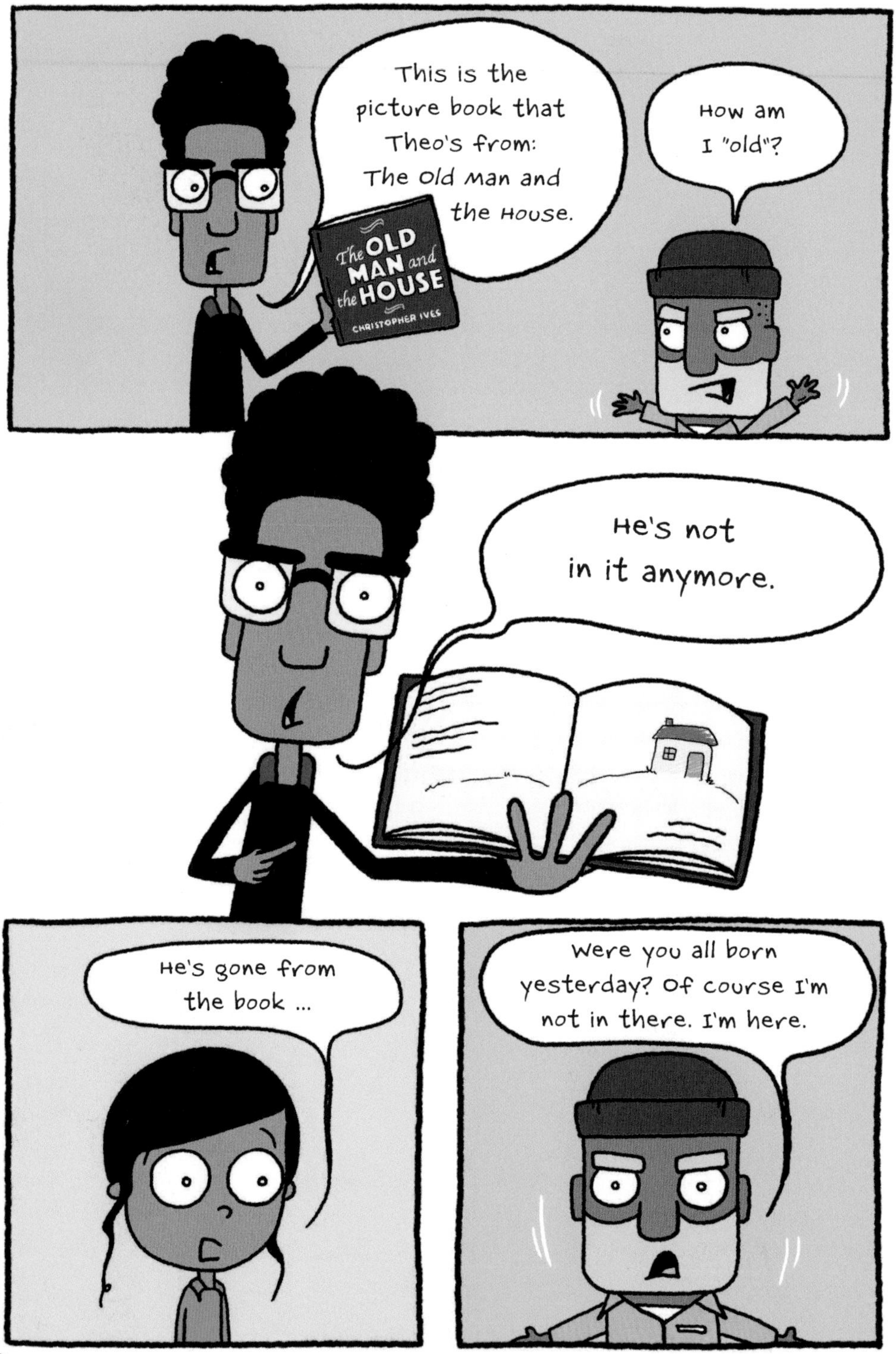
This is the picture book that Theo's from: The Old Man and the House.
The OLD MAN and the HOUSE
CHRISTOPHER IVES
How am I "old"?
He's not in it anymore.
He's gone from the book ...
Were you all born yesterday? Of course I'm not in there. I'm here.

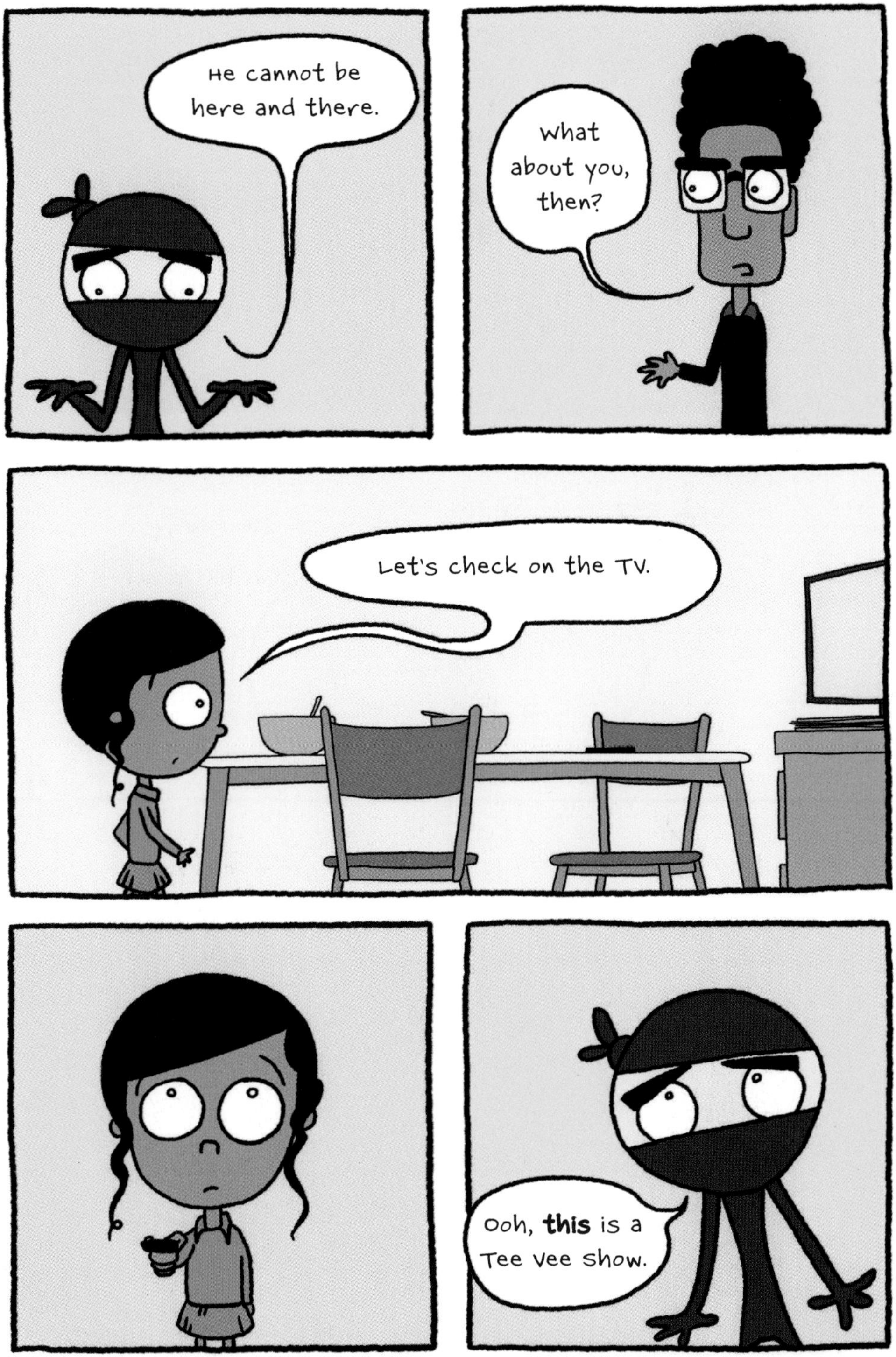
He cannot be here and there.
What about you, then?
Let's check on the TV.
Ooh, **this** is a Tee vee show.

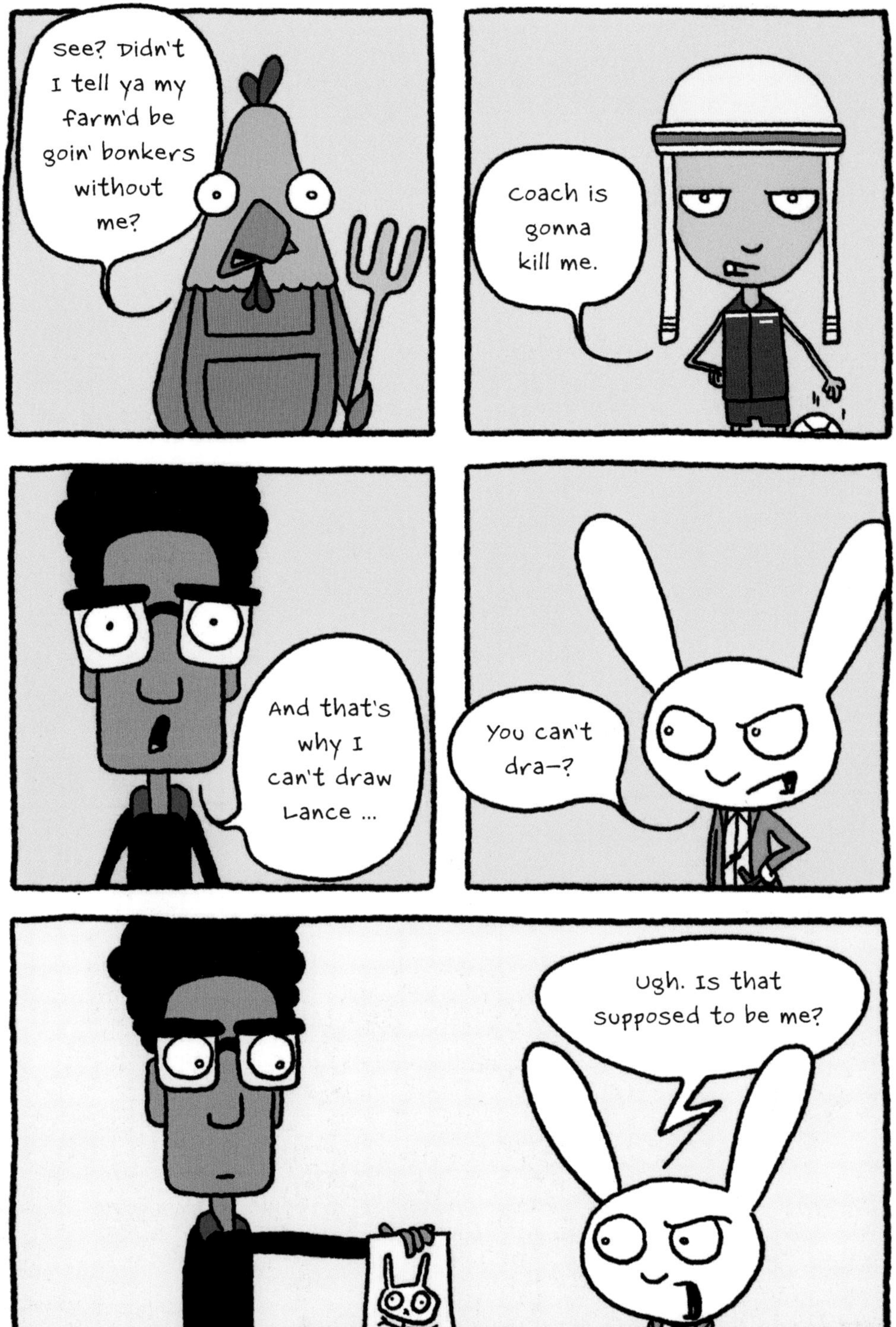
See? Didn't I tell ya my farm'd be goin' bonkers without me?
Coach is gonna kill me.
And that's why I can't draw Lance ...
You can't dra–?
Ugh. Is that supposed to be me?

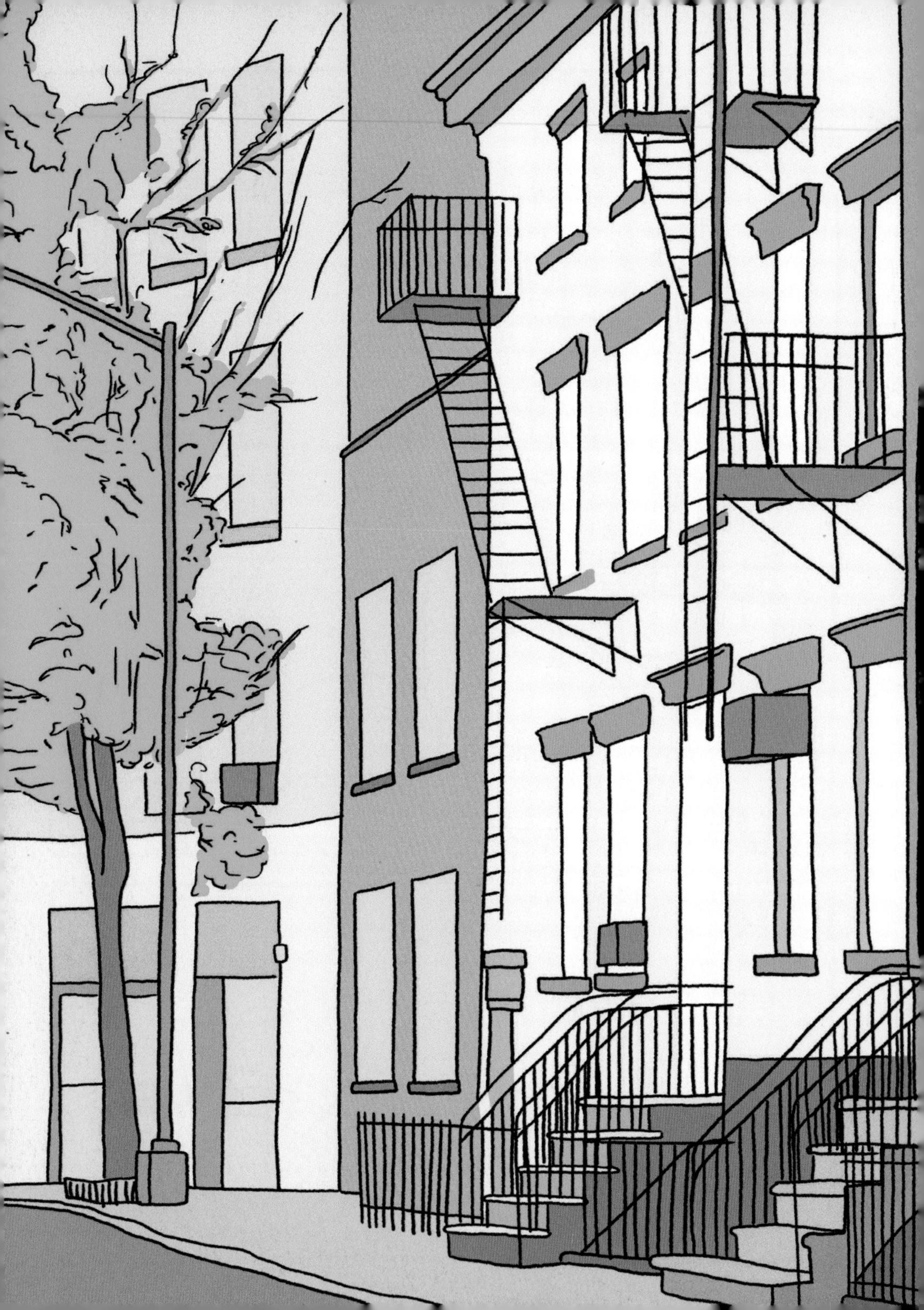

CHAPTER SEVEN

The Odds try everything

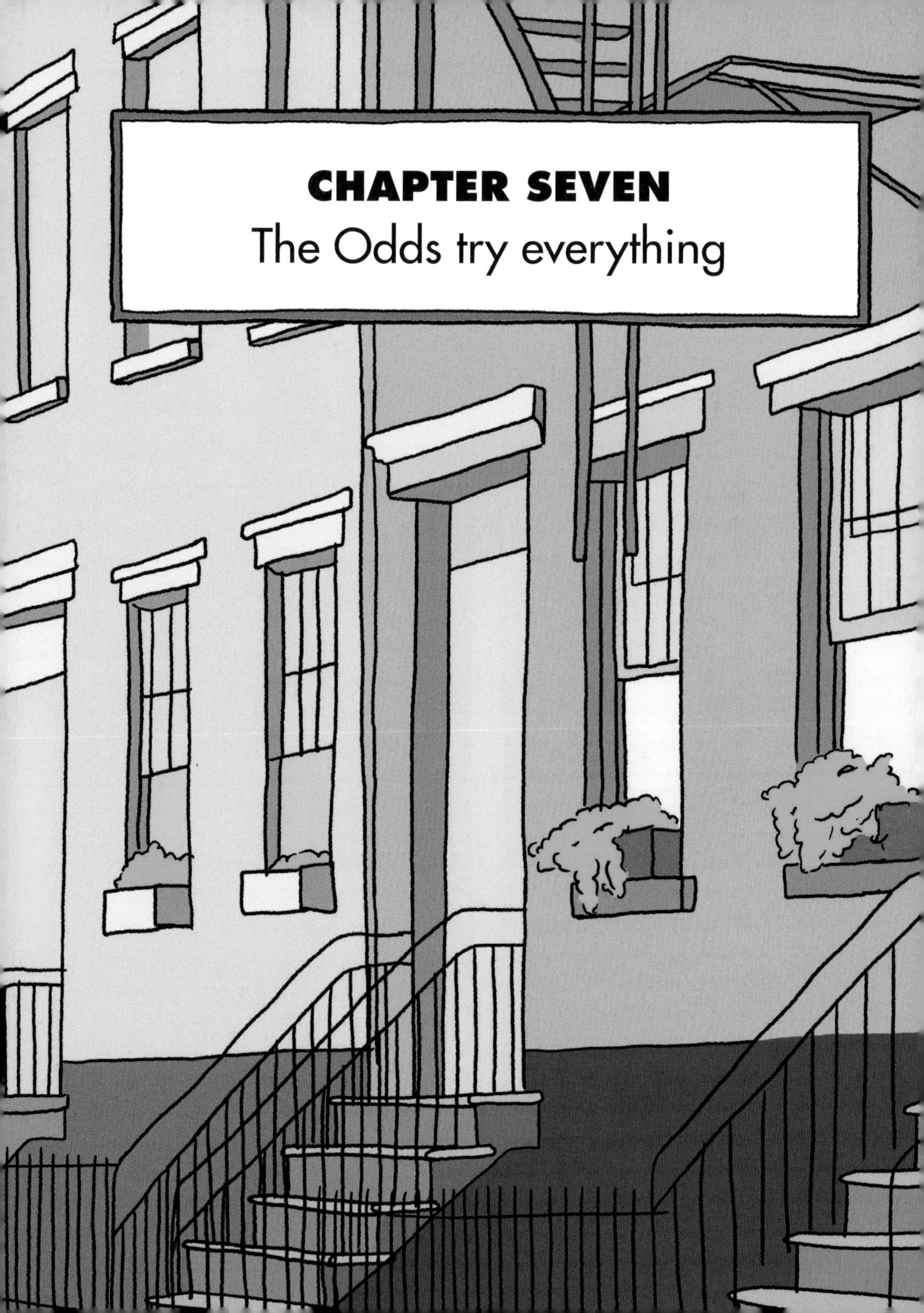

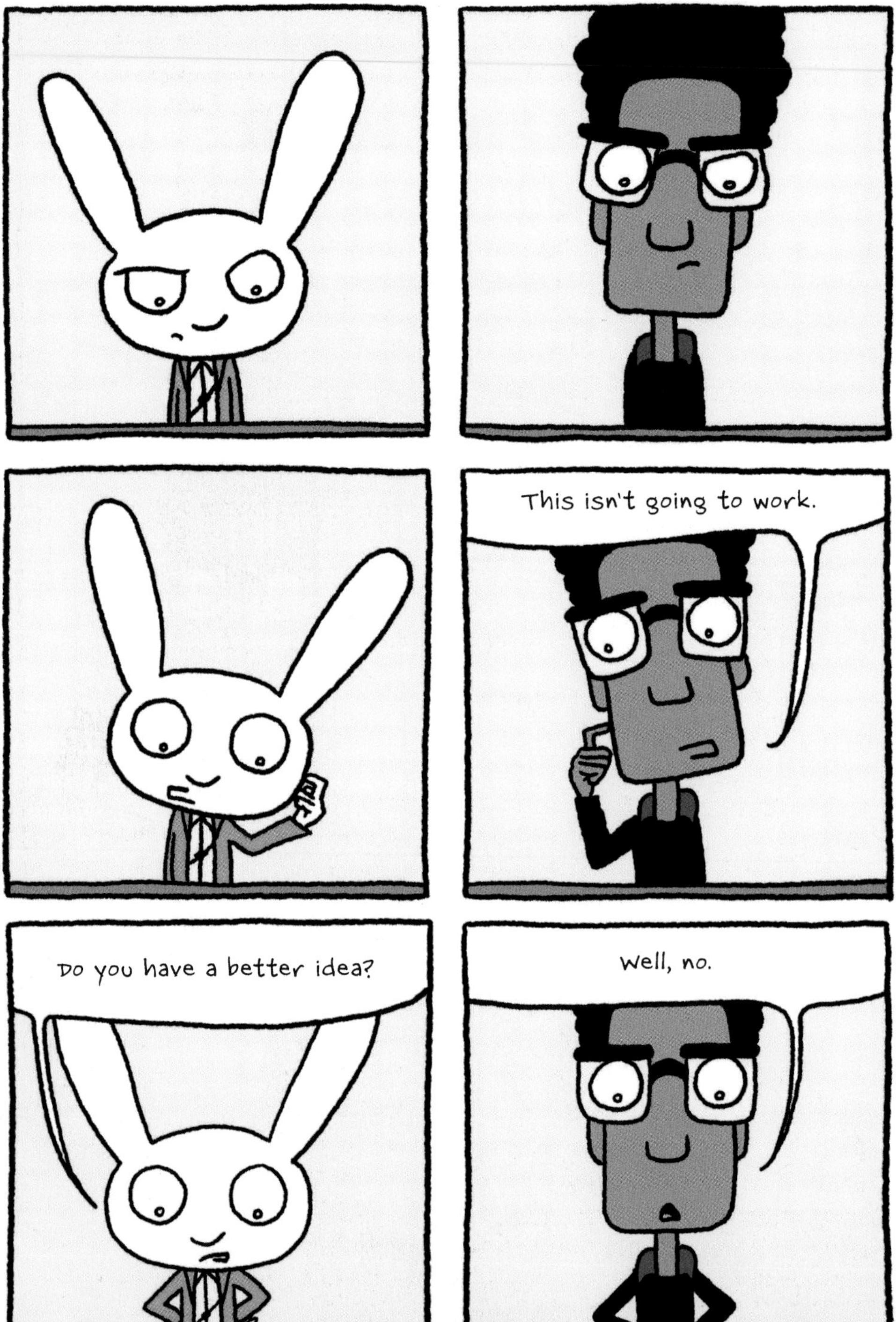
This isn't going to work.
Do you have a better idea?
Well, no.

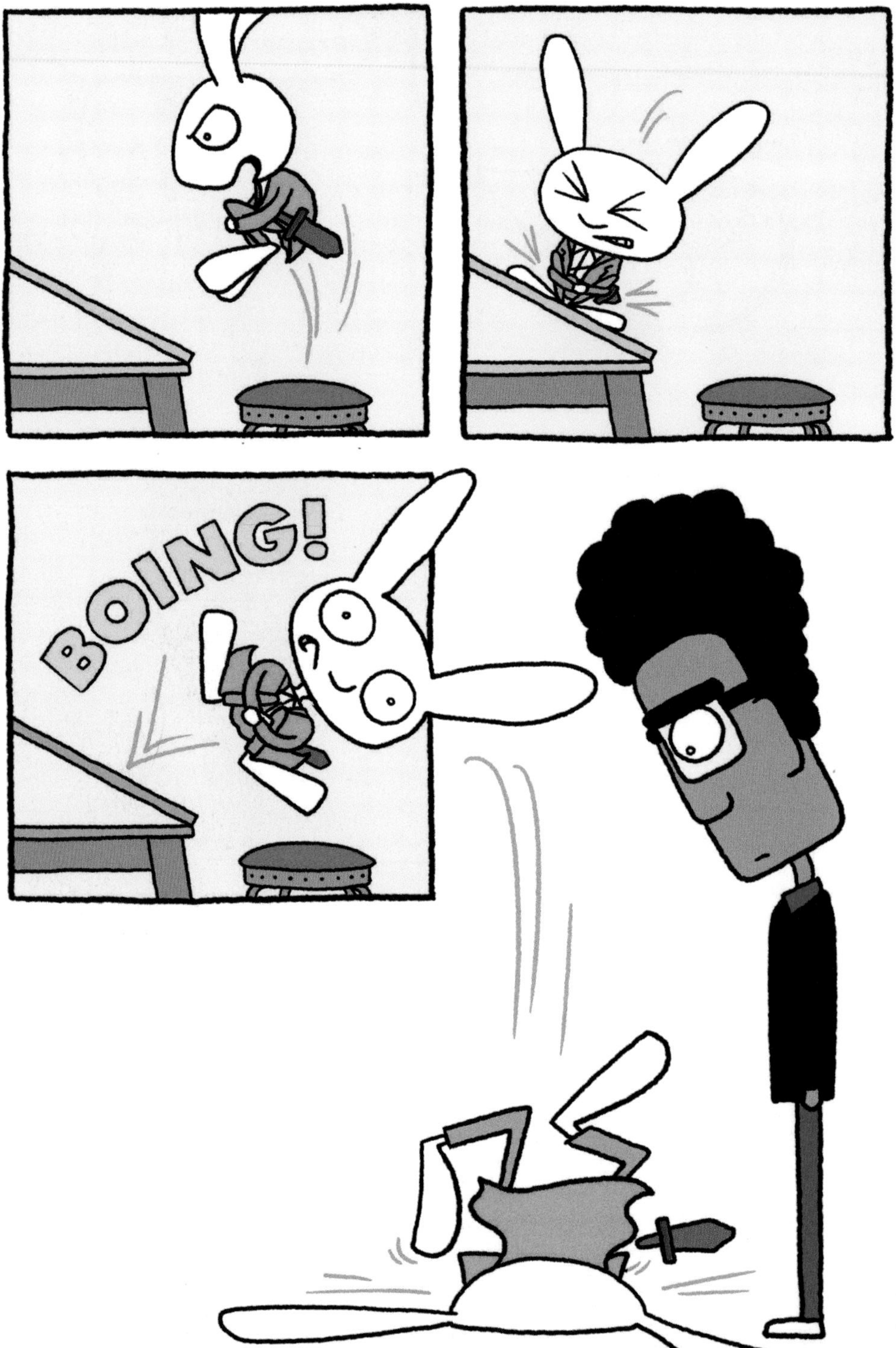
BOING!

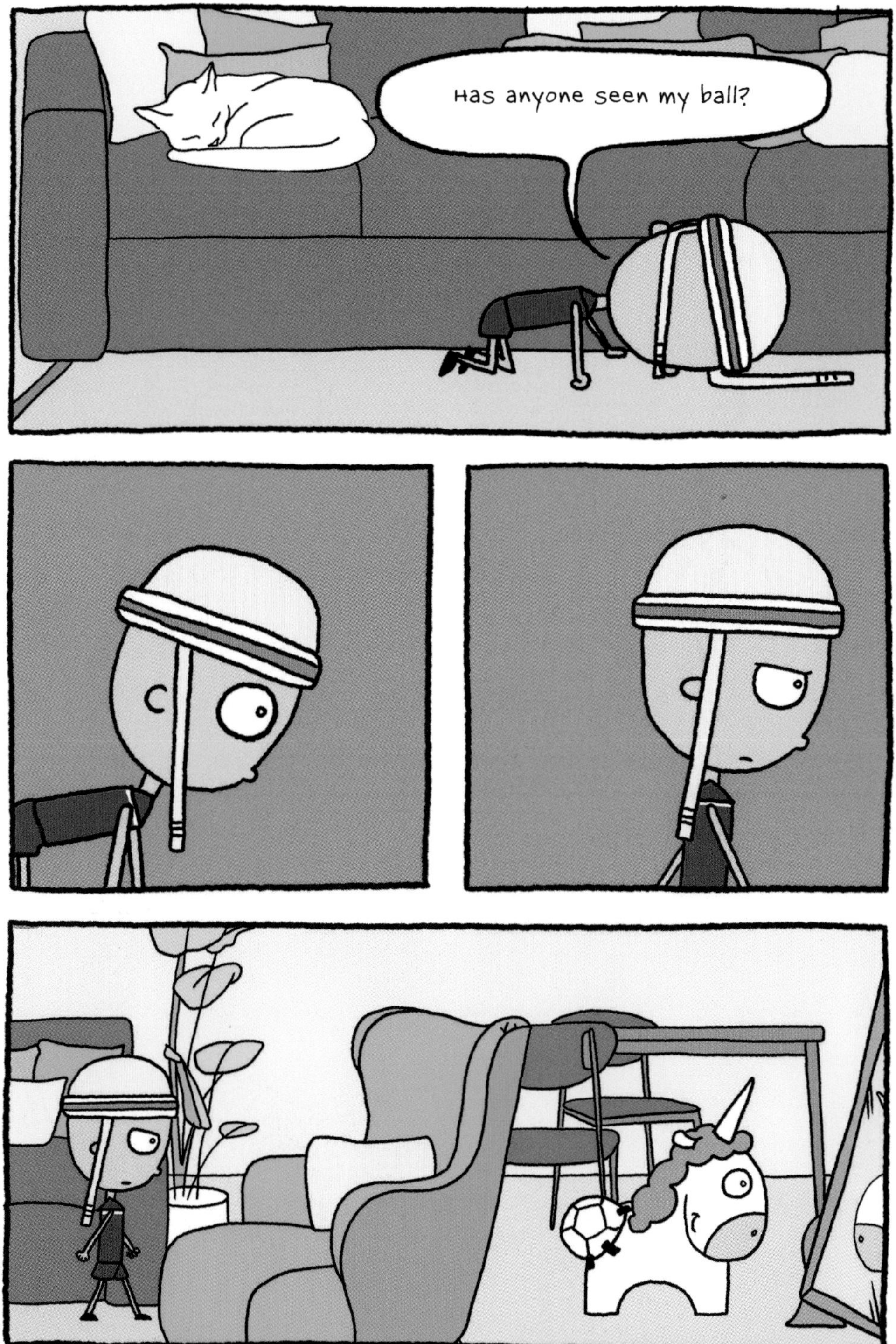
Has anyone seen my ball?

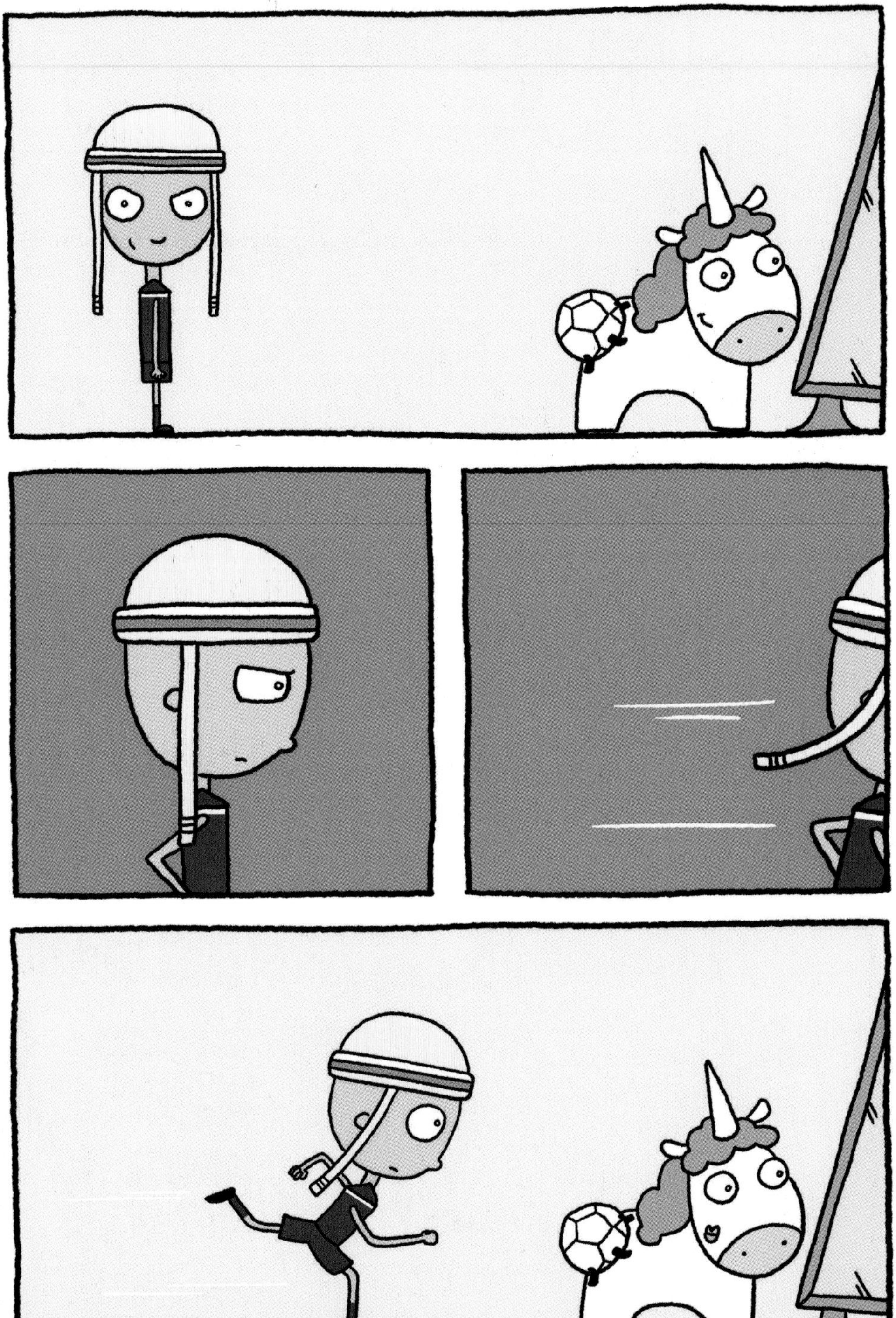

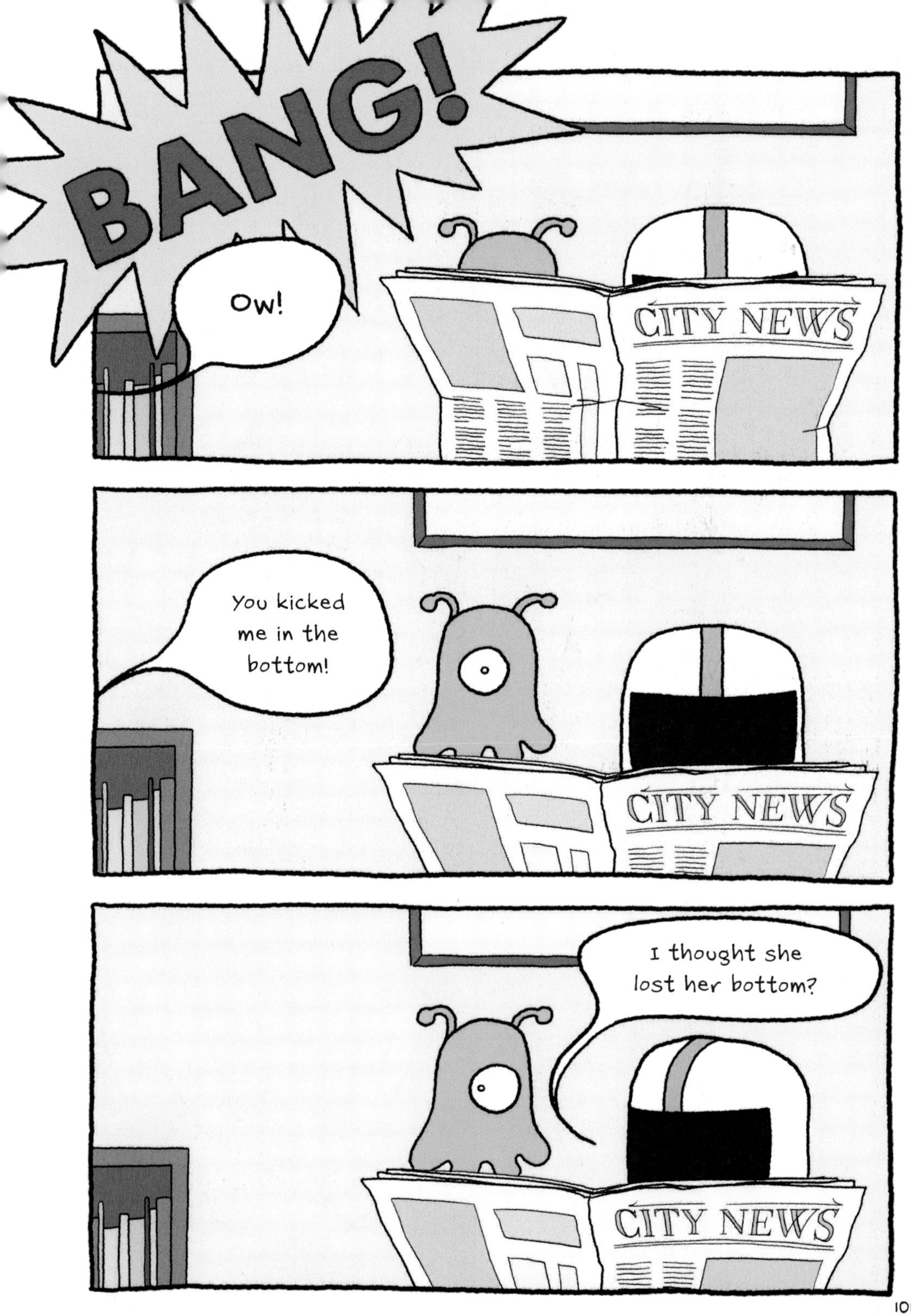
BANG!
Ow!
CITY NEWS
You kicked me in the bottom!
CITY NEWS
I thought she lost her bottom?
CITY NEWS

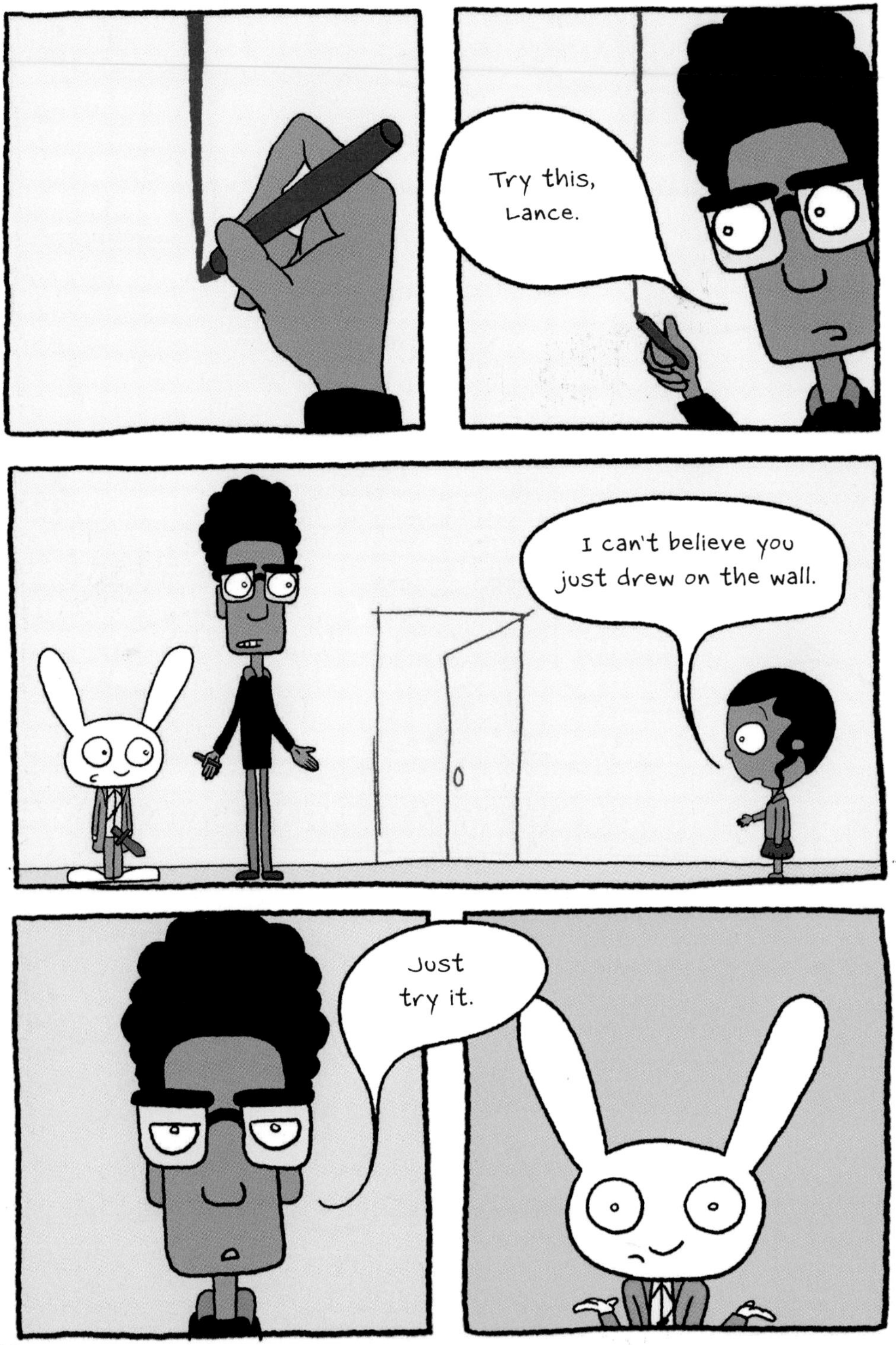
Try this, Lance.
I can't believe you just drew on the wall.
Just try it.

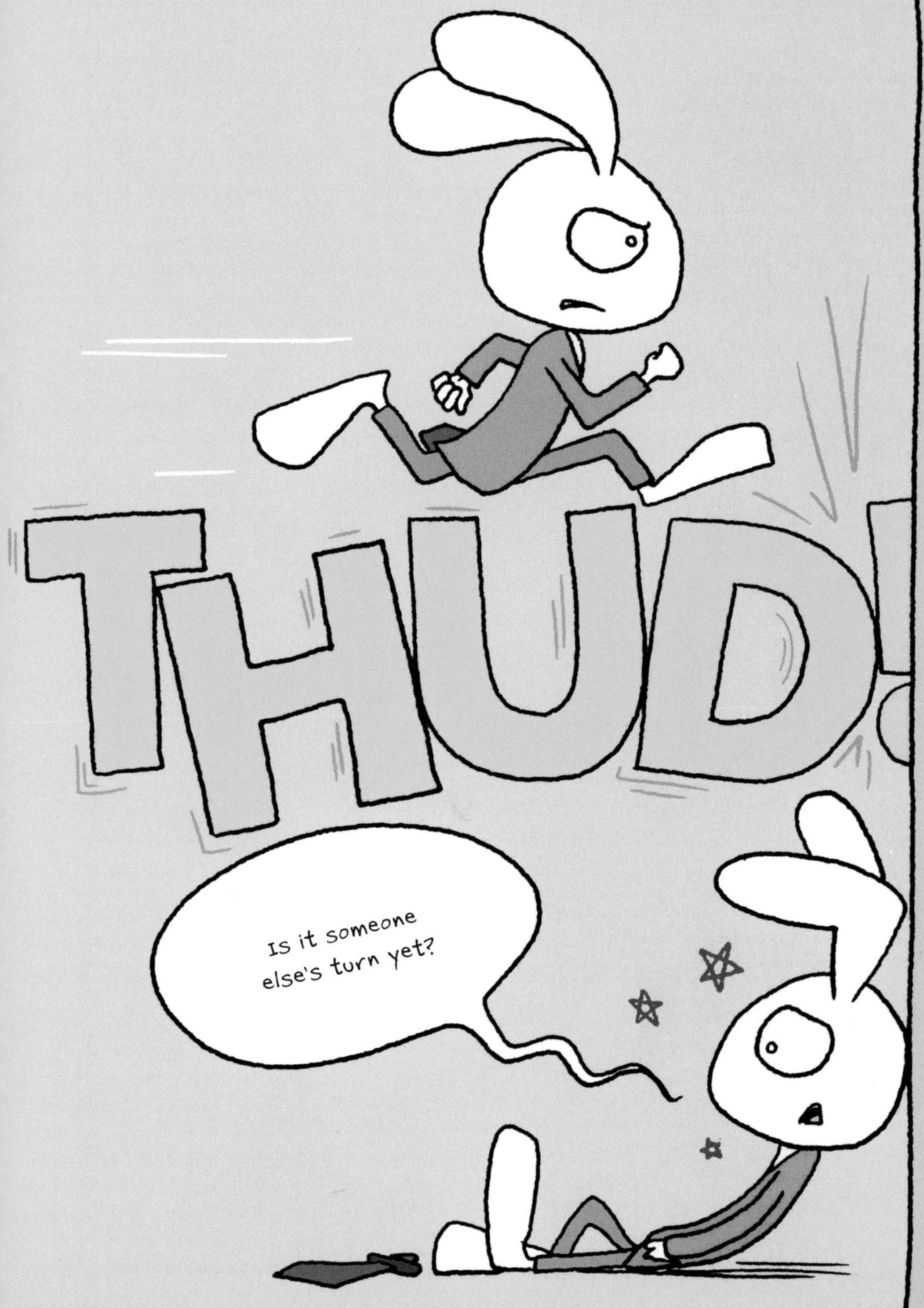
THUD!
Is it someone else's turn yet?

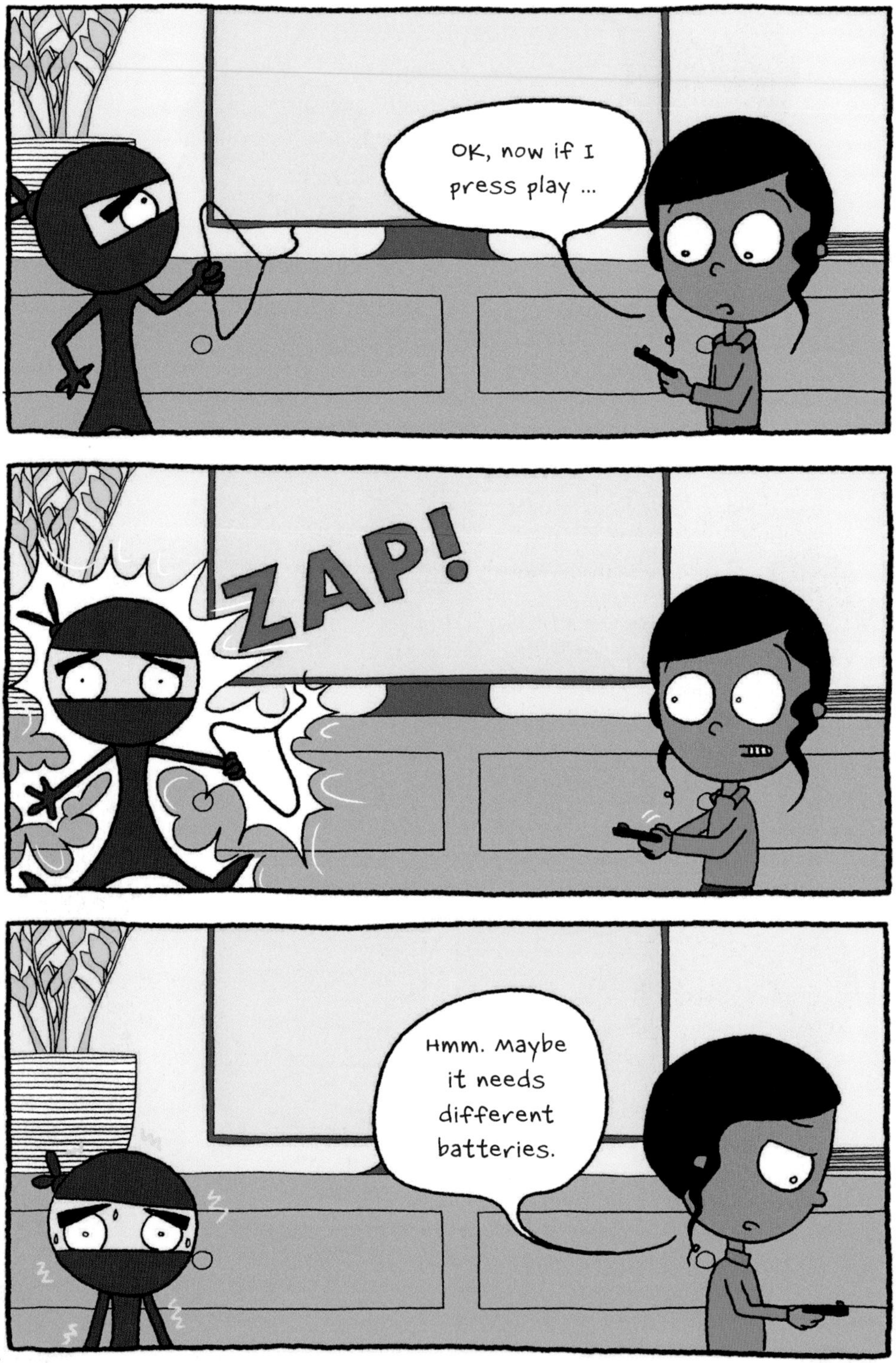
OK, now if I press play ...
ZAP!
Hmm. Maybe it needs different batteries.

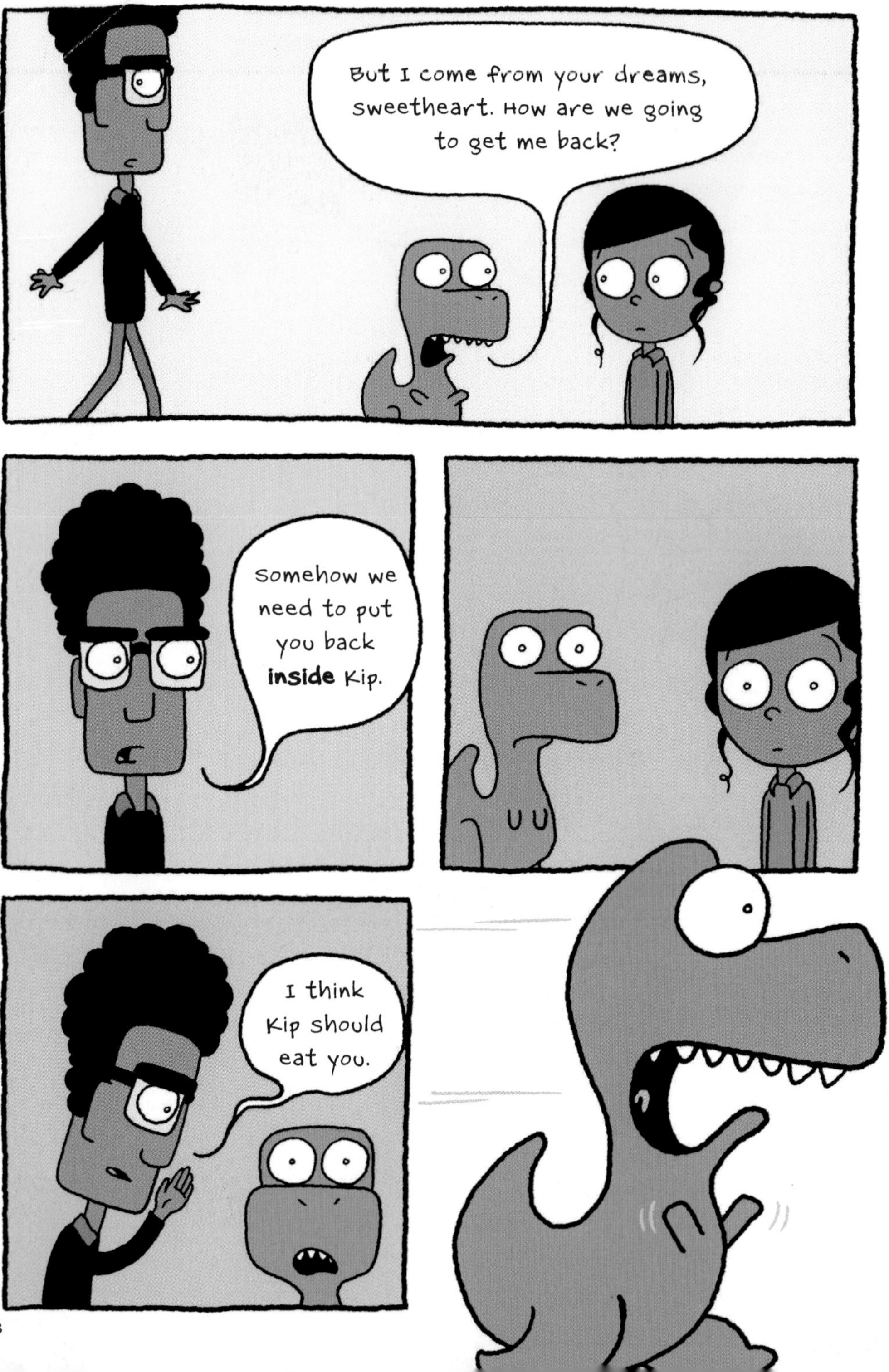
But I come from your dreams, sweetheart. How are we going to get me back?
Somehow we need to put you back **inside** Kip.
I think Kip should eat you.

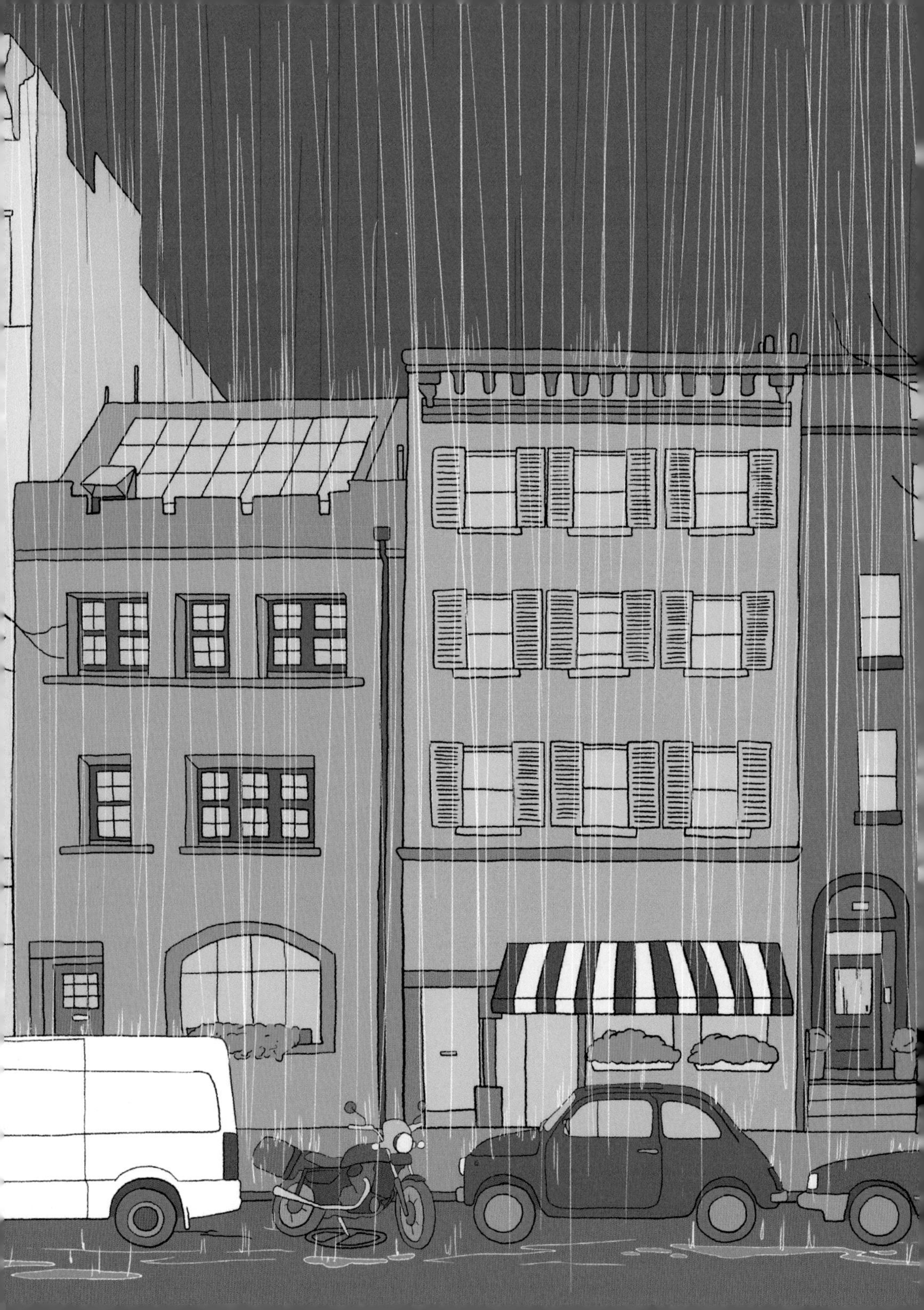

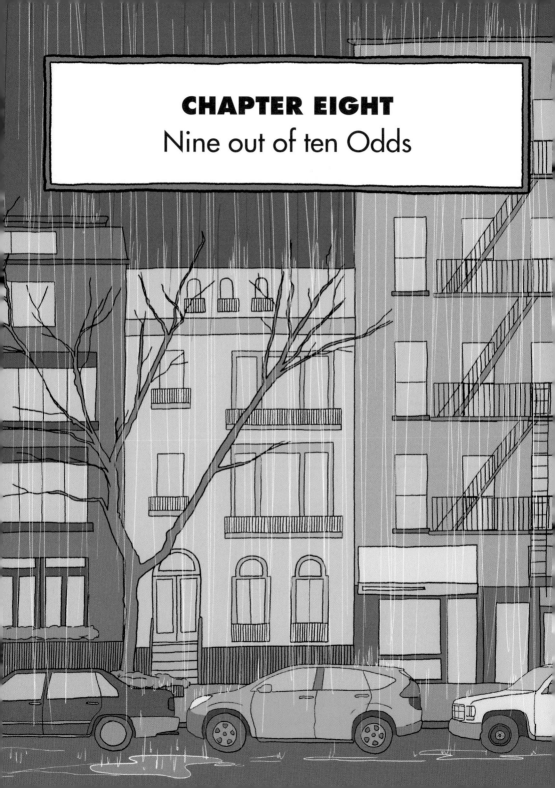

CHAPTER EIGHT
Nine out of ten Odds

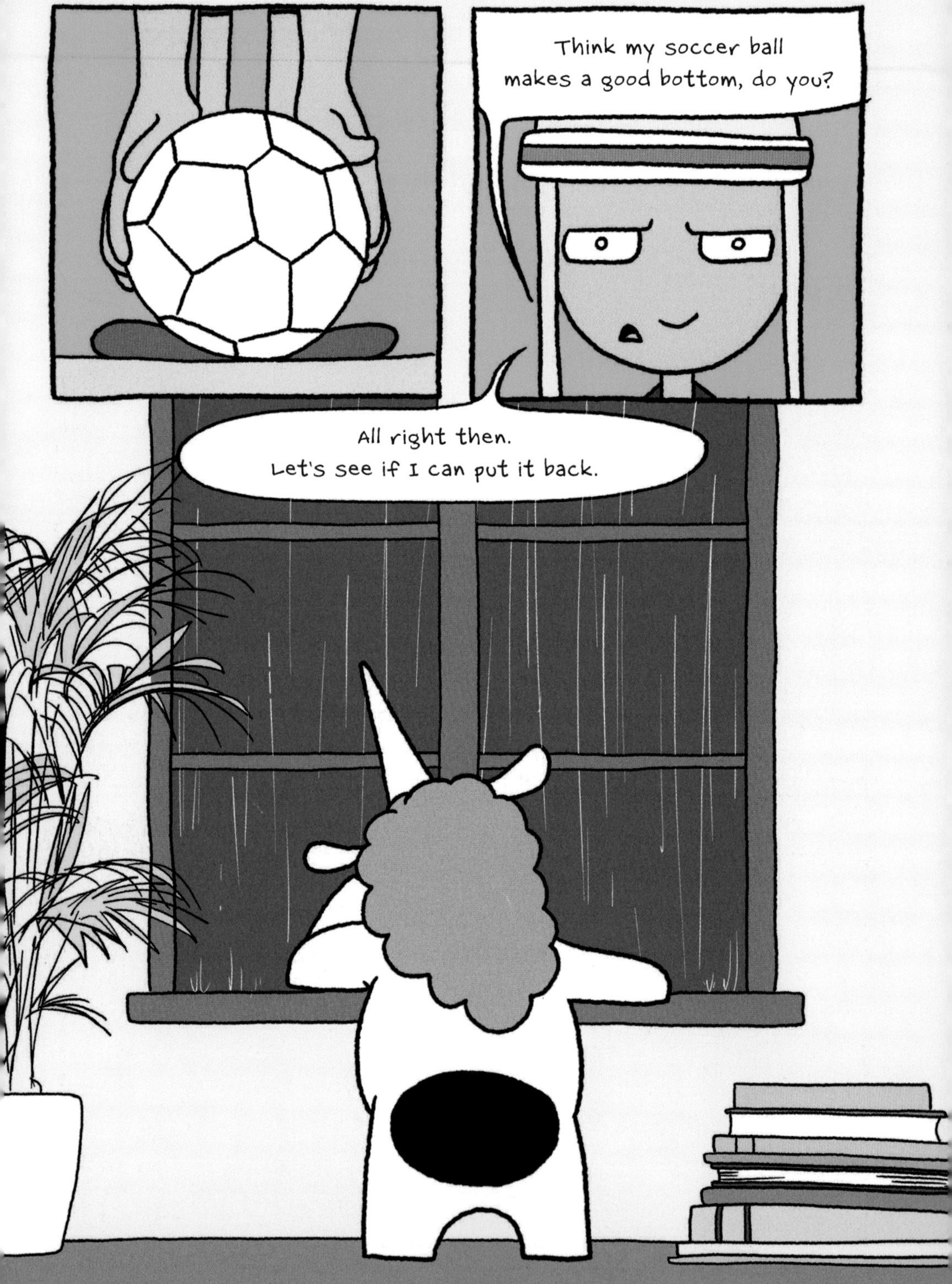
Think my soccer ball makes a good bottom, do you?
All right then. Let's see if I can put it back.

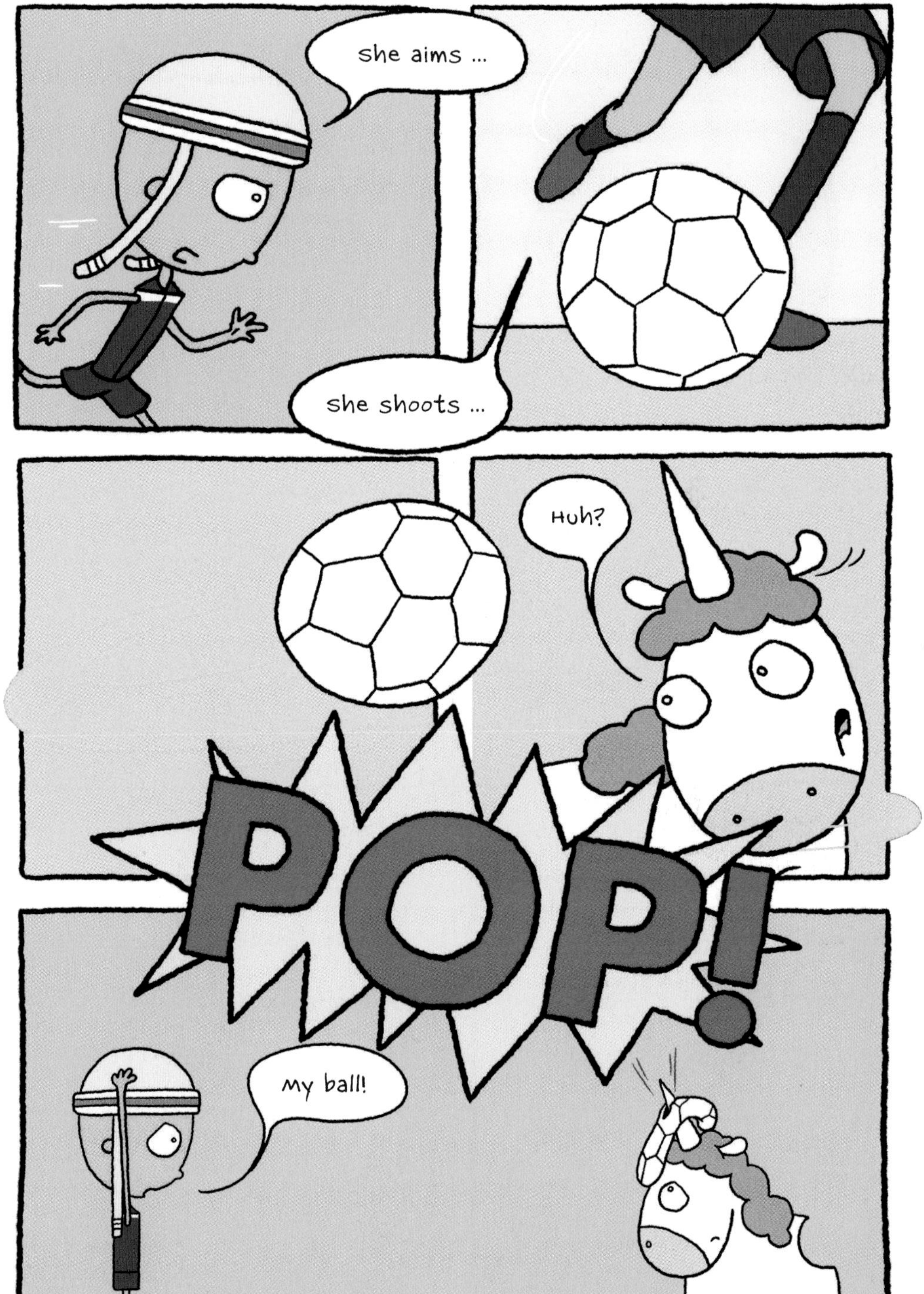
she aims ...
she shoots ...
Huh?
POP!
my ball!

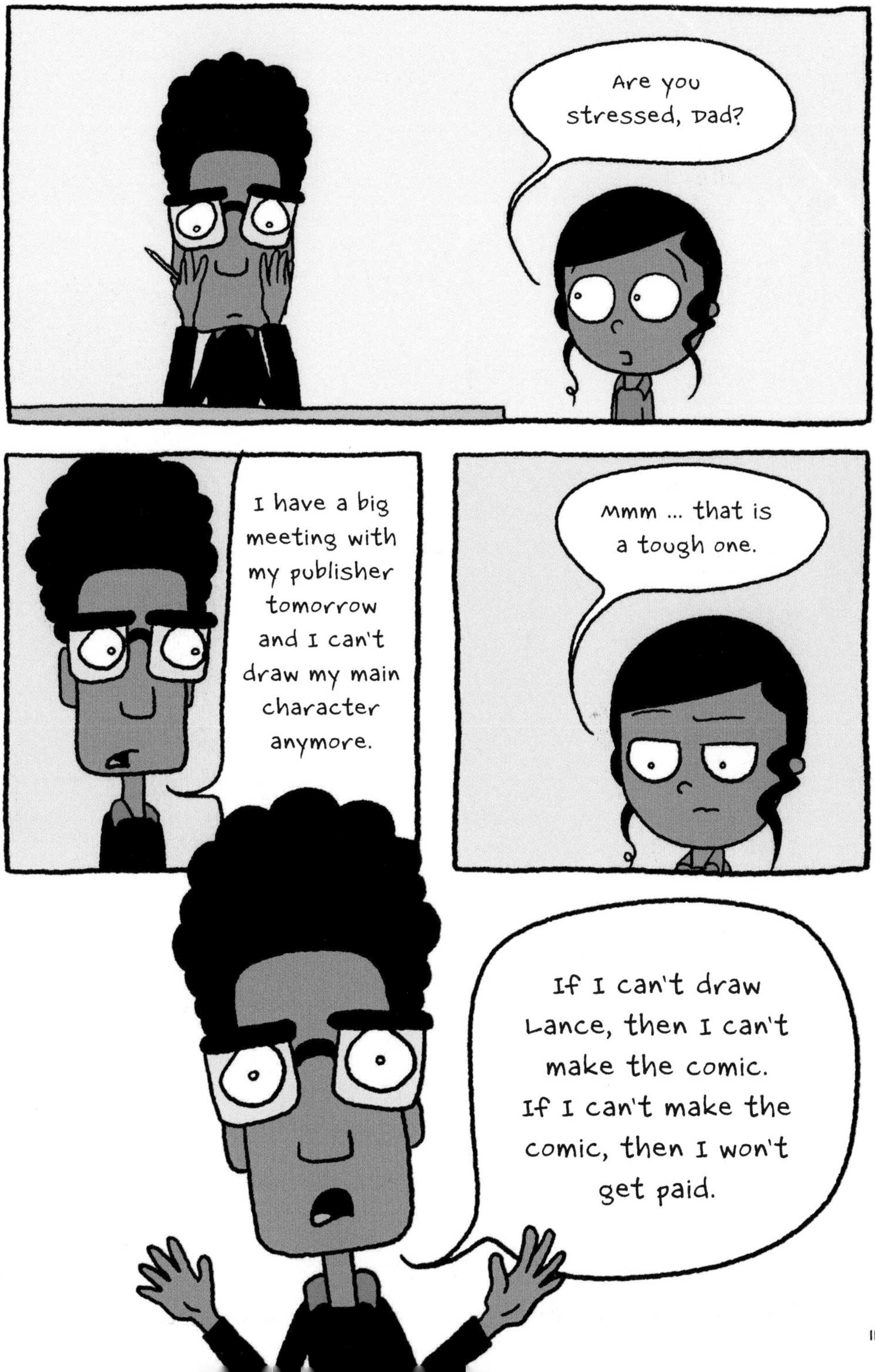
Are you stressed, Dad?
I have a big meeting with my publisher tomorrow and I can't draw my main character anymore.
Mmm ... that is a tough one.
If I can't draw Lance, then I can't make the comic. If I can't make the comic, then I won't get paid.

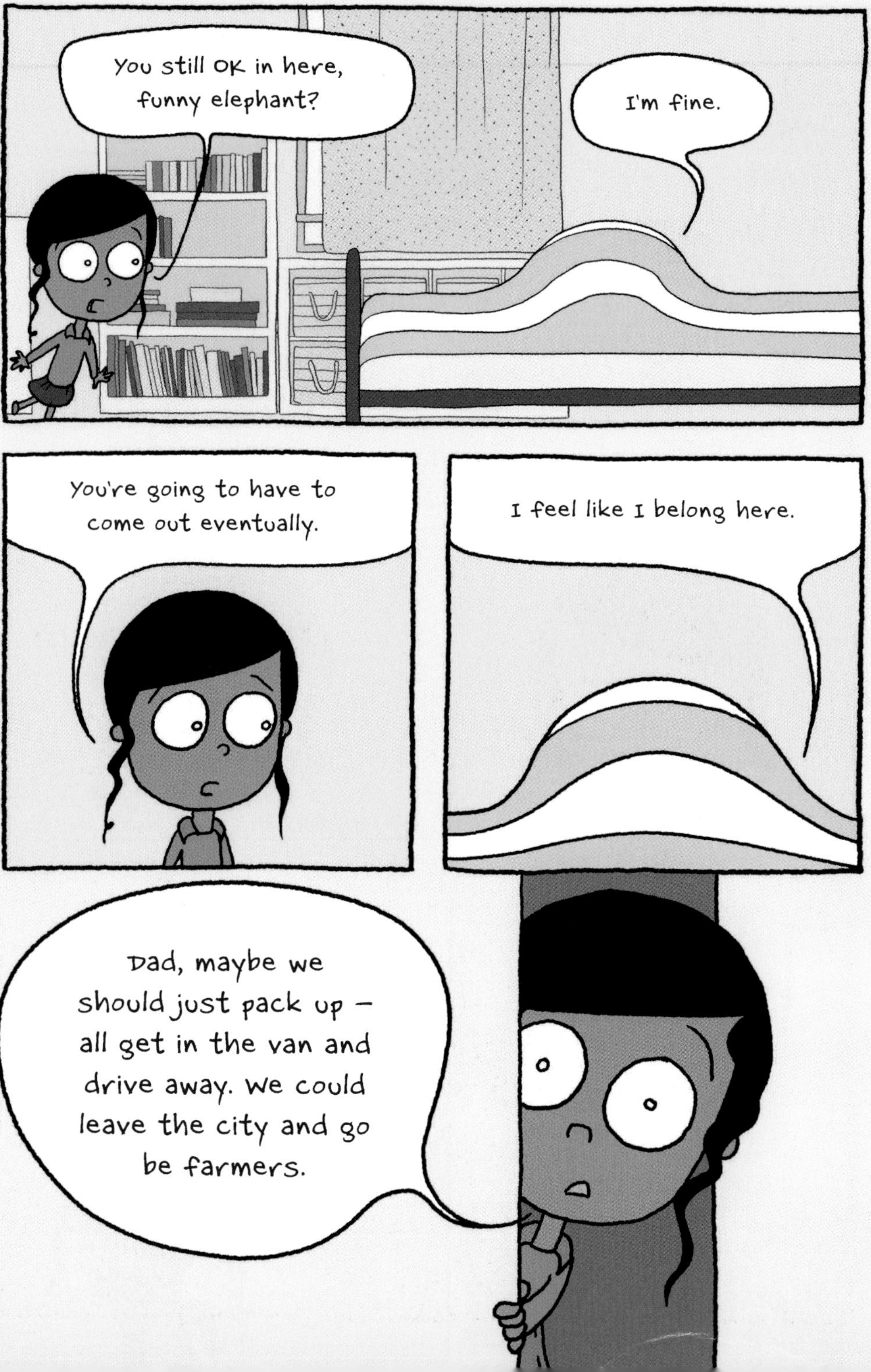
You still OK in here, funny elephant?
I'm fine.
You're going to have to come out eventually.
I feel like I belong here.
Dad, maybe we should just pack up – all get in the van and drive away. We could leave the city and go be farmers.

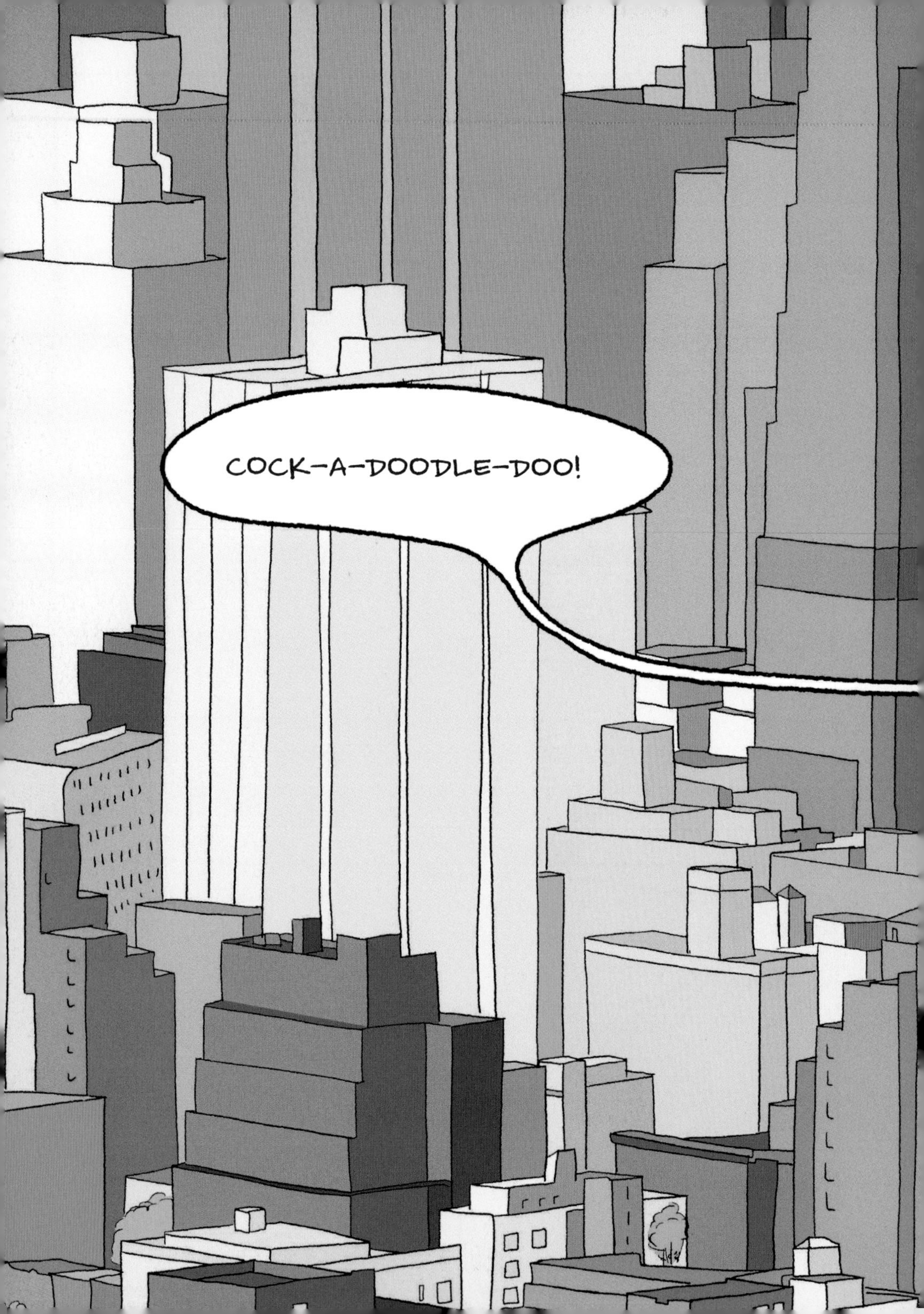
COCK-A-DOODLE-DOO!

CHAPTER NINE
The Odds get a secret base

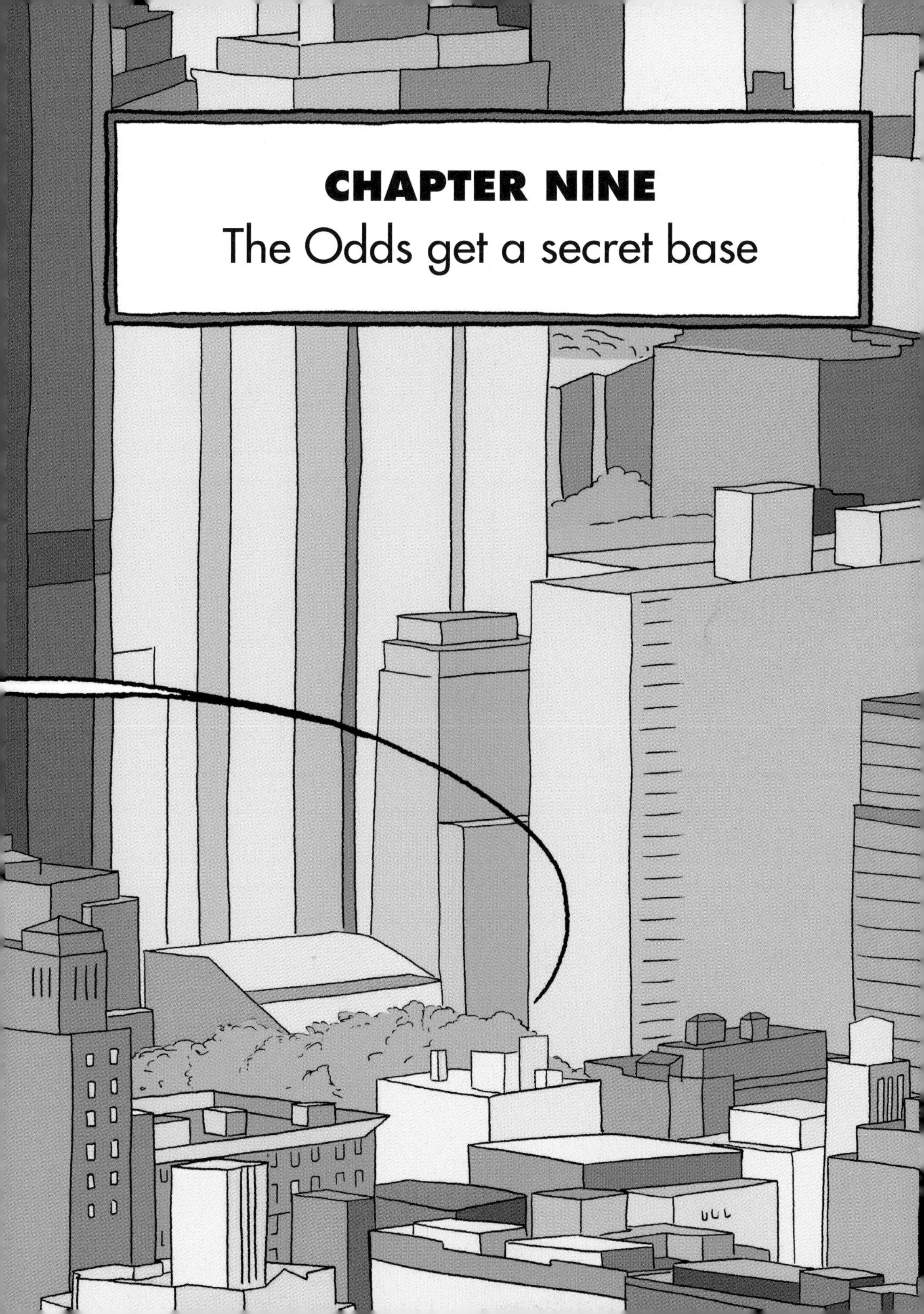

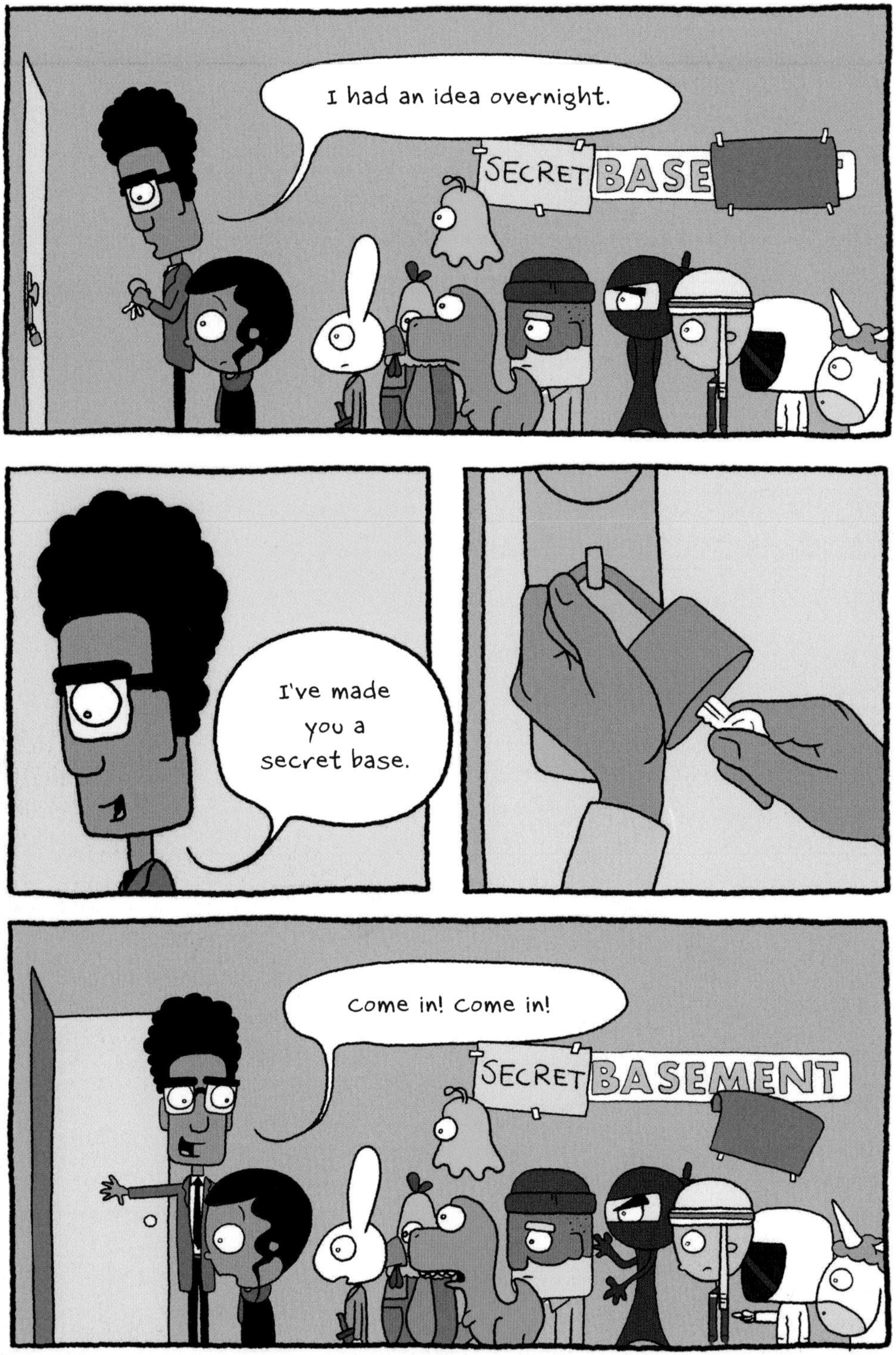
I had an idea overnight.
SECRET BASE
I've made you a secret base.
Come in! Come in!
SECRET BASEMENT

125

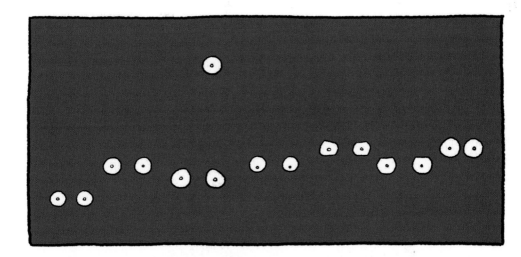

Booster! You're sucking my tail with the vacuum cleaner, you crazy rooster!

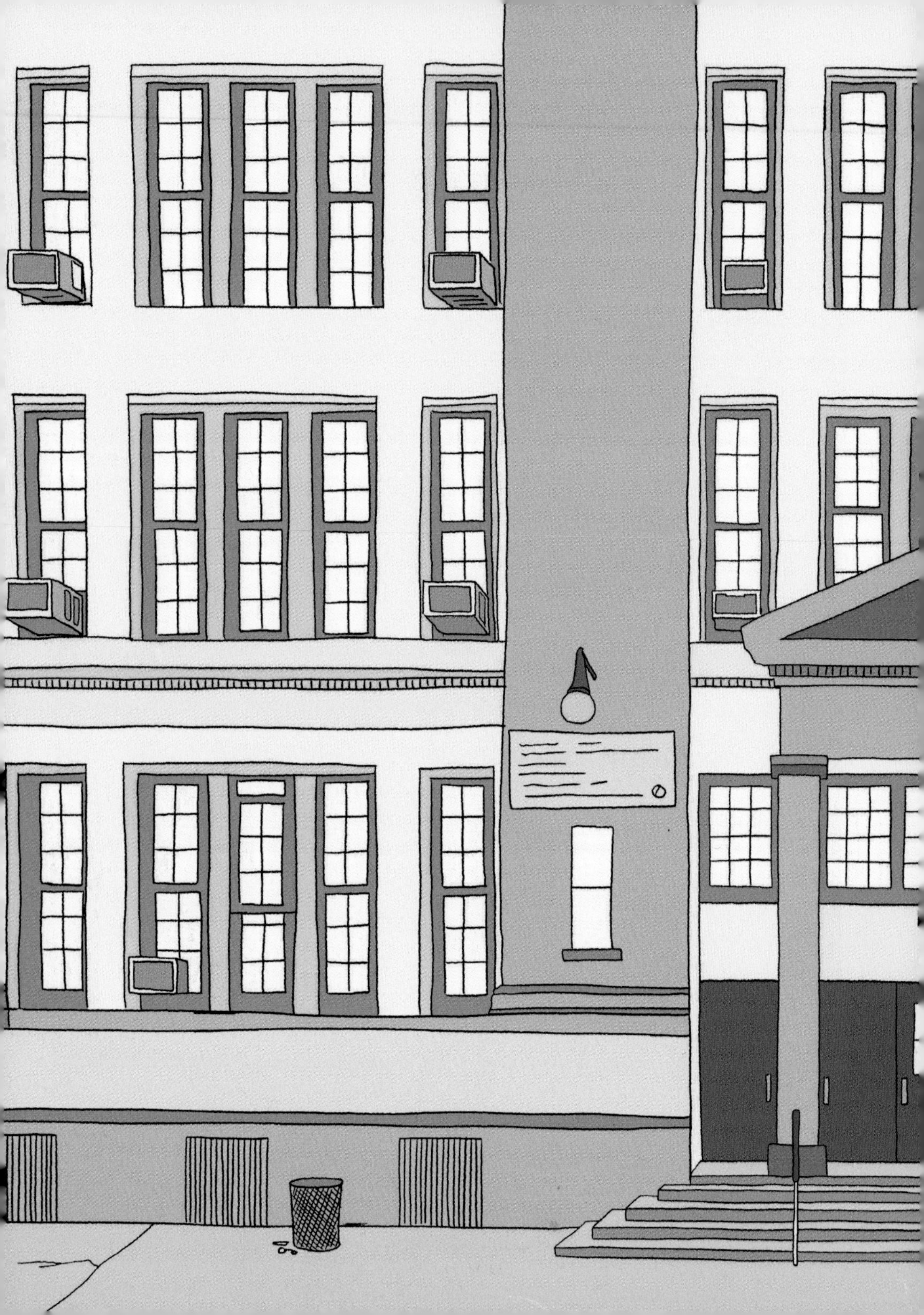

CHAPTER TEN
An odd imagination

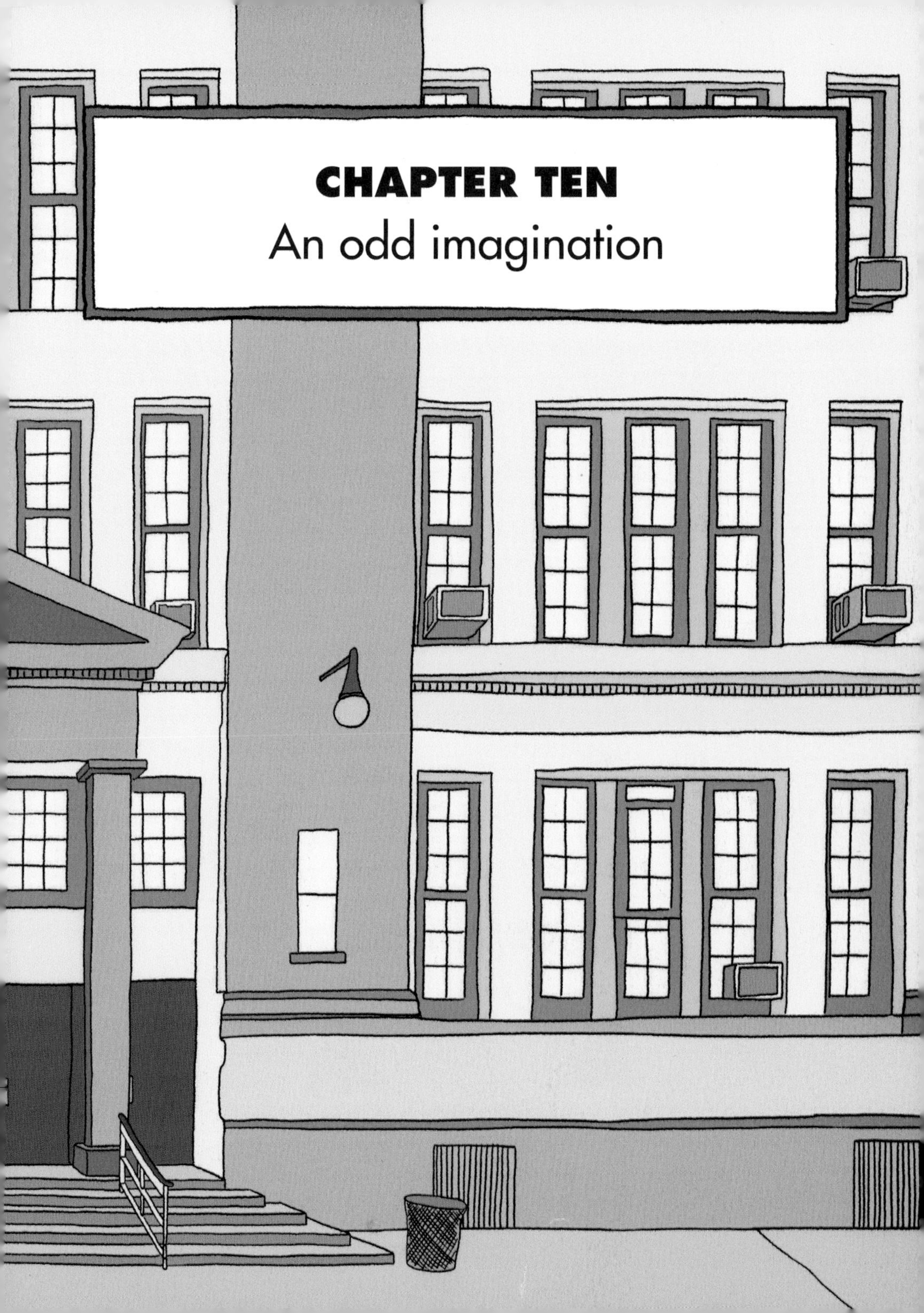

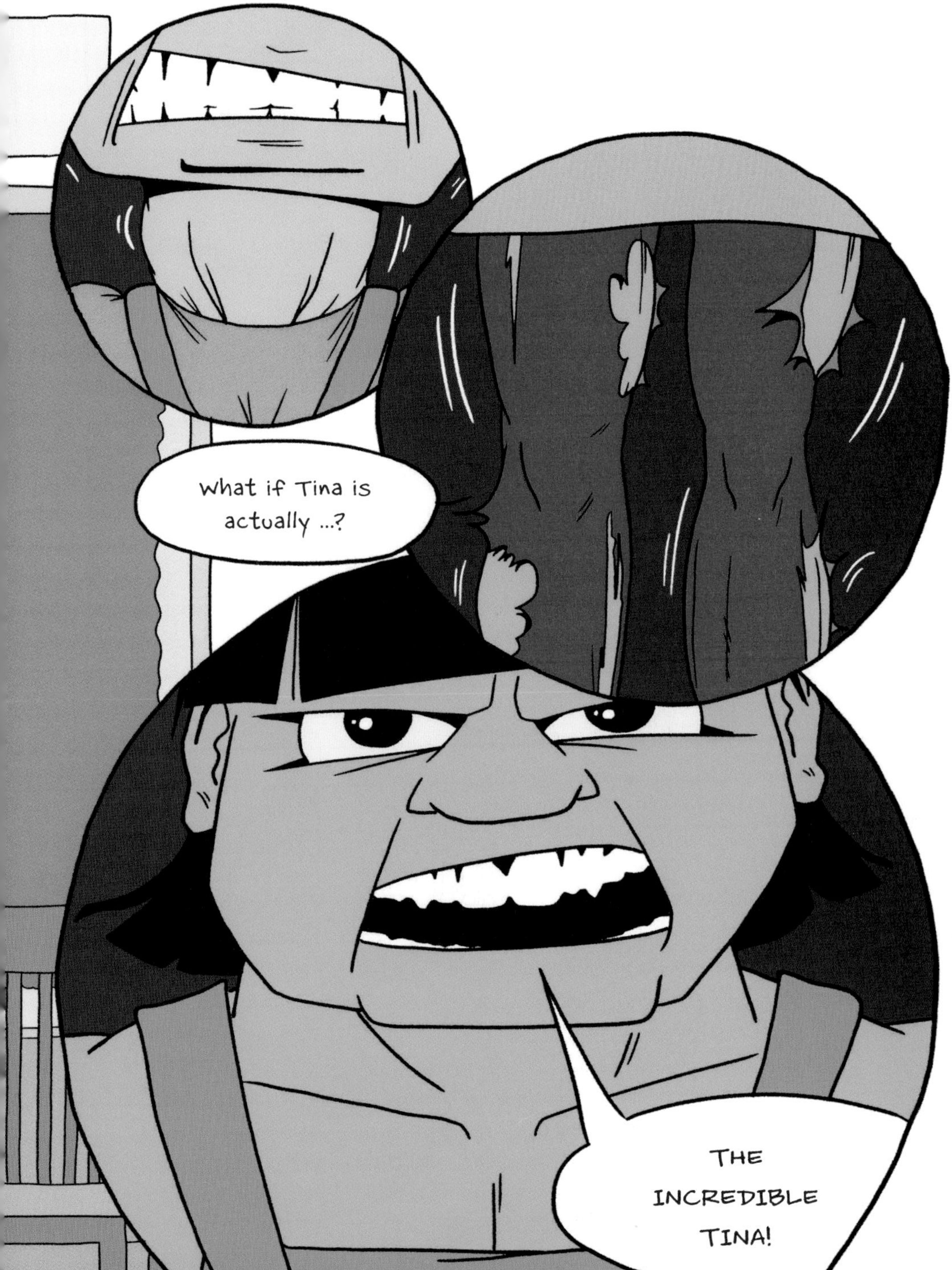
What if Tina is actually ...?
THE INCREDIBLE TINA!

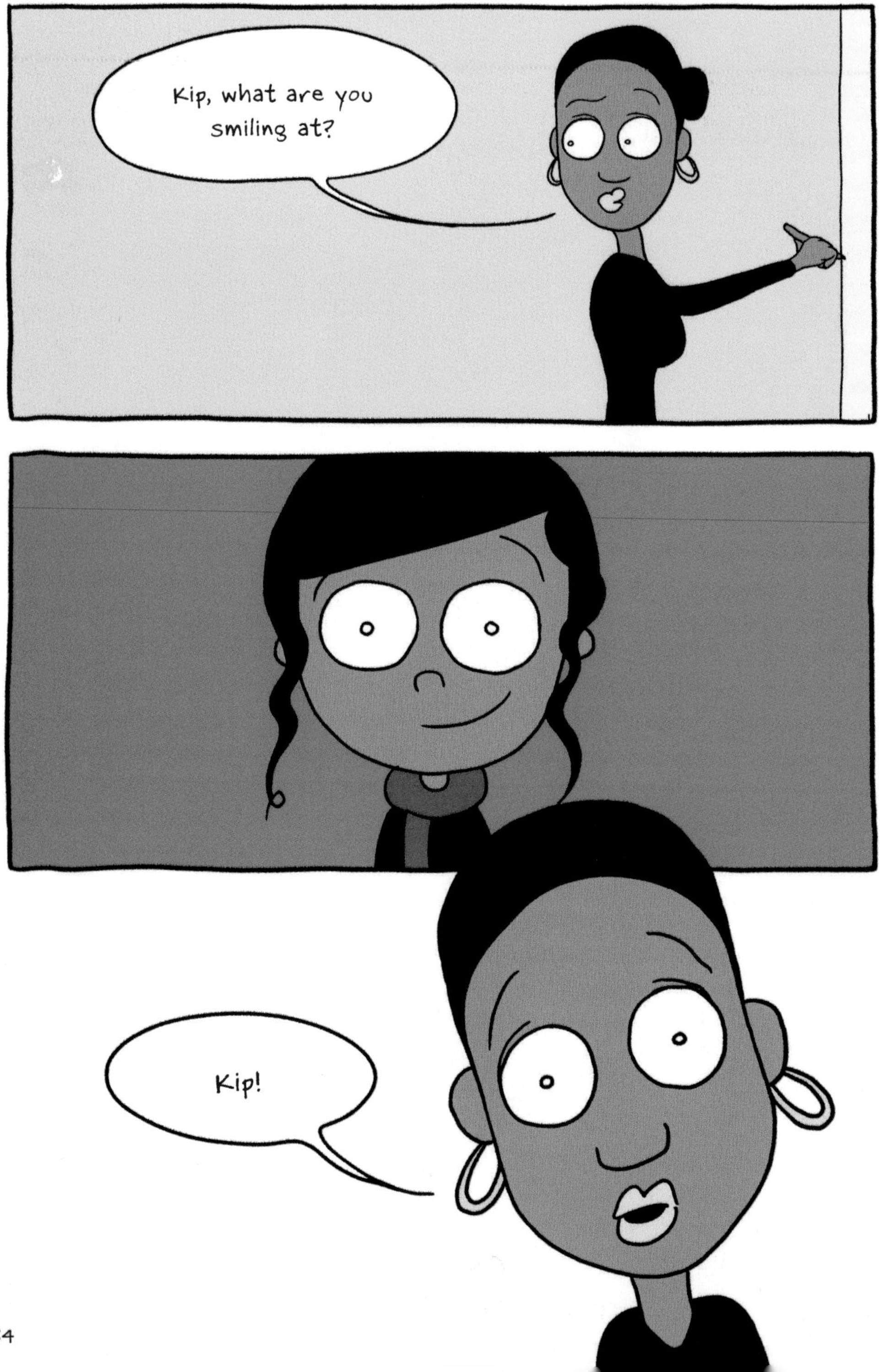
Kip, what are you smiling at?
Kip!

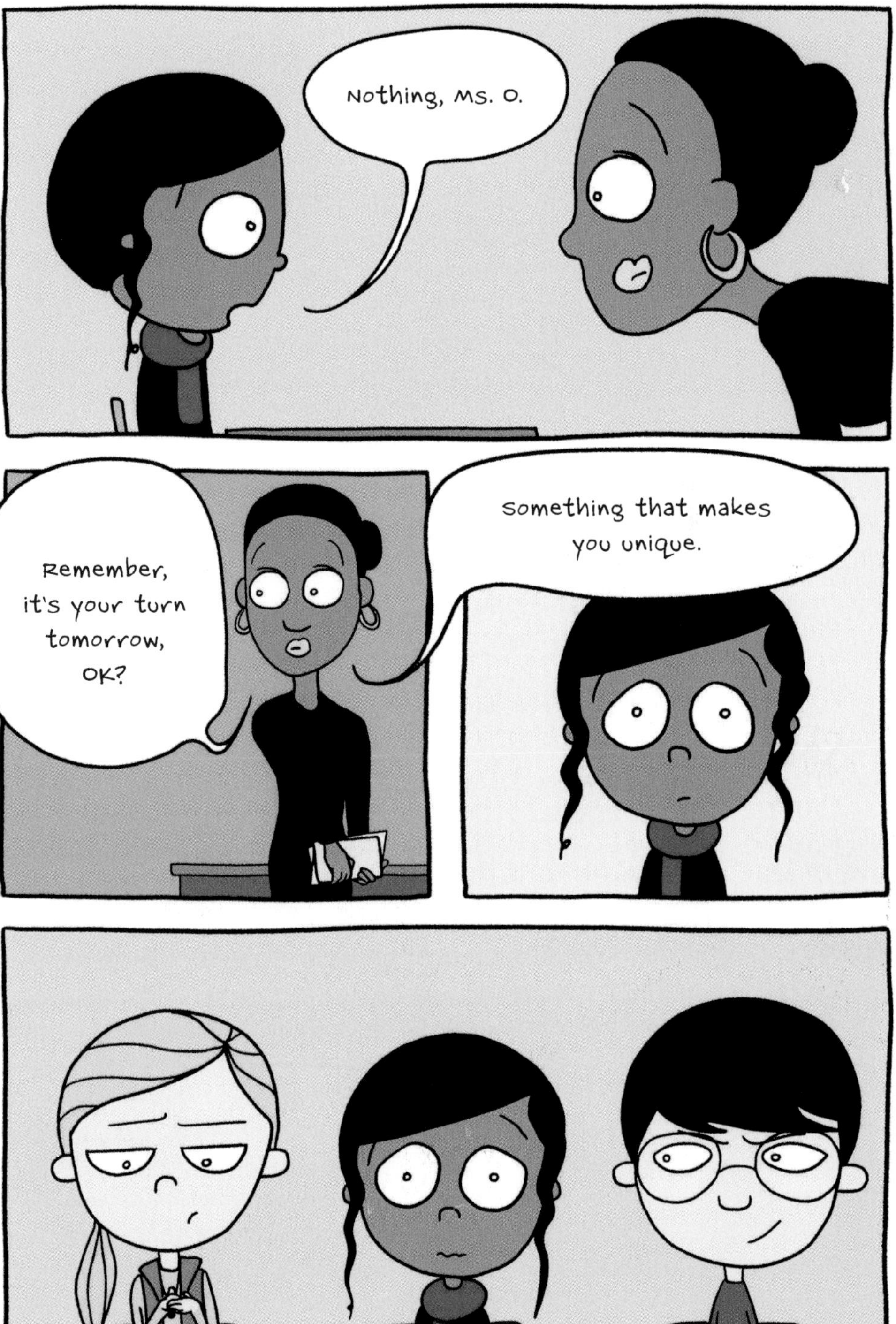
Nothing, Ms. O.
Remember, it's your turn tomorrow, OK?
Something that makes you unique.

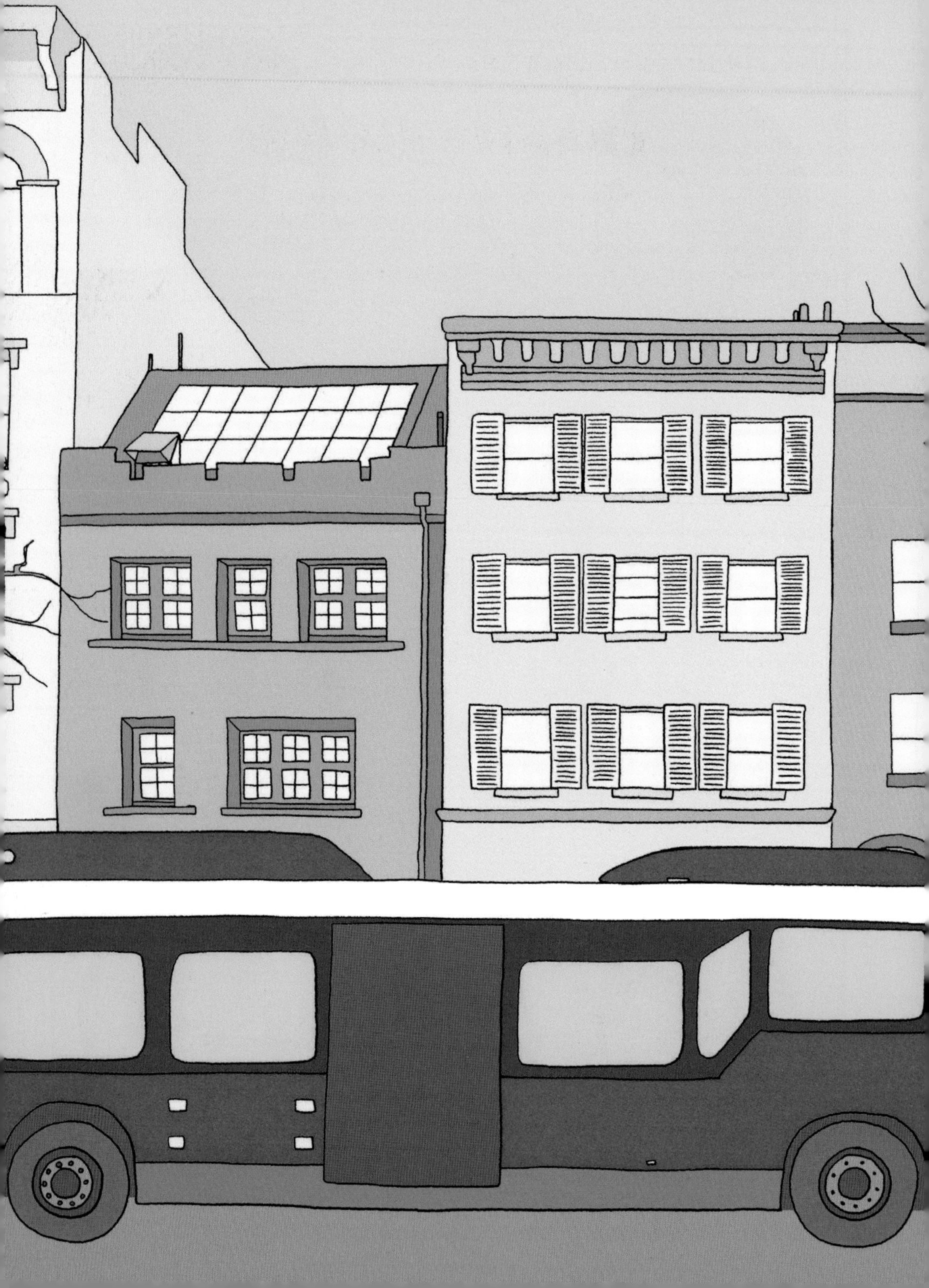

CHAPTER ELEVEN
The Odds escape

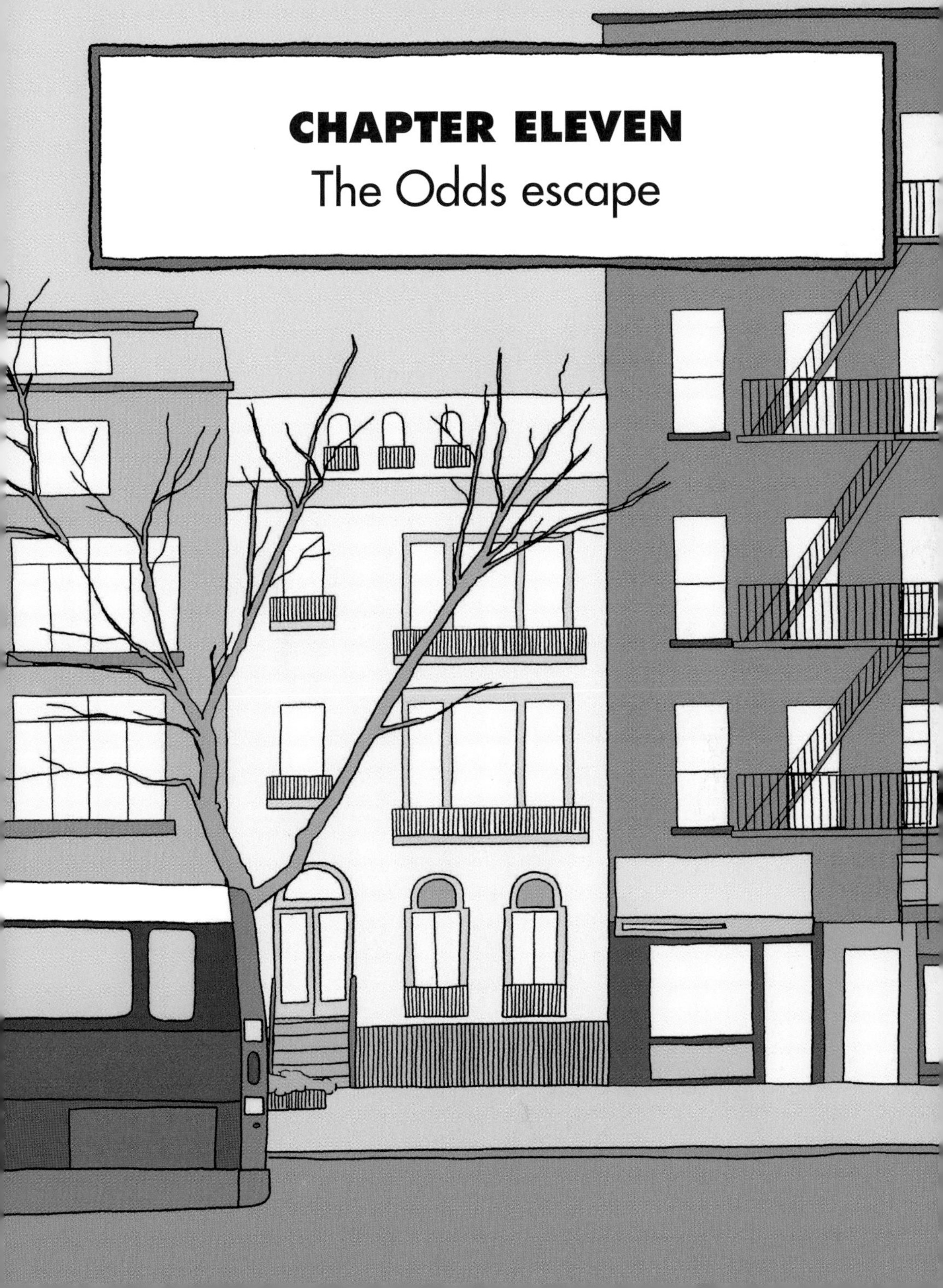

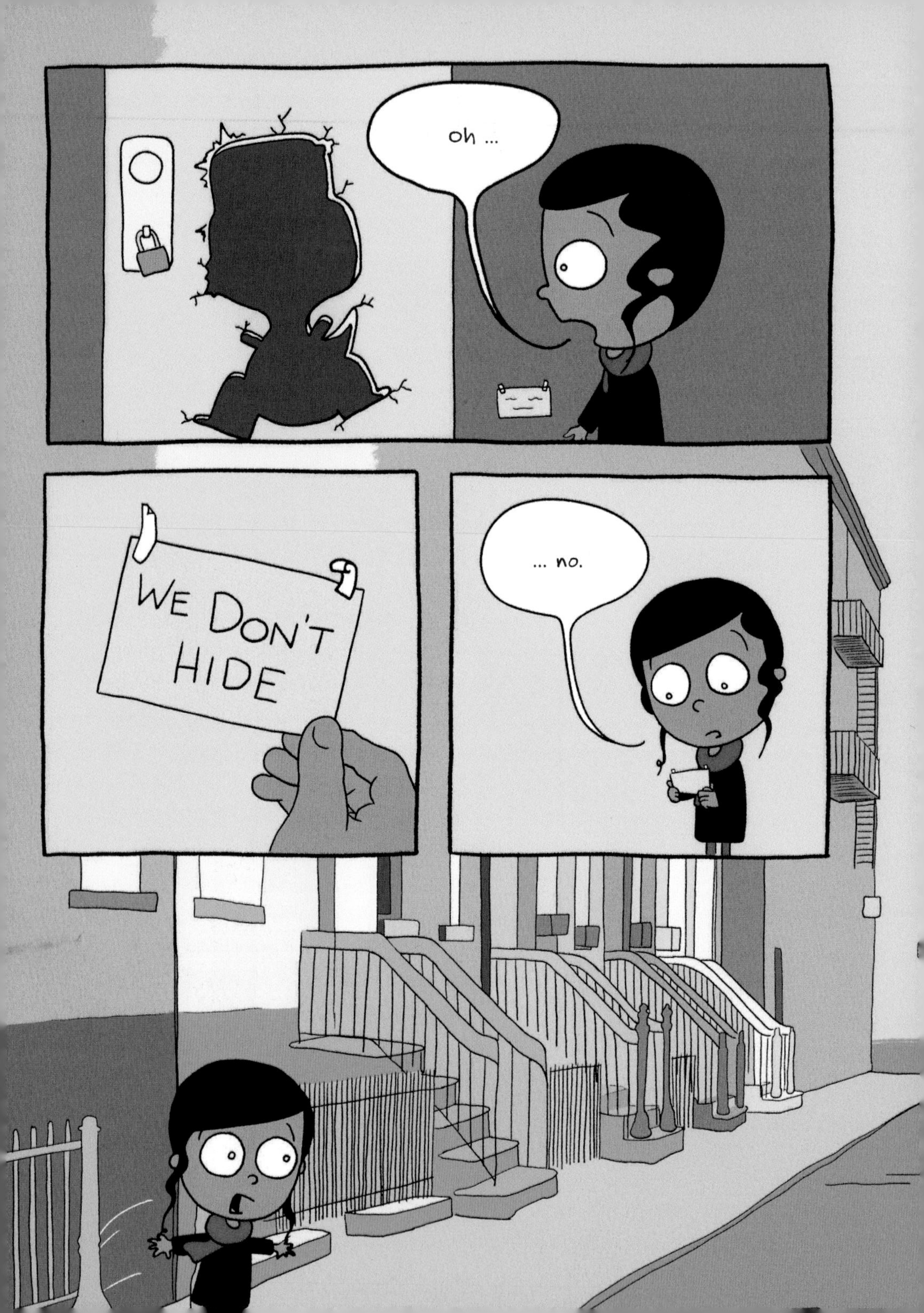
oh ...
WE DON'T HIDE
... no.

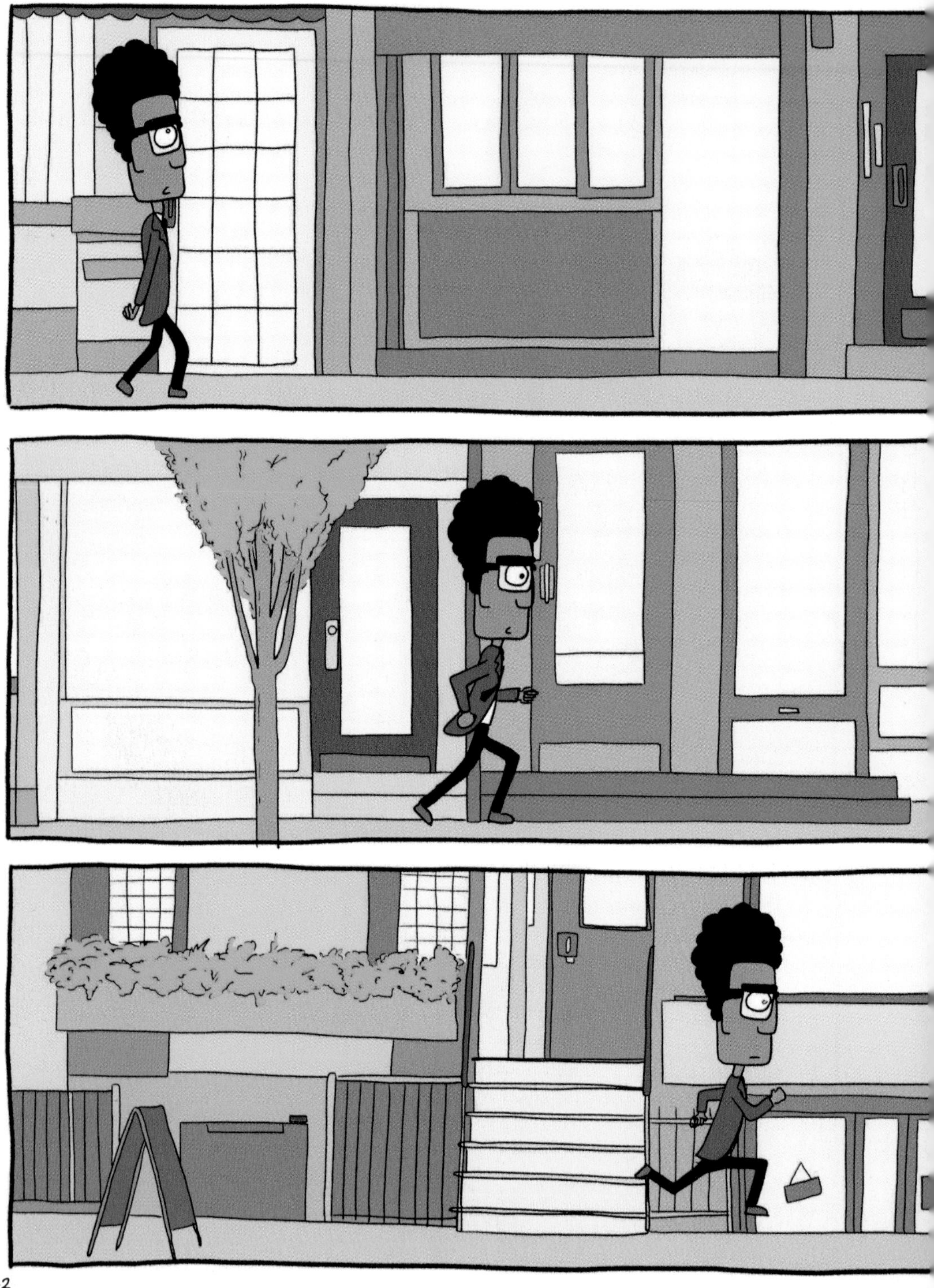

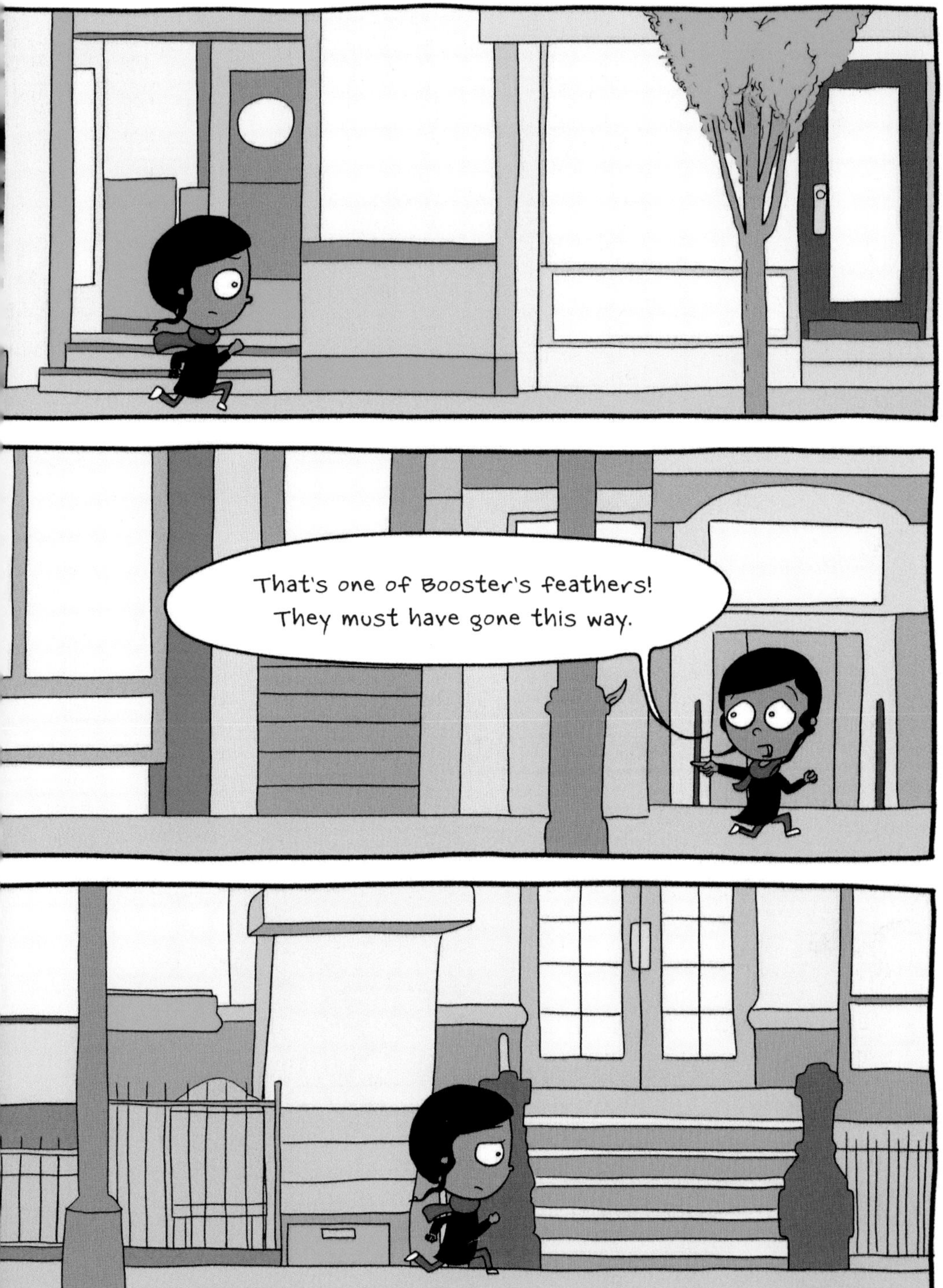
That's one of Booster's feathers! They must have gone this way.

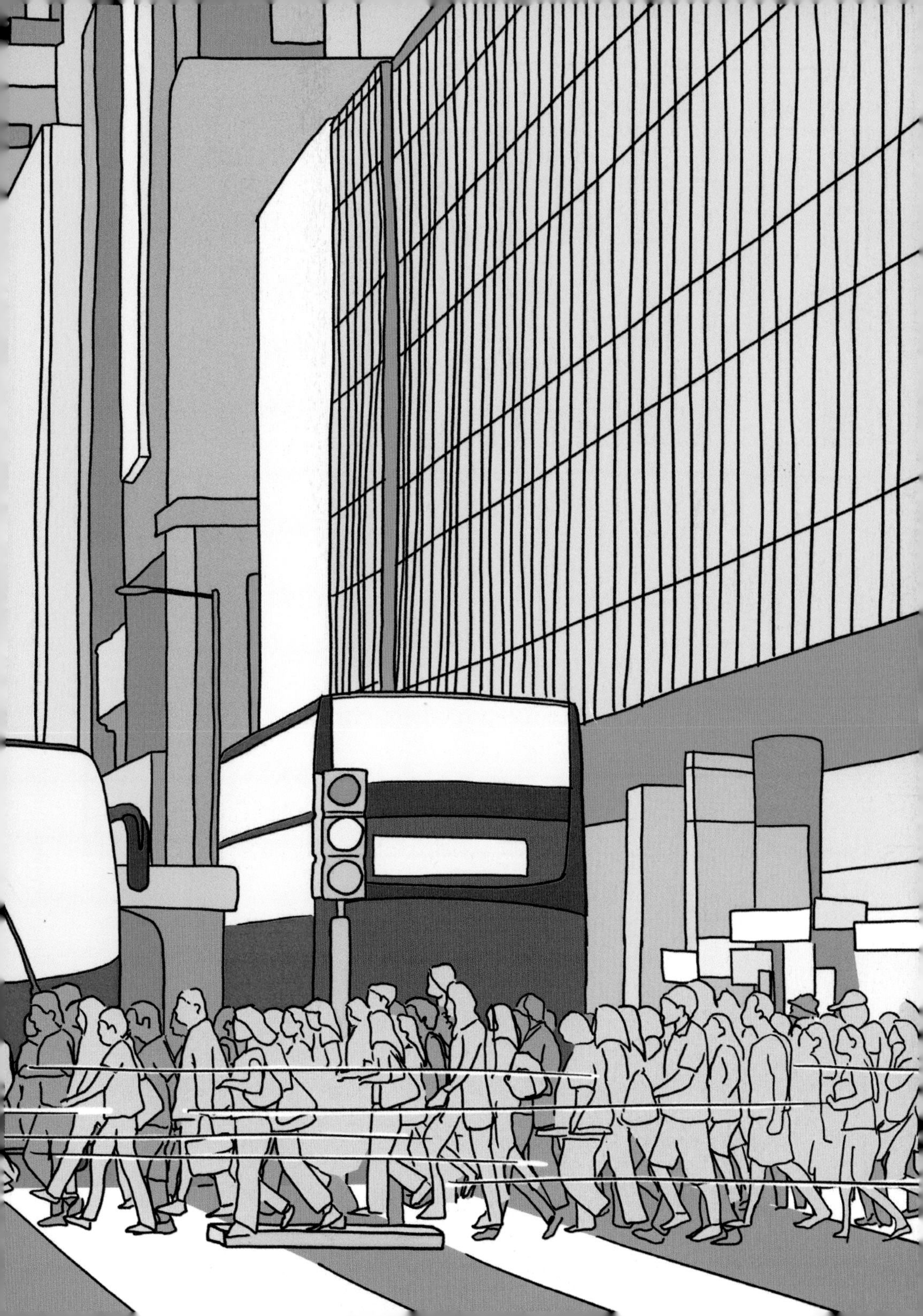

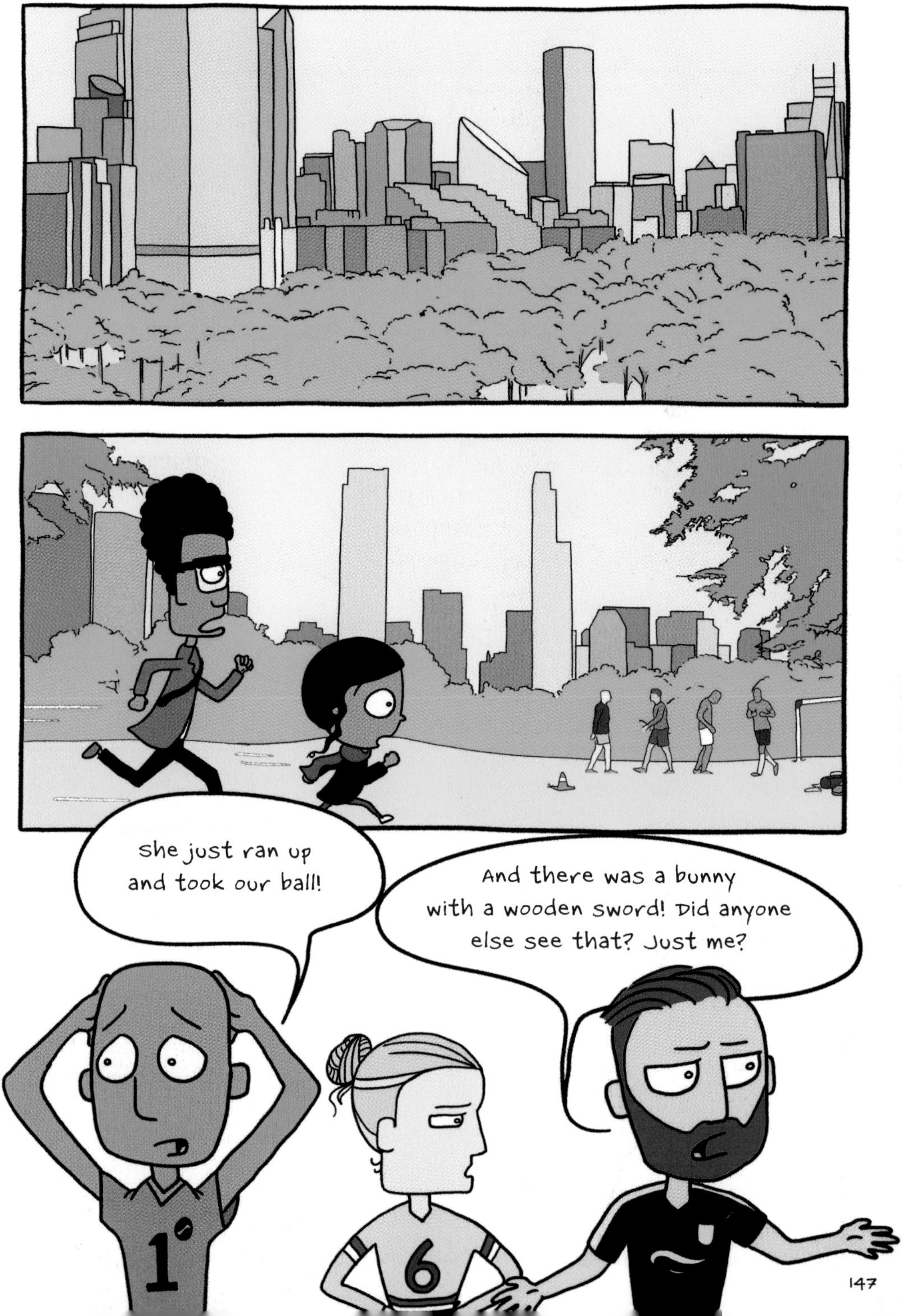
she just ran up and took our ball!
And there was a bunny with a wooden sword! Did anyone else see that? Just me?

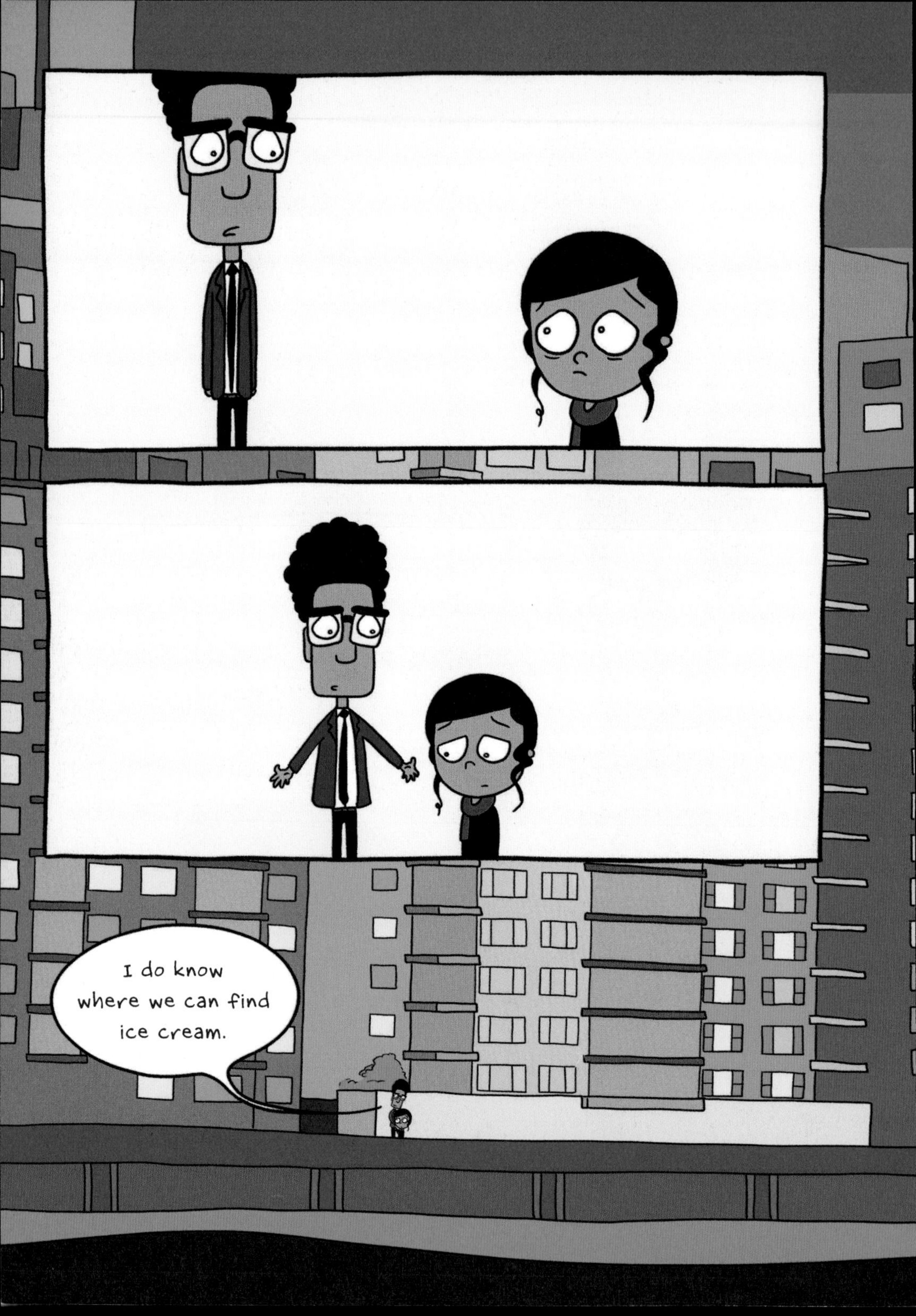
I do know where we can find ice cream.

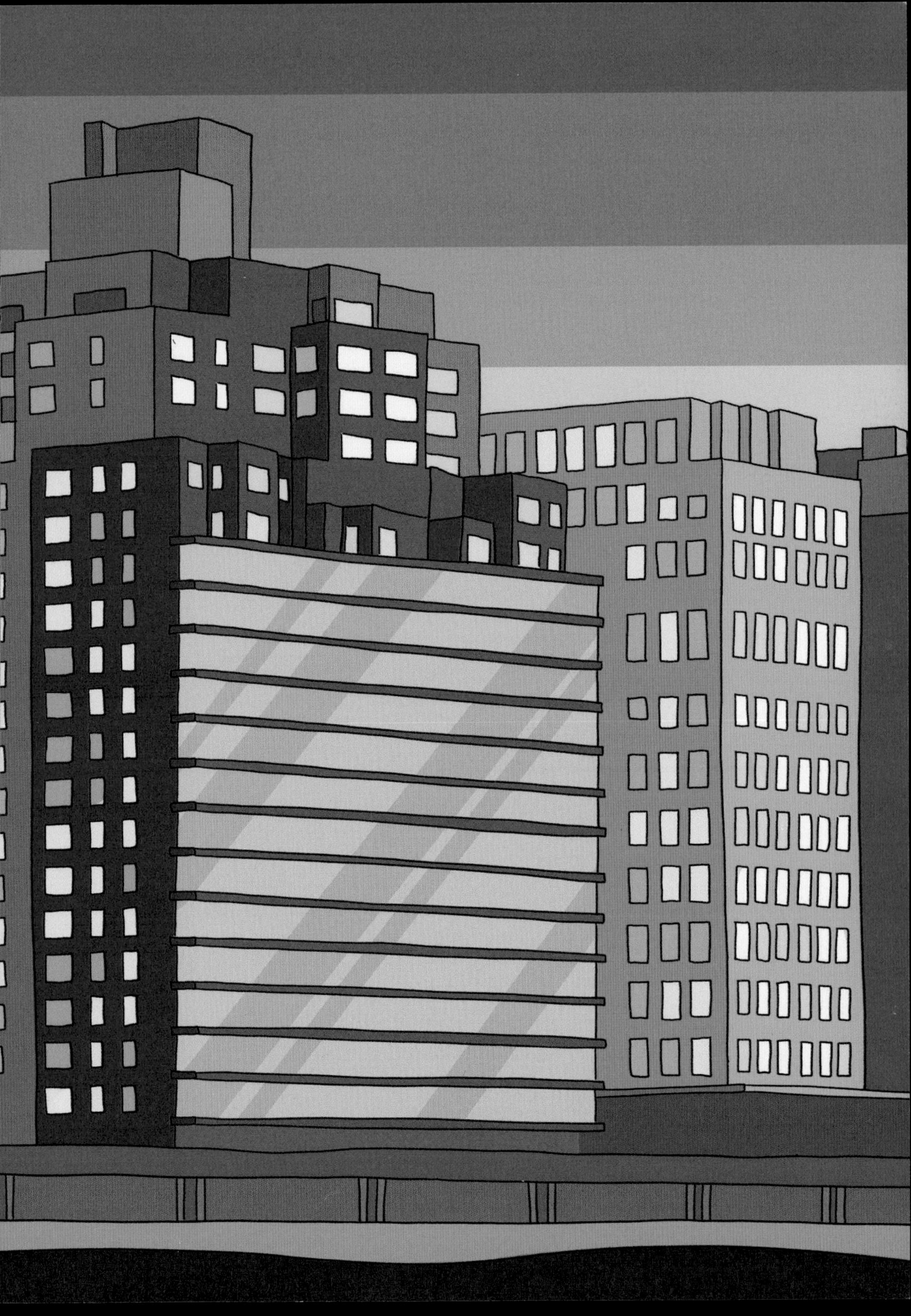

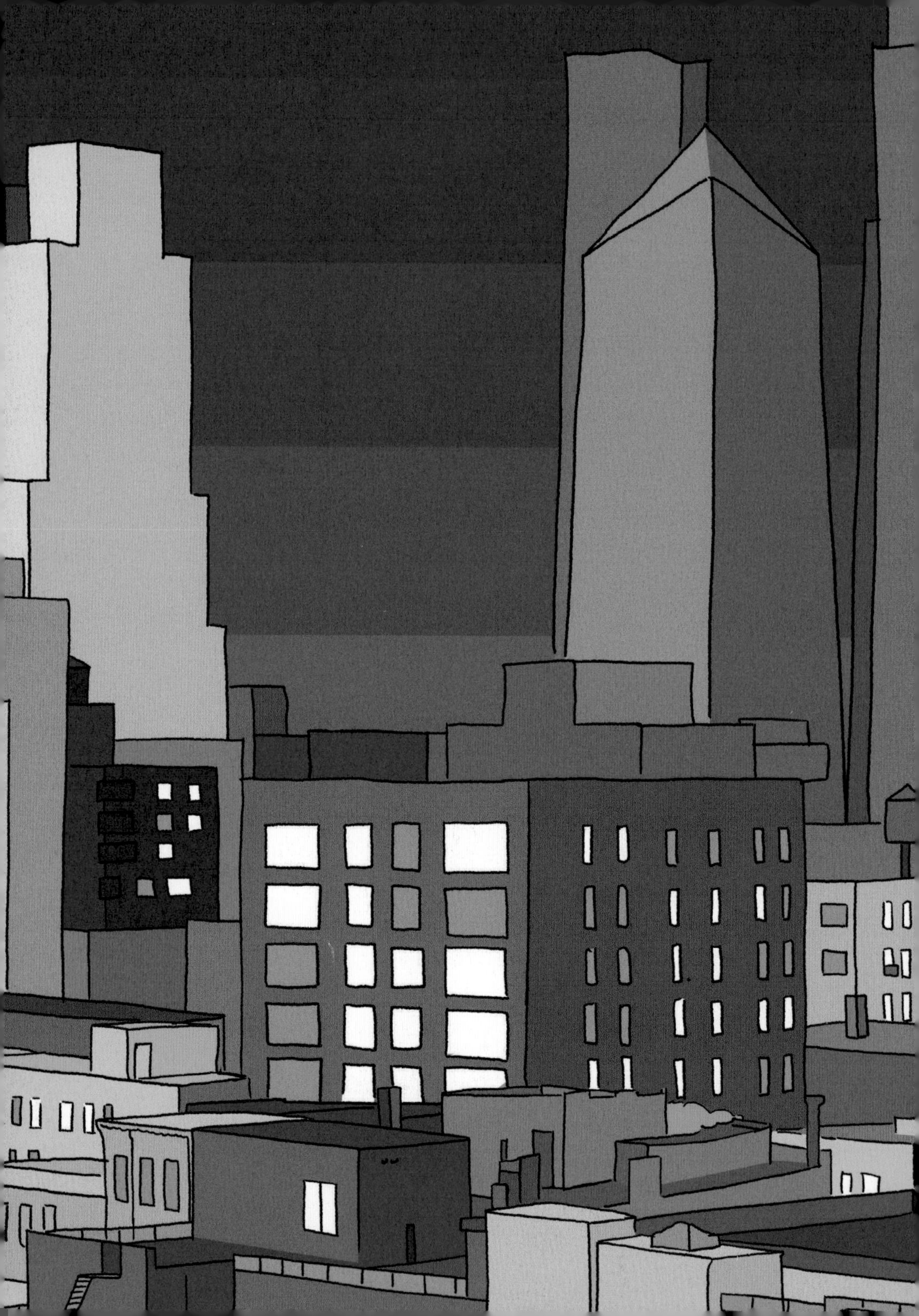

CHAPTER TWELVE
The lost Odd

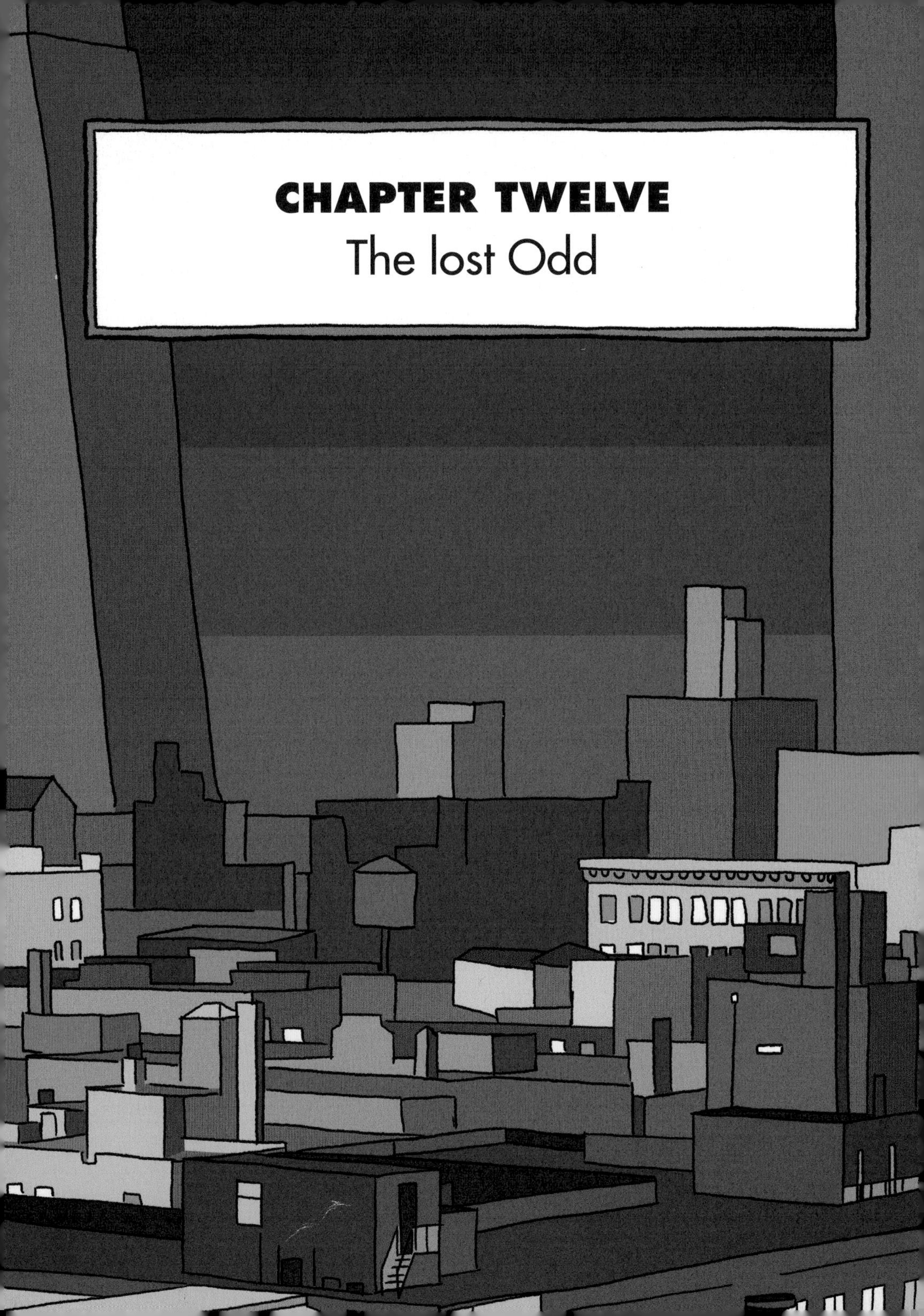

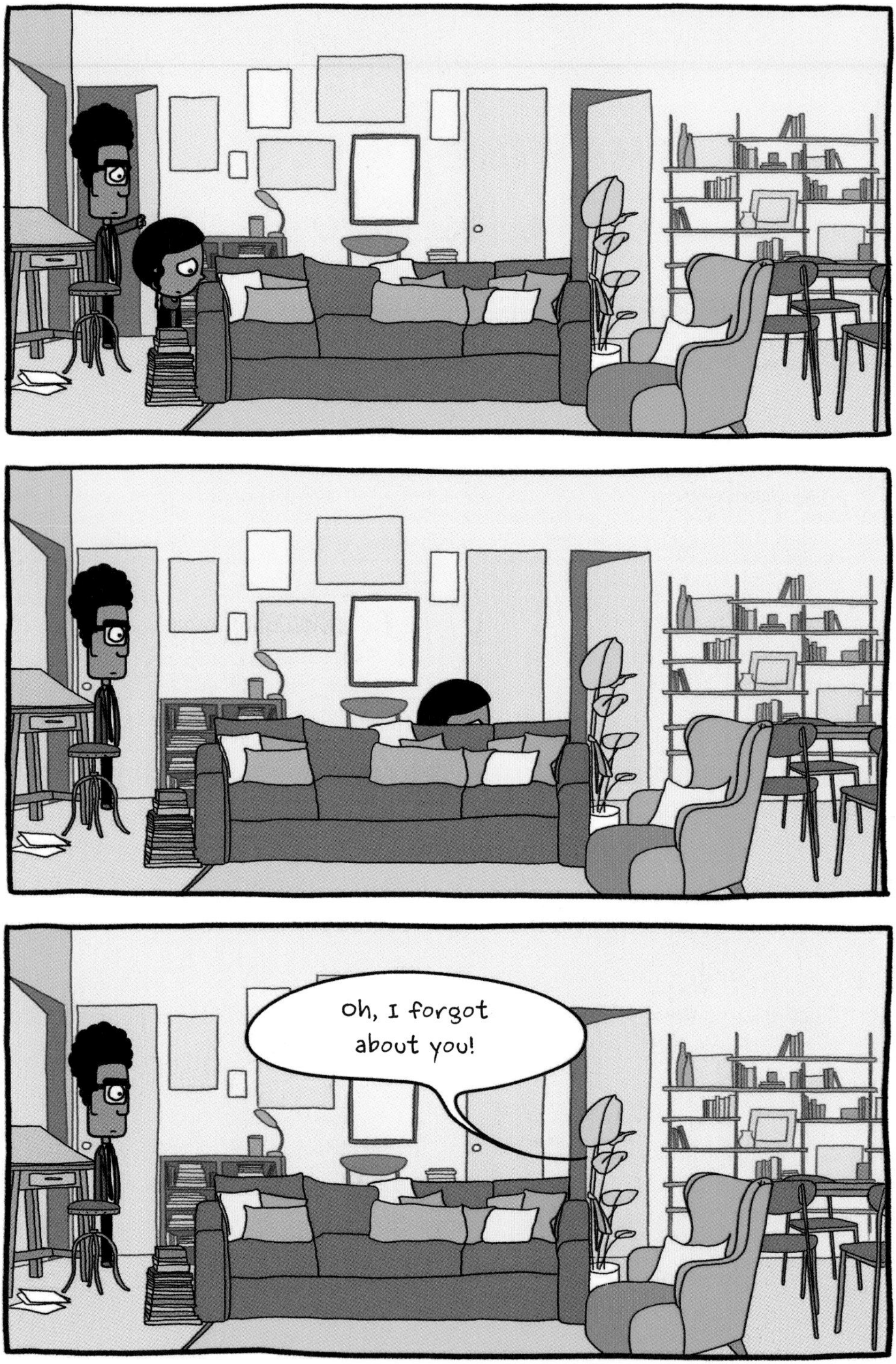
Oh, I forgot about you!

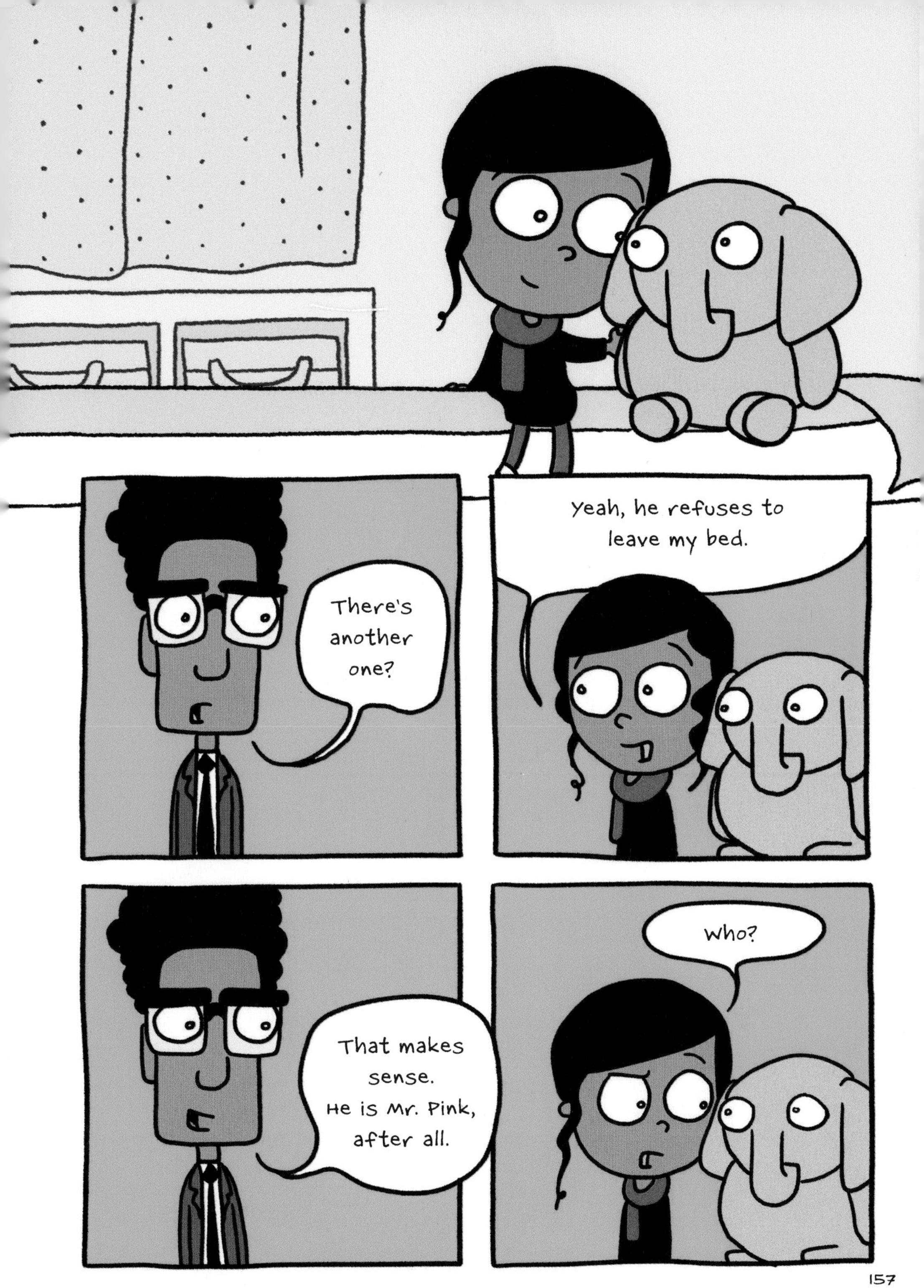
There's another one?
Yeah, he refuses to leave my bed.
That makes sense. He is Mr. Pink, after all.
Who?

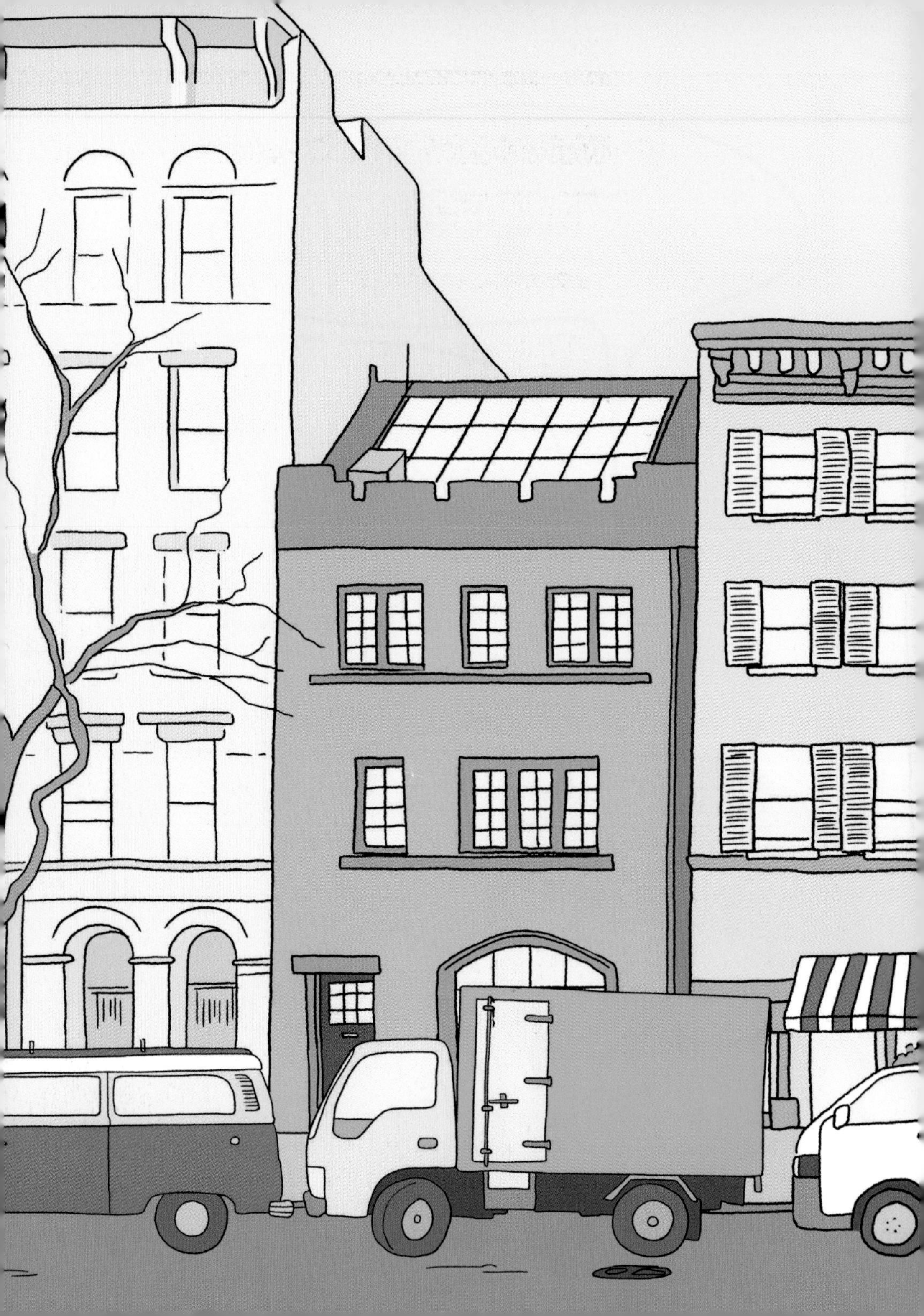

CHAPTER THIRTEEN
The Odds return

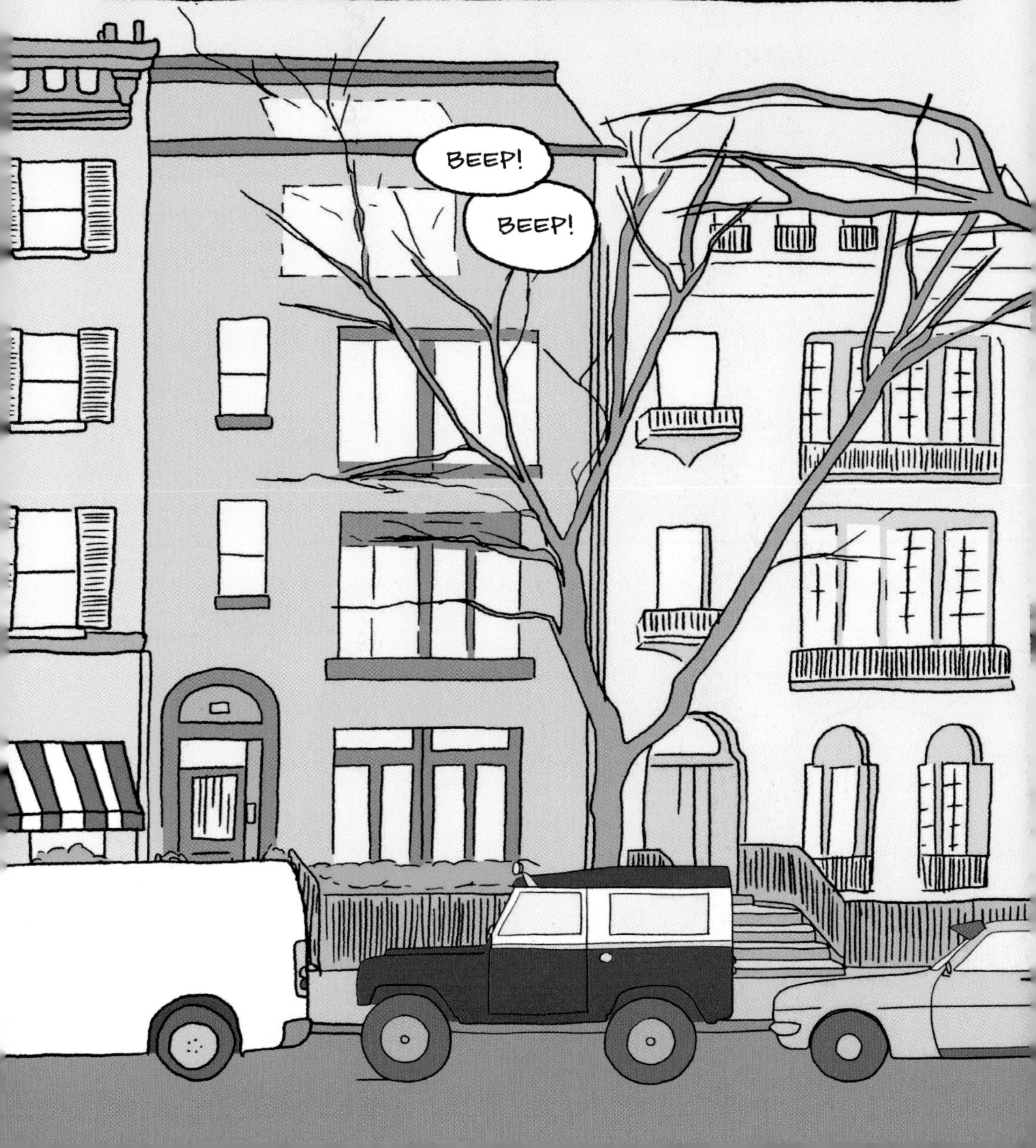

BEEP!
BEEP!

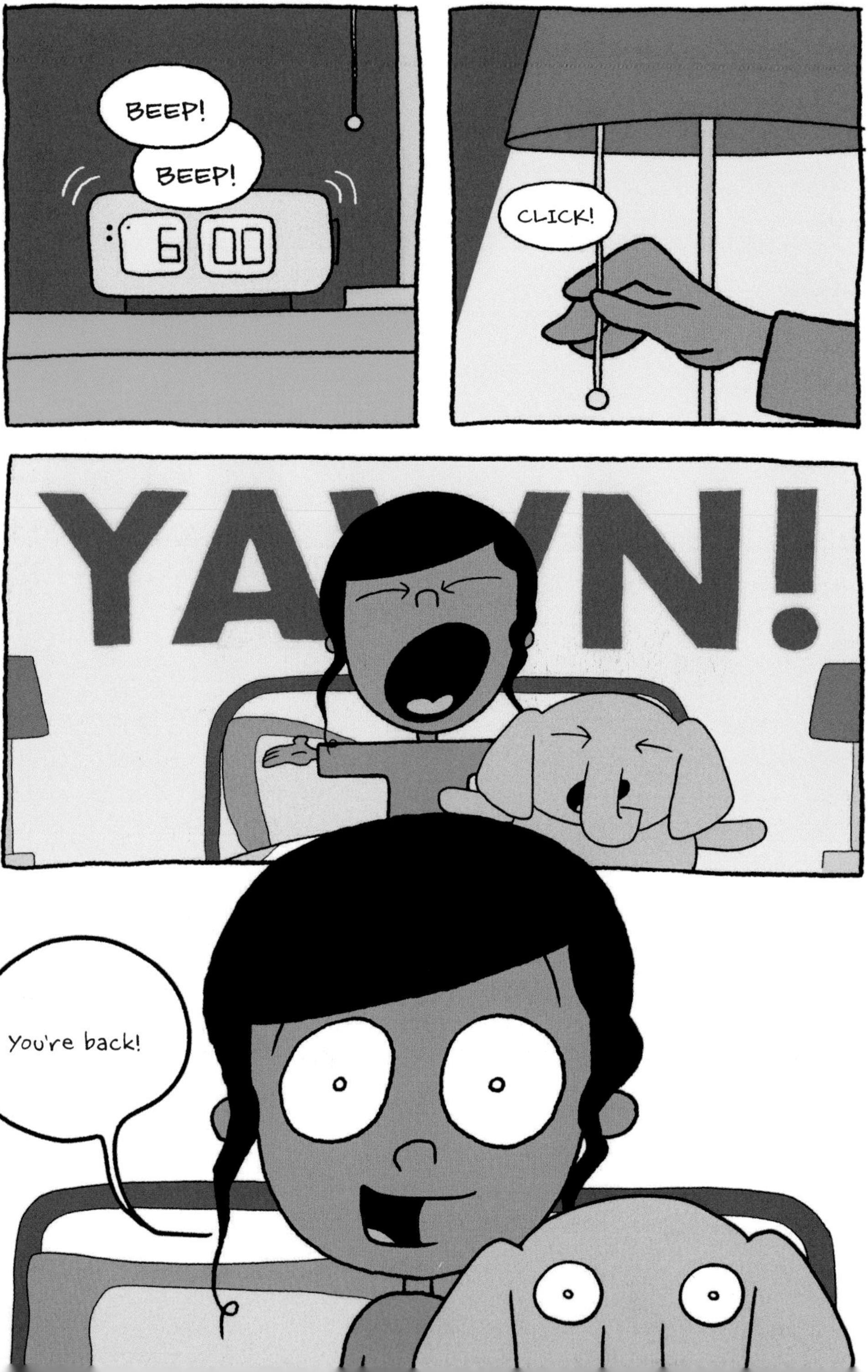
BEEP!
BEEP!
6:00
CLICK!
YAWN!
You're back!

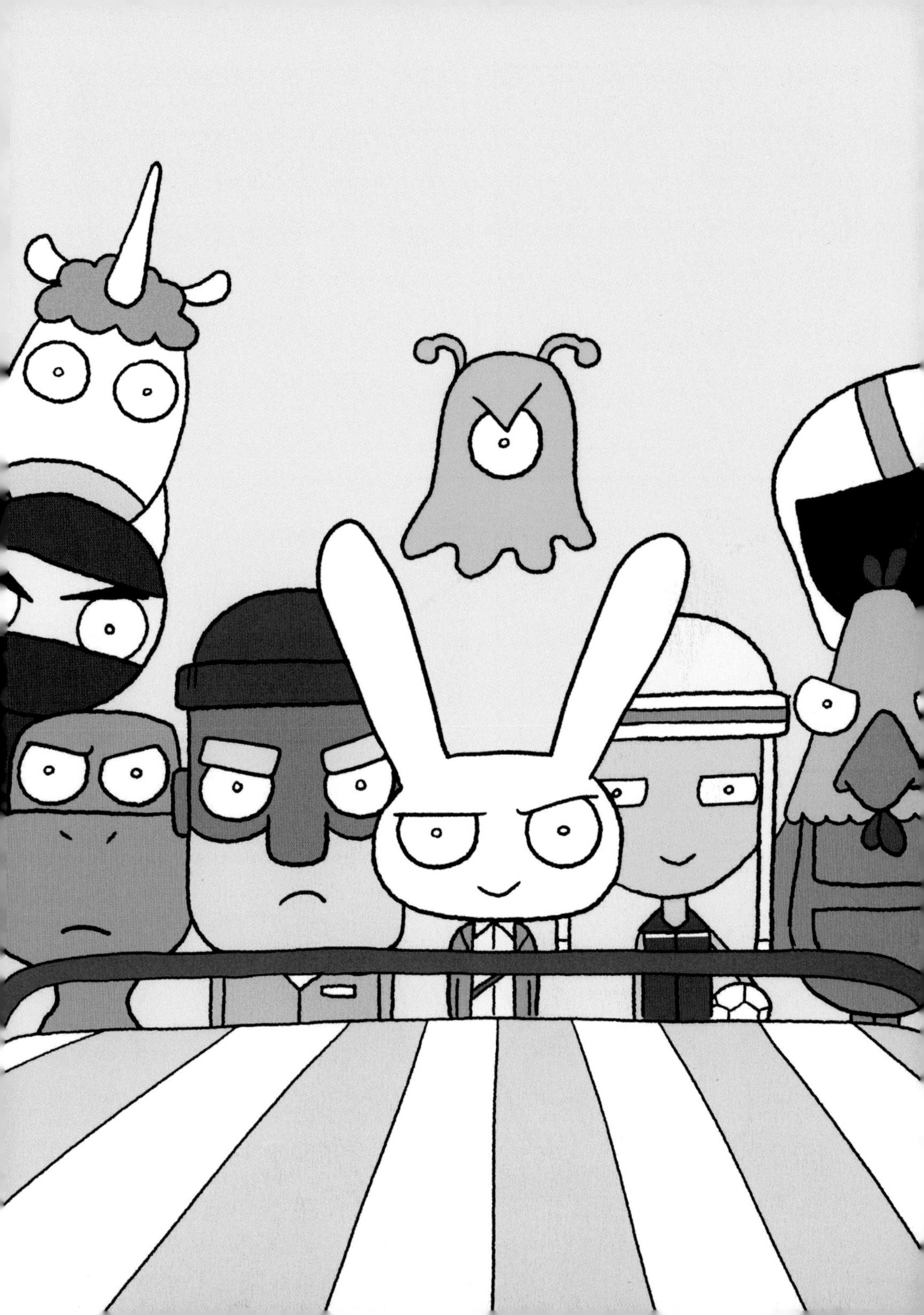

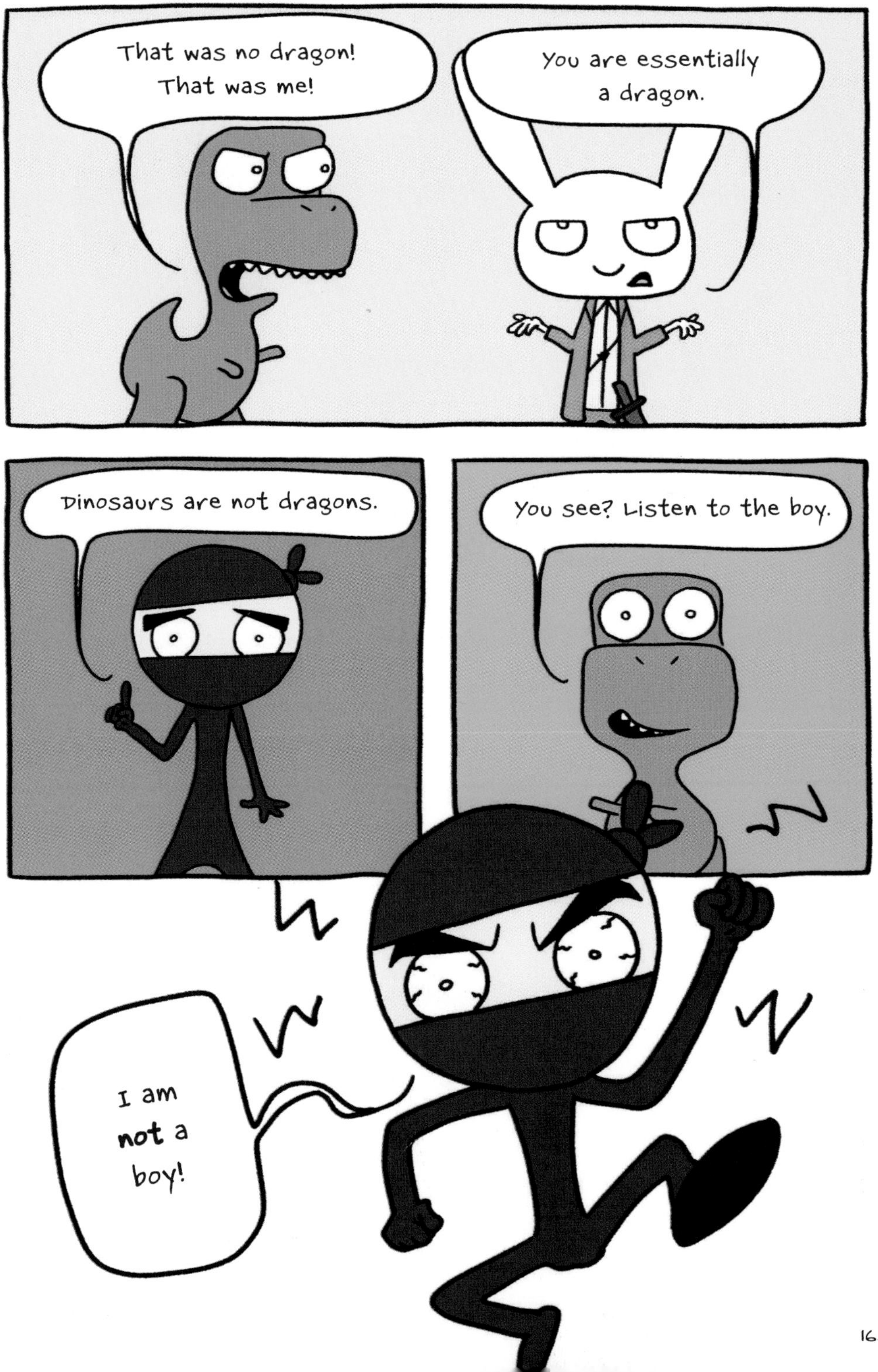
That was no dragon! That was me!
You are essentially a dragon.
Dinosaurs are not dragons.
You see? Listen to the boy.
I am **not** a boy!

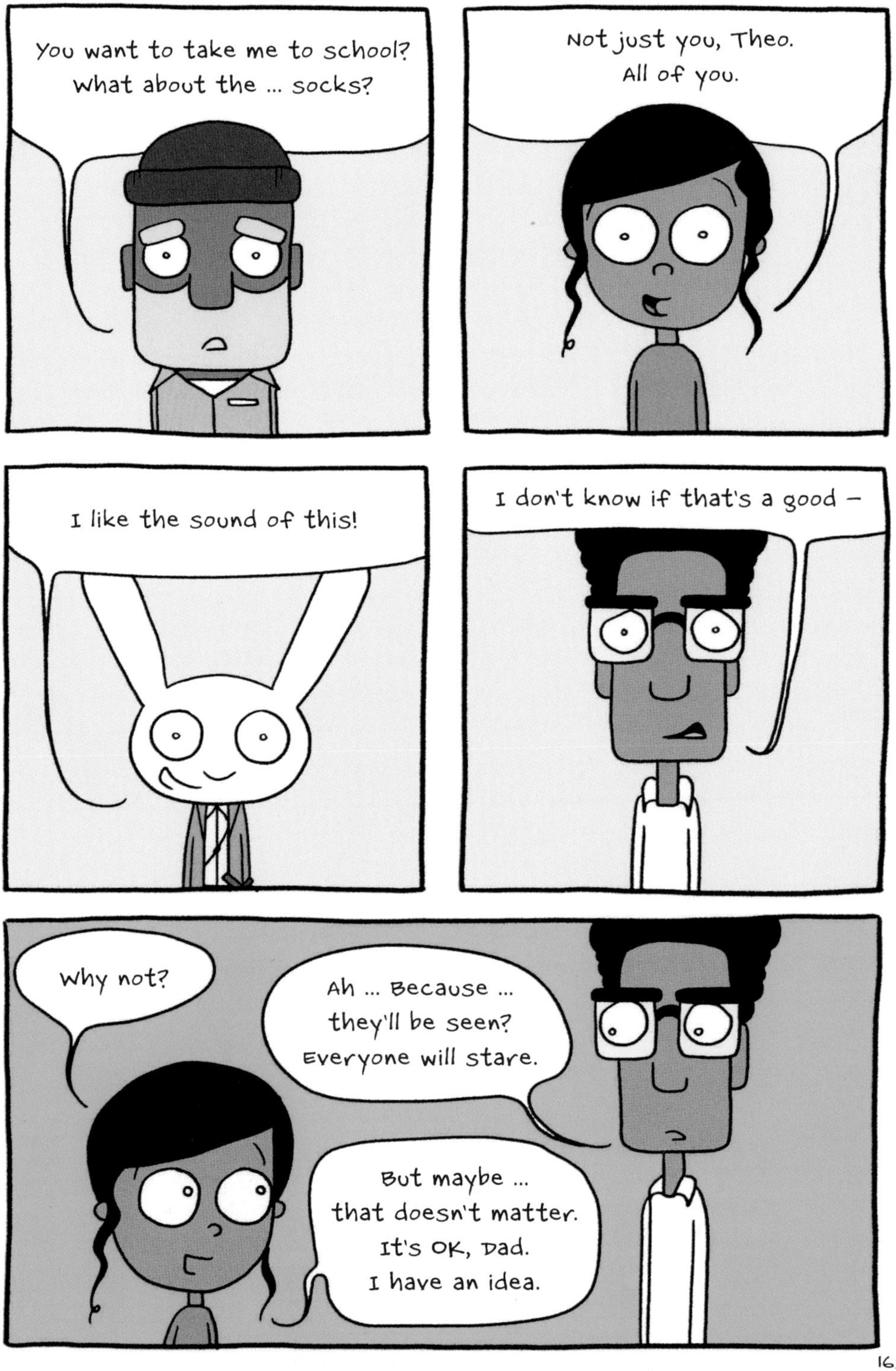
You want to take me to school? What about the ... socks?
Not just you, Theo. All of you.
I like the sound of this!
I don't know if that's a good –
Why not?
Ah ... Because ... they'll be seen? Everyone will stare.
But maybe ... that doesn't matter. It's OK, Dad. I have an idea.

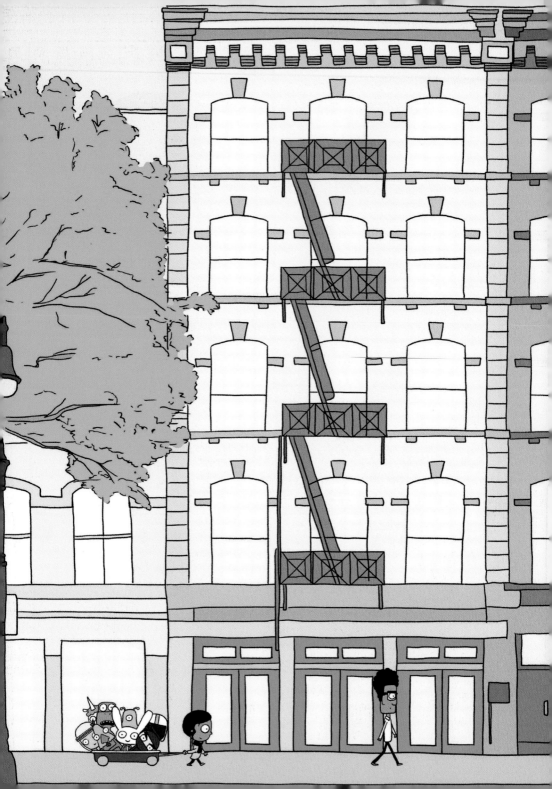

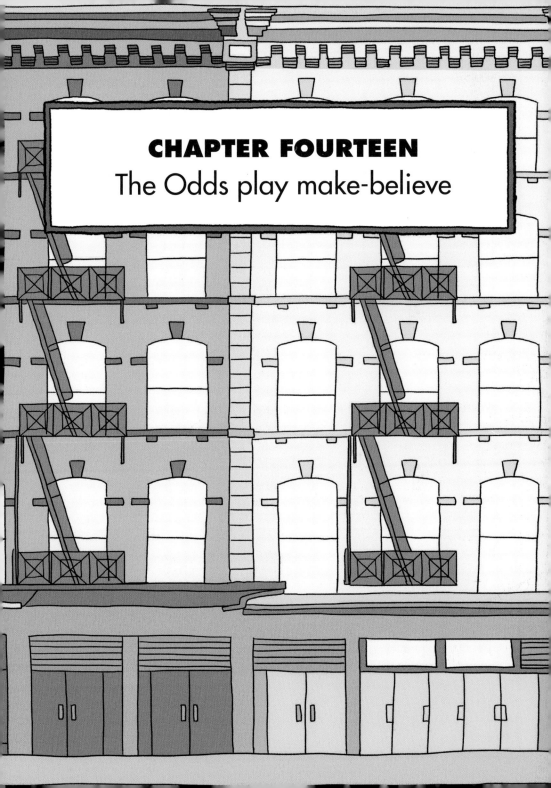

CHAPTER FOURTEEN
The Odds play make-believe

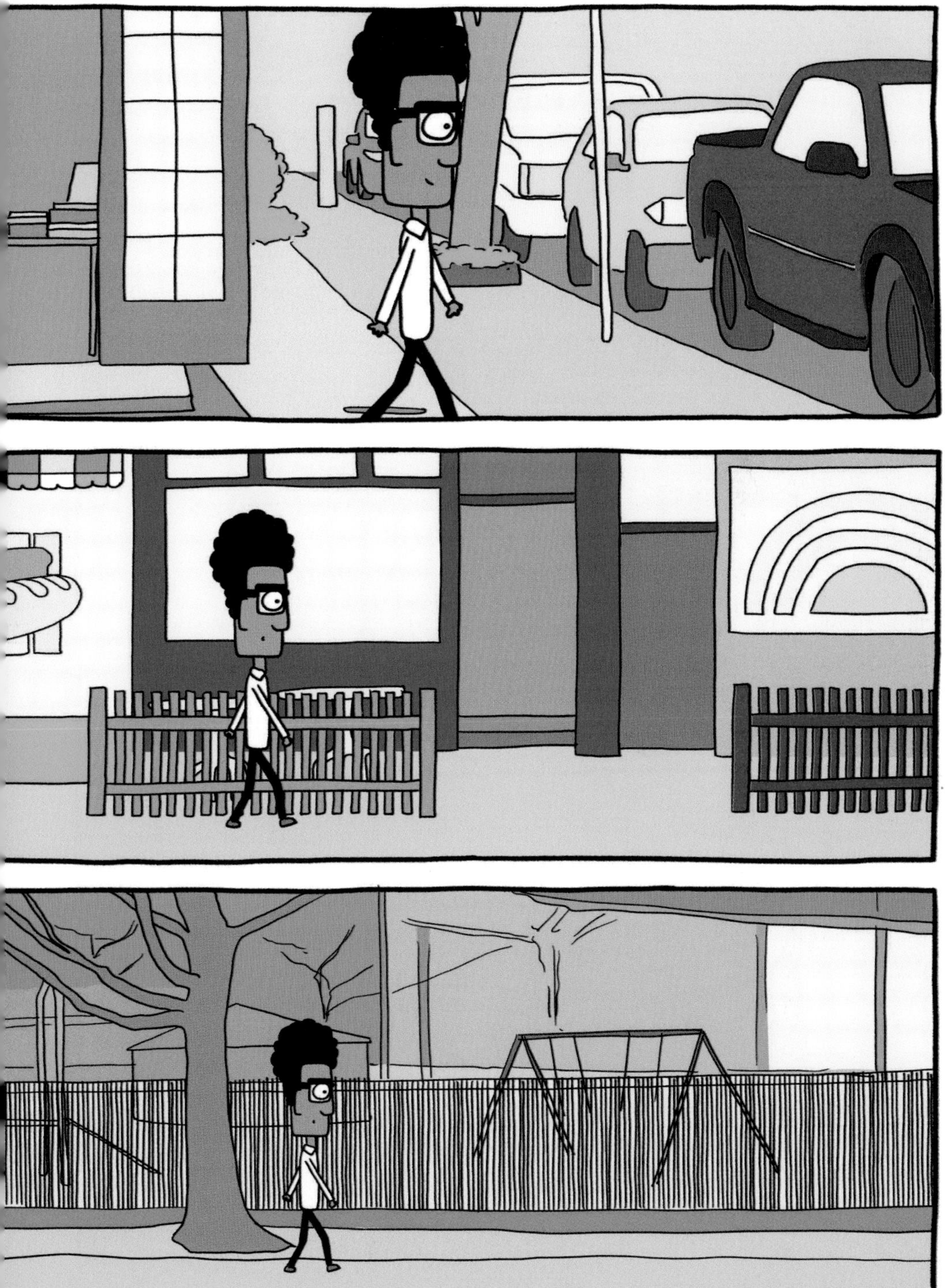

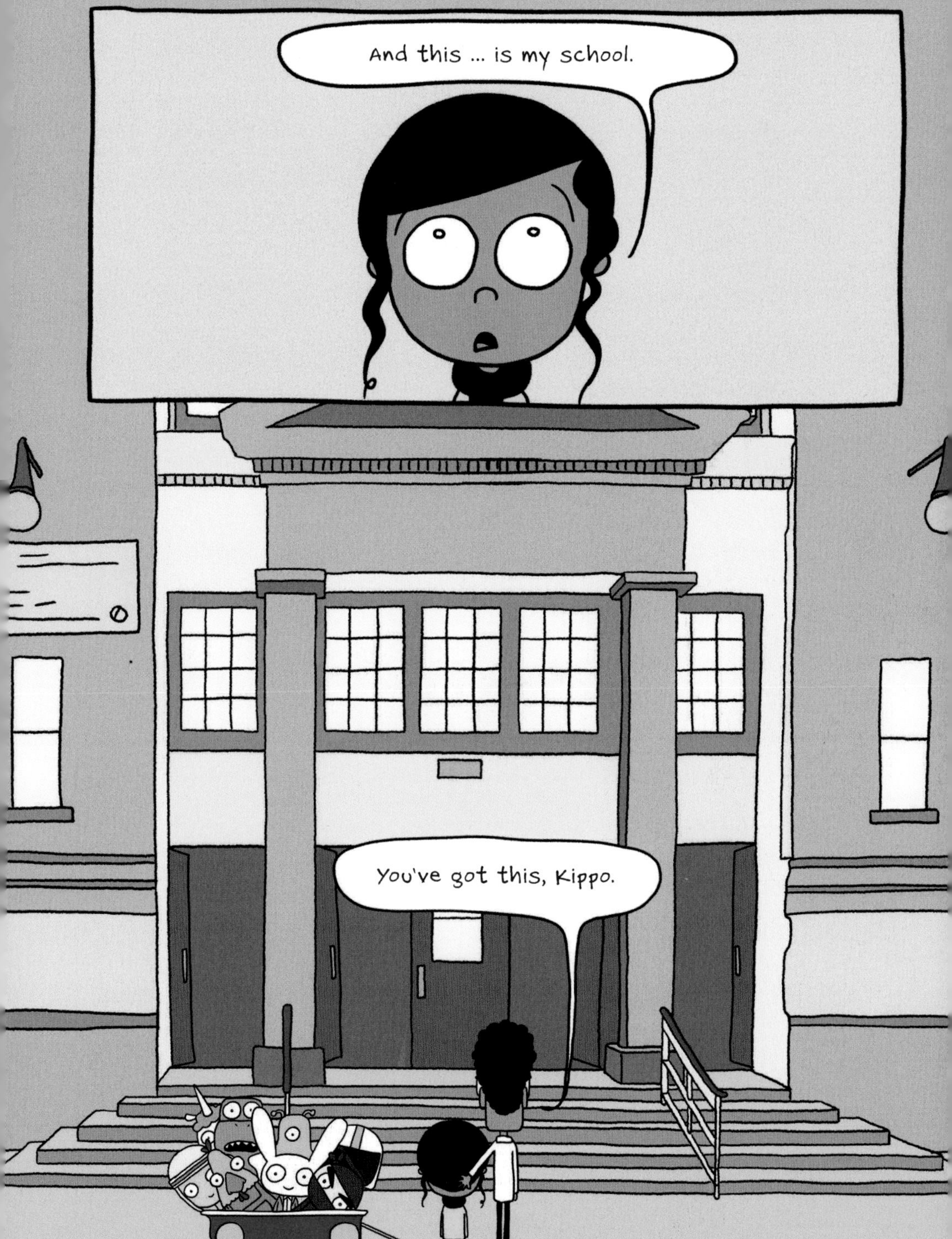
And this ... is my school.
You've got this, Kippo.

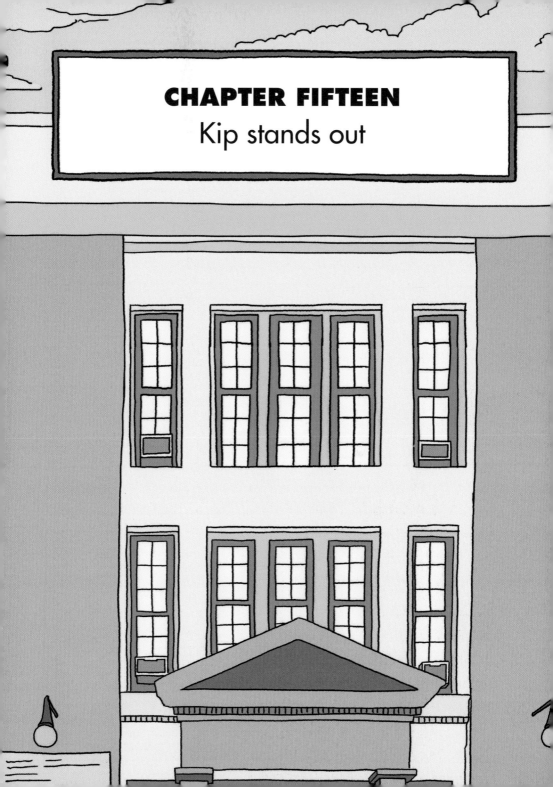

CHAPTER FIFTEEN
Kip stands out

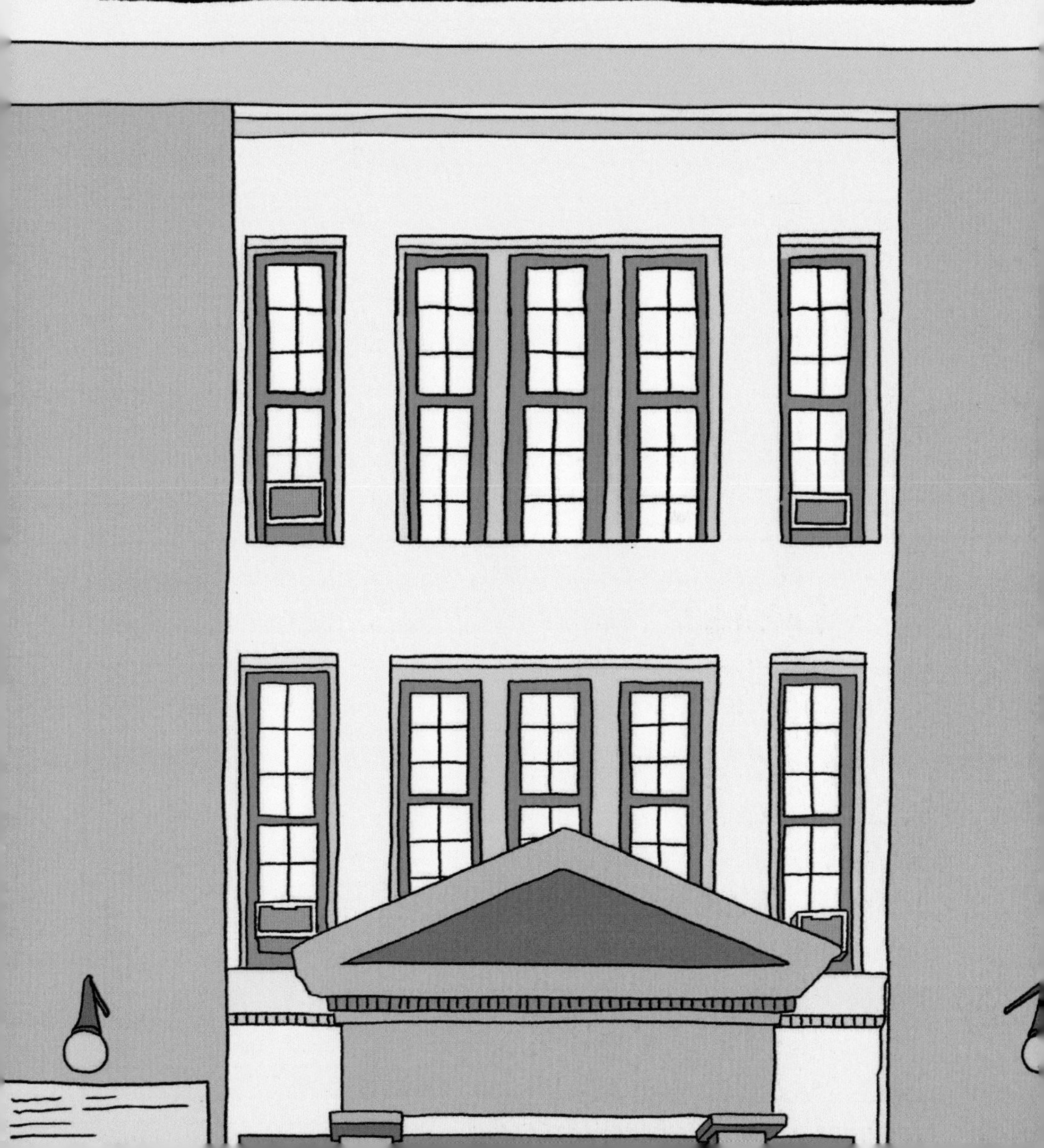

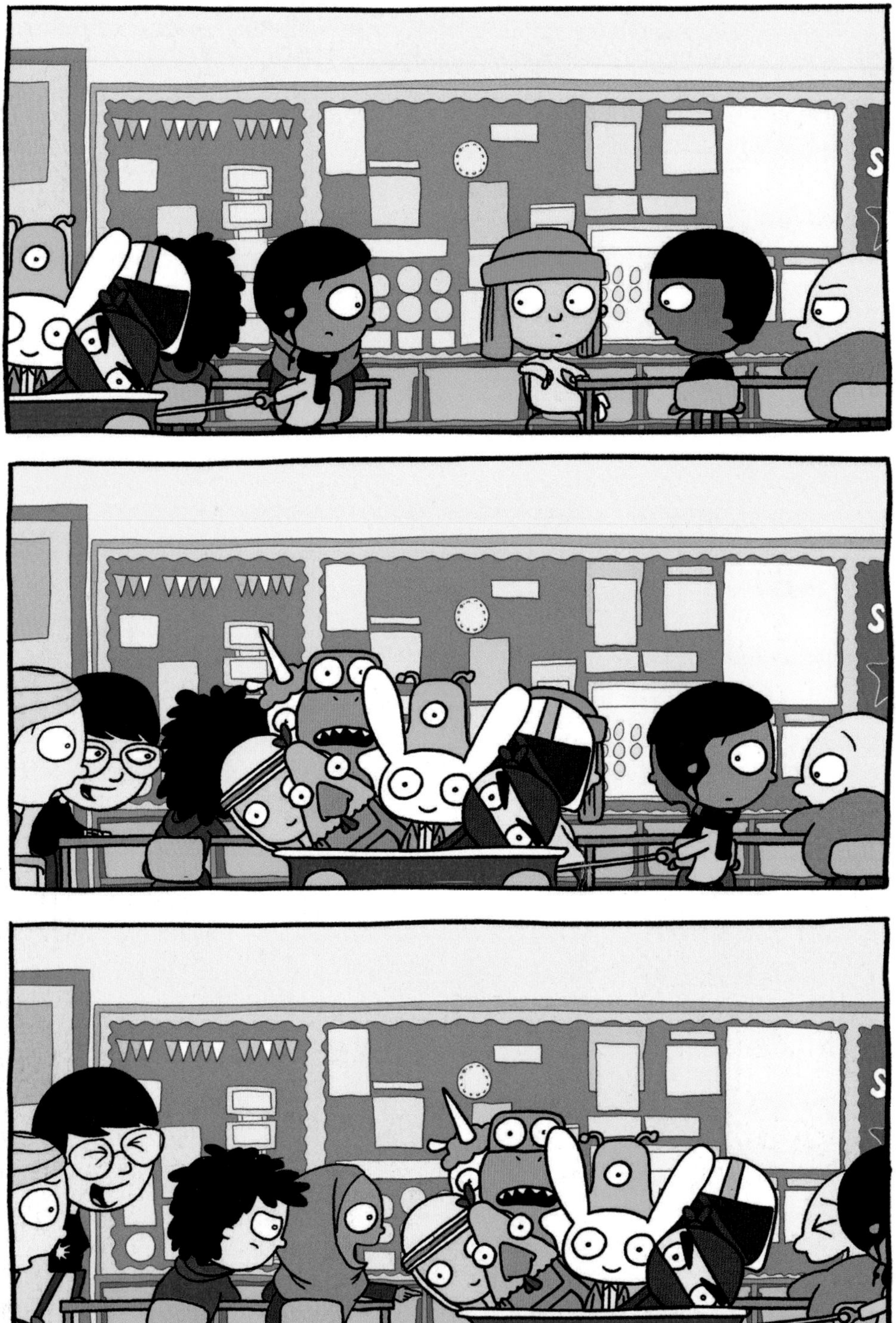

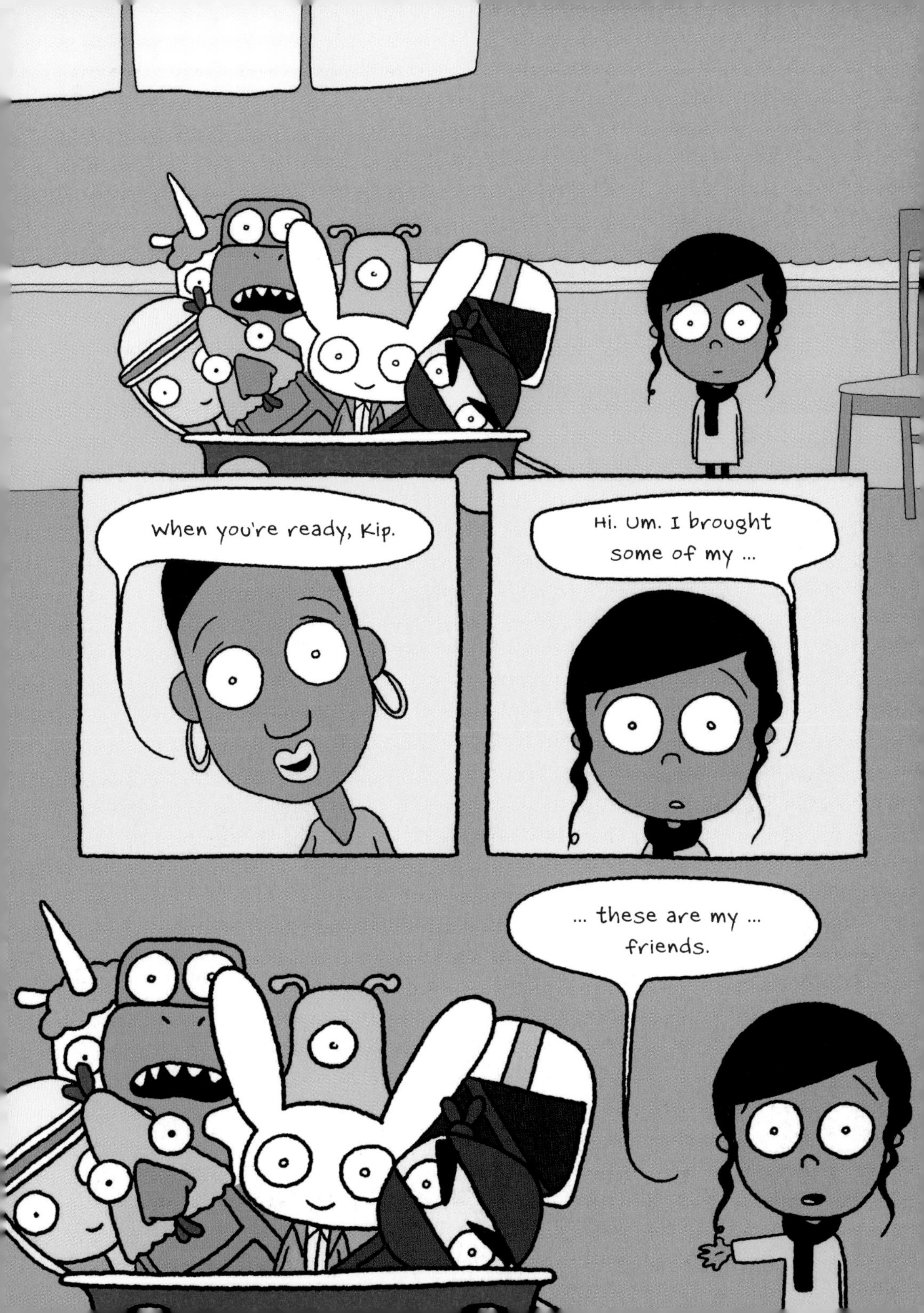
When you're ready, Kip.
Hi. Um. I brought some of my ...
... these are my ... friends.

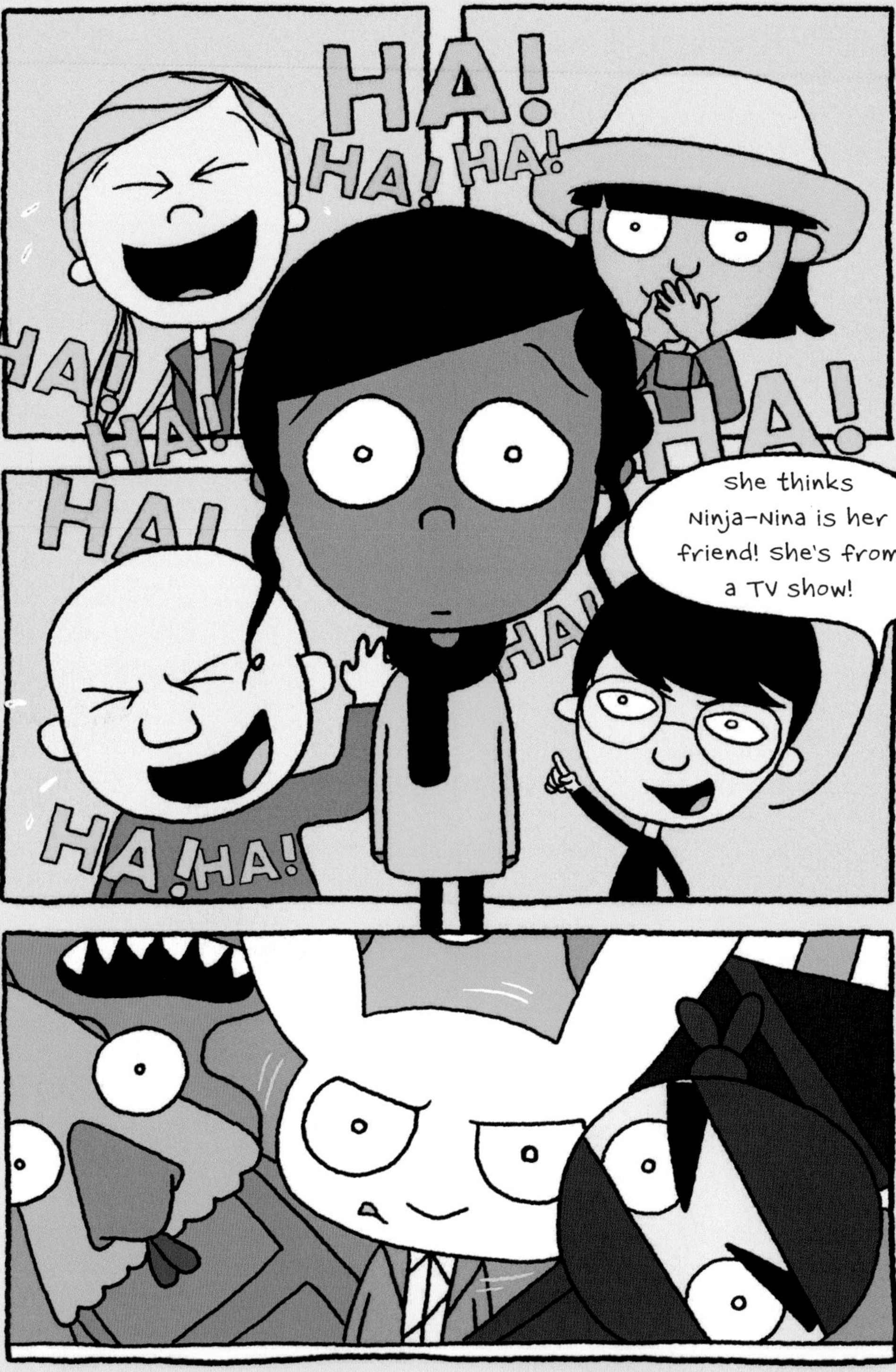
HA!
HA! HA!
HA!
HA!
HA!
HA!
she thinks Ninja-Nina is her friend! she's from a TV show!
HA!
HA! HA!

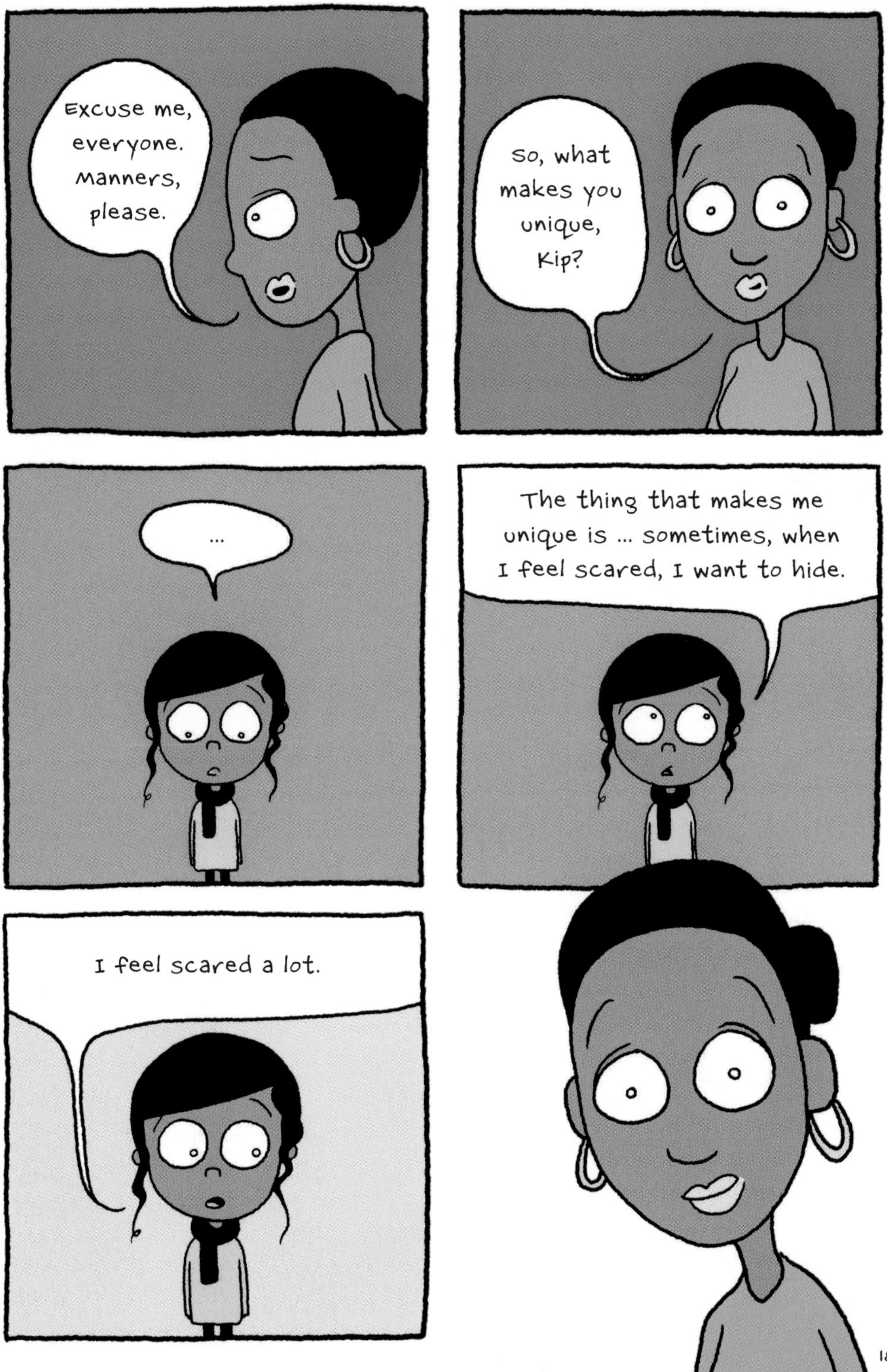
Excuse me, everyone. Manners, please.
So, what makes you unique, Kip?
...
The thing that makes me unique is ... sometimes, when I feel scared, I want to hide.
I feel scared a lot.

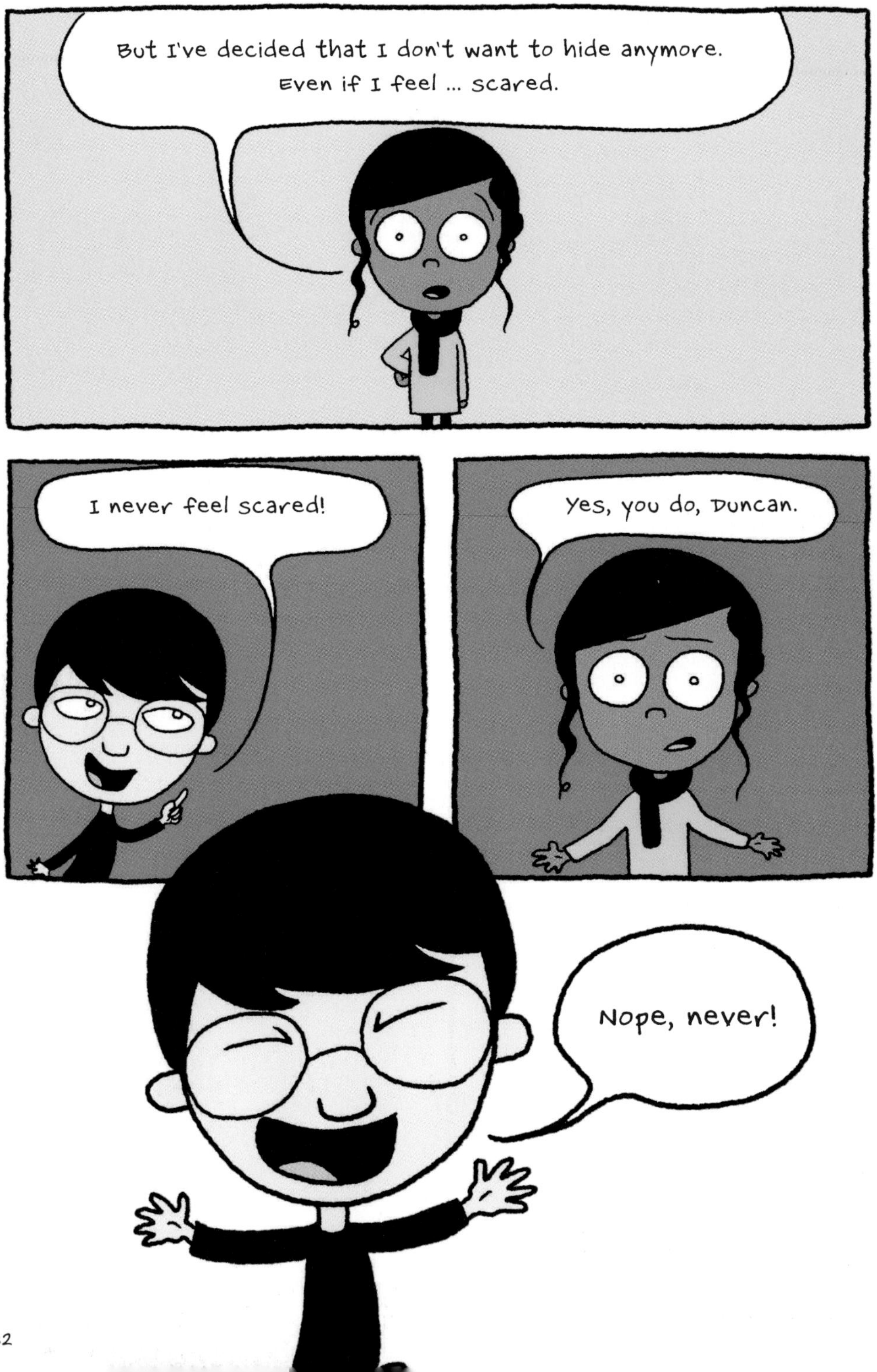

But I've decided that I don't want to hide anymore. Even if I feel ... scared.
I never feel scared!
Yes, you do, Duncan.
Nope, never!

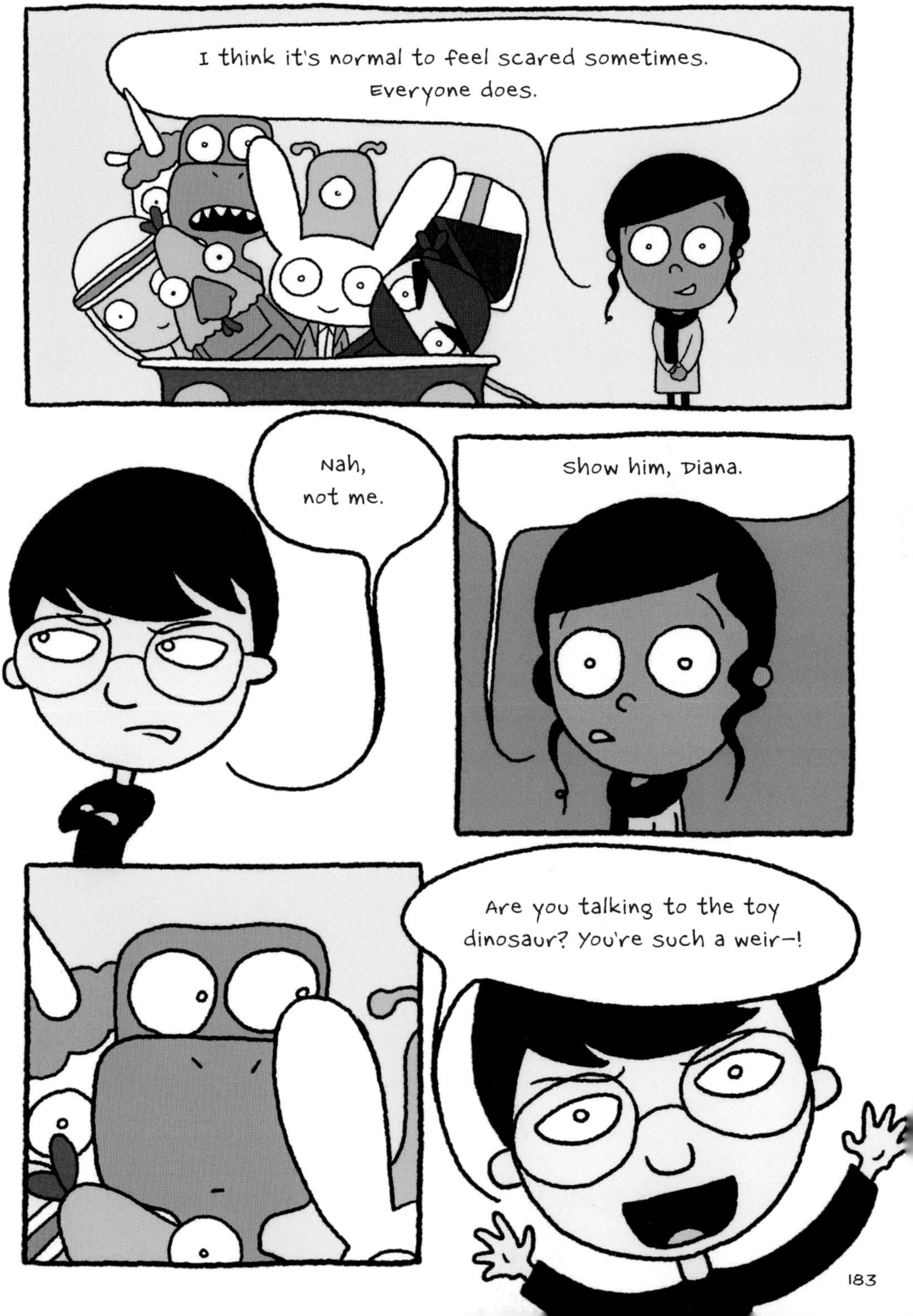
I think it's normal to feel scared sometimes. Everyone does.
Nah, not me.
Show him, Diana.
Are you talking to the toy dinosaur? You're such a weir—!

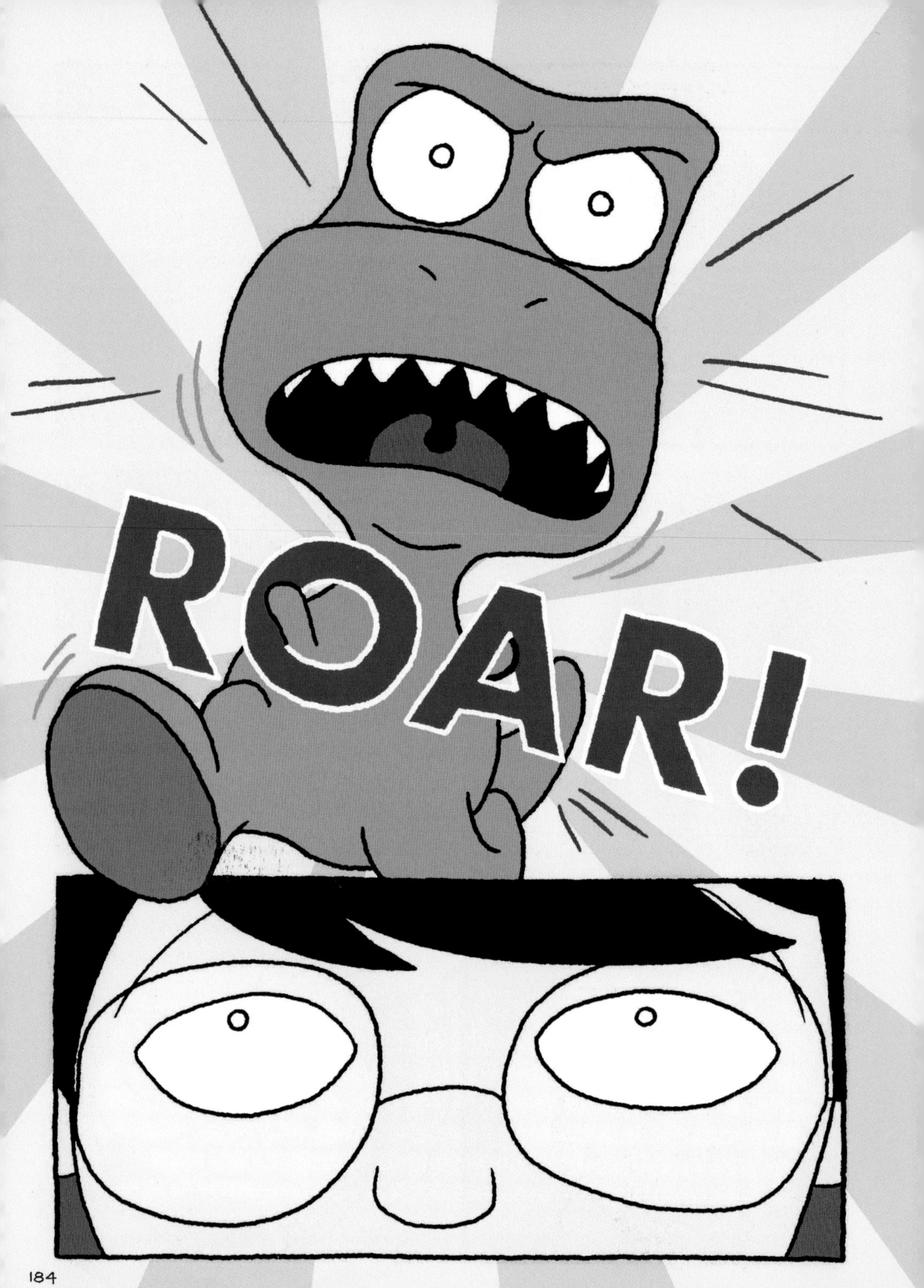
ROAR!

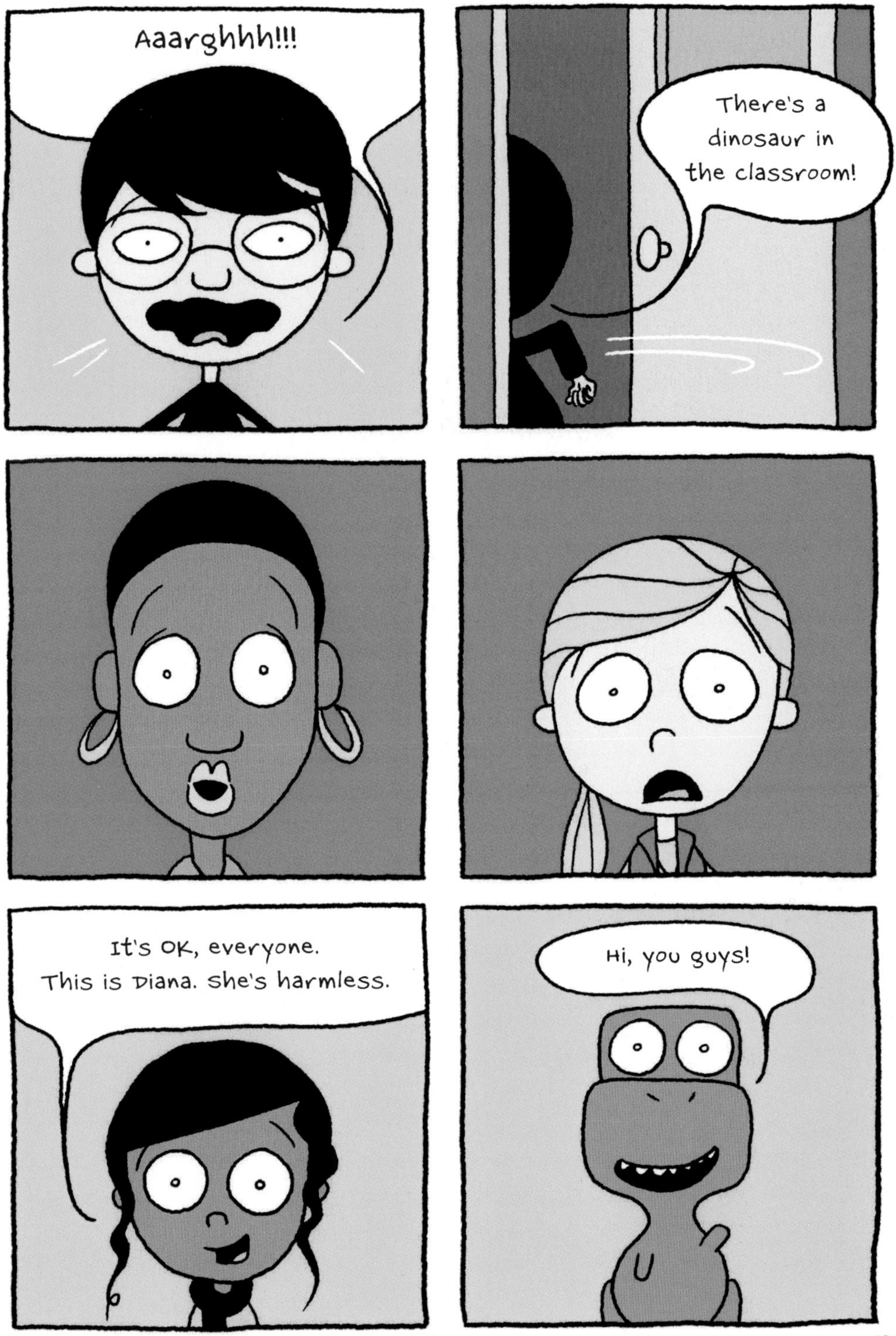
Aaarghhh!!!
There's a dinosaur in the classroom!
It's OK, everyone. This is Diana. She's harmless.
Hi, you guys!

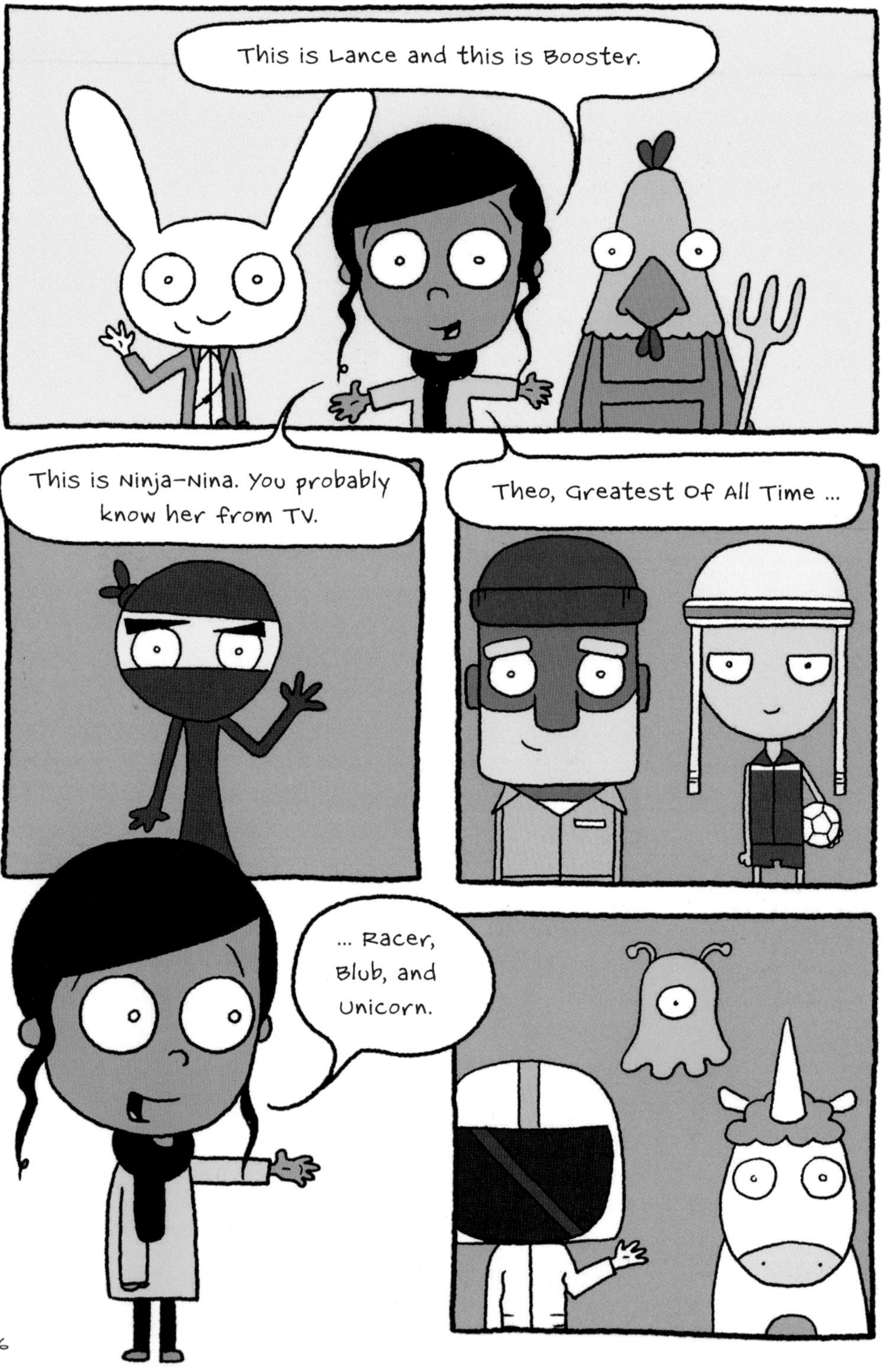
This is Lance and this is Booster.
This is Ninja-Nina. You probably know her from TV.
Theo, Greatest Of All Time ...
... Racer, Blub, and Unicorn.

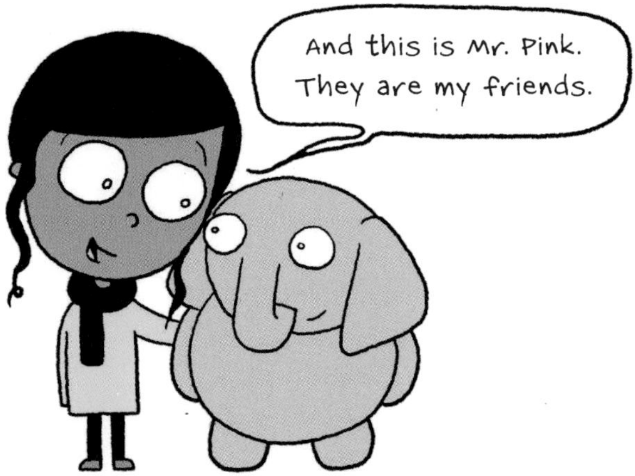
And this is Mr. Pink. They are my friends.

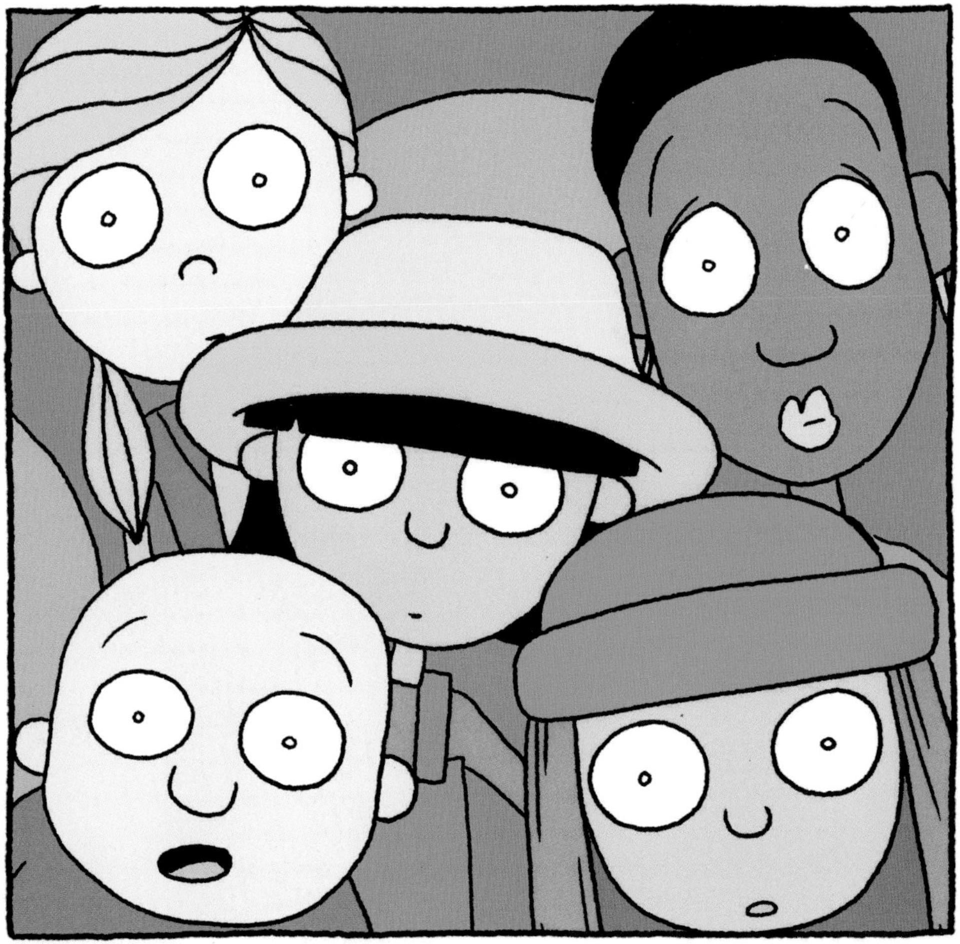

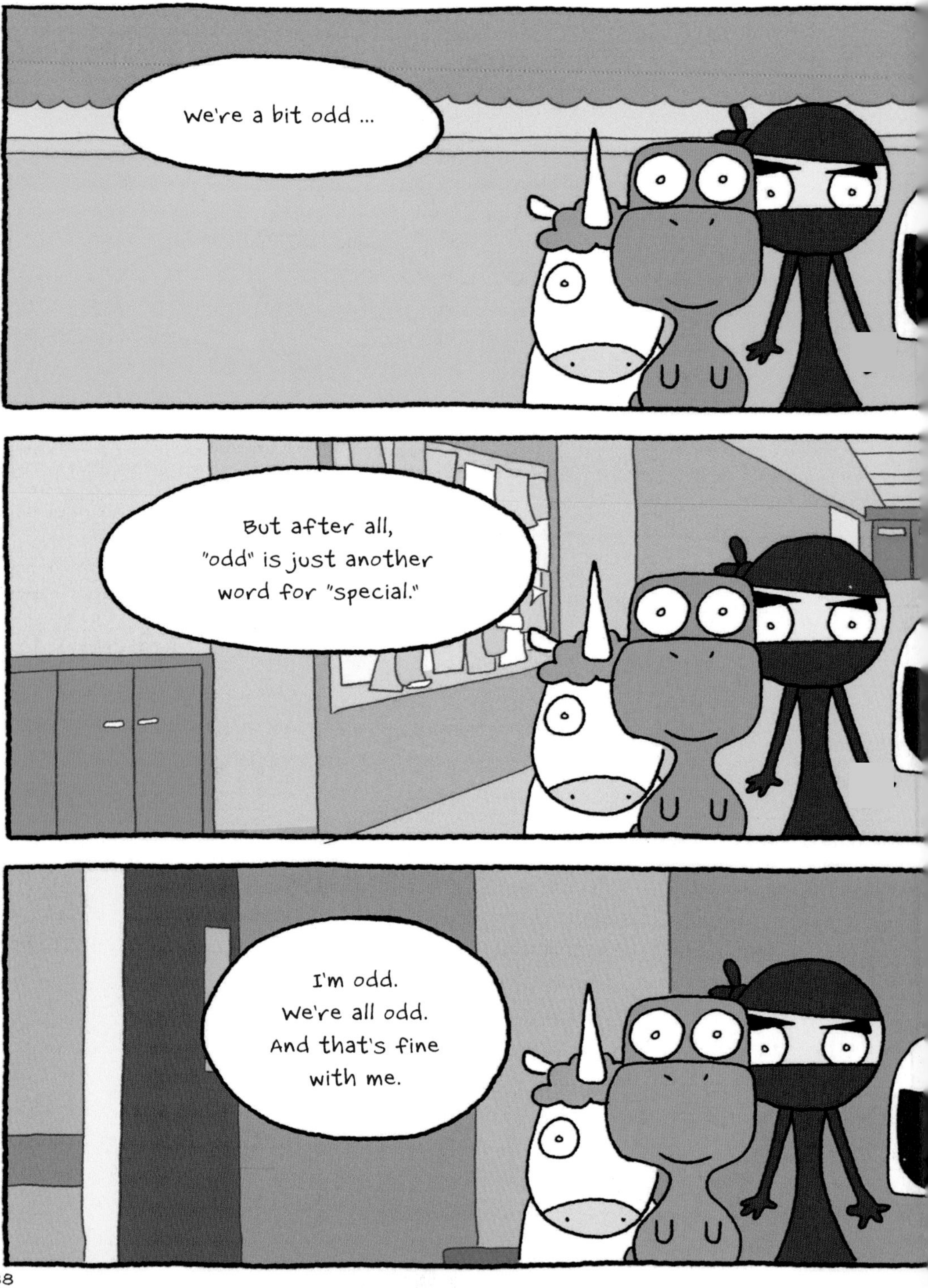
We're a bit odd ...
But after all, "odd" is just another word for "special."
I'm odd. We're all odd. And that's fine with me.

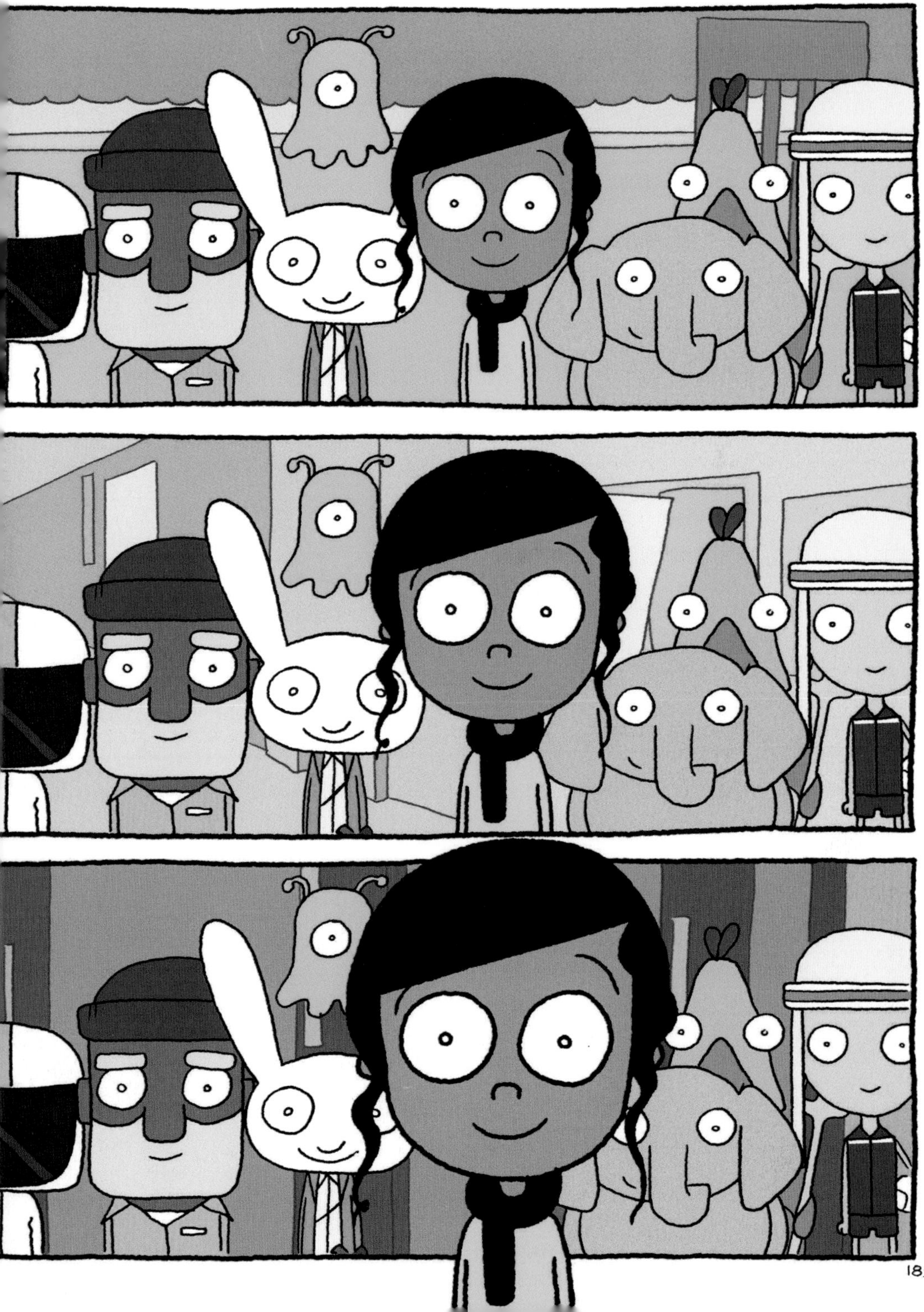

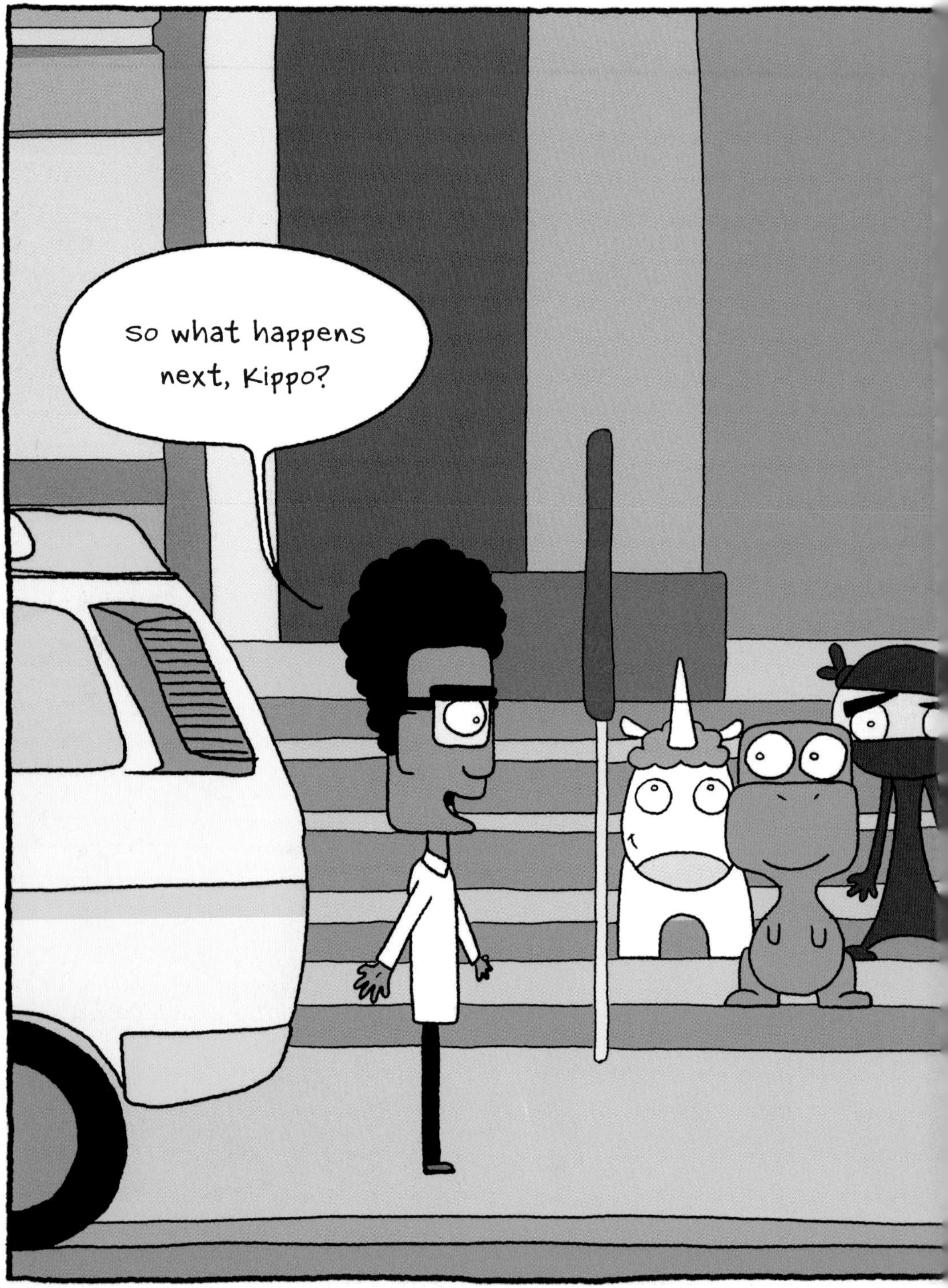
so what happens next, Kippo?

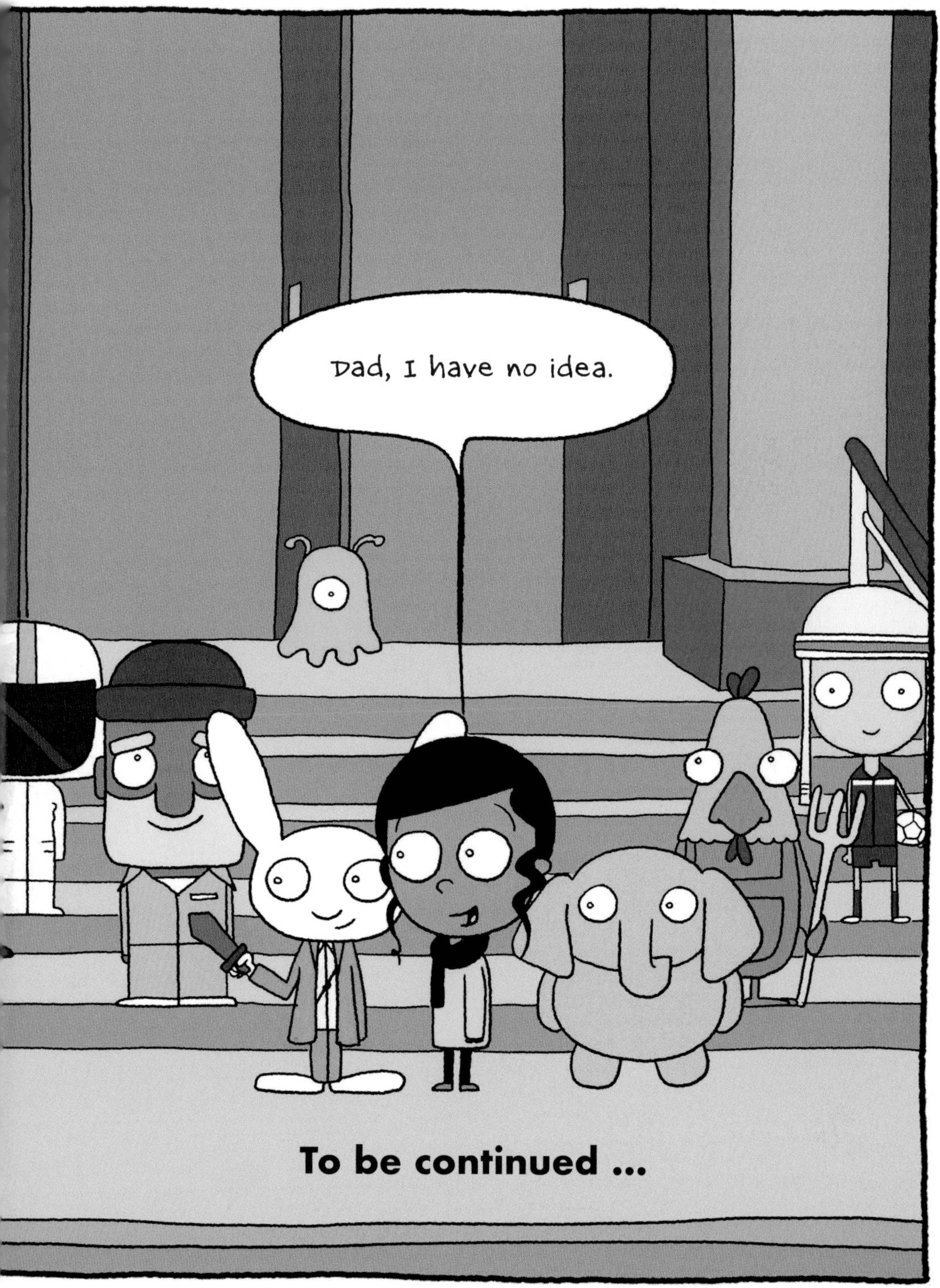
Dad, I have no idea.
To be continued ...

**Kids all over the world
are emailing Matt!**

**Who's your favorite Odd?
Tell Matt!**

matt.stanton@gmail.com

ACKNOWLEDGMENTS

This bit is like the credits at the end of a movie.

There are teams of people who work on getting this book from my imagination into your hands. They are some of the most wonderful people you could ever meet:

Chren Byng

David Linker

Emily Mannon

Anna Bernard

Andrea Vandergrift

Carolina Ortiz

Jessica Berg

Shannon Kelly

Kate Burnitt

Cristina Cappelluto

Jim Demetriou

Pauline O'Carolan

Elizabeth O'Donnell

Then there are teams at the printer, in the warehouse. There are fantastic people who talk to bookshops about *The Odds*. There are amazing humans working in bookstores, libraries, and schools all across the country who help make this book available for you to read.

To all of these people — thank you. You have made *The Odds* come to life.

To my publisher, Chren Byng. You helped me discover *The Odds* in one of my most difficult creative moments. From the bottom of my heart, thank you.

To my US editor, David Linker. I can't tell you how excited I am to see what you and your team have done with *The Odds*. Thank you.

To my wife and partner in all things, Beck Stanton. This book only exists because of you. You inspire me and compel me to create things that matter. Thank you.

To my kids, Bonnie, Boston, Miller, and Sully — you make my day, every day. Thank you.

And to you, the kids who have joined your imagination with mine in reading this book, you are so important, so creative, and you make the world a better place. Thank you.

Matt Stanton

Books by Matt Stanton

Funny Kid series
Funny Kid for President
Funny Kid Stand Up
Funny Kid Prank Wars

The Odds series
The Odds

Pea + Nut! picture books
Pea + Nut!
Pea + Nut Go for Gold!

Books That Drive Kids Crazy! picture books
with Beck Stanton:
This Is a Ball
Did You Take the B from My _ook?
The Red Book
Wait!
The Book That Never Ends

Self-Help for Babies picture books
with Beck Stanton:
Sleep 101
Whine Guide
Dummies for Suckers
One-Ingredient Cookbook

Fart Monster and Me series

with Tim Miller:

Fart Monster and Me: The Crash Landing

Fart Monster and Me: The New School

Fart Monster and Me: The Birthday Party

Fart Monster and Me: The Class Excursion

Fart Monster + Friends picture books

with Tim Miller:

There Is a Monster Under My Bed Who Farts

There Is a Monster Under My Christmas Tree Who Farts

There Is a Monster on My Holiday Who Farts

The Pirate Who Had to Pee

Dinosaur Dump

Don't Spew in Your Spacesuit

Burpzilla

Happy Farter's Day

Are you reading Funny Kid?

Matt Stanton is a bestselling children's author and illustrator who has sold more than one million books worldwide. His middle grade series Funny Kid debuted as the #1 Australian kids' book and has legions of fans across the globe. He has published such bestselling picture books as *There Is a Monster Under My Bed Who Farts*, *This Is a Ball*, and *Pea + Nut!*, and produces a daily YouTube show for kids. He lives and works in Sydney, Australia, with his wife, bestselling author Beck Stanton, and their children.

mattstanton.net

Come and subscribe to
Matt's YouTube Channel!

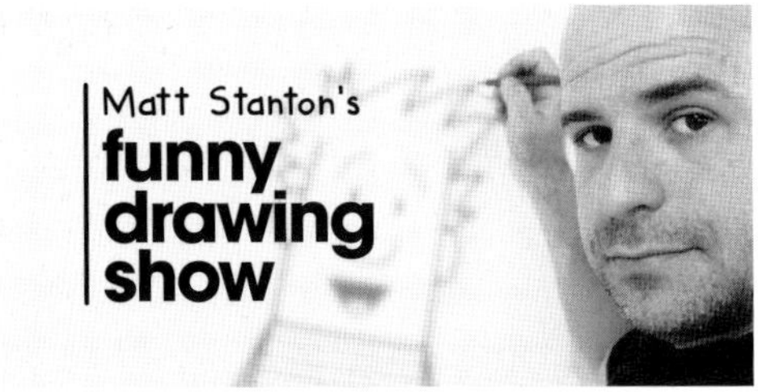
Matt Stanton's
funny
drawing
show

We learn to draw funny stuff!

Talk about how to write funny stories!

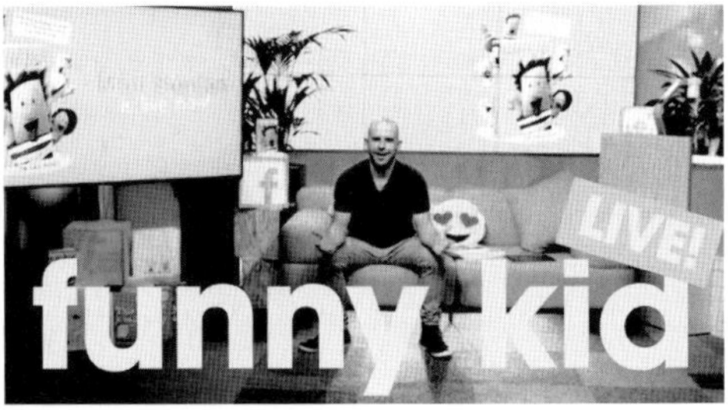
LIVE!
funny kid

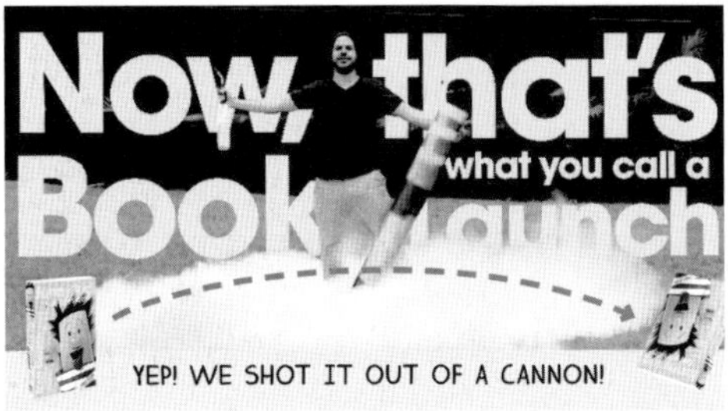
Now, that's
what you call a
Book Launch
YEP! WE SHOT IT OUT OF A CANNON!

And sometimes we launch a book out of a cannon!

MattStantonTV

youtube.com/mattstanton